GR!M
TIDES

GR!M
TIDES

TA PRATT

The Merry Blacksmith Press

2012

Grim Tides

© 2012 Tim Pratt

Cover art by Lindsey Look
lindseylook.com

For information, address:

The Merry Blacksmith Press
70 Lenox Ave.
West Warwick, RI 02893

merryblacksmith.com

Published in the USA by The Merry Blacksmith Press

ISBN—0-61563-578-4
978-0-61563-578-1

DEDICATION

For Anne,
who knows Marla even better than I do

Let Me Tell You a Story

THANKS EVER SO MUCH for seeing me. We may as well get started, don't you think?

Let's scroll through the mortal timeline and look in on Marla Mason, exiled sorcerer-queen, driven from her beloved city of Felport as punishment for her considerable sins and sent to languish in a tropical paradise, specifically Maui, second largest of the islands in Hawai'i.

We'll take as our focus one particular afternoon when she sat barefoot in the sand near the surf, behind the vast resort hotel where she lived in rather more luxury than she felt comfortable with, courtesy of her best (and almost only) friend, Rondeau.

He sprawled beside her on a towel printed with pictures of jolly green carnivorous plants, watching her wiggle her toes in the sand. Rondeau grunted. "You took your boots off. I didn't realize they came off. I thought they were permanently fused to your footmeat."

"I can kick your ass just fine barefoot," she said, but absently, her eyes on the waves, her mind even farther beyond.

"Feeling homesick?" Rondeau turned his head and slurped from a straw plunged into a plastic tumbler jammed in the sand, drinking a concoction that was mostly fruit juice but not inconsiderably rum. He didn't have the stomach for booze and drugs he once had, having inherited both a slew of psychic powers and a nervous constitution recently, but he imbibed as much as his body would allow.

Marla dug her feet deeper into the warm sand. "I live in Maui, in the kind of hotel where if you call room service at three a.m. and demand a well-done bison burger and a bucket of champagne, they bring it in fifteen minutes. My bills are paid by my rich best friend, so I never have to worry about how to pay for the buffalo and bubbly. I get to tell people, with a straight face,

1

that I'm an occult detective. I have an office in an old bookshop that I'm increasingly sure is actually magical. Nobody's tried to kill me in two months. I have absolutely no cares or responsibilities. The hardest choice I have to make on any given day is whether to spend the afternoon napping or swimming. My life is objectively wonderful, the sort of existence most people dream of. What do you think?"

"You really hate it here, huh?"

"Of course." Marla flopped back into the sand, exchanging a view of the endless expanse of blue-green water for the endless expanse of blue sky. "I know I'm ungrateful, but fuck it. I was sent away from the city I loved, where I had useful work to do, and now... I don't even know why I get out of bed in the morning. I mean, I'm sure Elba was nice too, but exile sucks."

Rondeau nodded. "Elba? You mean that black British actor? Yum. Is he staying at the hotel?"

"I love having you around. I never even finished high school, but you make me feel educated. Elba's the island where Napoleon was exiled, the first time. In the Mediterranean. He stayed there for about a year, then escaped and regained his empire."

"Ha. Are you getting ideas? I don't think I'd make much of an invasion force, but I'm up for it if you are."

"Napoloen got his throne back, but he only got to sit on it for about three months. Then he got beat down again at Waterloo. His enemies stuck him on a much uglier island after that, and he died there. So, no, Napoleon's not the model I want to follow. At least they made him king of Elba. What am I? I might as well be one of those tentacley things clinging to a coral reef, slurping microorganisms out of the passing waves."

"Aw, come on, like you said, you're an occult detective now—"

"I've had two clients, Rondeau. Two."

"Sure, but one of them was a shark god."

"I'm not saying they weren't quality clients. But helping a shark god recover his stolen teeth, and giving a snooty kahuna a hand dispelling a ghost? They don't exactly qualify as a life's work. I used to do stuff that mattered. I saved California from a frog god *and* a jaguar god, beat up the king of nightmares, and sent Death himself back to hell with his head hung low. And that was just this year. "

Rondeau took another slurp. "Business will pick up. You're still new here, and I get the sense the native Hawai'ian sorcerers don't like outsiders from the mainland much. Probably that whole history of invasion and subjugation and overthrow. But word will get around—you'll have more cases than you can handle. I'm sure at some point a squid god or a sentient volcano or a malevolent animate tiki statue will get out of control, and boom, you'll get the call."

"Promises, promises." Marla looked up at the perfect blue sky, a few fat clouds floating past in stately procession. A beautiful day, but every day here was beautiful, and what she wanted more than anything was to feel that autumnal bite in the air, like she would back home. It was October already, and back in Felport, the sidewalks would soon be covered in crisp, crackling leaves, people would be breaking out their scarves and coats, and in a month or so the first snowfall would begin. In a month or two here… things would be pretty much exactly the same as they were now. She'd have to take a trip to the east side of the island if she even wanted a reliable chance of seeing *rain*. "I don't even know if I'm cut out to be a detective. A protector, a guardian, sure—I can handle duty to a place, or even an ideal, in a pinch. But if you're a detective, you have to work for *people*, and you know I don't get along with those. Do you think it's a good idea for me to be working with the public?"

"I think you're good at helping people," Rondeau said. "Which is funny, since you mostly don't like them. But when you were the protector of Felport, what were you protecting, anyway? A bunch of buildings? Or the people who lived in them? Would you have stayed on as chief sorcerer if nobody lived there?"

Marla sighed. "Yes, fine, point taken. Mostly I just like getting in fights, and helping people out can make that happen. If you don't have enough enemies of your own handy, volunteer to take on somebody else's. But nobody's even asking for my help right now. What's the point?"

"Your whole life changed." Rondeau slurped the last dregs of his rum. "It's going to take some getting used to. But look: life is chaos. We both know that. If you don't like how things are going? That's okay. Things will change."

"Everything except the weather." Marla rose and walked off by herself, though Rondeau got the last word, or at least, the last long-suffering sigh. She couldn't blame him. Even Marla wasn't enjoying her own company lately.

She walked barefoot, letting the warm water lap at her feet. Sometimes she thought about walking the entire perimeter of the island, a journey of some 120 miles. The island was shaped something like a barbell, or the number eight, or an infinity symbol, and a better sorcerer could probably come up with some ritual purpose for such a walk, sketching out a symbol of power footstep by footstep… but Marla only considered the journey because it would be complicated and annoying and full of treacherous cliffs, and it would give her something to *do*. But doing that would be too much like a tiger pacing back and forth inside a cage, and when she finished the circuit, she'd just be back where she started. It was absurd to feel trapped, she knew.

She wasn't actually confined to Maui—she could go anywhere in the world, except for Felport, where she was forbidden to enter by magic. *Why did that sting so much?* There were billions of people on Earth who'd never go to Felport. Who'd never even *heard* of Felport.

But there was nowhere else in the world she'd ever felt needed, and nowhere else she wanted to be, and nowhere else she wanted to go.

Sad, isn't it? A woman of action, with no particular actions to undertake.

Clearly, something needed to be done.

Murder by the Sea

WE'LL SKIP AHEAD a bit and settle on the morning when Marla finally got her third case.

She sat on a stool behind the counter in her office on yet another fine autumn morning, sipping occasionally from a cup of coffee that had gone cold half an hour before, looking at a newspaper full of local news that didn't interest her. The office was actually an antiquarian bookshop in Lahaina, not far from the resort where she spent her nights. As a bookshop it was a failure, since it was situated in a bit of hidden space invisible to the eyes of passing tourists and local ordinaries. She'd inherited—or stolen, or maybe looted— the office from its previous occupant, a deranged sorcerer who'd made the mistake of antagonizing a local shark god—Marla's first case as a detective had ended with that man being transformed into a shark by his own magic and dumped into the sea, to contend with the furious spirits of those he'd wronged.

Because Marla had no interest in the traditional occupations of ordinary private detectives—outing cheating husbands, or doing background checks, or acting as stalker-by-proxy for jealous boyfriends—the bookshop acted as a useful barrier to entry. The first qualification she required of a client was the ability to *find* her in this hidden space, which required a certain amount of magical acumen.

Unfortunately, no one was looking for her, as far as she could tell. She'd hoped helping that kahuna on the Hana side of the island get rid of a ghost would lead to some word-of-mouth business, but Arachne had seemed profoundly annoyed to have to ask for assistance, and probably hadn't told anyone.

So on this morning, like so many others, Marla sat pretending to go through the motions of a morning at work while secretly brooding over the closed-down avenues of her life. Rondeau perused the shelves and tried to keep her spirits up. "I swear, there are new books here," he said. "Look at this one—a bound volume of old *National Geographics*, heavy on pictures of tribal men wearing penis-sheaths and not much else. I *know* I would have noticed this one before."

Marla spun her scythe-shaped letter opener around on the wooden counter. Not that she had any letters to open. She'd sent postcards to everyone she knew on this mortal plane when she first moved to Hawai'i, vicious bitchy missives for the most part, but no one had written back, not even her onetime closest allies. She gestured around the room, with its twelve-foot-high oak bookshelves, its rippled windows of old glass, its dangling brass light fixtures. "There's magic in this place, beyond the concealment spells. I haven't figured out exactly what yet. Something to do with small-scale matter transportation, some attractant associated with empty spaces on the shelves. I *think* the bookshop transports forgotten books here, maybe based on how long it's been since a human touched a particular volume. There are tons of ancient-ass books from all over the world here, and I think they've been snatched from libraries and garage sales and charity shops, most of them total junk, I'd guess—old medical textbooks, Reader's Digest condensed books, potboiler novels from the 1940s."

Rondeau laughed. He was wearing an aloha shirt patterned with sailboats in an eye-watering combination of reds and pinks and purples and blues. Back in Felport he'd favored whatever hideous things he could unearth from the back shelves of vintage clothing stores, and he'd adapted his fashion sense to life in the tropics admirably "So, what, the bookshop is magically looking for rare books by the dragnet method? Scoop up enough forgotten shit and you're bound to get a first edition of, I dunno, *The Hobbit*?"

"Or *Ulysses*. That's worth more." When Rondeau looked at her with a raised eyebrow, she shrugged. "I've got a bookshop now, so I looked it up, all right? I don't think there's a book in here that's even in the top one hundred most valuable first editions, though."

"Good thing I'm filthy rich. Especially since you've never had any customers, or sold a single book. Working in an invisible shop really cuts down on your walk-in trade. You could sell books on the internet, I guess, though that would require the ability to use a mouse, which I know you've never quite mastered." Rondeau had made a healthy sum when he'd sold his night club—a Felport institution that came with certain magical amenities, making it attractive to powerful sorcerers—before joining Marla in exile. Though in truth it was more that she'd joined *him*. She had no particular interest in Maui, or anywhere else, apart from Felport—the one place she was forbidden to ever return, upon pain of painful death. When Rondeau had asked her if she'd like to tag along with him to paradise, she'd shrugged and said "sure." This was as good a place as any to molder.

"You could advertise, you know," Rondeau went on. "Not for the bookshop, for the other job. I know you asked that shark god to tell all his friends you were open for business, but what kind of friends does a shark god *have*? Manta rays? Jellyfish? We need the kind of people who actually come up on *land*—"

Someone knocked on the door. Marla looked up and whistled. There was a blurring enchantment on the glass window set in the door, making the shapes beyond into shimmering blobs. "Whoever that is didn't trip my proximity alarms when they entered our fold in space. But they're announcing themselves now, which means they aren't outright hostile, or else, they're pretty dumb. That's… interesting. You get any psychic impression off of them?"

Rondeau's psychic abilities were substantial, but he hadn't possessed them for long, and was generally too lazy to work on developing them—after all, there were swims to take and massages to enjoy—so he just shrugged. "Something weird, not like a normal human mind, but if they found the shop, you already know they're some kind of magic, so that doesn't tell you much."

"Brilliantly insightful as always. All right, show them in—maybe you're a better greeter than a psychic."

Rondeau opened the door with a flourish. "Hello gentlemen. And lady. Uh, ladies? Wow, there are a lot of you." He stepped aside, ushering in five—no, six—or was it eight?—people, all young, tanned, and dressed in swimwear, from full wetsuits with reef shoes to barefoot and shirtless-with-trunks. They milled around, seeming to move in impossible ways, switching places with one another instantly in a bizarre series of interpositions, and sometimes their *bodies* stayed in the same place, but the *clothes* they were wearing switched, swifter than an eyeblink.

Marla gritted her teeth and closed her eyes. A certain god had gifted her with the power to see through illusions at will, and while the talent was useful, it was also disturbing. Sometimes it was a lot more pleasant to see the world as it *pretended* to be, not as it actually was, but since she combined an insatiable curiosity with a profoundly suspicious nature, she was reluctant to blind herself willingly. She couldn't talk to a bunch of people flickering like a strobe light, though, so she stepped down her vision. When she opened her eyes, her illusion-piercing gaze was deactivated, and she saw nothing but half a dozen surfer-types, two women and four men, dripping seawater on her hardwood floor. They were all still very attractive, but no longer so… interchangeable. "What can I do for you? Anybody want a towel?"

One of them stepped forward. "We are. Ah. Names. Leis. Ryan. Josh. Mad Gary—"

Marla took pity on him. "I don't need the full roster, really. I won't remember them all anyway. What's your name?"

"You may call… this one… Glyph." He was blond, square-jawed, blue-eyed, shirtless, and in the kind of shape only a very athletic twenty-something with unspeakably good genes could be. Rondeau was eyeing Glyph like the wolf looked at Little Red Riding Hood. (Rondeau's powers allowed him see through illusions, too, but he seldom bothered—misconceptions and lack of perception made the world more beautiful, as he always reminded her.) "A… friend of ours… was murdered." Something about Glyph's affect was deeply weird, his eyes not quite focused on Marla, his head titled just slightly—as if talking to another human with actual words was a significant effort for him.

Marla nodded. "Okay. Why come to me? They have cops for that."

Glyph shook his head. "Even if the police could help us… there is no body. Ronin was a devotee of the sea, and his remains returned to our mother ocean when he died—he became sea foam and salt, and washed away."

"Nice trick," Marla said. "Better hope organized crime doesn't figure out how to do that. But, again, why *me*? You kids are obviously carrying some pretty heavy magic around. Why not cast a few divinations of your own to find the guilty party?"

"The killer… he must be more powerful than all of us combined. We cast a dozen divinations, but we could find no trace of him."

Marla grunted. That was interesting, because she'd guess this group, combined, possessed rather a lot more magic than she did. Not that she'd ever let a little power imbalance stop her from getting into a fight. She'd kicked a hellhound across a room once, and outsmarted the god of Death, and imprisoned the king of nightmares, among other things, and those were all fights that, on paper, she should have lost. You didn't always have to be more powerful. Sometimes you just had to refuse to lose.

Of course, it helped to have something worth fighting for, which she didn't, not lately. The old cliché said "freedom" was just another word for "nothing left to lose," but if this life in exile from her home city was freedom, she'd take the prison of responsibilities anytime.

But, whether she really gave a crap or not, these people needed help, so it was time to stop moping and start asking semi-intelligent questions. "It's definitely murder, right? No chance it was an accident?"

Glyph nodded. "We saw him die. He… Ronin could not speak when we found him, his throat was cut, blood running into the sand and turning into seawater…" Glyph shivered, and all the other surfers behind him shivered an instant later—even draped in an illusion of normalcy, they couldn't entirely hide their group affinity. "Can you help us?"

"Sure, I could." Marla spoke with a certain amount of bland confidence. She'd recently defeated her own evil counterpart from a parallel dimension. *How hard could it be to find a murderer on an island that was only about 730 square miles all together?* "If you don't mind me asking, though, how did you find me? I don't exactly have a listing on Yelp or Craigslist."

"A god told us you might be able to help."

Marla nodded. "Shark god, right?"

Glyph shook his head. "No. He was not a god of the sea—or, not just the sea, anyway. We are unsure of his domain, or even his true name, but he is... not from around here. Not one of the Hawai'ian gods, we mean, who mostly slumber deeply now, anyway. He was friendly with Ronin, and when Ronin was killed, this god suggested you might be able to help. He spoke quite highly of you."

Marla frowned. She didn't know *that* many gods, nor did she want to. Apart from the shark god she'd helped soon after arriving in Hawai'i, there was just a snake god who'd pledged to kill her someday when he got around to it, and the god of Death, with whom she had a... complicated relationship. And there was her old apprentice Bradley Bowman, who was pretty busy maintaining the structural integrity of the multiverse since he'd ascended to a sort of meta-godhood. She didn't think any of them would be recommending her services as a detective to a pod of hive-mind surf-sorcerers, as such business was way below their pay grades. So this bunch had inadvertently brought her *two* things to investigate—who'd killed their friend, and which god was dropping her name.

"You are an outsider," Glyph went on, "and so we thought you might be more... objective? The kahunas here all have old alliances, grudges, and suspicions that could color their investigations if we sought their help. They look first to their own enemies, or those they have deemed undesirable, even if the evidence points elsewhere. You do not have any of their biases. We asked others about you, and were told... not good things, exactly, but things that make us think you can find out who murdered Ronin. Arachne said you knew your way around the dead."

Marla nodded. Arachne had only come to Marla at all because she was between apprentices and too proud to ask any of the other local kahunas for help—she could hire a *haole* like Marla without anyone knowing she couldn't handle the unquiet spirit on her own, though of course it had proven to be rather more complicated than an ordinary ghost. "Sure, I helped her out, but—"

"We talked to Zufi as well," Glyph said.

Ah. That made more sense. "The Bay Witch. That's what we call her back home—back in the city I'm from, I mean. We worked together for a lot of years."

"She used to ride the waves with us in the Pacific, before relocating to the Atlantic." Glyph frowned. "Her choice never made sense to us. Why leave the whole to be alone? And the waves over there are *terrible*. The god said Zufi could provide a reference for you, and when we sent word, Zufi said you are tenacious and capable and not very nice, but if you are on our side, you will be not very nice to people we do not *want* to be very nice to, so it is okay." He paused. "That is a direct quote. She also said to remind you that you still owe her a favor."

"Yeah, that sounds like Zufi. Okay. I'll take the case."

The surfers exchanged glances. It was like watching a meticulously choreographed bit of stage business. "What do you charge for your services?"

Marla grinned. Once upon a time, before being chief sorcerer of Felport, and then being an exiled *ex*-chief sorcerer, she had been a mercenary. She'd never worked for money back then, choosing a life of poverty in favor of accruing power. So her rates now were the same as they'd been back then: "If I solve the case, you'll have to tell me a secret I don't already know, and teach me a trick I've never seen before."

"That is acceptable," Glyph said.

Rondeau cleared his throat and glared at her.

"Oh, right," Marla said. "I charge a secret, and a trick—plus expenses." Rondeau had been funding her entire life since her exile, and even though he had more money than some gods now, he'd insisted that if she got a job she should at least not *lose* money in the process. As chief sorcerer she'd never worried about cash—all the other sorcerers under her protection had kicked up a percentage of the profits from their various legal and illegal businesses to her, leaving her free to look out for the city's well-being as a whole—but, as she kept discovering in new and annoying ways, this was a new world. If this kept up, she'd actually end up knowing how much a gallon of milk or a loaf of bread cost.

Glyph chewed his lip. "We do not have much in the way of actual money… what kind of expenses?"

That was a good question. "Like if I need to buy grave dust or a hand of glory or something, for a spell?"

He nodded. "May we pay you in black coral?"

Marla didn't know what that was, but she looked at Rondeau, and he nodded vigorously, so she said, "Yeah, that works."

"May we ask how you intend to proceed?"

"I should see the crime scene."

Glyph frowned. "Ronin's body melted, as we said, and we could find no trace magically—"

"Look, it's not that I don't have faith in you. Except, in fact, I don't know a damn thing about you, so I'm going to do everything you did all over again, just so I *know*. Okay?"

"You *do* work for us—" Glyph began.

"Nope," Marla said. "I work for *me*. On your behalf, yes, but not *for* you. I do this my way, and you don't get to bitch unless I don't get results. Understood?"

Glyph narrowed his eyes, glanced at his fellows, then nodded. "Understood. Just… find out who killed Ronin. He was our eldest, and the best of us, and he did not deserve to die that way."

"Sure," Marla said. "Give my assistant here the details about the crime scene, directions and all that. And it would be good if the directions were for traveling by *car*, and didn't start, 'Swim out half a mile east' or something."

"We can take you—"

"I'd rather see it on my own, without having my observations influenced," Marla said. "I'm going to go prepare my tools of the trade. Let Rondeau know how to get in touch with you, all right?" She stepped around the counter, shook Glyph's hand—strong grip, kinda damp—and nodded at his fellow sorcerer-siblings, or multiamorous lovemates, or hive-buddies, or whatever they were. She slipped through a curtain behind the counter into the little back room office, which didn't contain much but a chair, a smaller desk, a safe (unlocked and empty, except for a small silver bell), and a shelf on the wall holding a few books on Polynesian mythology and the Hawai'ian language. Marla didn't really have any prepatations to make, or any tools to pack—she just didn't want to deal with the logistics of shooing an anxious tribe of surfers out of her office. The prospect of a mystery to solve should have excited her, but she didn't actually give a crap about Ronin or the surfers, so the thought of getting in a car and looking at some sand a guy had died on made her tired. She didn't want to dwell on the negative, but… what if this whole occult detective thing didn't work out? What would she do with herself then?

A Conversation with Koona

ONCE HE'D GOTTEN RID of the surfers, Rondeau stepped into the office. "'I don't work for you, I work for me?'" He smiled. "You've been reading those Robert Parker novels about Spenser I gave you, haven't you?"

She scowled. "I have to learn to be a detective somehow, don't I?"

"Spenser *does* just wander around annoying people and getting in fights until he figures things out," Rondeau said. "Instead of using deductive reasoning and measuring the depths of footprints and collecting cigar ash and shit like Sherlock Holmes does. So he's probably a better model for your detecting style, if you can call it that."

"Yes, fine, you're hilarious."

"If you're Spenser, that makes me his buddy Hawk, right? A sexy, amoral badass?"

"One out of three ain't bad," Marla said. "So where are we going?"

Rondeau drove them north out of Lahaina in his little black convertible, past the West Maui airport, through the town of Kapalua, and along a route that curved gradually eastward along the northern edge of the island. The scenery along the coast road was absolutely gorgeous—great vistas of cliff and rock and sea—and Marla was sick to death of it. She liked to be in the shadow of old warehouses with the comfort of a vast continental plate beneath her, not out in the open under the sun on a speck of volcanic rock in the ocean.

"We both know I'm not going to learn a damn thing from looking at a spot where a guy died," Marla said. "Unless the killer left a confession written in the sand, and even then, it would have blown away by now. So here's what we'll actually do. You'll find an oracle, and ask it who killed our dead guy. Easy."

13

Rondeau sighed as he swung the car around a long curve. "You only love me for my vast psychic powers."

"Who says I love you?"

They approached the Bellstone, a boulder of volcanic rock that, when struck in just the right spot, made a sound like clanging metal. When Rondeau didn't even slow their pace as they passed the rock, Marla growled. "Seriously? There's no oracle we can talk to in the Bellstone? A great big hunk of rock upchucked from the fiery guts of a volcano? Rings like a bell when you smack it? You're telling me *that* doesn't have any magic?"

"Doesn't feel right," Rondeau said. "Sorry."

"You know, when Bradley wanted an oracle, he could find some ghost or demon or whatever in the first stinky dumpster or drain pipe or dark alley we passed." She was happy about her old apprentice Bradley's new gig as an immortal being who lived at the center of all possible realities, but it meant Marla didn't have his help anymore, and she was stuck with the infinitely less experienced (and lazier) Rondeau, who'd inherited Bradley's abilities, but not his skill at wielding them.

"I'm pretty new at this," Rondeau said. "But I'm learning. In my defense, I think there's a higher density of demons and dead people in a city. If you want me to turn around and go talk to the rock for a while and hope for the best, I can."

Marla sighed. "No, carry on, you're the one connected to the great grand mystical whatever. Something's seriously out of whack when *you're* the most spiritual person in the room. Or car. Whatever."

They drove in silence for a while, until Rondeau said, "Over here." He pulled the convertible onto a wide gravel patch on the shoulder of Highway 340. "There's definitely some magical stuff crackling down this way, by the Olivine Pools."

She frowned. "Isn't this where our dead guy died?"

"Yeah. That's convenient, isn't it? Maybe he left behind a ghost we can talk to. Go right to the source."

Marla grunted. She wasn't a big fan of ghosts. They weren't the souls or spirits or immortal residue of the dead, exactly—those went *elsewhere*, to whatever afterlife they expected to get, usually. Ghosts were more like... old photographs, or video loops, or echoes, or shit stains—psychic residue, persistent but slowly fading and degrading, and all pretty much crazy. But ghosts knew things, and they made reliable oracles, especially when you asked them about their own lives and deaths. Ghosts were pretty self-centered. Not every death resulted in wailing translucent psychotic ectoplasmic residue, but such manifestations were more likely in cases of violent death, so there was a chance some fragment of Ronin might still be hanging around, the magical-forensic equivalent of shed hairs or blood drops.

Marla and Rondeau picked their way down a steep, rock-scattered incline toward the Olivine Pools, a beautiful spot beloved of tourists and those locals who could abide the company of tourists: a group of lovely tidal pools, deep and clear, most big enough for swimming (though ideally you tried not to disturb the denizens of the pools), in an area scattered with the small greenish crystals called olivine. The pools were entirely deserted at the moment, though, and Rondeau wandered along the shore, pausing occasionally, squinting at nothing in particular, looking for ghost spoor. He eventually crouched down by one of the smaller pools. "Not a ghost." His voice was strained, like he was trying to do higher math in his head while operating heavy machinery. "But there's something... else. Something watery and dark and... in here." He pointed to the water, and Marla crouched with him.

One of Rondeau's powers was oracle generation. Marla wasn't sure whether he summoned existing supernatural creatures who possessed the power to answer questions, or whether the "oracles" were just external manifestations of his own abilities, a way for him to get answers out of his own powerfully psychic brain, like a crazy guy in a comic book who took orders from his own ventriloquist's doll.

Either way, the process worked, so Marla peered into the water—and jerked back when a gargantuan white moray eel rose up from the suddenly bottomless depths of what should have been an ordinary tidepool. The eel's eyes were the size of teacups, black and dead, its mouth a horrorshow of overlapping fangs. The water rippled as the eel spoke, but the voice that emerged was perfectly clear, a deep bass with no underwater qualities at all: "I am Koona, the death of sharks, the thief of fish. What do you seek?"

Rondeau cleared his throat. "A man called Ronin died near this spot two days ago. We want to know who murdered him."

The eel swayed a bit, almost hypnotically. Its jaws were big enough to swallow a human head in a gulp. After a moment, it said, "That knowledge is closed to me. I see a figure, but it is shrouded in mist. The killer is a being of power."

Marla sighed. Well, yeah. The guy had murdered a member of a badass hive of wave-mages, so the power was self-evident. "Thanks anyway," she said.

"I *do* have knowledge that may interest you," the eel said. "Glad tidings, and grim ones. Do you wish to know?"

"Uh, sure," Rondeau said.

The eel opened its mouth. "You must pay."

"I always pay," Rondeau said. The oracles he summoned were transactional creatures. "What's the price?"

"Blood."

Rondeau sighed. Marlas passed him one of her many knives, this one more suited for slicing mangos than throats. He pressed the blade to his palm, winced, and made a fist over the water, drops falling in and turning to drifting streamers in the water. The eel closed its eyes for a moment, then spoke, gazing not at Rondeau, but at Marla. "An old friend will soon return to you, to gladden your hollowed heart. But others are coming, and they seek not to soothe your heart, but to tear it from your chest. One you once loved, whose love for you has soured. Old enemies returned. Strangers who shall become new enemies. They sharpen their knives for you, and gather their powers."

"What friend?" Marla said. "And what enemies? Come on, give me names." But the eel just sank down into the pool, vanishing into the blackness, which shimmered, and became just an ordinary tidepool again, with nothing more remarkable at the rocky bottom than anemones and a scuttling crab. She looked at Rondeau. "That oracle sucked."

Rondeau wrapped his wounded hand in a handkerchief. "It sucked my blood, anyway. What now?"

"I guess we go back to the office, and try to find out who this 'friend' is."

"You're not more concerned about the enemies?"

"Enemies, I'm used to. I've got lots of those. I don't have that many friends."

"True," Rondeau said. "And most of the ones you used to have don't like you anymore."

"Honestly, it makes me wonder why you still hang out with me."

Rondeau shrugged. "What can I say? I have profoundly horrible judgment."

There was no one at the bookshop, and no familiar faces lingering on the streets in Lahaina town, and Rondeau refused to call up another oracle just to satisfy Marla's curiosity about this mystery friend—summonings like that gave him headaches and insomnia even at the best of times, and two in one day would give him nosebleeds and the kind of migraines that come with auras and last for a week. "Maybe your long-lost pal is at the hotel, kicking his heels in the lobby, wondering where the hell we are?"

Marla shrugged. "Sure. It's as good an idea as any." The resort was the closest thing she had to a forwarding address.

Rondeau lived in a two-bedroom suite at a hotel in Kaanapali, a stretch of gorgeous coastline dominated by giant resorts. It was a long way from the traditional Hawai'ian experience, but Rondea was an unapologetic tourist and hedonist. He let Marla stay in the suite's extra room, at least when she didn't sleep on the hideous brown couch in the bookshop. She knew she should find a place of her own. That would be a pain in the ass, but hotel life just wasn't to her taste. Too many people had keys to their room. Back in Felport, she'd owned an entire apartment building and lived in it alone, with her personal effects scattered in the empty apartments around her own to create a cloud of psychic chaff if anyone tried to divine her precise location within the building. Oh, beautiful privacy. That kind of real estate was rather beyond her reach here on Maui, unless she asked Rondeau for a major loan, and she felt beholden enough to him already.

Rondeau drove up along Highway 30 from Lahaina, leisurely covering the short distance to the hotel. Marla was in the passenger seat, doing her habitual (if paranoid) scan of her surroundings. She peered into the side mirror. "Someone's following us."

Rondeau glanced up at the rearview. "Marla, that's a taxi. People take taxis to the resorts, and this is the main road to the resorts from Kahalui airport. What makes you think they're following *us*?"

"I've got a sense for these things. Besides, you're going so slow that any taxi driver worth a damn would have passed you miles ago. Why put up with your pokey ass unless he's following us?"

"You *told* me to slow down," Rondeau said, outraged and aggrieved—or at least affecting to be. "You said I drove like a maniac, so I brought it down to the speed limit, just like you *asked*—"

Marla pointed. "Pull over in the park there."

Rondeau sighed, paused to await a break in the oncoming traffic, and turned left into the lot of Wahikuli Park. The long, narrow strip of public ground boasted a few picnic tables overlooking the ocean but little else, and didn't have much going for it except all the scenery you could eat. Marla barely noticed the deep blue vistas of ocean and sky anymore. She wasn't sure it was true that you could get used to *anything*, but you could certainly get used to beauty.

"Well, hell," Rondeau said, as the taxi pulled in and parked next to them. "What do you think? Is this the world's least subtle assassin? Or—"

Marla was already getting out of the car, just as the taxi's back door swing open. Friend, or enemy?

When the cab's passenger climbed out, Marla stopped dead, then broke into the biggest, most genuine smile she'd worn in weeks, if not months.

Rondeau got out of the convertible, too, and bellowed "Pelly!" He raced around the car and picked up the short, middle-aged man who'd emerged from the cab. He spun Pelham around twice, then put him back down on his feet, where he wobbled a bit.

"A pleasure to see you, sir," Pelham said, and then looked at Marla. "And you, too, Mrs. Mason."

The cab driver emerged, leaning over the roof of the car, squinting. "You going to ride the rest of the way with your friends, pal?"

"I wouldn't presume," Pelham murmured, but Rondeau was already saying, "Yeah, we got this, pop the trunk." Pelham reached into the cab and removed a battered-looking canvas backpack, and a gnarled black walkingstick that might have passed for a wizard's staff. The cab driver helped Rondeau wrestle a familiar-looking trunk out of the cab, then accepted his fare and a generous tip from Rondeau before driving off.

While Rondea was wrangling luggage, Marla walked around the car and looked Pelham up and down. He still had his wispy hair, his mild eyes, his mostly-unlined face, his general air of affable harmlessness, but he'd changed some, too. "You got some sun on your travels, huh? I never even imagined you with a tan."

"I did indeed, Mrs. Mason, in Africa, mostly," Pelham said. "Though the snows in Nepal reflected a glare even brighter."

"What are you doing *here*?" Marla said. "I told you to spend a couple of years on your, ah, mission, and it's only been a few months."

Pelham nodded. "I am still traveling. I landed this morning on the Big Island, as part of a journey through the Pacific. But I could *sense* you, nearby. I took a flight to Maui, and frustrated my cab driver immensely by refusing to tell him my final destination, guiding him instead in the direction where I felt your presence, and... Why are *you* here? Have you finally agreed to take a vacation?"

"I was going to send word to you," Marla said, "Except I wasn't sure *where*, since we warded you so well from divination, nobody could tell where you were, exactly. I left word for Hamil to pass along my contact info if you called in, but—"

"Don't mind me." Rondeau heaved the steamer trunk into the convertible's too-small trunk and fussed with bungee cords to tie it down. "I've got this."

"My apologies." Pelham stepped in with his customary competence, swiftly strapping his luggage in and tying the trunk lid partly closed with the bungees. He turned back to Marla. "Then... this isn't a vacation? Oh dear. Does something here in the islands threaten the safety of Felport? Volcano gods with strange grudges? A tentacled creature of ancient lineage stirring on the sea floor?"

Before she could answer, Rondeau yelped, and jumped like someone had stabbed him in the ass with a pin. "Marla... something's happening. Something's *coming*."

Marla had a knife in each hand before he finished speaking, and she put her back to the convertible, scanning the area. Unless the picnic tables were about to come to life like Japanese tsukumogami, she didn't see any potential threats. "What is it?"

Rondeau shook his head. "How should I know? Call it bad vibes. Some kind of... I want to say... eruption? No, I shouldn't use that word on a volcanic island, it's not that kind of eruption. Something's coming, or actually it's already here, but it's about to make itself known—"

"Oh, dear." Pelham chewed at his lower lip. "Not these again." He pointed with his walkingstick toward the ground beneath a tree. The dirt was beginning to rise up in little cone-shapes, like molehills. "I'm terribly sorry, Mrs. Mason, I thought I'd gotten rid of them."

Marla frowned. "Of what?"

"Should I be wishing I had a gun?" Rondeau said.

"I don't think a gun would be much—" Pelham began, but then a strange chittering emerged from the three mounds of black dirt, and at least a dozen cat-sized creatures poured out, like ants boiling up from a hill. The creatures moved fast enough that Marla couldn't get a good look at them, but they seemed both insectile and mammalian, with hairy bodies and too many limbs and grinding mandibles and antennae and weirdly humanlike eyes.

Knives were not ideal for fighting off a swarm of rat-bug-people, and she was stepping to the side so she could unleash a fire spell without catching her friends in the spray when Pelham stepped forward and began to spin his stick in a blur. He caught the first of the creatures with a blow hard enough to send it sailing right out of the park and into the sea, and flattened half a dozen more in seconds using his stick and his feet, spinning with a fluidity and grace that Marla couldn't quite wrap her head around—after all, Pelham looked like the manager of a small branch bank, or a longtime certified public accountant, but now he was become death; or if not death, then at least grievous bodily harm. "If I might ask you to destroy the mounds?" Pelham shouted, as more of the creatures came scrambling out of the dirt. Marla caught Rondeau's eye, shrugged, and moved with him toward the source of the invasion.

She considered just stomping, but she didn't like the idea of one of these things climbing up her leg, so she knelt, scooped up a handful of sand from the ground into a little heap, took a deep breath, and *believed* the mound she'd made was the same as the mounds the creatures were coming through.

Then she stomped on her little mound, and the other three flattened, smashed by the weight of Marla's sympathetic magic. Rondeau watched the collapsed mounds warily, then nudged one with the toe of his foot. Nothing came out. "There's not even a hole under here. What the hell?"

Pelham had finished bashing the little monsters, and those that survived burrowed into the ground, dragging their dead after them, and soon they'd all vanished from view, seemingly pulling their holes in after them, leaving the ground unmarked and unmarred. Pelham mopped his brow. "I am so very sorry. The creatures have not troubled me in weeks, and I had assumed they were gone forever. They are deucedly persistent beasts."

"What the fuck are they?" Marla said.

"Nuno sa Punso," Pelham said. "Frightful things, but really just a nuisance, incapable of doing real harm. I… picked them up during my time in the Phillipines."

"Pelly," Rondeau said. "Tell me these things aren't some kind of supernatural STD you picked up in a Filipino cathouse. Or, better yet, tell me they *are*, because that would be hilarious."

Pelham bowed slightly. "Loath as I am to disappoint you, the origin of this infestation is less lascivious. I spent a week in the Malay archipelago, studying the martial art known as Silat. I have long been proficient in Bartitsu, which incorporates elements of Malaysian stick-fighting, and I thought to refine my technique by studying at the source."

"You seem to have gotten the hang of it," Marla said. "You could have played eighteen holes using those little Nuno things as golf balls."

"Yes. Thank you. Alas, that is not the first time I have needed to forcibly dispel the creatures. While I was out walking in the countryside in the Phillipines, I inadvertently disturbed an ant hill, or perhaps a termite mound, with my stick. I expected insects to emerge, but instead—out came several Nuno. They looked more human, then, though they were still very small, appearing as tiny men with long ragged beards. They are local spirits, called 'ancestors of the ant hills,' though I think they are more closely aligned to imps than to true ancestral spirits. By which I mean, their resemblance to humanity is superficial and conditional."

"Lots of supernatural creatures start to look more like humans when they have more contact with humans," Marla said. "Or else people just perceive them that way. I looked at them in their true forms, and they weren't much like people at all, apart from the eyes."

Pelham nodded. "The Nuno are mostly used as a story by the locals, to keep children away from ant hills. If you disturb their homes, the Nuno can curse you—either trivially, to cause pain in the foot that kicked their hill, or more seriously, to… ah… this is indelicate… to urinate a viscous black fluid, or vomit blood. Most people never encounter the creatures, and only the superstitious believe they exist. I suspect they were attracted by the magical spells on my luggage." He gestured toward the convertible's trunk "Or perhaps I simply stumbled onto the one mound where they *actually* live. The Nuno have chosen to punish me more creatively than usual, it seems. They appear occasionally and attack me, wherever I am. I attempted to dispel them in Malaysia, paying an alularyo to perform a tawas ceremony. She poured molten wax into a bowl of water, interpreted certain signs beyond my understanding, and said I must make offerings of fruit at the site of the hill I'd destroyed, and beg for forgiveness. Unfortunately, I had difficulty finding the precise location again, and though I did make offerings… ." He shrugged. "I may have gotten the location wrong. Or perhaps the alularyo was a fraud. I did not realize the ritual had failed until I was a thousand miles away, when the creatures attacked me in an outdoor market. They are easily defeated, but terribly persistent, appearing days or even weeks apart. Though I lack your ability to pierce illusions, Mrs. Mason, they seem less and less humanoid to me with each appearance, as I've gone farther and farther from their home. Perhaps familiarity is enabling to see me more as they actually are."

"They look pretty much like pissed-off garden gnomes to me," Rondeau said, helpful as always. "I didn't bother to try and see their true forms. Stuff pretty much never looks *better* that way."

"I send you on a trip around the world," Marla said, "and you come back with a case of supernatural fleas. Well, curses can be lifted. We'll see what we can do."

"I would appreciate that," Pelham said. "The Nuno are most unseemly. But I do not mean to burden you with my problems, Mrs. Mason. Please, tell me, how are *you*? Why are you here?"

"You ride up front with Rondeau." Marla climbed into the convertible's comically undersized back seat. "*He'll* tell you how I am, and what I'm doing in Hawai'i."

A Visit from Death

"**THE FIRST TWO THINGS** you need to know," Rondeau said as he pulled out of the parking lot, "are that I'm crazy rich now, and Marla's been exiled from Felport."

Pelham turned around in the passenger seat and looked at Marla, his eyes owlish and wide, and she nodded, then looked away, concentrating on staring out the window.

On the ride back to the hotel, Rondeau gave Pelham the rundown on everything that had happened since he left Felport to go on his world tour. The recitation was enough to make Marla exhausted all over again. Rondeau told the valet about Marla's run-in with her con artist brother Jason, about Bradley Bowman's murder at Jason's hands, about Marla's ill-conceived (or, if you were feeling charitable, daring) plan to bring Bradley back to life. And, finally, about the horrible consequences of her meddling in such cosmic affairs, including a rip in the fabric of space/time and the subsequent emergence of her villainous counterpart from a parallel universe, the Mason. "She looked just like Marla," Rondeau said, gesturing animatedly with one hand as he drove with the other. "Well, Marla when she was twenty, maybe, because the Mason didn't age after that. Only... well, you know Marla's white-and-purple *cloak*?"

"I am familiar with the cloak." Pelham sounded thoughtful, but not especially freaked out. This was probably a lot for the guy to take in—but then again, he'd once literally traveled to Hell with Marla, and lately he'd been battling a repeated infestation by Malaysian ant-monsters, so he was used to rolling with the punches. And the kicks. "Indeed, I think of the cloak often. I find its very existence rather disturbing."

"Don't we all," Marla muttered. When she was twenty, she'd found a magical cloak hanging in a thrift store, and she'd felt compelled to buy it, sensing it was an item of magic. The cloak was more than merely magical, though—it was an *artifact*, a conscious object of uncertain origin and mysterious motivation. The cloak had granted Marla profound powers, both healing magics and viciously destructive battle prowess… but the latter came at a terrible psychic cost. Every time she used the cloak for violence, its alien intellect tried to subjugate her mind and possess her body for its own destructive ends. Essentially, it was a parasite, and Marla was the host, though it had taken her a long time to realize that. Marla's will had been strong enough to resist the cloak's attempts to possess her, but she'd never been comfortable wearing it, not once she was old and wise enough to realize how dangerous it could be. She'd eventually discovered it wasn't a cloak at all, but a malevolent entity from another universe that chose to *look* like a cloak, and that in its true form, it was so scary it even frightened gods. When she finally glimpsed the cloak's true form—something like a many-eyed devil ray with extra tentacles and fishhook fangs—she'd been horrified and vowed to never wear it again. The thing couldn't be destroyed, though, and she'd dispatched Pelham on his world tour, with the mission to hide the cloak somewhere deep and obscure, someplace no one, even Marla, could ever find it. Except—

"The Mason made Marla look like Miss Congeniality," Rondeau was saying, so Marla swatted him on the back of the head. He went on, unperturbed. "Imagine a version of Marla who put on the cloak at twenty, didn't bother to fight the cloak's influence at *all*, and just let herself get possessed by the evil alien mind inside it. That version of Marla, over in that hell of a universe next door, pretty much literally conquered the *world*. And then… we fucked up, trying to save Bradley, and tore a hole in the fabric of space-time. That set the Mason loose over here, and she went on the warpath. Shit got ugly. A lot of people in Felport died before Marla managed to outsmart the Mason. Viscarro, and Ernesto, and Granger… ." He shook his head. "Don't worry, the Chamberlain's okay, and all your friends on her estate are fine too, the Mason didn't go near her place."

"I am relieved." The Chamberlain had been Pelham's… employer, sort of? Or maybe foster mother? Pelham came from a long line of professional servants, pledged (and magically bonded) to serve prominent sorcerers. Marla hadn't wanted a valet, even a supernaturally savvy one, but the Chamberlain had insisted that, as chief sorcerer, Marla required such help, and she'd "given" Pelham to her. Pelham had turned out to be amazingly competent, and soon became a friend, but Marla wasn't happy with the notion of servants, especially supernaturally-bound ones. Which was one of the real reasons she'd sent him on his world tour—

"Oh, and check it out," Rondeau said. "The Mason had a sidekick who was like an evil version of *me*, called Crapsey, with a creepy wooden jaw and a nasty trick where he could jump into people's bodies, shove their souls into the void, and walk around in their skins—"

"Get to the exile part," Marla snapped. Rondeau was breezily reciting events that had left some pretty brutal wounds on her, psychically if not physically.

"Right." Rondeau coughed. "The, uh, sorcerers in Felport who survived the Mason's attacks blamed the whole interdimensional invasion thing on Marla, and... they kicked her out of the chief sorcerer job. Exiled her here. Well, not here specifically, they just forbid her to ever set foot in the city again. I didn't see the point in staying in Felport with Marla gone, so I sold my nightclub and decided to retire in style. Marla didn't have anything better to do, so I asked her to come along, and... here we are."

"Mrs. Mason." Pelham twisted around in his seat again, and this time, put his hand on her knee. "I am profoundly sorry for your loss. For *all* your losses."

"Me, too," Marla said. "Look, Pelham, the Chamberlain is actually the chief sorcerer of Felport now, and me... I'm *nobody*. If you want to go to Felport, I'm sure the Chamberlain would be happy to take you in—"

"I am bonded to you, Mrs. Mason." Pelham voice was gentle, his eyes placid and sure. "I could not break that bond if I wanted to, and I do *not* want to. Even if I did care about status, well, you *are* greater than any mortal nobility—"

"Shush," Marla said sharply. Pelham knew a secret about her that no one else in the *world* besides Marla herself did. It was bad enough he kept calling her "Mrs."—that would be a giveaway to anyone more attentive than Rondeau.

"Shush what?" Rondeau said.

"He was going to say something about my amazing natural gifts," Marla said. "And you know I hate being complimented."

"Whatever," Rondeau said. "Now that Pelham's back, he can keep you company at the bookshop. That'll really open up my afternoons for spa visits."

"I am pleased to serve in any capacity you wish," Pelham said. "Shall I stay here, Mrs. Mason, or do you wish me to continue my travels?"

"Did you, ah, dispose of that thing yet?" Marla said. "The thing in the trunk?"

"Do you mean the bedsheet you glamoured to look like your cursed cloak?" Pelham said politely. "No, ma'am. That is still wrapped in bindings and wards in the steamer trunk."

Marla groaned, and Rondeau whistled. "I was trying to figure out how she was going to break that to you," Rondeau said. "Sending you off on a mission to get rid of a *fake* cloak."

"Pelham, listen, I wasn't trying to screw with you, I wanted people to *think* the cloak was gone from the city," Marla said. "There were powerful people who wanted it, and I was afraid of what would happen if it fell into their hands. But at the same time, the cloak was so powerful, I couldn't bring myself to really get rid of it. I wanted to keep it in reserve, just in case I needed it, like… a nuclear weapon or a vial of super-flu. And I didn't let you in on the secret because I wanted you to—"

"I understand," Pelham said. "Truly. You wanted me to experience the real world. Before I joined your service, I'd never even left the grounds of the Chamberlain's estate. Though I was educated, and learned to serve at a formal dining table, repair cars, and cause permanent nerve damage with a well-aimed strike of the fist, I was provincial and unworldly. You wanted to expand my horizons."

"Yes," Marla said. "I mean, pretty much. I thought it would do you good, I guess."

"You are also profoundly uncomfortable with the very idea of having a lady's personal gentleman in your employ." Pelham sniffed. "I am confident you will overcome that reticence in time. May I stay with you now, then, or do you prefer me to continue the pantomime of looking for a safe place to hide your cloak?"

"No need for pretense anymore. The cloak is *really* gone now. Once I met the Mason, and saw what the cloak wanted to do to the world, what it hoped to use me for, what it *had* used me for in another dimension… I didn't have any qualms about getting rid of it, permanently, even if it did mean giving up my best weapon."

"I hope you buried it deeply," Pelham said. "Such things have a way of rising to the surface."

"Ha," Rondeau said. "Remember Bradley Bowman? How trying to bring him back to life caused all this trouble? Well, he didn't come back to life, exactly, but he ended up ascending beyond the mortal plane and whatnot. Now he's, like… the guy in charge of maintaining the structural integrity of the multiverse. Immortal, and existing simultaneously in every possible reality and in *none* of them, which is a nifty trick. We gave him the cloaks, both Marla's and the Mason's, and he put them both at the North Pole in a parallel universe where life never even developed on Earth. They are *gone*."

Pelham exhaled. "That is a relief. Then… may I stay here?"

Marla reached out and touched his shoulder. "Of course. It's good to have you back, Pelham. You'll be a great help."

"Marla's a detective now," Rondeau said. "Solving mysteries. Or, ah, failing to solve mysteries, mostly, but it's a start."

"A… detective?" Pelham said, in the tone of voice someone else might say, "A… rat turd?" "Is such an occupation truly suitable for your station?"

"What station is that?" Rondeau said. "Poverty stricken ex-chief-sorcerer? No offense, you know I love Marla to pieces, but she's not exactly an aristo, Pelly."

"Mrs. Mason." Pelham's voice was stern. "How can you expect Rondeau to give you the respect you deserve if he does not *know* you are due such respect?"

"Why do you keep calling her 'Mrs.'?" Rondeau said. "You always used to call her 'Miss Mason,' and even that was weird, but—"

Marla closed her eyes, covered her face with her hands, and groaned. "I hate you both. Take me back to the hotel."

"You got *married*," Rondeau said for the third time, sipping a rum-and-pineapple juice on his balcony. They had a great view of the ocean up here, but Rondeau was staring at her instead.

Marla sank down further in the padded chaise longue, looking up at the underside of the balcony attached to the room above them. "Okay, yes, but see—"

"To a god," Rondeau said. "To the god of Death. You're the bride of Death. You're a *goddess*."

"Only by marriage. And it's not like it was a love match. Pelham and I were in the underworld, and, well… it was a marriage of convenience. I needed to use the god of Death's sword, and in order to do that, I had to take certain aspects of his power as my own—had to become a member of the family, a god by association. Don't think of it as a marriage, it was just… a ritual."

"So you're saying you didn't consummate?" Rondeau waggled his eyebrows.

Marla made a face. "That incarnation of Death was pretty much falling apart when I met him, hanging on way past the end of his natural span. He was a wreck, and he should have made way for the new incarnation of Death years before. He wasn't exactly alluring. He couldn't even stand up from his divine throne—he was holding onto his office by pure force of will and butt-in-chairness."

"You missed out on throne sex?" Rondeau said. "I bet that thing was all encrusted with jewels, too." He paused. "And I'm not talking about the chair."

"Mrs. Mason was widowed soon after the wedding." Pelham appeared with a silver tray and placed a drink—more juice than rum—on the small round table beside Marla. *Where had he found that tray? Did he have some kind of emergency valet-kit in his backpack?* "When the old god of Death was replaced by his newer incarnation."

"Oh, I remember *him*," Rondeau said. "The Walking Death. Now *he* was yummy, even if he was kind of a dick. Shame you couldn't have married him instead of his dad. Or predecessor. Or whatever."

"A little of both," Marla said. In reality, she *was* still married to Death—it turned out the marriage ceremony had wedded her to the *office* of the god of Death, not to any particular incarnation, and the being known as the Walking Death was now her husband. Which was sort of like marrying a father, getting widowed, and marrying his son, but, hell, mythology was full of weirder sorts of incest. She hadn't consummated her marriage to the Walking Death, either, though the idea wasn't entirely unappealing, and he certainly wanted to. Her wifely duties—ha—were supposed to wait until after she died, when she'd take up the mantle of her goddesshood and sit on her own throne deep under the ground. (Well, metaphorically, and metaphysically. You couldn't actually dig a hole and get to the underworld, but it definitely had a subterranean quality.) She wouldn't really be the bride of Death until her *own* death… unless she figured out a way to wriggle out of the obligation first. Not that spending her afterlife as a terrifying goddess sounded so bad, but she was opposed to destiny in principle.

"It is a shame," Pelham mused. "If your husband still existed, you could simply *ask* him who murdered this Ronin person. Solving murders would be much simpler with the god of Death at your beck and call."

Marla stared at him. The idea had never occurred to her. She pretty much hated to ask for assistance with anything, but it wasn't like she'd be asking the Walking Death to fight her battles for her—she'd just ask him to answer a question. Surely that wouldn't shift the balance of power in their relationship too much? Though worrying about that was probably asinine. He was a god, tasked with overseeing the end-of-life and afterlife of every living thing in the universe. The "person" called the Walking Death that she interacted with occasionally was just an insignificant splinter of the god's true vastness, an externalized physical presence created to interact with humans and other lesser beings. He probably had all the power in the relationship anyway, by definition. Still, no reason to give him more. But maybe if she spun it the right way…

She cleared her throat. "Um. Maybe I'm not so widowed after all. See…"

Rondeau insisted on accompanying her back to the bookstore, and Pelham murmured that he'd be happy to join them, if she had no objection, so she just gave in. They were both giving her a lot of crap about how she shouldn't have lied to them, Rondeau gleefully, Pelham morosely. But, damn it, a woman's marriage to a chthonic deity was nobody's business but her own, and she refused to apologize.

In the back room of the bookshop, she opened up her safe, revealing the silver bell inside. It was a perfectly ordinary bell, not magical in the slightest… but Death was always listening for it.

She rang the bell.

The Walking Death never appeared before her in a puff of black smoke, or descended from the heavens like a sinking balloon. True to his name, he always just walked in, though strictly speaking, it wasn't always clear where he walked in *from*.

He walked in now, emerging from a black door in the exterior wall (which was, usually, utterly doorless.) The Walking Death stood well over six feet tall, his long brown hair falling just past the shoulders of his impeccably tailored midnight blue suit, no tie. Marla knew next to nothing about menswear, but his dress always struck her as vaguely European and timelessly fashionable. His face was pale, narrow, and aristocratic-looking, his lips curved almost perpetually into the hint of a smirk. The look should have been maddening, and it was, a little, but it was also cute. He had rings on each of his fingers, as usual, eight glittering gemstones in different colors—but, no, now he had an extra ring on the third finger of each hand, just simple silver bands.

"Darling." He kissed Marla on the cheek and took her hand in his own—cold, no surprise—before turning to look at Pelham and Rondeau. "The servant and the sidekick. How pleasant to see you both." They stared at him, apparently more overawed by the company of a god than Marla was... or at least more than she allowed herself to appear to be.

Marla pulled her hand away from his. "Sorry to call you here. I was hoping you could help me out with this... murder investigation I'm doing."

He raised one elegantly arched eyebrow. "Really? I'm to be your informant, am I? I suppose that makes a certain amount of sense. I do have access to the material witnesses in any suspicious death. I am not unwilling to assist you, if you choose to indulge in such trivialities. But I was actually planning to come see you anyway. I have something to tell you. It's wonderful news, actually."

She frowned. "What's that?"

"A number of your enemies are conspiring to kill you." The Walking Death broke into a wide smile, and swept Marla into a tight embrace. "Isn't it *wonderful*?" he breathed into her ear. "You'll be dead soon, my darling!"

The Bad Doctor

LET'S LEAVE MARLA and her friends for now, and take a few moments to talk about Dr. Leda Husch.

You don't know her? There's no reason you should; she's not alive, exactly, and will never die, though she often wishes she had. For many years now Dr. Husch has run the Blackwing Institute, a hospital of sorts for mentally ill sorcerers, located a bit outside the city of Felport, Marla Mason's old holdfast. Marla and Dr. Husch have had their disagreements, but they were essentially allies, and business associates, and occasionally even friends—as two strong women with difficult jobs, they had certain things in common, after all. But shortly before Marla's exile, something very bad happened to Dr. Husch. Her assailant was a woman from another universe—a woman who was only in *this* universe because of something Marla did, a certain selfish act that ripped a hole in the fabric of reality and let bad things cross over, specifically a bad thing called the Mason. But you know about *her*. She sent a lot of people your way, didn't she?

The Mason did a great deal of damage on her rampage through this reality before Marla stopped her, but the only damage that concerns us just now is what happened to Dr. Husch:

The Mason tore her to pieces. Literally. Small pieces. Hundreds of them.

For most people, being dismembered so thoroughly is fatal, but as I mentioned, Dr. Husch isn't exactly alive—she's a fully sentient and self-aware homunculus, created long ago by a powerful sorcerer, and as such, she cannot die. Though she was ripped to shreds, she retained awareness throughout her ordeal and the aftermath. She was later reassembled by a biomancer named Langford, and she—oh, but listen to me, going on and on. Better to show you.

While Marla is investigating a murder in Maui, back on the mainland a pair of people are on their way to meet Dr. Husch, and they should suffice for our introduction to the other side of this story. These two people were *never* friends of Marla: the first is a one-armed chaos witch named Nicolette, who holds a longstanding grudge against Marla, and the other is Crapsey, the Mason's old lackey and the dark doppelganger to Rondeau. Crapsey was stranded in this world when Marla killed his mistress the Mason, and after that he began clinging to Nicolette's coattails, because some people are only happy when they're being told what to do. Let's see how things look through Crapsey's eyes…

"Aren't you even a little bit afraid Dr. Husch is going to throw you in a cell again?" Crapsey said. "The Mason and I just broke you *out* of this place not so long ago."

"I've got you to protect me, big boy." Nicolette kicked at the massive oak doors of the Blackwing Institute, her boot thumping with the regularity of a metronome.

Crapsey winced. "Dr. Husch isn't going to be too happy to see *me*, either—I was just following orders, but I did some not-so-nice stuff to her myself, the morning she got all torn up."

"The divinations say this is the place to begin our campaign," Nicolette said. "My dice and mouse bones and toad stones don't lie."

"I still say we could've just done some recruiting," Crapsey said. "We should be looking for Marla's *enemies*, not her allies."

"There aren't that many enemies left, ugly. Even though she doesn't usually kill them herself, Marla's rivals have pretty lousy life expectancies. There's me, and there's you, and maybe her brother, but even though he's a hell of a con man, he's not much of a fighter. Mutex is dead, Todd Sweeney is dead, Ayres is dead, Joshua Kindler is dead, Reave might as well be dead. The Mason was exiled from this reality, and you two idiots killed Susan Wellstone and Viscarro on your little cross-country rampage. My old boss Gregor is dead, Bulliard and Marla reached an understanding, I don't exactly have a phone number for the so-called King of the Fairies, and—"

"All right, all right!" Crapsey touched the butterfly knife in his pocket. It had seemed so simple, when Nicolette first brought up the idea—Marla was in exile, stripped of her powers, all but friendless. What better time to try and kill her? They'd join forces with some other people who hated Marla, fly down to Hawai'i, and unleash murder most foul. Except they'd had trouble finding anybody to fill out their team, which led Nicolette to cast a divination spell to suggest a course of action, and now, here they were, on the doorstep of one of Marla's old allies. Maybe not a suicide mission, but probably an *imprisonment* mission, which was better, but not by much.

The door swung open, and Nicolette squinted inside. "What are you, a beekeeper in mourning now? Part of a Goth hazmat squad?"

The figure in the foyer wore a broad-brimmed black hat with a long black veil, the cloth thick enough to obscure her features entirely. She also wore a floor-length black dress of severe cut, and leather gloves to match. Not an inch of skin showed.

"Nicolette." The voice that emerged from beneath the veil was cracked, broken, and jagged, but comprehensible. "Have you come to commit yourself?"

"Why, Doc? Do you miss me that much?"

"You never really belonged here." Dr. Husch sounded somehow placid despite her shredded voice. Almost peaceful, Crapsey thought, even though she'd been cut to pieces. "I never believed you were mentally ill. You are vile, contemptible, and selfish, but sane. No, you were a political prisoner, kept here because of your repeated treasons against Marla Mason." The doctor shrugged. "But Marla isn't in charge anymore, and our new chief sorcerer has no particular interest in you. You're lucky—you have a chance to start over. You're just fortunate that Marla chose not to kill you. I used to share her compassion, but no more." The hat and veil shifted, and Crapsey knew the doctor was looking at him. "And you. The last time you came to my door, I… suffered. I do not like suffering. I abhor it."

Crapsey took a step back. "Doc, it wasn't my idea, the Mason *made* me go after you. I kinda liked you, honestly, and anyway I didn't catch you, you smacked me on the head—"

"I know," Dr. Husch said. "You are a lackey. And I understand your more… promiscuous tendencies… have been curtailed, making you a *harmless* lackey as well."

Crapsey winced. Once upon a time, he'd had the power to leave his flesh and take over the bodies of others, overwriting the consciousnesses of the original owners, and tossing their souls into the darkness of oblivion without hope of resurrection or afterlife. He'd murdered hundreds that way, on the Mason's orders, and changed bodies the way most people changed their shirts… but Marla had cast a spell that trapped his mind in this body, like a fly buzzing around in a glass jar. Worst of all, when this body died, there was no reason to think his consciousness would die too—he might just be trapped in his own rotting corpse forever, awake and aware. Probably justifiable punishment for his crimes, he could see that, but still: fucking harsh, to go from immortality to… well, an entirely more horrible form of immortality.

"Yeah, he's been neutered," Nicolette said. "He's totally housebroken now. I don't even know why I keep him around. He's a born lickspittle, and as you can see, I'm in greater-than-usual need of a right-hand man." She grinned and twitched her stump.

"Yes, I noticed your lack of limb. You should have stayed in the Institute. You had both arms when you were under my care."

Nicolette ran her remaining hand over her scalp. While she was captive, Crapsey knew, they'd kept her head shaved—Nicolette used to have dreadlocks, with wicked charms woven into the locks. She was letting her hair grow back in, but all she had now was a pale duck-fuzz, which looked even dumber than a bare skull. "Not that I don't miss your tender ministrations," Nicolette said, "but I'm here about something else. A certain mutual enemy. Mind if we come inside and talk?"

"If that crosses my threshold—" she pointed at Crapsey "—it will be confined, forever, in the blackest cell I have. The one in the basement. The one I used to be too enlightened to keep *anyone* in. And you aren't welcome through this door, either, chaos witch."

"Uh, okay." Crapsey took another step back. Much farther and he'd be back in the driveway. "We can talk out here. Or we can just… go. Probably it was a mistake to come here—"

Nicolette interrupted. "The divinations don't lie, Doc. I did three different readings, with entrails and dice and butterflies, and they all told me— you're the one we need."

"And what were you trying to find with this divination? Someone to lock you both up for your own good?"

"Nah." Nicolette leaned in close, not quite crossing the threshold. "We were looking for somebody else who wanted Marla Mason dead bad enough to do something about it."

The veil and the hat made reading expressions impossible, so it took a moment for Crapsey to realize that Dr. Husch was shaking with silent laughter, which finally bubbled forth in a harsh little series of caws. "Oh, dear," she said. "Well, yes, divination doesn't lie, assuming an augur skilled enough to read the signs correctly, but there's nothing to stop a witch from asking entirely the wrong question."

"What's that supposed to mean?" Nicolette demanded.

"You should have asked, 'Who would *help* us kill Marla Mason?' Because my name would not have appeared in a list of answers to that query. I do mean Marla Mason harm. Her selfishness unleashed the Mason on the world, and that led directly to me becoming… *this*." She drew out the last word in a hiss, and Crapsey steeled himself for a dramatic raising of the veil to reveal the horror beneath, but Dr. Husch settled for shuddering and hugging herself. "And Marla doesn't *care*. She didn't even come to see me after her exile, even though my hospital is outside the borders of Felport, and open to her. If she'd come… if she'd *apologized*… Well. I don't know that it would have mattered, really. But she didn't. Exile is far from sufficient punishment for her transgressions, and her selfishness. So, yes, I do mean her harm—but why on Earth do you think I'd need help from *you* two idiots to kill her?"

"No offense," Nicolette said, "but every time one of the more dangerous loonies in this bin of yours got loose, you always went crying to Marla, and before her, you went crying to Sauvage, and I'm sure before that, you went crying to whoever was chief sorcerer before him. You're a healer, right, and a *jailer*, and when it comes to fixing broken things and locking up the things that can't be fixed, you're pretty badass, and I'm full of respect for that. But killing Marla Mason? Doc, you just don't have the *chops*. Neither do I, and neither does Crapsey, not alone. But together? Striking now, when she's weak and friendless? We can all get revenge. Crapsey for getting stranded in this stupid universe he hates, all his powers stolen, his boss sent away to another universe. And me? She locked me up *here*. Before that she backed me into a corner so tight I had no choice but to kill my own mentor Gregor just to stay alive myself. Hell, indirectly, she's the reason I lost my arm. What do you say? You, me, Crapsey, maybe we round up a few others, and go all legion of supervillains on her ass?"

"Not really legion of supervillains." Crapsey flinched away when they both swiveled their heads toward him. He couldn't help it—he'd read a lot of comic books in his home universe, and he wanted to get the metaphor right. "More like the… Marla Mason Revenge Squad. "

"I am well aware of my limitations," Dr. Husch said. "I do not intend to attack Marla personally. But as you pointed out, I am a *jailer*. This is the foremost magical containment facility on the East Coast, and I have in my care some of the most lethal sorcerers to ever grace this continent. Norma Nilson, the nihilomancer. Gustavus Lupo, the skinshifter. Roderick Barrow, who rules a dark realm of his own imagination, and yearns to loose his armies into this reality. Roger Vaughn—*both* Roger Vaughns, the original and his young reincarnation—and their terrible oceanic magics. The nameless madman who calls himself Everett Malkin, and claims to be Felport's first chief sorcerer, displaced in time. The immortal Beast of Felport *itself*. And, of course, I have your hero, Nicolette, locked in the most potent cell I possess, at the center of a cube wrapped in bindings of order—the witch Elsie Jarrow. You would be *amazed* at what some of these people are willing to do when you dangle the prospect of freedom before them. So, no—I won't be needing your services. Good luck with the rest of your miserable, pointless lives." The doctor started to close the door.

Nicolette stuck a boot in the way, and Dr. Husch made a noise of distaste and opened it again. "Do you want to lose a foot along with your arm, woman?"

"We want in," Nicolette said. "If nothing else, we can help wrangle the crazies. Besides, don't bullshit me, there's no way you can let Elsie Jarrow out, you'd never be able to control her, she's too—"

"I am well aware of her condition—indeed, as her doctor, I know far more about her situation than you do. As I said, your services will not be needed. Why hire Vasari when you can work with Michelangelo?"

"I'm going to assume that's an insult," Nicolette said. "Like 'why listen to Rush when you can listen to Led Zeppelin?' But I don't mind—I'm not fit to touch the hem of Elsie Jarrow's garment. But that just means I'm even more eager to lend a hand. Let us join in. What could it hurt?"

"My chances of success," Dr. Husch said.

Nicolette laughed. "Not bad, Doc. Being disfigured has given you a sense of humor. But what'll *really* hurt your chances of success is me going to Marla and telling her what you have planned. And sending word to a few of the reigning sorcerers—I don't think the Chamberlain or Hamil would be happy to hear you've decided to switch your patients from art therapy to murder-for-hire. That's the kind of thing that could seriously impact your funding at the next meeting of the council, don't you think? Or maybe you want to get locked up in one of your own cells?"

"You would help Marla? Protect her from me? Even though you want her dead?"

"Doc," Crapsey said. "This is Nicolette. You can't trust her to do *anything*. Messy unexpected stuff just makes her more powerful. She's got a roulette wheel instead of a soul, you know?"

"Hmm. What makes you think you can escape the grounds of this estate?"

Nicolette drew a small hatchet with a curved blade the color of the moon from behind her back, and held it up to catch the light. "I did a little looting while I was running around with Crapsey and the Mason. I found this beauty in one of Viscarro's vaults. It's sacred to some moon god, I forget his name, but the point is—it is *awesome*. All those years I was jealous of Marla's cloak, and her dagger of office, and now I've got an artifact of my own, and Marla doesn't have *any*. Anyway, sure, sic your orderlies on me, whatever—if you feel like getting chopped into fucking little *bits* again."

Dr. Husch didn't move. You could have cut the tension with a knife. Or a really terrifying axe.

"Look, we want the same thing," Crapsey said, holding up his hands in a gesture he hoped was soothing. "There's no reason for us to fight. Just let us help. We can lend a hand."

"Three hands, even," Nicolette said.

To Crapsey's surprise, Dr. Husch snorted with laughter. "Fine. I can see you won't go away. I suppose I could use people to carry boxes and fetch coffee. But you take orders from *me*, understood?" She turned and started into the Institute, then paused, and called back over her shoulder, "You can come inside now."

"No trying to lock us up, Doc," Nicolette said, stepping in.

"I wouldn't worry," Dr. Husch said. "Haven't you heard? Nowadays, it's fashionable to let the inmates run the asylum."

A Mother's Love

"**I CAN'T WAIT.**" Death smelled of cut lemons and tarnished metal. "We can finally start our afterlife together—"

Marla resisted the urge to knee Death in the crotch, but she did disentangle herself from his embrace and push him away. "We've been over this. I'm not eager to shuffle off this mortal coil yet, and like you always say, the rest of my long and natural life is just a drop in the bucket of eternity, and all that—you promised you wouldn't rush me into an early grave."

He held up his hands, rings twinkling in the light from the brass chandeliers. "I'm not! I have no hand in this at all, darling. But there are forces gathering against you, and, well... while there are no certain futures, there are certainly *likely* ones, and it doesn't look like you'll live to see the new year here in the upper world."

"Huh." Rondeau turned to Pelham. "So, if your mistress dies, what happens to you? Do you, like, crawl onto the funeral pyre? Or serve her in the afterlife like an unlucky Egyptian servant?"

"The bond is broken by death." Pelham wrung his hands. "But—but surely—"

"Surely for *sure*." Marla crossed her arms. "Who's coming after me, Death?"

He sighed. "I'm not certain. I can tell when someone is going to die—or when they're *likely* to die, though the possibilities have always proliferated rather wildly for you—and gradually those lines of probability narrow into certainties. Your death is... increasingly likely. I know some other people who will almost certainly die *with* you, in the same place, around the same time. Perhaps that might give you a hint?"

"Shoot," she said.

"A witch named Nicolette," Death said. "And, ah... your brother, Jason."

Marla whistled. "Both of them? They don't even know each other."

Death shrugged. "Perhaps not yet, but they will probably die within half-a-dozen yards and a few minutes of one another, and your odds of lasting long beyond their demise are quite slim."

Marla nodded. "But now I *know* about the threat. That changes the equation, right? Forewarned is forearmed and all that."

Death spread his hands, and gazed down at the rings. The gems glowed faintly in various colors, from sky-blue to the red of strawberry wine to a necrotic pulsing black. He slowly shook his head. "Here, in this physical form, I have only limited access to my full powers, but from what I can see. . . . No, sorry. Your knowledge doesn't change things substantially. Oh, the place and time, those have shifted, but death is still rushing toward you. None of this is *written*, nothing is ordained, but... you don't need to believe in fate to know a dropped billiard ball is going to hit the floor. It's simple physics. Objects are in motion, and it is possible to chart the trajectories of those objects, barring outside interference."

"Like someone kicking the billiard ball through a window." Marla rounded on Rondeau. "You! You're supposed to be my seer. Haven't you been having any crazy prophetic dreams? Bradley used to have visions if I was about to stub my toe!"

"Bullshit," Rondeau said. "Anyway, I take *way* more opiates than Bradley did. I've had a few of *those* dreams, the prophetic ones, and they're cryptic as fuck and scary as hell. I don't like them much. Is it any surprise I pop some downers before bedtime?"

Marla sat down on the padded stool behind the counter, happy to put a slab of oak between herself and the Walking Death. She stared at the rippled windows of the bookshop, and after a moment, she smiled. "All right. Okay. What's my timeline looking like?"

Death reached into his vest pocket and tugged on a chain. Marla expected a pocketwatch, but instead, he pulled out a small hourglass, filled with white sand, and held it up to the light. Marla rolled her eyes. "An hourglass? Really?"

"There's nothing wrong with tradition. I should show you my scythe sometime. I'd say you have... three days? Perhaps a week? It varies, there's some slippage, so it could be a bit more, or a bit less."

"Around Hallowe'en, then?" Marla said. "Isn't that a little, I dunno, over-the-top?"

"For a witch's duel? Someone has a taste for the classics, anyway."

Marla cracked her knuckles methodically. "All right, then. I get the general idea. Nicolette and Jason both have reasons to want me dead. I figure this is a revenge thing, kick me when I'm down, then keep kicking me until my insides come out. I don't know how *they* got together, or will get together, or whatever, but I'll roll with it. I can make plans."

"Mrs. Mason," Pelham said. He glanced at Death. "Or, er... Mrs. Death?"

"I believe my wife would prefer to keep her own name," Death said.

"She would. What is it, Pelham?"

"Forgive me for saying so, but... you seem almost *pleased* at the prospect of your imminent demise."

"Nah," Rondeau said. "She's pleased at the prospect of a fight. Aren't you?"

She reached under the counter and took out a Samoan war club, three feet of intricately carved black wood curved at the end like a blunt hockey-stick, the whole thing heavy as a sledgehammer. "Beautiful, isn't it? A kahuna over on the Hana side asked me to help out with a ghost problem, and gave me this as payment. I haven't had a chance to hit anybody with it yet. I don't know that I could bring myself to use it on Jason, despite everything he's done… but I could sure as shit split Nicolette's skull with this."

Death sighed. "I hate it when you get all bloodthirsty. It's unbecoming in a queen of the dead."

"I'm not dead yet, loverboy." She put the war club away. "Thanks for the heads-up about my imminent demise. But while I'm alive, I've got a job to do, which is why I called you here in the first place. There was a wave-mage named Ronin. Somebody cut his throat and let him bleed out into the waves. His cohort want to know who did the deed. Divinations don't turn up anything, and Rondeau even summoned an oracle that couldn't help us. The killer has whipped up some kind of big obfuscating magic—but I figure *you* can just pop in on the dead guy's private hell or heaven and *ask* him who cut his throat, right?"

"I'll do almost anything for you." Death leaned across the counter, bringing his face close to Marla's. "But the price is a kiss."

"What would she have to pay to get you to kill Nicolette and Jason before they come after us?" Rondeau said, and just grinned when Marla glared. "What? It's worth asking."

"We have an agreement," Death said, glancing at Rondeau. "I will do nothing to hasten Marla's demise… but I will not intervene to delay it. This life of hers is important, of course, but from my point of view, it's all just… prelude." He looked back at Marla. "The underworld is *dull* without you. The place could use—"

"If you say 'a woman's touch,' this is one woman *you'll* never touch," Marla warned. Death chuckled, and Marla leaned in and planted a quick kiss on his lips.

"Would it be so bad, spending eternity with me?" Death murmured.

"I'll be honest," Marla said. "It's not the thought of being dead that bothers me. It's the thought of being beaten." She shook her head. "You wouldn't want to spend eternity with me if *Nicolette* manages to kill me. That's one bad mood that would never end. Hell would become a genuinely unpleasant place with me in charge."

"You'll be a good queen." Death stepped away from the counter. "It's a shame the qualities that make you worthy to stand beside me also serve to delay the time until you *do*. All right. I'll check on this—Ronin, was it? I'll be in touch when I find out something." He ambled across the room, opened a door in the corner, and stepped through, shutting the door after him, where-upon it turned into nothing more than a slanted shadow.

Marla grinned at Rondeau "There. That's a detective-type thing to do, right? Working informants, using sources, all that stuff? I rule at this."

"I can't believe you married *Death*," Rondeau said. "How do you not mention that?"

"Probably because it leads to conversations like this one? So what do we do with the rest of the afternoon? I can't do much about this investigation until I hear back from, ah—"

"Your DH?" Rondeau said. "That's what the happy homemaker types call it on the internet—'dear husband.' Or 'dead husband' I guess in this case."

"Go swim in a shark tank." Marla looked up at the ceiling. "I should prepare for the attack that's coming, too, but... well. Back in Felport I'd call the seers and sibyls, I'd tailor the pattern recognition sensors on the border guardians to look for Jason and Nicolette, I'd put all the snitches and street kids on alert... but what the hell do I do *here*?"

"Well," Rondeau said. "Death says your brother is coming. So maybe, I don't know... call him?"

Marla snorted. "You want me to reach out to Jason? Are you forgetting he *shot* you?"

"He did worse than that—he used me, said he'd teach me to be a con artist, said I'd be part of his *crew*, and then tried to kill me as soon as I got a little bit inconvenient." Rondeau shook his head. "But he's still your family. If nothing else, calling him up is an *unpredictable* thing to do, right? An un-likely thing? Some of that, what do you call it, lateral thinking, it might shake up some of the paths of probability your DH was talking about."

"It's not like I even have Jason's number. He had a cell in Felport but it was a burner, he tossed it—"

Pelham cleared his throat. "Mrs. Mason, if I may... there is an interme-diate connection you might exploit."

"Who? I don't know anybody who knows Jason. Nobody alive, anyway. Cam-Cam is dead, Danny Two Saints is dead—"

"Mrs. Mason," Pelham interrupted. "I meant that you could call your *mother*."

Marla put her head down on the counter and brought out some of her choicest curse words, the ones she saved for special occasions.

When they'd reunited after their long estrangement, Marla's brother Ja-son had told her their mother was dead, passed on years ago from cirrhosis of the liver, leaving behind an inheritance of exactly jack-shit. He'd used that news to both guilt-trip Marla into some family bonding and as a way to scam his way into becoming the beneficiary of Marla's own last will and testament, acting on the mistaken impression that she was a rich crime boss. After Jason's treachery was revealed, Marla realized nothing he said could be trusted, including the potential life-or-death of her mother, so she'd made some discreet inquiries. It turned out Gloria Mason still lived in the same shitty trailer in the same shitty Indiana town she always had.

Marla remembered her childhood phone number just fine. The voice that answered was smoke-roughened and way too old, but it had an aggrieved and peevish tone she recognized instantly: "What?"

"Nice to talk to you too, Mom," Marla said.

"You got a wrong number, girl."

"Don't hang up!" Marla shouted, glad she'd sent Rondeau and Pelham out of the shop. Making this call was hard enough. "It's me, mom. It's Marla."

A long silence, and then an inhalation that probably involved a cigarette. "Well, well. What kind of trouble are you in?"

Marla gritted her teeth. Her relationship with her mother wasn't the only reason she'd run away from home before turning sixteen, but it had been in the top five. Gloria Mason had been a roadhouse beauty with a string of drunken boyfriends, and as soon as Marla hit puberty, her mother started to view her with a combination of distrust, suspicion, jealousy, and entirely unhealthy competition. "No trouble at all. Just… thought it was time I got in touch."

"After nearly twenty years? Isn't that sweet of you, to remember the woman who gave birth to you and kept you clothed and fed. I just naturally assumed you were dead, murdered by some psychopath the first night after you ran away. Nice of you to call and set my mind at ease."

"I sent money," Marla said. "A few times."

A laugh. "Did you now? Jason told me he was the one who sent it."

Of course he did. "He ran away too, you know"

Her mother's voice was patient, and as condescending as a god talking to a wayward worshipper. "No, dear. He told me he was leaving. He kissed my cheek and gave me an address where I could reach him. He *moved* away. That's not the same thing. I guess all this time you've just been confused about the difference. So now you know you should feel bad. I'm sure you'll get right on that."

Marla leaned forward in the chair, resting her forehead on the smooth wooden surface of the desk. She'd rather kick a hellhound than do this, any day. "You're right. I'm sorry. I was young, and stupid, and ungrateful." *And you were an evil bitch who was either willfully blind to the way your boyfriends groped me, or who thought I deserved it, or who thought I wanted it.* But saying that wouldn't get her what she wanted, so she didn't. "Listen. I ran into Jason a few months ago. That's why I'm calling—I've been thinking about family."

"Blood isn't much, but I guess it's something. So this is just a call to catch up? Let me know whether or not I have any grandbabies?"

"No babies here."

"Learned to keep your legs closed, did you?"

Marla had to literally bite her tongue to keep from saying something nasty—*I was a virgin when I left home, no thanks to the efforts of your thousand asshole boyfriends.* She almost hung up the phone, and her hands started to shake, but she took a deep breath and powered through. "I... we should talk. Try to get past this... all this time and distance between us."

"You abandoned this family." Gloria's voice was cool and poisonous. "Now you think you can make one phone call and get back on the Christmas card list?"

"I have to start somewhere, don't I? And like I said, I saw Jason. We were supposed to get together again recently, but I got sidetracked and couldn't make it, and now the number I had for him doesn't work. Do you have a way to reach him?"

A long silence. "I see. This is about money, isn't it? Jason always was a soft touch, he'll probably even give you some, the fool boy."

"It's not about money," Marla said. "It's... more a matter of life and death."

Another harsh laugh. "His, or yours? I can tell you which one I'd favor. Never mind, never mind. Give me your number. I'll call Jason and tell him you're trying to reach him."

Marla rattled off Rondeau's cell number—no way she was giving her mom one of *her* numbers, and they could always throw Rondeau's phone in the ocean later. After performing an exorcism. "Thank you. I know I wasn't the easiest daughter in the world, and this means a lot."

"You were plenty easy, and don't think I didn't notice. I'm glad this means something to you. It doesn't to me." There was a click as she hung up the phone.

"That went well," Marla said to the empty office.

Marla was crap at waiting, and she had nothing to do *but* wait—for Death to get back in touch, and for Jason to call her back, assuming her mother even tried to pass on the message. So she locked up the bookshop and went out out onto Front Street. She walked down a couple of blocks, then crossed to the ocean side, going down a short flight of steps next to a mediocre cheeseburger restaurant with spectacular views. Just like that, she was on the beach, and what a beach: pale sand, views of the sea, sailboats, and the island of Lanai, that last partially obscured by clouds. A far cry from the bay of Felport, with its iron-gray water fizzing and sloshing with pollution by the shore, and the scraggly wooded islands farther out. Marla would never admit to liking this view better than the one in her old city—but she could grudgingly admit it was lovely enough in its way, even if she was sick of looking at it by now.

She took off her boots and stood in the surf, gazing at the leaning mast of a dead sailboat that had been reefed a few score yards out and abandoned years before. "I know how you feel," she told the boat.

"And how's that?" The voice was cheerful enough, but so unexpected that Marla reached for a knife before turning her head.

A shirtless, athletic Hawai'ian man wearing knee-length blue shorts and rubber sandals sat down in the sand next to her feet. A long black ponytail, bound with colorful elastics along its length, hung down between his shoulderblades, straight as a plumb line. He was somewhere north of twenty and south of fifty, but Marla had trouble pinning his age down any more precisely than that—his face was young, but something about his calm dark eyes suggested they'd seen a lot of things over a lot of years. He looked up at her, smiling. "Will you sit and talk with me?"

Marla sat. "Have we met?"

"We have now. My name is Reva." He offered his hand.

She didn't take it. "I'm Marla." She didn't get any whiff of bad crazy off him, or any intimation of power, either—which meant he was either an ordinary man, or strong enough in magic to hide every trace of the uncanny.

"Oh, I know. I told Glyph and the others of his tribe about you. How's the job going, by the way?"

"I shouldn't discuss an ongoing investigation." She looked him over. "Glyph told me a god recommended me."

"Yes." Still calm. But crazy could be very calm under certain circumstances.

"Reva's your name? Can't say it rings a bell. I've heard of Pele, and Lono, and Uli, and—"

"Oh, they're all much greater than I am. I'm the sort of god only a hipster could love—so obscure, almost nobody's ever heard of me."

"I always thought the big gods were sellouts anyway. So what exactly are you supposed to be the god *of*?"

"I *was* the god of a little island in the Pacific, far from here—far from anywhere, really. Not many people lived there, but there were enough inhabitants to kindle me into specificity, to expect the local power to have a mind and a personality, and so draw me into being. I lived a simple life of storms, and fishing, and births, and deaths. But, alas… my island sank."

"Wait, what? You mean *sank*? Like Atlantis?"

"Atlantis was a great city. My island was little more than a village and some trees. But, yes. It sank. That happens sometimes. Volcanic activity. Earthquakes. Land rises, land falls."

"Huh. So all your worshippers died?"

"Oh, not that many. Most just left. Islands don't sink overnight. They departed, and left me behind. I found myself a genius loci with no loci, or no worshippers anyway."

"Isn't that a death sentence for a god?"

"Eh. Not necessarily. Belief is a factor in the birth of gods—some gods, anyway, sometimes. Others seem to exist because the universe needs them to exist. Those gods were around before there were people, though they've come to resemble people more and more over the years, at least in some of their aspects. I mean the big gods—sea gods, storm gods, like that."

"The god of death."

Reva nodded. "That's another one. But smaller gods, yes, we emerge from raw magical power, taking on specific forms based on the beliefs and expectations of our worshippers. But that belief just starts us going, like crumpled up newspapers are used to start a fire. After it's started, the fire can continue burning long after the original source of fuel is gone—as long as it can find something else to keep it going. So, with my home and original purpose gone, I had to find another niche."

"And more worshippers to consume, oh burning bush?"

"All right, the fire metaphor was ill-chosen. I do not consume my followers. Nor do I look for sacrifices. Since I became a wandering, displaced god, I became the god of wanderers and the displaced. Exiles, and the homesick, and the expatriate. I'm the god of people who aren't from around here—wherever 'here' might be."

"Uh-huh. No offense, but I don't get a real godly vibe off you." Marla squinted, letting Death's gift of true seeing fill her. The man before her wore no illusions—he was just what he appeared to be.

Reva nodded. "Good. That means it's working. When I come to a place, I like to take on a shape that conforms to local norms—this body is perfectly human and quite unremarkable here, as it should be, even though I made it from dust and sand and dead animals and sea salt. Everything is just atoms, after all, and it's trivial to assemble the atoms this particular way. Just be glad I didn't appear as a loudmouthed middle-aged sports fisherman instead. That shape would fit better on the Big Island anyway."

"Yeah, okay, whatever. I'm not in the market for a new god, anyway, so you can take your pitch elsewhere."

"Oh, Marla Mason. You've lost heart, haven't you? Lost your purpose, along with your home. A man once told me, 'a person needs a purpose like a car needs a driver.'" Reva rose, brushing sand from the seat of his shorts. "I'm already your god, Marla—because you are an exile, and far from home. I'm not asking for worship or tax-deductible donations. Just know that, when I can, I help my people."

"What makes you think I want your help?"

"I know you don't want it." Reva began to walk south along the shore-line, and called after him: "But I also know you *need* it."

Marla watched him until he was just a speck in the distance, then flopped back on the sand to look at the sky and the clouds. Maybe he really was a god. She'd met enough of them, more than most people ever did—maybe some god-stink had rubbed off on her, attracting others.

Someone cleared his throat discreetly, and a flash of anger rushed through Marla. Gods*damnit*, couldn't she have a few minutes alone to con-template her mortality and think about who she might have to kill to stay alive? And what she'd do with herself if she did manage to survive? And if it was even worth *bothering* to survive?

"What is it, Pelham?" she said, calm as calm.

"Your husband appeared in the grocery store where Rondeau and I were shopping. He is now waiting at the bookshop." Her valet paused. "He told me to let you know he has bad news."

"Of course he does. Why ruin a perfect streak?"

Death Makes an Offer

RONDEAU HAD, REMARKABLY, never needed to make small talk with a god before. "What do you do for a living?" and "Which kind of massage do you like better, hot stone or shiatsu?" seemed like fruitless lines of inquiry. But Pelham was off looking for Marla—it was weird that the god hadn't managed to show up where Marla actually *was*, but presumably Death didn't need to be omniscient about anything except maybe actuarial tables—leaving Rondeau here alone with one of the more powerful personifications of an impersonal force in the universe. Probably better to keep mum, but Rondeau had a pathological aversion to silence, so he had to say something. He settled for, "So, did you find that dead guy? The one who got murdered?"

"Mmm? Yes, I spoke to Ronin." Death sat in a soft, red leather armchair beneath a light-filled window. He looked like something from a Renaissance painting (specifically the sort of portrait commissioned by wealthy and amoral merchants). Death must have brought the chair with him, or conjured it into existence, as the chairs that normally furnished the bookshop were straight-backed and wooden. Rondeau hadn't actually seen the chair appear, but that was Death's whole modus operandi. He insinuated himself. By the time you started wondering where he'd come from, he was already in place.

"Ronin," Rondeau said, leaning against a bookshelf. "Something about that name has been bugging me, it sounds familiar. It's Japanese, right? Wasn't there a movie called *Ronin*?"

"I wouldn't know. But yes, the man was born in Japan, though that is not his given name—he chose it."

"Right. I don't know much about Japanese mythology. Ancestor worship and stuff, right? What kind of hell, or heaven, or whatever, do they favor?"

"Once upon a time, Japan had some interesting visions of the afterlife. The ten judges of Hell, and the old hag Datsueba, who would rip the clothes from your back as you passed by—and if you weren't wearing clothes, she would rip off your skin." Death took an art book featuring pictures of the moon from the shelf and began flipping through it idly as he spoke. "Many Japanese are quite secular now. The religious ones tend to be Buddhist or Shinto, and Shintoism eschews the issue of death almost entirely—they leave that for the Buddhists. But neither faith is known for its rich and complex visions of the afterlife. Nirvana for some, or the purgatory of the bardo, followed by reincarnation—which does happen, sometimes, it's very strange, and I don't entirely understand it, but I usually don't interfere. Nothing of the original personality seems to remain when a soul is reincarnated and returns to Earth. It's more like… recycling a plastic bottle into a plastic bag. The raw material is the same, but the end product is quite different. When those people die again, and come back to me, they're like a wholly different soul."

"Huh. So is this Ronin in the reincarnation queue?"

"Oh, no. His spiritual inclinations lay in a different direction, and his afterlife is… rather more unique. I never cease to be amazed by the heavens and hells people conjure for themselves. Ronin made himself into a sentient ocean on a watery planet. I had to create a boat of reeds and papyrus and ply his waters for a while before he noticed me, and even then, it took a while before he consented to talk to me. I could have made myself into an asteroid and smashed into his surface, and really gotten his attention, but… he was so beautiful. Blue and vast. I couldn't bring myself to do something so crass. Besides, there was no hurry. Time in the eternal realms functions differently from time in this world. Things are much slower down there." He sighed. "That's part of why waiting for Marla to die is so tedious—"

"Wait," Rondeau said, standing up straighter. The moment he spoke he realized he'd just interrupted *Death*, but, shit, too late now. "So you're telling me everybody gets to create their own afterlife?"

Death shrugged, closing the moon book on his lap. "People get what they expect, mostly, or what they think they deserve. Very few realize they're the ones creating the afterlife they live in—shaping the raw magic of my realm into appropriate shapes."

"Huh. So the bad guys come to bad ends because deep down they know they deserve it? But there are plenty of evil people who don't think they're evil."

"Yes."

"So, what, they just get to cavort in the corpse gardens of Pedophile Island or whatever, happy and depraved for eternity?"

Death shrugged. "Sometimes. And why not? It's not as if rehabilitation or punishment really matter—occasional reincarnation notwithstanding, eternity is eternal. It doesn't matter if the souls are reformed, or tormented. They can't hurt anyone while they're locked in the palaces of their own imaginings—every figure they conjure is an aspect of their own selves. Anyway, when freed from the pressures of the flesh, and the poison of bad brain chemistry, people can be remarkably different, and some very nasty folk have felt profound remorse for their actions in life. Still, as someone who once dabbled in cruelty and later saw the error of my ways, I… occasionally intervene, and try to bring a certain amount of moral clarity to the truly repellent souls. But you'd be surprised how seldom it's necessary. Most people realize, on some level, when they've done unforgivable things."

"But if I ever manage to die, you'll totally hook me up, right?" Rondeau said. "I mean, I *assume* I'm an immortal psychic parasite who wears human bodies like you wear pants, but I'm not a hundred percent sure. You can't know the unknowable and all that. I could die someday."

"I doubt you'll have any trouble in the underworld." Death leaned forward. "Although, if you'd like to make *sure*, I'd be open to making an arrangement. Not just limited to the pleasures of the afterlife, either—I can make sure your days on Earth are pleasant beyond your imagining."

Rondeau frowned. "I'm… pretty rich, and just as bone idle as I'd like to be already."

Death snorted. "You can afford to live well on a nice island, Rondeau. But I could give you the wealth to buy your own islands, and the influence to rule them, and the power to shape them to your whim."

Rondeau licked his lips. He knew, instinctively, that he wasn't the kind of person who should be trusted with reality-altering powers. But he was exactly the kind of person who found them very tempting. So: why was Death trying to tempt him? "I'm guessing this would be more in the nature of a transaction than a gift?"

"I wouldn't ask for much," Death said. "Only, if there comes a time when you could do something and save Marla Mason's life, or do nothing and let her die, I'd ask you… to choose nothing."

Rondeau whistled. "You want me to betray my best friend?"

"I suppose you could put it that way," Death said. "But you're free to say no. The fact that you're almost certainly immortal is one of the reasons I'm willing to ask you this—there's no implied threat, you see, since I can't take your life. Still, I hope you consider the option. Marla would never know, after all—your failing to act in time to save her would hardly strike her as unbelievable. You often fail to act in a timely fashion, don't you? It's not as if dying would be the end of Marla—she'd ascend to her goddesshood, and begin her truly important work." Death sniffed. "Not that investigating murders isn't important, I suppose, but from my point of view, one more dead person is hardly anything to get worked up about."

"Thanks for the offer, really, but I think I have to pass." Rondeau wanted to go crawl behind the counter and hide. This was Death; he wasn't human. He didn't *get* humans. If you wanted to be technical, Rondeau wasn't a human, either, but he'd lived as one long enough to get a pretty good handle on the subtleties.

"No, no, don't decide now, mull it over. Dream about the kind of power I could give you. I'm not asking you to raise a hand against Marla, I'd never ask you that—but *not* raising a hand? Just... standing by? All I'm asking you to do is... nothing at all, at the right time, if the situation arises."

"Seriously, I—"

"Do not *answer*." Death's voice was like an ice gale, freezing Rondeau's words in his throat. "Just... act, or do not act, as the circumstances warrant."

"Okay," he croaked.

Death rose and strode over to Rondeau, putting a hand on his shoulder. It was like being touched by a marble statue: heavy and cold. "I'd appreciate it if you kept this conversation between us. I want what's best for Marla, that's all, but I don't think she would understand. If you saw someone you loved wasting their life on trivialities, when you knew they could be doing much greater things, wouldn't you want to steer them toward greatness?" His face was long, pale, and earnest; his eyes lively and bright; but all Rondeau could imagine was a void behind those eyes, an everlasting blackness. Eternity was eternity. As far as Death was concerned, everything before eternity was just a waste of time.

"I'm, uh, a pretty big fan of trivialities." Rondeau resisted the urge to squirm away from Death's touch. "String together enough trivialities, and you're talking about something pretty substantial."

"Disappointing." Death let go of Rondeau and spun around just as the door to the bookshop opened. "Marla, darling! I come bearing news from the worlds below."

"Anything useful?" Marla entered, followed by Pelham, and she sat right down in the chair Death had vacated. She looked worried, and thoughtful, which was a nice change from the way she'd mostly looked lately—namely, bored and pissed-off.

"Alas, I have little to report." Death sat on the arm of the chair, putting his hand on Marla's shoulder, prompting her to roll her eyes. "Ronin declined to tell me who'd murdered him."

"What, he doesn't know?"

"He knows—he just doesn't want to say. He informed me it was none of my business."

"But you're Death," Rondeau said. "It seems like his murder would fall under your jurisdiction."

"He disagreed, and politely asked me to leave him to his eternity. So I did."

"Don't you have some kind of kill-o-vision you can access to see the dirty deed done?" Marla said. "I thought you were present at the moment of every death."

"I am present for every death the way a bank is present for every credit card transaction, my love. In a highly-distributed, extremely abstract, and basically impersonal fashion. Oh, I sometimes make a personal appearance, if the deceased interests me particularly, but that's a rarity. Don't pout, Marla."

She shruggled his hand off her shoulder. "I don't pout. I'm not pouting. I'm *fuming*. You're telling me there's no way you can find out who murdered Ronin?"

"Marla, I'm *Death*. Of course I could find out, if I expended the effort. But Ronin asked me not to do so, and I am granting his request."

"You'd favor some dead guy over your own wife?"

"I'm not just the god of Death, Marla—I'm the god of the *dead*. One of my subjects made a reasonable request, and I see no reason to deny it."

"You *want* me to have to do this the hard way, don't you?"

"It is lovely to see you interested in something again, I admit. Be honest. Did you take this case because you have a burning desire to see justice done, or because you thought investigating a supernatural murder would be interesting?"

"You know me well enough to know the answer to that one."

Death spread his hands. "Then where's the fun if I just *tell* you who killed Ronin?"

"What, it'll mean more to me if I earn it? That what you're trying to say?"

"Hmm. I suppose so."

Marla sighed. "I prefer to be the one teaching people lessons, Mr. Mason. You'd do well to remember that in the future. But, fine, point taken. If you're not going to help me, beat it. I'll see you at my funeral. Which won't be for a *long* time, so don't get excited."

Death stood. "Before I go, I wanted to give you this." He slipped the silver ring off his right hand and held it up. "You lost your cloak—and good riddance to the vile thing—but I hate to think of you with only *one* artifact in your possession."

Marla grunted. She still had a magical dagger that could cut through anything physical and many things that weren't, including ghosts and astral bodies; it was an exact replica of the dagger of office she'd had as chief sorcerer of Felport, and it was also a gift from Death. Being married to a god had advantages, Rondeau had to admit.

"What is it?"

"A wedding band."

"Well, yeah. What's it do?"

"Again—where's the fun if I just *tell* you?"

Marla actually smiled. "Ha. Fine. I never read instruction manuals anyway. It won't kill anyone it touches, will it? Give me *that* much of a heads-up."

"No touch of death," he said. "I have to reserve some of my powers for myself." He kissed Marla on the forehead—if Rondeau had ever tried doing that, Marla would have kicked his balls up through his ribcage—and then left, this time walking out the actual front door.

Marla squinted at the ring, shrugged, and slipped it into her pocket.

"Are you going to wear that?" Rondeau said.

"I put on a wearable artifact once before without knowing what the hell it did," Marla said. "And that cloak eventually dumped an ocean of shit on my head. That's not a mistake I'm going to make again." She shook her head. "Never get married, gentlemen. It's a peculiar institution."

"So what now, Poirot?" Rondeau said. "Since the shortcuts failed us, what? We take the long way around?"

"I guess we go *investigate*." She began pacing up and down the room and talking to herself while Rondeau lounged and Pelham worked on re-organizing the bookshelves according to some arcane system of his own. "So," she said. "Let's look at the evidence. I haven't made plaster casts of any footprints or taken any fingerprints, but that doesn't mean we don't have any clues. The murderer is someone powerful enough to deploy supernatural forensic countermeasures, to shroud their identity even from one of Rondeau's oracles. Ronin doesn't want to give up the killer, which maybe means it's someone he wants to protect, for whatever reason. So what's that tell us?"

"You need a violin to play or some cocaine to inject or something," Rondeau said. "Your pacing around is making me tired."

"It's obviously someone in the magical community," Pelham said, without looking away from his work. Rondeau wanted to ask if he was sorting by the Dewey Decimal or the Library of Congress system, but since he didn't actually know what the difference was, he didn't bother. "Any murder investigation would start with the victim's closest associates, wouldn't it? If a woman dies, you look at the husband. If a child dies, consider the parents."

"You mean he might have been killed by one of the other surfers? Huh, maybe, but I get the feeling they're pretty closely bound-up together—it's hard to imagine one of them could do the dirty deed without the others finding out. Still, it's worth looking into."

"We could see if there are any *ex*-surfers, too," Rondeau said, getting into it now. "After all, where there's a group, there's usually an outcast."

"Ha." Marla paused for a moment, then tromped on, up and down. She was going to wear a groove in the hardwood if she made a habit out of this. "Speaking as an outcast, I can sympathize with murderous impulses. So that's a good idea. We'll ask our clients a few questions. Not that I can necessarily believe anything they say—for all I know they're a cult worshipping dark sea gods and practicing human sacrifice..." She snapped her fingers. "Rondeau.

Get in touch with the Bay Witch, would you? Call Hamil, he can reach her. She knows these guys, but she's not *of* them anymore, so maybe she'll have some insight."

"Insight? From Zufi? Maybe if her brain worked even remotely like a normal person's…"

"It can't hurt to ask," Marla said. "Come on, we're working our contacts here, this is good. Probably worth asking some of the *other* magic types in the area about Ronin and the rest of the wave-mages, too—try to get an objective sense of the group."

"Do you know many people in the local magical community?" Pelham asked. "Is there a chief sorcerer here?"

Marla shook her head. "I don't know if they were ever all that hierarchical, but things are extra messy around here now—we told you about that lunatic hunting and killing other sorcerers not too long ago, turning them into sharks and letting them drown in the air? He left a lot of holes in the local scene, or so I understand. I only really know one of the kahunas." She sighed. "Guess we'd better go see her. Arachne. She lives way the hell on the other side of the island, just off the road to Hana. I'm not up for that shit tonight. What do you say, Pelham—how about tomorrow morning we go for a drive?"

Pelham, of course, felt like doing whatever Marla wanted—and people thought *Rondeau* let Marla push him around. At least he wasn't, like, genetically engineered to be enthusiastically obedient. "That's enough work for one day," Marla said. "I'm going to take Pelham to get some seafood, Rondeau. You coming?"

"I'll catch up with you," Rondeau said. "I should call Hamil about the Bay Witch before it gets too late in Felport." After they left, Rondeau went into the office and sat down behind the desk. He took out his phone and dialed Hamil, Marla's old consigliere back in Felport, and asked him to pass on a message to Zufi.

Hamil agreed without asking too many questions, then said, "How's Marla doing?" in his bass rumble.

"She's staying alive," Rondeau said. He asked after a few of his acquaintances in Felport, trying to sound casual, hoping Hamil wouldn't realize there was only one name on the list he really cared about. After he hung up, he sat for a few minutes looking at the scythe-shaped letter opener on Marla's desk, sighed, and then dialed another number. It rang half-a-dozen times before being picked up.

The voice said, "I didn't expect to hear from *you*."

"Yeah," Rondeau said. "Hamil told me you were, you know, all recovered. After everything that happened."

A chuckle. "I'm good as new."

"I'm glad to hear it. The reason I called is... you know that counseling you gave me when I was all broken up after Bradley Bowman died? You really helped me out a lot, gave me some great advice. Some pretty heavy shit is going on here, and I don't really have anyone I can talk to about it, so I was wondering... does that doctor-patient confidentiality thing we had still apply?"

"Of course, Rondeau," Dr. Husch replied. "Tell me your troubles."

Meet Elsie Jarrow

"**You can't be serious.**" Nicolette stared at the immense cube of granite, twenty feet to a side, decorated with inlaid gold in eye-watering patterns and etched with strange runes that seemed to shift and writhe without every losing their essential symmetry. "You're really going to let her out? I thought you were just screwing with me."

Dr. Husch walked around the cube, her long black dress rustling. Crapsey wasn't sure what was going on, but from the way Nicolette was acting, it was pretty major. They stood in a large gray room in the basement of the Blackwing Institute, lit by harsh white overhead lights, looking at the world's most boring sculpture, as far as he could tell. They were attended by at least a dozen orderlies—a whole harmony of human-looking homunculi—arrayed and waiting in the room's shadowy corners.

"You don't think I should release her?" Dr. Husch said.

"No, I think you definitely *should*. I just can't believe you *will*."

Oh, Crapsey thought. *It's a box.* "Who's in the box? Or, what?"

"Her name is Elsie Jarrow," Dr. Husch said. "She is easily my most troubled patient."

Nicolette gave a long raspberry, spraying spittle. "Please. She's so far beyond ordinary notions of sanity that calling her 'troubled' is like calling cancer psychopathic."

"If cancer were sentient," Dr. Husch said, "it would *be* psychopathic. Speaking of cancer… I'm not sure if you're aware, but Jarrow's body died some months ago. She was absolutely riddled with tumors—she had been more cancer than clean flesh for years, of course, but her own mastery of chaos magic kept her physical form in more-or-less working order. Unfortunately… she tried to escape, as I think you know, this past winter, and she expended the last reserves of her power when she attempted to break through the wards on

55

the Institute's walls. She had precious little strength left for life support, and couldn't control her own decay. I was unable save her physical form."

Nicolette whistled. "She transcended completely? I mean, I knew she could leave her body behind to cause trouble in disembodied form, but she doesn't even have a home base made of skin and bone and meat anymore? She must be like a wind made of *fire* now."

"The death of her physical form doesn't seem to have diminished her presence at all, no," Dr. Husch said. "She had been experimenting with astral projection anyway—she tried to get out of the Institute via the phone lines once, and it almost worked. She's still trapped in the cube, now, though the bed and the chairs and tables inside don't do her much good anymore. She is wholly bodiless, and... she doesn't like it much. She says the pain of the cancer made her crazy, and now that she has no body, and thus no pain, she's thinking more clearly. It could even be true, I suppose—she was never capable of a ruse before, being far too irrational for deception. But she seems lucid, and wants a new body, and she's willing to do almost *anything* if I can get her one."

"What, you want an organ donation? And my whole body's the organ? Elsie's my *hero*, but I'm not willing to die so that she might live." She glanced at Crapsey, who swallowed hard.

Shit. How many bodies had he stolen over the years, at the Mason's orders, or—be honest—at his own whim? How many souls had he consigned to infinite oblivion, how many bodies had he used like puppets? Letting Elsie have his body would probably count as justice. "Fuck that," he said. "Nobody's taking my body, you got it?"

"Both your vessels are too weak." Husch stood staring at a spiral of gold twelve feet high. "When she was free, in those last days before her capture, anyone who came within a dozen yards of her developed tumors. She was chaos walking, and cancer is nothing but cells who have lost all sense of order—she became a living carcinogen, and that poisonous aura was a side effect of her power that she couldn't turn off. She caused bone marrow cancer, mostly. That's why some people called her Marrowbones." Dr. Husch paused. "That, and because in a moment of... I won't call it clarity, but, maybe, misguided compassion? She had the idea that she could save the people she'd poisoned with her presence by magically *removing* all their diseased marrow."

"Human osso bucco," Nicolette said. "Yum."

Husch's dress rustled as she turned toward Crapsey, though with the veil it was impossible to tell if she were really looking at him. "Do you know what happens to a person when all the marrow in their bones instantly vanishes?"

"Uh. No."

"Bone marrow produces red blood cells, platelets, and white blood cells, and regulates the lymphatic system. Let's just say the people she 'cured' would have preferred the cancer. They at least had a chance of short-term survival with treatment."

Crapsey furrowed his brow. "So she's a, what... disease sorcerer? A cancer-mancer?"

"Cancer-mancer!" Nicolette said, and guffawed, actually bending over and slapping her knees. "That's a little rhymey-wimey, there, Crapsey-wapsey."

"What *would* it be called?" Dr. Husch mused. "An... oncomancer? No, 'mancer' is Greek and 'onco' is Latin, not that a little thing like that ever stopped people from talking about 'polyamory' or 'genocide'—"

"Okay, professor boring," Nicolette said. She turned to Crapsey. "Nah, cancer's not Elsie's thing. I mean, it's *one* of her things, but it's just a side effect. The purpose of a tea kettle isn't to *whistle*, that's just something it does in addition to its purpose. See, Elsie Jarrow is just like *me*."

"Elsie Jarrow is to you as the sun is to a forty-watt lightbulb," Dr. Husch said. "She is a force of unstoppable entropy with a will. But, yes, she is a chaos magician. She gets her power from disorder, and she is excellent at *generating* disorder as well. So powerful that, after she lost her mind and her self-control, her mere proximity was enough to drive cell division mad in the bodies of any creatures unlucky enough to come within range. And her mortal form was never much good at containing such a force of disaster."

"Huh," Crapsey said. "So she's basically a tsunami made of tumors, but she's on our side. Okay. What's the plan?"

"We have to find a body that can withstand the stresses of having a woman who is essentially the living incarnation of chaos bound inside it."

Nicolette snorted. "What, like a robot body? Sounds like anything fleshy would turn into tumor soup in a few seconds."

"Elsie is very... sensual. She wants flesh."

"Flesh is weak, lady," Nicolette said. "Take it from the chick with one arm. Flesh is *grass*."

Crapsey whistled. "Wait. You're... you're going to use *her*, aren't you? The... the host?"

"Very good." Dr. Husch might have been praising a bright student. "My orderlies are bringing her down right now."

"What?" Nicolette was annoyed, and when Nicolette was annoyed, things tended to get broken. "What are you talking about? Crapsey's not even from this *reality*, how the hell does he know anybody who could withstand—oh." The chaos witch blinked, and a smile crept across her face. "No shit. That's wicked. I *like* it."

"I'm so glad you approve." Dr. Husch spoke with enough condescension to wither even the mightiest egomaniac, though it didn't dent Nicolette's sudden good humor.

A few moments later, a pair of orderlies appeared, one pushing a wheelchair that held a slumped, apparently catatonic woman, the other holding a shotgun with the barrel wrapped in copper wire and plastic flowers—some kind of magical ordnance, Crapsey figured. The woman in the chair hardly seemed like a threat, but it was definitely better to be safe. She had once been a destroyer of worlds, an unstoppable conqueror—or, at least, the host for one.

"Evil mirror-universe Marla," Nicolette said, walking around the chair and shaking her head. "She doesn't look so scary now."

"The cloak was the scary thing," Dr. Husch said. "This poor child was just the host the cloak chose." She knelt before Beta-Marla, lifting up her chin with two fingers, and looking into her blank-staring eyes. "She's spoken a few times during her stay here, but just whimpers, really, and mostly, she's been like this. I don't think she's ever going to recover."

Crapsey just stared at the woman in the wheelchair, awash in memories. This was the Marla Mason from his home universe—the version of Marla that put on the white-and-purple cloak and then never taken it off again, her mind utterly dominated by the cloak's malevolent intelligence, reduced to a puppet for an alien master. She still looked about twenty, smooth-faced and with the beauty of youth, because the Mason hadn't seen any incentive in aging, and had woven her defensive magics strongly. The Mason was un-matched as a sorcerer, and claimed it was because magic in her home uni-verse was *denser* than magic here—she could brush aside spells in this world as easily as a man brushes away cobwebs. But she needed a human host to op-erate in this reality—said it was like a scuba diver's air tanks, or an astronaut's space suit. The Marla from *this* universe had managed to trick the Mason into temporarily separating from her host, and defeated her that way—but it had left the host an almost-empty shell, with Beta-Marla's long-dominated mind tattered and shredded and almost entirely gone.

"I just hope she'll be strong enough to survive possession by Jarrow," Dr. Husch said. "She looks so frail…"

"Let's find out." Nicolette drew her glittering silver hatchet.

"No!" Dr. Husch shouted, but Nicolette stepped past her and swung the weapon down in a smooth, swift arc toward Beta-Marla's skull.

The blade just barely touched the skull, shearing away a few strands of hair, before rebounding hard enough to rock Nicolette back on her feet. Beta-Marla didn't react at all.

"*Damn*," Nicolette said. "You know, when I stole this hatchet, I thought I might be able to use it to kill the Mason. Guess that wouldn't have worked."

"The Mason told me it's an impressive weapon," Crapsey said. "But she said unless it was wielded by a god, it wouldn't be able to hurt her, not re-ally."

"Huh. Well, apotheosis is on my to-do list anyway."

"Please refrain from swinging axes at my patients," Dr. Husch said wearily.

Nicolette shrugged, a strange-looking gesture from a one-armed, hatchet-wielding woman. "Whatever. If this axe had hurt her, there wouldn't be much point in giving her body to Elsie anyway. I don't really understand why she's still invincible though—the cloak is *gone*, Marla sent it off to a whole other universe, supposedly. This thing in the chair is just a husk."

"The host body was soaked in the Mason's magic for over a decade," Crapsey said. "Marinated in it. Irradiated. Whatever. And the Mason wrapped that body in every kind of protective spell she knew—and she knew a *lot*. You could drop an atom bomb on this body and it would come walking out again without a scratch—assuming it has a mind to tell it to walk."

"So it's safe to say she would be immune to cancer? And… other stresses?" Dr. Husch said. "I have speculated, but…"

"I'm not a doctor, or even really a sorcerer, but, shit, yeah. The Mason thought bodies were *disgusting*, so she made this flesh as unchanging and impregnable as possible."

"Then let's give Jarrow her new vessel," Husch said.

"Uh." Nicolette cleared her throat. "I'm all for unleashing devastating horrors on the world, but… Elsie's just gonna *eat* us, then take this body, and leave. This is Marrowbones we're talking about. She's not trustworthy."

"Nicolette, shut up, please. I have access to objects of power that make your little hatchet look like a fingernail clipper. Precautions have been taken. If Jarrow doesn't do what I want, she'll be back in this cube in moments. I do not need your advice on how to contain my patients. I am a *professional*."

Professionals don't let dangerous prisoners loose on murder-for-hire gigs, Crapsey thought, but didn't figure that was a productive line of argument, so he kept his mouth shut.

"Now then," Husch said. "Let's crack open the seals." One of the orderlies handed her a hammer and chisel, and Nicolette took out her hatchet again.

Beta-Marla moaned, and whispered something. Crapsey knelt down beside her, and her vague eyes seemed to fix on him. He should look familiar to her, at least, assuming she'd had some degree of consciousness during her long years of being dominated by the Mason. "What is it, sweetie?" he said, though looking at her face reminded him of his old boss and tormentor.

"Kill me," she whispered, eyes fixed on his.

"What did she say?" Dr. Husch demanded.

"She wants us to kill her," Crapsey said.

Dr. Husch clucked her tongue. "Can't be done, dear. I'm sorry. But this should be oblivion, which is the next best thing." She placed the chisel at a seemingly arbitrary point on the face of the cube, and struck it with the hammer.

The face of the cube split open, dividing one of the spirals of inlaid gold into asymmetrical not-quite-halves. White light poured from the inside, which was furnished like a rather Spartan dorm room or an upscale prison cell—single bed, sink, toilet, shower stall, desk, chair, polished steel plate for a mirror. There was nobody inside, but there *was* a sort of disturbance in the air, something like a heat shimmer, but streaked with colors... the most beautiful *colors*—

"Avert your eyes," Dr. Husch said, and Crapsey wrenched his gaze away to stare at his feet. "There's a force field preventing her from getting out, but it's permeable from this direction—there's nothing to stop you from going inside if you're entranced. As homunculi, my staff and I are immune to her charms, but the two of you aren't, probably. Orderlies, wheel in the new vessel."

Beta-Marla reached out as if to clutch Crapsey's sleeve when the orderlies pushed her wheelchair toward the cube, but she either didn't have the strength, or didn't have the strength of will. Poor thing. She'd just escaped from hosting one malevolent parasitic entity, and here she was, about to be enslaved by another. The kid never had a chance.

Then again, if she hadn't been possessed by the cloak, she probably would have turned out a lot like the Marla Mason from *this* universe, and she was pretty much a total bitch, so whatever.

Crapsey risked a glance at the cube. The orderlies pushed the chair inside and stepped back, but they couldn't get out, of course, because of the force field—theirs was a suicide mission. Good thing they were mindless man-things and not actual people. That close to Jarrow's essence, the orderlies slumped like melting snowmen in hospital scrubs, their flesh liquefying into a slurry that stank like rising bread mingled with melted plastic.

"Does the vessel suit you?" Dr. Husch called.

The shimmer in the air vanished, and then Beta-Marla began to *glow*, a bright green aura enveloping her, and sparks started to fly up in the air.

"Shit," Dr. Husch said, and Crapsey was actually surprised to hear such a basic profanity from her. "I was afraid the Mason might have made her host impregnable to possession." Crapsey nodded, because the one time he'd tried to take control of the Mason's body himself, he'd bounced off her protective barriers like a handball hitting a stone wall—

The green shimmer vanished, and Beta-Marla stood up from the chair, her back to Dr. Husch and the others. She stretched her hands up in the air, rolled her head around on her neck, then did a few toe-touches and deep knee bends before turning to face them.

Crapsey was astonished. He was used to seeing this woman's face, of course, but while in the Mason's control, it had almost always been blank and expressionless, more masklike than animated flesh. As the semi-catatonic Beta-Marla, her face had been slack and empty of everything but flashes of despair. But *this*—

This woman looked happy. More than happy. *Joyful*, all twinkling eyes and dazzling smiles.

"I *like* it!" she shouted, and did a little pirouette, twirling on one foot. "Wowza! This body is *cherry*, Dr. Jigsaw, truly fine, damnfine, *really* fine. I had a little trouble getting in, I couldn't pop the locks with any finesse, so I had to break a window with a brick, more or less, but that's okay, I didn't mess up any of the optional extras." She pressed her hands against the invisible barrier keeping her inside the cube and grinned, so widely it looked like her face might split apart. "Knock, knock? Who's there? Let me. Let me who? Let me OUT!"

"You have... control of yourself?" Dr. Husch said. "You know if I suffer injury, or lose consciousness, you'll be snatched out of that body and back into the cube—"

Elsie Jarrow rolled her eyes, then flopped onto her back on the floor dramatically. "It's *okay*, Doctor Mom, I know, if I melt you I'm totally grounded, the deal is done, lemme free, lemme free!"

Dr. Husch made a series of arcane gestures—she looked like a guy on a runway waving in three or four planes at once—and Elsie did a little somersaulting roll out of the cube, springing to her feet. "New friends!" she shouted at Crapsey and Nicolette, then whirled toward Dr. Husch. "First thing's first! Give me the stuff! The stuff the stuff the *stuff*!"

Dr. Husch summoned another orderly who'd been lurking in the shadows, and he came forward carrying a bottle of dark red fluid.

"Is that blood?" Crapsey said. "Is this some blood magic thing?"

"Ha," Elsie Jarrow said. "You ever try dyeing your hair with blood? It's total crap! Gets all crusty and when it dries it ends up looking *brown*."

"It's hair dye," Dr. Husch said as Elsie snatched the bottle and a proffered comb and went back into the cube, to the sink.

"If I can't be a redhead, I'd rather be dead," Elsie said. "Help a girl out, would you, baldie?"

Nicolette, who'd been uncharacteristically speechless during this whole exchange, smirked, then stepped over a melted orderly to help the most deadly chaos magician in the world dye her hair.

"Is she for real?" Crapsey said. "She's, like... not what I expected. I mean, she's not... all supervillainous and everything."

"She's always tended toward the manic," Dr. Husch said. "It would not be correct to call her bipolar—she is *mono*polar. Elsie Jarrow can be warm, and vivacious, and even *fun*... but she's responsible for rivers of blood. Half the time she doesn't even mean to cause the damage she does. The other half of the time... she does mean it. And it's a lot worse when she means it." She sighed. "This is going to take a while. We'd best make ourselves comfortable." She summoned an orderly, who carried over a couple of plastic lawn chairs.

After nearly an hour of hair ministrations, Elsie declared herself satisfied with the dye and stripped off the red-stained shirt she'd been wearing, dropping it on the floor. Crapsey found himself getting a little aroused at the sight of her in just a bra, even if it was boring hospital-issue underwear—hell, it wasn't like he'd had much experience with fancy lingerie in the nightmarish dystopian world he'd called home. A girl with no festering sores on her body had been a big treat over there, and he hadn't exactly been rolling in willing scantily-clad women since he crossed over to this universe.

"Husch. Lipstick me. I know you like to wear that red red red. Or you did before your lips got torn into little pieces. Which means you don't need it anymore. Give."

Husch handed her a tube, and Elsie lavished her lips in scarlet, then took the hem of Husch's veil and used it to blot. "Perfecto." She turned to Crapsey and gave him a dazzling smile. "You. Want to have sex with me right here on this concrete floor? I've got this *body*! Gotta use it!"

Crapsey winced. "I would, I mean, but that body used to belong to my monster-boss—"

"Okay, too much talking, you missed your window, big boy." She turned to Nicolette. "You? And me? And the floor? I like the one-armed thing, I bet only having five fingers makes you work a lot harder, am I right?"

"I'm not into girls, and I hate *both* the people you look like in that body, but you are Elsie Jarrow, and I will so absolutely fuck you," Nicolette said.

"Stop!" Dr. Husch said. "We have work to do, things to discuss, plans to make."

"Dr. Jigsaw is a buzzkill," Elsie Jarrow said. "Lift that veil, pretty lady. "

"I am not sleeping with you."

"Oh, don't worry, I'm not in the mood anymore, but you're pretty prudish for a sexbot, even one with a PhD." She glanced at Nicolette. "The doctor here was invented as a *sex* homunculus for her creator, did you guys know that? He gave her all those smarts so she could read the Kama Sutra or recite lyric poetry while she gave him handjobs or whatever, and then she goes to college and gets advanced degrees, just like she's *people*. Her maker wouldn't like banging her now, though, she's all damaged. The veil. Up."

Husch backed away, arms crossed, the faint blot of scarlet lipstick on her veil reminding Crapsey of a spreading bloodstain. "You don't give me orders—"

"I'll kill Marla for you, okay? And anybody else who annoys you. Don't get all unyielding, it makes me cranky. Just. Lift. The. Veil. Let me get a look at what they did to you."

With trembling hands, Dr. Husch raised the black netting and revealed her face. She was worse than Crapsey had expected. He hadn't been the one to cut her up, but only because she brained him with a blunt object before he could carry out his boss's orders. The Mason had done the deed, tearing her into pieces. She'd been stitched back together… but her face was a nightmare of bright red lines, a map of scars so pronounced they looked drawn on with red Sharpie. Her face was like a photo shredded and taped back together, with none of the edges quite lining up anymore.

"They sure did a number on you, didn't they?" Elsie said. "These hands, right here, they ripped you up, didn't they?" She wiggled her fingers. "Well, let me fix you up, then."

Husch tried to jerk away when Elsie reached out for her, but some magic snared her, and the chaos witch pressed her palms against the doctor's face. Husch twitched and writhed and moaned for a moment, battering uselessly at Elsie, then tore free and fell to her knees. The doctor looked up.

"Uh," Crapsey said. "Doc. Maybe look in that mirror over there?"

"What have you done to me?" Dr. Husch said, her voice no longer rough and shredded. She rushed to the mirror, and looked at herself—at her smooth face, restored to its original classical perfection.

"Fixed you." Elsie sat down in the middle of the floor, pulled one of her feet up close to her face, and sniffed her own toes. "Not just your face, either. The whole caboodle. Boobies and nethers and all. Did you guys know she's hairless as a hypoallergenic cat from the neck down? Her maker was a perv."

Husch paid no attention, just staring at her own face, touching her cheeks with her fingertips. "The biomancer, Langford, he said there was no hope, that my skin couldn't heal like a human's, that it lacked the elasticity—"

"Eh, all true, but broken things are my whole, um. Thing. I can increase disorder, but you know how double-edged magic is, I can run the progression back the other way, too, and create order. There, poof, you're pretty again, yay." Elsie seemed bored with the whole situation now—she was chewing on her big toenail—and Crapsey got a sense of just how unsettling it could be to work with her. She was changeable as the moon, as the sea, as...

Well, the whim of a lunatic devoted to chaos.

"No offense, but what the fuck?" Nicolette said. "You *fixed* something? Increased order? That just... isn't something I'd expect the great Elsie Jarrow to do."

"That's exactly the point." Elsie spat out a toenail. "Half my power comes from doing the unexpected. A lot of the time even *I* don't know what I'm going to do. That approach has worked out for me so far. Except for killing everyone I ever knew and loved or even liked, and being imprisoned for all those years, and everything. Otherwise it's been a rock-solid strategy. Besides, I don't mind creating order. I like it! Build those towers high! The more complex you make something, the bigger the mess it makes when it collapses."

Crapsey was mulling that over when Dr. Husch's cell phone rang. She looked at the screen and said, "What in the world..." She put the phone to her ear. "I didn't expect to hear from *you*," she said, walking toward a corner of the basement, presumably for privacy.

"We're gonna have fun," Elsie said, standing up, and walking toward Crapsey and Nicolette with her arms outstretched. "I'm in the mood again. What do you say? Three-way, right now? We've only five hands among us, but we can make do, right?"

Seeing the World

PELHAM ROLLED ACROSS a one-lane bridge on the winding, narrow, gloriously scenic road to Hana, then adroitly squeezed the black convertible onto the minuscule shoulder to let an impatient local in a mud-stained Jeep swoop around them and speed away.

"I was worried this drive would stress you out," Marla said. They were only travelling about fifty miles, but it was going to take between two and three hours, because the Hana Highway was as twisty as a grifter's wit, following the coastline through tropical rainforest on a route that included something like sixty bridges, many of them one-lane, plus an effective infinity of blind curves. The trip was stressing *Marla* out, because two parts of her nature were in conflict: she hated driving, but she was also a control freak. At least with Pelham she was in good hands. When Rondeau had driven this way, they'd nearly died about 125 times, by Marla's count. This wasn't a trip to take when you were in a hurry... but unless you had a helicopter or a boat handy (or were willing to brave the risks inherent in teleportation), there was no other way to reach the eastern side of the island.

"Oh, no, this is lovely," Pelham said. "I suppose it might have made me anxious when I first left Felport... but since then I've driven the road of death in Bolivia, and the Deosai National Park Trail in Pakistan—after driving across a wood-and-rope bridge suspended over a chasm, a few blind curves and one-lane stretches are nothing to get worked up about."

"Ha. I guess not. I'm going to have to get used to the new you, Pelham— I'm still thinking of you as the guy who never left Felport, who'd barely been off the Chamberlain's estate."

"The past few months have been most instructive, Mrs. Mason. During our time together I gained some inkling of the divide between my theoretical knowledge and the practical application of that knowledge." He had a far-

65

away look in his eyes—a trifle worrisome in a man driving along the edge of a cliff towering over the ocean. "I have experienced so much since then. Great kindness and casual cruelty. Amazing food and filthy rooms. Learning a language from books and tapes is quite different from speaking the language with *people*. I was groomed for service, but the world is so much larger than I ever realized. Thank you for that—for sending me out."

Marla had been a few places over the years, but always for business, and she'd never explored like Pelham had—had never *wanted* to, with all her attention focused on Felport's well-being. "You don't have to stay here now," Marla said. "With me, I mean. We can be—bonded, or whatever—without you having to live in a little room under the stairs emptying my chamber pot and cooking me rashers of bacon."

"With your permission, I may go traveling again," Pelham said. "But for now, you are in danger, and you are my friend as well as my mistress, and I would prefer to stay and assist in whatever way I can."

"Ha. 'Mistress.' Careful calling me that in public, all right? But I'm glad to have you. I could use the help."

He glanced at her sidelong. "Mrs. Mason. *You've* changed, too, if you don't mind me saying. I can scarcely remember you ever admitting to needing help before."

She sighed, gazing out the window as they passed the burned-out hulk of an old pickup truck someone had shoved into the trees on the side of the road. "I don't claim to be the smartest person in the world, but if there's one lesson I've learned this past year, it's that there are some things you can't do on your own. Being self-reliant is still important to me, don't get me wrong… but losing almost all my friends and allies has given me a new appreciation for the ones I have left. You included."

"Aren't we on our way to see another of your friends now?"

Marla snorted. "I wouldn't go that far. She's a kahuna named Arachne, though she's not as… spidery as the name would imply. She's into the weaving thing, though, mostly magics of binding and separating. She weaves together nets and rugs and whatever else as part of her ritual. Arachne's native Hawai'ian, pretty much a nature magician—you know how much I love *those*—and I helped her out with a ghost not long ago. She wasn't too grateful, though. I think she was pissed off that she needed help at all—and, yes, I know, I can relate to that. Seeing me again will probably annoy her—but apart from the surfers who hired me, she's literally the only sorcerer on the island I'm on speaking terms with. The local kahunas aren't big fans of haole sorcerers from the mainland. Hard to blame them, since the last haole magus to show up on Maui was an asshole of a guy who turned rival sorcerers into sharks. But you've already heard that sob story, and I don't feel like telling it—we've got a long drive ahead of us. Tell me what you've been up to."

Pelham recited the list of places he'd visited—Malaysia, South America, bits of Eastern Europe, a lot of Southeast Asia, none for more than a few days at a time—and some of the difficulties he'd encountered. Apart from the Nuno, he'd also had run-ins with the iron-toothed Abaasy of Turkey, a Tokoloshe in South Africa, and a Colo Colo in Argentina. The glamour Marla had placed on the steamer trunk had proven an irresistible attractant for minor magical beings, something she hadn't anticipated—there weren't a lot of loose supernatural creatures in the streets of Felport, and she hadn't realized quite how wild some of the remaining wild places in the world could be.

"Did you see anything *nice*?" Marla said. "I'll feel like crap if it was all monsters, all the time."

"Oh, no, it wasn't all being chased by terrifying or bewildering creatures," Pelham said. "And, given my extensive studies in magic, I generally knew what I was dealing with, and how to banish them, or at least avoid being harmed. There were many beautiful things. A forgotten temple in Indonesia, still intact, and more ancient than some civilizations. The Hang Son Doong cavern in Vietnam, where holes in the ground above admit water and light sufficient for a small forest to grow over the centuries, creating what is essentially a jungle under the earth—that was like something out of an Edgar Rice Burroughs novel. The Metéora monasteries in Greece, built atop towering pillars of rock, almost literally castles in the air." He smiled, his expression going all soft and faraway. "I even met a woman. Nothing serious, of course, just a fellow traveler, but… . Yes. There were beautiful things."

"Good for you, Pelham. I'm glad to hear it."

Pelham blushed, adjusted the convertible's mirrors in a completely unnecessary way, and continued briskly. "I went to Lake Paasselkä in Finland, thinking it might be a good place to sink the glamoured trunk—the lake was formed by a meteor impact, and there are strange magnetic anomalies associated with the place, along with other purportedly supernatural qualities. I decided the magics on the trunk and in the lake might interact badly, alas, but before I left, I saw the Paasselkä devil—a ball of light that seems to move almost consciously. Eerie, and beautiful, and despite the fierce name, I did not find it frightening at all."

"What is it? The devil thing, I mean."

Pelham smiled. "I have no idea. Isn't it wonderful? The world is so *big*, Mrs. Mason. So full of mysteries, vistas, experiences. At home on the estate, growing up, I thought the world was very small—after all, I could see the whole thing on a globe, or a map. I read books, and believed the whole world could be contained in those books, and in a sense, I suppose they can. But the guidebook is not the *experience*. Knowledge received cannot compare to knowledge directly perceived."

"Damn, Pelham," Marla said. "You've managed to make me feel positively provincial, which is a pretty good trick for a guy who didn't leave the grounds of a mansion for the first few decades of his life."

"Oh, I wouldn't say that. There is something to be said for the intense knowledge you have about Felport as well. My experiences were wonderful, but in many ways they were shallow. Spending only a few days, or sometimes only a few hours in a place, I could take away only surface impressions—startling and moving impressions, often, but not deep ones. To *truly* know a place takes a long stay, and the sort of devotion you gave to Felport. When, in my youth, I expressed dissatisfaction with the constraints of living on the estate, the Chamberlain told me that the world was small, but the gardens were vast—meaning, or so I understood her, that close attention could make a place seem to expand, containing multitudes. In my perfect world, I would spend a few months, perhaps a year, living in a place, thereby going a level or two deeper than the average tourist does, before moving on. Combining breadth and depth of experience, and trying to achieve some sort of balance."

"But wouldn't you feel, I don't know, adrift? Not having a proper home?"

"I think home is where you make it, Mrs. Mason. Even if you make it in the inside of your own head."

"Huh. I—oh, wait, this is close enough." Marla directed Pelham to pull over into the big gravel parking lot, still half full of cars even this early in the day, surrounded by verdant hills. "Arachne likes to hang out in the woods around here. If I wander around a bit she'll notice me soon enough."

"We're near the Seven Sacred Pools, aren't we?"

"Yeah, that's right, you read guidebooks. It's a pretty place—waterfalls feeding pools, tropical birds, all that. Rondeau likes it over here, except for the drive being a pain in the ass, and all the walking you have to do to see everything. He'd be happier if they'd move the whole park closer to the hotel so he could wander over after his morning Bloody Mary."

"The effort to get here is surely some of the appeal, though," Pelham said. "If it were easy, wouldn't it be less satisfying?"

"Huh. If you say so. I've always been more results- and destination-oriented myself. Look, I'm going to head up that hill over there, and try not to kill myself scrambling around on the lava rocks. Arachne doesn't hang out on the hiking trails with the tourists. But if you want to go hike around, feel free."

"Shouldn't I accompany you?"

Marla shook her head. "Not yet. Arachne can be… prickly about outsiders. She pretty much sits in the woods and broods about tourists from Japan and the mainland US all day, as far as I can tell. The ghost we had to banish was some haole who jumped down a waterfall, landed badly, drowned, and ended up haunting the area. She doesn't mind the ghosts of locals, but haoles like you and me… We're *all* invasive species as far as she's concerned. She probably hates the surfers, too, which is why I think she might be able to give me some nasty gossip about them. I figure nasty gossip is a good thing to hear in a murder investigation."

"I can find no fault in your methodology," Pelham said. "I have my phone if you need me. I suppose it might be pleasant to walk. And if you get in any trouble, I should sense it."

"Arachne doesn't scare me. Nobody's managed to kill me with withering scorn yet, and I doubt she'll be the first." Marla got out of the convertible, tightened the laces on her boots, and gave Pelham a wave before going up the hill.

It was great to have Pelly back… but he was different. Probably he was just changed from having his horizons expanded and everything, but he seemed preoccupied, too, like there was something weighing on his mind. Pelham wasn't the sort to share his troubles—having been trained all his life to ease trouble for others—but if he wanted to suffer in silence, that was his business. He did say he'd met a woman on his travels—maybe that was it. Nothing could mess with you like romance, in Marla's experience, which was why she avoided it as much as possible.

A long green frond brushed her cheek as she tromped up the slope among the greenery. Nature. She'd never even liked going to the park back in Felport, and now she lived on an island that was half jungle. She liked to say that all of civilization was based on the effort to get *away* from nature, but talking to Pelham had made her reconsider certain of her bedrock assumptions. Maybe her dislike for wild places was just part of her need for control, and her distrust of things she *couldn't* control. But she'd believed herself in complete control of Felport, and look how that had turned out.

The surfers who'd hired her were wave-mages, like the Bay Witch, and that meant they didn't try to dominate the waves: they just worked with them, and chose the right one to get them where they wanted to go. Maybe they had a point. And maybe, damn it, she *was* kind of provincial.

Marla was so deep in thought that she walked right into a spider web. She wiped the threads from her face, scowling. Life had been a lot easier when she was absolutely dead certain about everything.

Pelham carefully locked up the car, adjusted his broad-brimmed hat— he'd gotten a terrible sunburn on his scalp in South Africa, and didn't want to repeat the experience—and started toward the nearest trailhead. While he would never be able to dress down to the level of, say, Rondeau—those Aloha shirts!—he'd realized early in his travels that his preferred garb of waistcoats and cravats and perfectly-creased slacks and mirror-shined black dress shoes was impractical, regrettably anachronistic, and tended to draw attention. He had adjusted. Life was about adjustment.

Today he wore a white linen shirt, a tropical-weight sports coat in pale tan, and khakis, with (of all things) hiking boots. He'd felt a bit disloyal dressing down to such a degree while once more in his mistress's direct employ, but Marla hadn't commented, and he knew intellectually that she didn't care what he wore. Overcoming decades of training on the proper attire and behavior of a valet was difficult... but he'd come a long way.

A Hawai'ian man, wearing a blue rashguard and long black shorts, fell into step behind him as Pelham walked along the trail winding through the trees. "Aloha," the man said.

"Good morning," Pelham said politely, still walking.

"How's Marla doing?"

Pelham stopped, scrutinized the man, and shook his head. "I am afraid I do not know you, sir."

"You do, though. We met in Nepal. I was a little shorter then." The man paused. "And female. And, you know. More *Nepalese*. You were feeling awfully homesick, and I made you feel better."

Pelham exhaled. "Of course. Ms.—Mr.—Reva. I should have realized your... demeanor would be different, here."

The god shrugged. "Not 'Mr. Reva,' please, just 'Reva.' You and me, after how close we've been, it's kind of silly to be formal." He leaned close, put his hands on Pelham's shoulders, and gazed into his eyes. "Let's talk."

Pelham took a step back, clearing his throat. "Ah, can we talk without... such intimacy? I mean no disrespect, and I realize our past history might cause confusion, but I confess I find it disconcerting now that you are in a different body—"

Reva frowned. "Now that is weird as *hell*, Pelham."

"What is, sir?"

"You didn't—look." He called out to a middle-aged man trudging past on the trail with a grim expression on his face. "Hey!" Reva shouted. "Come here for a minute. I want to talk to you."

The man walked over, a strange, faraway look in his eyes, and stopped in front of Reva.

"Where's your home?" Reva asked.

"Hot Springs, Arkansas," the man said.

"Beautiful little town," Reva said. "There's a swimming hole near there, deep and still, in an old quarry, as nice as any tropical lagoon, isn't it?"

"Sure is," the man said, eyes locked on something far off, perhaps in the past. "Went there with my wife on our first date, if you could even call it a date—we were both about sixteen. We swam out to the float in the middle, and she kissed me, and..." He sighed.

"Tell me what troubles you, friend." Reva rested a hand on the man's shoulder.

"This is supposed to be our second honeymoon. Our first honeymoon was just a hotel room in Little Rock, nothing special, so we thought for our twentieth anniversary we'd do it up right, but my wife got a stomach bug from some bad fish I guess. I was moping around the room all morning, and she was moaning in the bed, and finally she yelled at me to go do something so we wouldn't *both* waste the whole day, and here I am, did that whole long drive by myself, and now I'm just walking in the jungle, and what's the point, when she's not here?"

"Head on back," Reva said. "When you get there, she'll be feeling better, and she'll be sitting out by the pool, wearing that new swimsuit she bought, and she'll be just as pretty to you as she was when you were both sixteen. Go into the pool with her, slip back behind that little fake waterfall they have, and believe me, you won't regret it." He paused. "And you'll get a free upgrade to first class on the flight back home, how's that?"

"That sounds good," the man said, and Reva took his hand off his shoulder. The man shook his head, eyes focusing, and looked around. "Ah. I should get back to the hotel and check on my wife."

"Safe travels, my friend," Reva said, and the man gave a wave and hurried down the hill.

"Magic," Pelham said. "And a rather kind sort of magic, too. But what was that meant to show me?"

Reva looked around, then sat on a big rock by the trail. Pelham eased down beside him. The god said, "When I meet somebody who's not in the place they consider home—one of *my* people, whether they're a traveler, an exile, or just a tourist—I can sort of... cut through the bullshit. I talk to their deepdown parts. They can't lie to me then. They tell me their true feelings. And I help them when I can. Since I'm a god... I usually can. I talked to you the same way in Nepal, at first."

Pelham frowned. "I have no memory of that. But I suppose I wouldn't, would I? I don't think I'm comfortable with you having direct access to my secret thoughts, to the levers and axles of my mind. Especially considering what happened between us later—"

Reva shook his head. "No, Pelham, there was no coercion—that's not how I do things. I can't make you do anything you don't want to. I did get a sense of your loneliness from our talk, and in *that* body, with that brain, I thought you were cute, and one thing led to another... but everything that happened was consenting adult stuff. Don't worry, you don't do much for me now, this body is pretty firmly heterosexual."

"Even so," Pelham said. "To be laid bare that way, to have no choice but to answer your questions... ." He shuddered. "You are not human. You cannot understand why your actions trouble me. It is important for me to remember that."

Reva sighed. "I guess you could see it as an invasion of privacy. And you'd be right. I am an invader of privacy. It's just how I get things done, right or wrong—it saves time, and gives me confidence that I have all my facts straight. You can disapprove. I don't mind—all I can tell you is, I try to use my power to give people better lives. Anyway, I thought I'd talk to you the same way here, but… it doesn't *work*. Which is weird, because Hawai'i isn't your home, and if someone's away from home, my power *always* works—"

Pelham shook his head. "But I am home. I am back with Mrs. Mason. Wherever she is—*that* is my home."

Reva clapped his hands together, delighted. "Right! I've seen that before, in some lovers, but never in a case like this. But you and Marla have a magical connection, a supernatural bond… it makes sense. She's *your* home, but you're not hers." He winced. "No offense, I'm sure you're important to her—"

Pelham shrugged. "It is the nature of our relationship. It does not trouble me. Unlike non-consensual hypnosis and seduction by a god." His shuddered at the thought. No wonder he'd felt so instantly comfortable with Reva in his—her—previous form; the god had known just what to say to him, just how to behave, to win Pelham's trust and affection. It was horrible, but perhaps no relationship between a mortal and a god could ever be truly consensual—there was always going to be a fundamental imbalance of power in the god's favor. Something withered deep in his heart. A beautiful memory had been made ugly forever.

Reva winced. "Look, I promise not to try to shortcut around your conscious mind again, okay?"

"How noble of you to promise not to do something you are no longer able to do, immediately after trying and failing to do that very thing."

"Look, we have to move on from this, all right? We've got other things to talk about, and anyway, I'm glad you've found your home again. So how's our plan working?"

Pelham closed his eyes. He was involved with this creature now, and he believed Reva *did* mean well when it came to Marla, so he tried to suppress his revulsion. He said, "Marla seems interested in finding out the murderer's identity. You were right, I think, that having a difficult project would help take her mind off her exile. But she is still not quite herself. She has renewed her connection with her consort, the god of Death, which may prove beneficial to her outlook, but I am unsure. She seems… uncomfortable in her relationship with him. He did bring another distraction, though—he says her death is imminent. Her enemies are coming for her."

"My powers aren't much good when it comes to looking into the future—I'm a here-and-now sort of god—but I've gotten a sense of forces gathering, too. From everything I've observed, Marla's tough. The future's not fixed. Don't give up hope."

"I have not." Pelham was offended at the suggestion. "She has faced terrible foes before, and triumphed. I just worry… she does not have as much to fight *for*, now. Her city is lost to her. Death is trying to woo her with tales of how wonderful her afterlife will be, in his company. I do not believe she would willingly let her enemies kill her, but what if she lacks the fire, the passion, that has always given her an edge? What if, at the crucial moment, she cannot muster the will to stop her foes from killing her?"

"That's why she has friends like you." Reva clapped him on the shoulder. Pelham remembered the god's touch, using different hands, and shuddered. "And friends like me, though she doesn't seem to appreciate it. And you say her husband is trying to convince her to choose death? I might have to go have a talk with him."

"Are the two of you acquainted?"

"Nah, he doesn't even know I exist. On the scale of gods, Death is like a crowned head of Europe, and I'm chief of an island village so tiny it doesn't even have a name. Compared to a mortal, or even a sorcerer, I've got a lot of power—but compared to Death, I'm an insect."

"Then what does that make mortals, or sorcerers, to Death? Microbes? Parasites?"

"Exactly," Reva said. "That's why things like him shouldn't be giving mortals advice about their life choices. Which is something I might point out to him."

"It is brave of you to confront him," Pelham said carefully

Reva sighed. "You're thinking things like *me* shouldn't be giving advice to mortals, too, aren't you?"

"The thought had occurred to me."

Reva nodded. "You have a point, but I do know what it's like to be human, unike Death. When I instantiate like this, take on a local form, I become a person, with the drives and limitations of a person… mostly. Anyway, talking to Death isn't all that brave. When you can't die, Death is a lot less intimidating. I doubt talking to him will do me any good, but I can try. Marla may be his wife… but she's one of my *people*. Her home is lost, but if we can help her find a new home, or at least realize that she might *someday* find a new home, she'll be okay. Keeping her busy is a good first step."

"Trying to find a murderer, and prevent yourself from *being* murdered, is certainly one way to keep occupied. Tell me, Mr.—ah, Reva. Do *you* know who killed this man, Ronin?"

Reva nodded. "I do."

"Will Marla's investigation lead her to ask you?"

The god of exiles stroked his chin. "Hmm. It's possible, sure. I already introduced myself to her. She knows I know the surfers. She might get around to interrogating me."

"Will you help her, if she questions you?"

"Depends on whether or not she can figure out the right questions. Just keep an eye on her. I'll be around."

"I don't like deceiving her," Pelham said. "I had a hard time telling her I just happened to come to Hawai'i, when you are the one who told me she'd been exiled, told me she might need help. And now, having met you again, to keep *that* fact from her as well—"

Reva hmmmed. "I think it's better if she doesn't know we're trying to guide her life—she strikes me as the contrary type, one who'd say 'no' just because we asked her to say 'yes.' But if you feel like it's a betrayal to keep the conversations we've had a secret, do what you must."

"I was taught to be utterly trustworthy. But I was also taught that there are things one's master or mistress need *not* know, things they shouldn't be bothered with, things they would not benefit from knowing, that might trouble them, and that can therefore be concealed... but it is so hard to know whether *this* qualifies."

"You'll do the right thing, Pelham. Whatever that turns out to be."

"Mrs. Mason will be most unhappy if she finds you've been meddling in her life."

"I'm a god. Meddling is what I do. It's what *she* does, too—I'm just trying to find new things for her to meddle with. Take care, Pelham. Enjoy the scenery. And remember, we're not conspiring against Marla—we're conspiring for her."

"I an unconvinced Mrs. Mason would appreciate the distinction," Pelham said.

Revengers, Assemble!

The first thing Crapsey heard when he woke up, slumped on the couch in Dr. Husch's office, was Elsie Jarrow saying, "They're so adorable when they sleep. Like lobotomized little puppies."

"Do you mean Crapsey and Nicolette in particular," Dr. Husch said, "or just... those who require sleep?"

"I know!" Elsie said. "I love unclear antecedents too!"

Crapsey sat up, groaning. His tongue felt like it had been replaced in the night by a mummified rodent—which, given his proximity to Elsie Jarrow, wasn't an impossibility. "Buh," he said.

Elsie sat perched on the edge of Dr. Husch's desk, dressed in a dark green pencil skirt and a white blouse, clearly raided from Husch's wardrobe. Her lips were heavily lipsticked crimson, and her hair—dry, now—was red as molten rock. Crapsey looked down at his hands, saw the streaks of red on his fingers, and tried to remember if things had gotten *that* crazy. He sniffed, and was relieved: not blood, just dye from Elsie's damp hair. Nicolette was sleeping on the floor by a potted ficus, and while she was dressed, her shirt was on inside out. Crapsey had slept with Nicolette a few times before, because even though her weird shoulder-stump-thing freaked him out, she was the only game in town, but he'd never seen her as passionate as she was last night. Probably the way Crapsey would feel if he got to sleep with one of *his* idols. Except he couldn't think of any idols he'd want to actually sleep with. He loved the comics of Jack Kirby and Steve Ditko, but...

Nicolette's eyes opened, she sat up, and grinned. "Today we eat the world, yeah?"

"First we torment and kill Marla," Dr. Husch said. "After that... what you do is your own business."

Elsie had an oversized coffee mug in her hands, and she put her nose close to the rim, inhaling deeply. "Did you know, Nicolette, now that the good doctor has unshackled me, I can draw enough power from the Brownian motion of the steam rising from this coffee to light up an entire city? And by 'light up' I mean 'devastate with a relentless storm of fireballs'?"

"That's badass," Nicolette said. "You're badass."

Crapsey rolled his eyes. One of the few things he liked about Nicolette was her absolute refusal to be impressed—she'd even backtalked the Mason a few times, until she realized one more slip of the tongue would get her turned into a smear on the old monster's boots. But she was kissing Elsie's ass. Sometimes literally.

"You'll learn a lot from me," Elsie said. "Just be sure you do what I want with that knowledge. You showed me last night you can take direction, so keep that up, and we'll be fine."

"What happens now?" Crapsey croaked. "And where can I get some of that coffee?"

Dr. Husch pointed at a large French press on the edge of the desk, and pushed a cup toward him. Crapsey grinned at her, but she looked away, a lock of blonde hair falling across her eyes in a seriously fetching way. She'd declined to take part in the debauchery the night before, withdrawing in disgust—though presumably keeping them under observation and guard—and Crapsey was bummed about that. Elsie still looked pretty much like his old evil boss, and sleeping with Nicolette was always a one-way-ticket to Regretsville, but now that her wounds had been healed, Dr. Husch was irresistible.

"Doctor Prettyface agrees I get to run operations," Elsie said. "After all, telling me how to kill somebody is like telling a Django Reinhardt how to tune a six-string."

"What's a Django?" Crapsey said.

Elsie crossed her legs, gave him a smile patronizing enough to wilt his traditional morning erection completely, and said, "We'll put our team together, and then we'll teleport over to Hawai'i, and start making Marla's life miserable."

"Uh," Nicolette said. "I don't... I mean... I'm not a big fan of teleporting. Last time I did that..." She gestured at her empty sleeve.

Elsie's look of concern was so convincing Crapsey had to concede it might be real. "You poor thing! One of the nameless many-limbed horrors of the in-between ripped your *arm* off?"

Nicolette nodded, looking away, clearly embarrassed. Crapsey had only teleported a few times, when the Mason really needed to get somewhere fast, and he'd never had any problems... but ripping holes in space and stepping through to somewhere else was dangerous, and there was a double-digit-percentage chance that some interdimensional predator would try to eat you on the way through. Or maybe not predators, and maybe not eating—the Mason had told him once that teleporting took you through the machine room of the universe, and it was possible Nicolette had lost her arm to the whirring gears of some incomprehensible cosmic engine, like a kid in a factory getting his hand caught in a drill press.

"Something tried to tear my leg off once when I teleported," Elsie was saying. "But I just ripped its arms off instead. Nasty things, they melted into a sort of silvery sludge as soon as I brought them through the portal with me. I dumped the remains in a pond, it killed like a thousand fish, really interesting, they grew extra eyes and then their brains exploded, poof!" She laughed, deeply and genuinely. "Nasty fuckers, those beasties-in-between. I actually learned another way to travel somewhere quickly—a Sufi mystic taught me the secret of Tayy al-Ard, 'the folding of the Earth.' Instead of ripping holes in reality and stepping through, you stay in one place, and the Earth moves *under* you, and puts your destination beneath your feet. Doesn't work for groups, though, so I couldn't pull you along. Besides, I prefer the old hole-tearing Western form of teleportation—it comes with a much bigger chance of disaster."

"You could teach me the... Tayy, whatever," Nicolette said.

Elsie chuckled. "Oh, that's cute. No, I couldn't. No more than I could teach a toddler to fly a fighter jet. Actually, the results would be equally hilarious. If you're too scared to teleport, you can book a ticket on Hawaiian Airlines or something and catch up with us on your own time."

Nicolette narrowed her eyes. "No, I want to go, it's fine, I'll teleport. I got one arm ripped off already, so what are the odds of it happening again?"

"Exactly the same odds you'd have if you still possessed both arms," Elsie said kindly. "The fact that it happened once before doesn't affect the probability of it happening again—not in the slightest. That's simple statistics. But there's no reason you should know about statistics or probability, after all. They're only fundamental underpinnings of chaos magic."

"I love what a bitch you can be," Nicolette said, with apparent sincerity. Crapsey looked at Dr. Husch and raised an eyebrow, but there was no making a connection with her—she just turned up her nose and looked away.

"I'm as changeable as the colors in an oil slick all right," Elsie said. She hopped off the desk and clapped her hands. "Dr. Husch has given us the run of the asylum. I figure we'll fling a couple of the inmates—sorry, patients—Marla's way, just to cause trouble. Then we'll step in more directly and have some fun."

"Can't we just kill her?" Crapsey said. "And Rondeau, too. Especially Rondeau."

"So many vendettas! Who can keep track? No, just killing her is *boring*, it would not fatten me up or make me drunk with power at all. We will have a *plan*, and it will be an extremely complicated plan—"

Nicolette raised her hand. "Not to agree with Crapsey or anything, but... a plan? Really? Shouldn't we just jump in and make some moves and see what happens, surf the probability waves, stir up some shit and cause a ruckus?"

Suddenly Elsie had a wooden ruler in her hand, and she slammed it down on the desk with a resounding *crack*. "Nicolette! What is chaos?"

Nicolette blinked. "Disorder?"

"Yes. What necessarily precedes disorder?"

"Um. Order?"

"Good girl! Chaos magicians don't hate order, silly, we *love* order. If we were just relentless champions of entropy, you know what we'd get? A static universe, with all the particles evenly distributed, and no heat. Everything still, and unmoving, and dead. That's the kind of world the Mason, the *last* inhabitant of this fine body, wanted. It's not the kind of world I want. I *love* plans, Nicolette, and the more complicated the better. I want a big crew, and lots of moving parts. A team of criminally insane sorcerers, and assorted other malcontents and grudge holders, all secretly pursuing their own agendas, looking to backstab and scheme and further their own interests, working at cross-purposes and getting into fights and squabbling and storming off in a huff..." Elsie's eyes rolled back in her head, and she shivered all over.

"Is she... having an orgasm?" Dr. Husch asked. "Because she looks like she's having an orgasm."

"Either she is," Crapsey said, "or she was faking it exactly the same way last night."

Elsie pushed a hank of hair out of her face, bit her own thumb hard enough to draw blood, then smiled. "Sorry. Just thinking about all that potential disaster gets me.... Ahem. The more complicated the plan, Nicolette, the more possible ways it can fall apart. And that falling apart is basically the kinetic energy that feeds my power—and yours, too, I guess, not that I've seen any power out of you yet."

"I did not release you to grow fat off disaster." Dr. Husch glared. "I want Marla miserable, and then I want her *dead*. Your plan is useless to me if it doesn't achieve those ends. And, much to my surprise, it turns out I have an informant of sorts in Marla's camp. Rondeau called me last night for a friendly conversation, unaware of how my loyalties have shifted. Marla knows you're coming." Husch paused. "Not you, specifically, Jarrow, but her enemies—Rondeau summoned an oracle, which gave Marla a warning, in general terms. You will not be able to take her unawares."

"It'll be way more fun with an informed opposition anyway!" Elsie said. "What's the point of a war if one side of the conflict thinks it's a vacation instead?" She leaned over the desk and patted Husch's folded hands. "It's okay. If the plan works, misery and death, just like you wanted. If the plan fails spectacularly, I'll get a nice power surge, and, eh, then I'll just pop Marla's head like Nicolette pops her pimples, okay?"

"I care only for results," Husch said.

"I guess we'd better get started, then! Let's meet the new recruits."

"I think these are the best prospects." Husch pushed over a pile of folders, and Elsie picked them up and flung them at Nicolette, who snatched one out of the air but, lacking a second hand, got smacked in the chest with rest.

"Read!" Elsie barked. "Summarize!"

Nicolette sat down on the floor and scanned through the files. "Uh, Norma Nilson, the nihilomancer. She projects her emotions, making others feel what she feels, and since she thinks life is horrible and meaningless, she's kind of a bummer to be around. Everybody in her apartment building died of starvation before she was locked up—they just stopped caring enough to eat. All the people who came to check on their friends or family who lived in the apartment got caught in the field of depression, too, until somebody with magical connections figured out what was going on. Ugly stuff."

"She's a maybe," Elsie said. "Nihilism is boring. If we could get her to project, say, Dionysian frenzy, that could be something. Might be possible. Brain chemistry can be hacked." She sat back down on the desk and turned to Husch. "What about that other psychic, Genevieve? The one who knocked me out last time I tried to escape? She's got some power we could use."

"She escaped herself," Husch said. "Her current whereabouts are unknown."

"She's friends with Marla anyway, I hear," Nicolette chimed in. "Marla helped de-crazy her."

"Hmm, that could be a real challenge, if she got involved on Marla's side," Elsie mused. "It would be nice if this wasn't a total one-sided blowout. Okay, who's next?"

"The Beast of Felport." Nicolette opened a folder and removed a single sheet of paper. "Not a lot of info here. An animal unknown to science. Relentless killing machine, cunning, difficult to contain, apparently immortal, seems to be connected to this area somehow, though nobody's sure why— maybe a supernatural protector? Ha, kind of like Marla was, except whatever it's protecting isn't the populace. Hates people, tries to kill them all, pretty indiscriminately. Wants to wipe the city off the map, it looks like. Maybe it just really like trees and mud. Currently wrapped in a dream that makes it believe it's running around primal uninhabited Felport, all happy and unconscious."

"Hmm. No, I don't think so. I like people I can talk to. Relentless killing machines don't scheme or plot, anyway. Capital B Boring. Next."

"This guy calls himself Everett Malkin—claims to be the first chief sorcerer of Felport, from hundreds of years ago." Nicolette shook her head. "He's got some kind of magic, but it's not clear if he's super-powerful or anything, and apparently Marla tricked him into getting locked up here without much trouble. He really hates her, though, so he's got that going for him."

"I think we have enough personal grudges against Marla in this crew already," Elsie said. "One more and we'll be in danger of having a quorum, far too much unity of purpose. Next!"

"Roger Vaughn, and his reincarnation, the younger Roger Vaughn—"

"Vaughn? That idiot?" Elsie blew a raspberry. "He worships an evil sea-god that doesn't even exist.. Pathetic. If I worshipped an imaginary sea-god, you'd better believe it would *start* existing, and quick. Next."

"Gustavus Lupo, the skinchanger." Nicolette looked up from the pages in her lap. "Didn't he make a giant body out of corpses or something once?"

"That was just a rumor," Dr. Husch said. "It was an unrelated flesh golem. No, Lupo is…"

"I told *Nicolette* to summarize," Elsie said and, amazingly, Husch fell silent—possibly because she was afraid the chaos witch would ugly her up again. Crapsey didn't like the way the power dynamic was shifting here. It felt kind of like an ocean liner starting to capsize.

"Lupo can… Ha! You ever hear of the Napoleon complex? When a crazy guy thinks he's Napoleon?"

"Yes. I also know about people trapped on desert islands, men lying on psychiatrist's couches, people crawling through the desert, and other gag comic-strip clichés."

"Well, if Lupo thinks he's Napoleon, he turns *into* Napoleon. Like, physically, it's not just an illusory light show, he *really* changes. And he has the strategic and tactical knowledge that Napoleon had, and he speaks French, and all that."

"His impersonations are more convincing when the subject is living," Husch said. "I think he establishes a sort of… psychic link, and mirrors their minds directly. For the dead, he gets the knowledge from *somewhere*, perhaps the minds of some scholar or relative somewhere, but the artifice is less perfect."

"What's Lupo doing in here?" Crapsey said. "Sounds like he's a crime boss's dream. Perfect impersonations on demand."

Husch shrugged. "He lost control. Replicating so many minds grievously damaged his own—when he impersonated someone, he forgot almost entirely about himself and his own identity. He'd turn into people he encountered randomly on the street, sometimes. Then he would become convinced they were doppelgangers, monsters impersonating *him*, and he would try to murder them. Any actual identity he once had is in shreds and fragments. I've tried to coax out the 'real' Gustavus, but… it's been a long time, and we've made almost no progress. His rooms are full of mirrors, so he can see his face, and remember who he is, but if he so much as sees a photograph of another person, he takes on their form, and in the absence of external rein-forcement or new people to imitate, he just... blurs."

"So what good is he to us?" Nicolette said. "If he's too crazy to follow orders?"

"Oh, I can control him," Elsie said airily. "I can't *heal* him, or anyway I won't, but I can pick a person for him to impersonate and stir in a little com-pulsion to lock down that shape until we want it to change, not a problem. But who should we turn him in to? Does Marla have any dead lovers? Ooh, maybe her dead apprentice?"

"Her brother," Nicolette said. "They've got some kind of messed-up his-tory. Lupo could impersonate—"

"No, no, we're going to recruit her *actual* brother," Elsie said. "It's on my to-do list for later this morning."

Husch frowned. "Jason Mason is just a criminal—a confidence man. He has no real knowledge of magic. You want to recruit him to your team?"

"Of course!" Elsie said. "It'll be a *disaster*. I can't wait." She reached out and touched Husch's cheek. "Your skin, I swear, it's like porcelain. Which is to say, I could shatter it with a hammer. Now, I'll do this job for you, I've made an agreement, and I'll stand by it since I haven't figured out a way to knock down your binding spells yet, but you have to give me the good stuff, quit holding back. Who do you have locked up in here who can do some *real* damage?"

Dr. Husch sighed. "Yes. I thought it might come to that. Let me show you."

"Elsie Jarrow and Roderick Barrow?" The chaos witch laughed. "I can't decide if that sounds like a firm of lawyers or a vaudeville duo." They were in a small room just off a remote hallway of the estate, a space unremarkable in most respects—except for the fact that one wall was an unbroken sheet of black volcanic glass, so imbued with magics that it made Crapsey's wooden jaw ache.

"He calls himself Barrow of Ulthar now," Dr. Husch said. "Though his full title is Lord of the Maggotlands, Protector of the Ravenous Dead, Dis-penser of Injustice, Bestower of Maladies, Emperor of the Cinderlands and the Megalith Isles... well, I can't remember the rest of it. He's a Dark Lord, basically."

"Of an imaginary fantasy universe," Elsie said.

"He is very good at imagining. Barrow was a pulp science fiction writer in the 1930s, and after he suffered a mental breakdown, he began to imagine him-self living in a sword-and-sorcery world of his own devising." Husch spread out a few photos on the desk—they showed swords, animal pelts, some kind of giant dead snake, and misshapen skulls. "These are all… imports, you might say, or rather *apports*, from his fantasy world. He is delusional, but he's *exother-mically* delusional. I almost tried to recruit him to run this operation, but I was afraid I might accidentally unleash his monstrous horde upon the Earth."

Elsie smiled. "And, what, you thought I'd be *safer*? I wonder about your sanity, doctor. Maybe my craziness is contagious. Though I'm feeling much better in this body. Chronic agony tends to distort your worldview."

"He's also very resistant to direct communication," Husch said. "Any-one who enters Barrow's physical presence is pulled into his fantasy world. The results are seldom pleasant for those so absorbed. He incorporates visi-tors into his narrative, generally as enemies. And Barrow of Ulthar's enemies don't tend to live long. His fantasy alter-ego used to be a hero, actually, with a destiny, on a quest to save the universe. But I sent Marla Mason into his dreamworld in an attempt at therapy, hoping she could thwart his quest, and show him his world was an illusion. This was many years ago, back when she was just a mercenary, really…"

"She fucked it up?" Elsie said.

"On the contrary, she did just as I hoped. She showed Barrow he was not a hero fated to save a world—that he was just a man, fragile and flawed and entirely capable of being defeated. Alas, he did not respond by becoming lucid and returning to this reality. Instead he decided that, if he didn't have a destiny, he would make his *own* destiny, and that if he couldn't be a hero, he would become a conqueror."

"I'm so over conquerors," Crapsey muttered, running his fingers along the wall of obsidian glass that separated Barrow's room from the rest of the Institute.

"We could still use him," Elsie said. "Or his power, anyway. Let me in to see him."

"He'll think you're a rival sorcerer," Husch warned. "He'll try to kill you."

"Many have tried," Elsie said. "Few have triumphed."

Few? Crapsey thought. Then again, how surprising was it that Elsie had died already, and more than once?

Husch removed her necklace, revealing the small golden key that had been hanging between her breasts all this time. *Lucky key*, Crapsey thought.

"Ooh, there's power there." Elsie leaned forward and sniffed. "You've got yourself an artifact, don't you?"

"This object maintains Barrow's captivity," Husch said. "Among other things. It's called the Key of Totality. An item of power that comes from Bar-row's own imaginary universe, actually, which might be why it's so effective against him." She put the key into a small hole in the black glass wall—though Crapsey wasn't entirely convinced the hole had been there a moment ago—and gave it a twist. A rectangular section of rock slid away, revealing darkness inside. "It's basically an airlock," Husch said. "The door to his room will open after this door closes behind you. Are you sure you want to do this? Our Dark Lord is more powerful than you realize."

"I love meeting new people." Elsie stepped into the wall of black glass, and the door slid closed after her, the whole becoming seamless and solid again.

"I hope she doesn't die," Husch said. "Or… I don't suppose she's solipsistic enough to want to usurp Barrow's power?"

"Elsie's not really a builder," Nicolette said. "Or, if she builds something, it's just for the joy of demolishing it later. I've been spending my whole life kicking over sandcastles, but Elsie likes to build the sandcastles herself and then kick them over—probably because she makes better sandcastle than your average asshole with a pail and shovel does. But she's been trapped in a box for a long time. I doubt she'd want to be stuck in another box, even one made of imagination."

"Uh. How will you know when she wants to come *out*?" Crapsey said.

Husch shrugged. "The spells of binding here are meant to keep Barrow and his various emanations in captivity. It should be possible for Jarrow to get out—assuming she isn't murdered in my patient's dreamworld. But either way, we should—"

A knocking sound came from beyond the obsidian wall. "Yoo hoo!" Elsie called, voice muffled but cheerful. "Open, says me!"

Husch touched the key, which pulsed golden light, and twisted it again in the keyhole, making the door in the wall slide open again. Elsie came out, hair mussed but otherwise unchanged. She had an object the size of a soccer ball, wrapped in a brown fur, tucked under her arm. "Okay," Elsie said, "Barrow and I made an arrangement. I'm done."

"You were there only moments!" Husch said.

Elsie waved a hand. "Messing with time is a specialty of mine, and in a fantasy world? Please. The rules are so much more elastic there, you don't even really have to break them, just stretch them a little. I spent a couple of weeks with the Dark Lord, and helped him deal with some rebellions in the provinces—I think he's killing externalized representations of inconvenient parts of his psyche, like guilt and empathy, in the form of peasants and revolutionaries, it's pretty interesting—and this is my payment." She patted the object under her arm. "It should come in handy."

"What is it?" Husch said.

"I know!" Elsie said. "I love surprises too! All right, it's time to get things going. I know not much time passed here, but subjectively it feels to me like we're running late, so you're all on Jarrow time now. We've got a bit more work to do on the mainland, but there's no reason we can't start softening Marla up now. The road to hell wasn't built in a day. Let's go see Gustavus

Lupo, teleport him over to Maui, and put him to work." Elsie draped her free arm around Nicolette's shoulder. "What were you saying before, about how most of Marla's enemies were dead? What are their names? And do you think we could get some pictures of them?"

The Dead, Walking on the Beach

MARLA FOUND ARACHNE seated on a broad, flat stone beside a pool of water fed by a stream that plummeted off a higher cliff, and could have been called a waterfall by someone feeling sufficiently generous. The kahuna was weaving together a mat of vines and leaves and grasses. That was how she worked her magic, apparently, though Marla didn't know the details—she'd never been much of a maker, so it wasn't a discipline she favored. "Aloha," she said, leaning against a tree, after making sure there weren't any bugs or lizards on the trunk. Hawai'i was too damned fecund by half.

Arachne ignored Marla until she'd finished plaiting together a few more bits of plant fiber, then looked up. She was in her forties, probably, with long black hair woven into intricate (and, doubtless, magically significant) braids, dressed in a skirt of ti leaves. She was topless, apart from a cascade of shell necklaces, which was actually more modest than the swimsuits a lot of the tourists wore on beaches. She looked at Marla, her face expressionless. "Aloha," she said after a long moment. "What can I do for you, Marla Mason?"

"I was wondering if you know anything about a pack of surfers, led by a guy named Glyph?"

"They have no 'leader,'" Arachne said. "They are a collective. Glyph is more connected to the secular world than some of the others, so he is often their spokesman. I suppose they showed a certain deference to their eldest member, Ronin. He has, sadly, passed away."

"I know. He was murdered, and they've hired me to find out who did it. Any ideas?"

"Why ask me?" Arachne said.

Marla thought about that, and decided she might as well go with honesty. "I don't know anybody to ask. The locals haven't gone out of their way to make me feel welcome.."

Arachne half-smiled. "All right. You did me a good turn, and you have been discreet about our dealings, so I am willing to help. I fear I cannot offer much: the wave-mages have no enemies, as far as I know. They spend most of their time in the water, drawing their power from the sea—its motion, its depths, the life that teems within it, the deaths that sink down. They use their power to help the very sea that gives them that power. They have no *goals*— they just want to be connected to the ocean, which they know is their mother, and their father, and their confessor, and their grave. How can people with no goals make enemies?"

"Good question." Marla crouched down and leaned her back against the tree. "I guess that's been my problem all along—too many goals. What can you tell me about Ronin?"

"He was old. Older than I am, and I am older than I seem. He came from Japan, originally, though he has lived here for a long time. Do you know what the name he chose means?"

"Ronin? It's some kind of samurai, right? My friend Rondeau made me watch a movie called *Ronin* once, but it was just some crime thing."

"A Ronin is a *masterless* samurai," Arachne said. "It means 'wave man,' which is appropriate for a sorcerer devoted to the sea, but more specifically it means someone carried by the waves. Someone given *over* to the waves, and taken wherever those waves take him. I met him a few times. I gather he had a dark past, that he had performed terrible acts, and that he had chosen to give up his own personal agency in favor of letting the sea guide his actions." She shrugged, and began weaving again. "How can a man who makes no decisions make an enemy? A mystery."

"It couldn't have been a random attack, though. Whoever did this has big magic, and used it to cover their tracks."

"Perhaps a dark sorcerer hoped to steal his power?" Arachne said. "We've had experience with such people before, as you know. Everyone who comes to Hawai'i wants something, it seems. Our fish. Our soil. To own the beauty of our islands, and make them ugly in the process."

"Right. So it must have been an out-of-towner, then." Marla had read enough mystery novels to know that people *always* wanted to blame atrocities on outsiders.

"I suppose it's more likely it was someone close to him," she said. "Aren't most murders committed by those who know the victim? Though I hate to think so. One of the others in the collective, perhaps? It is hard to imagine any of them striking against Ronin, but they are certainly powerful, and probably capable of hiding the signs of such a crime. As I said, they aren't hierarchical, so there couldn't have been much of an advantage in killing Ronin... but there may be currents and schisms and conflicts in their group that are unknown to me. It's hard to know how close they are, truly—if they're more like a family, or more like a nest of ants."

"Families kill each other all the time," Marla said, thinking of her brother.

"This is true," Arachne said. "Is there anything else I can help you with?" Her tone said she hoped not.

Marla brushed a many-legged, winged thing away from her face. "You ever heard of a guy named Reva? Claims to be a god of the lost and the exiled?"

Arachne frowned. "I sensed the arrival of a minor power, and heard rumors, but I have not encountered this being myself. You have?"

"He introduced himself, yeah. He thinks I'm primed to become one of his worshippers, I guess."

Arachne grunted. "Serving a god is a tricky business."

"I don't serve *anyone*," Marla said. Or anyplace. Not anymore. "Anyway, thanks. Sorry to bother you." She stood up.

"Wait," Arachne said. "I doubt it is important, but… the wave-mages, they occasionally recruit, and they have been grooming a new member, a boy named… John? Luke? Something like that. He shows some natural aptitude for magic, and has the appropriate reverence for the sea, but he is not… hmmm… 'assimilated' yet? He may be able to give you a more informed perspective on the group than I can, since he knows them, but is not yet fully *of* them."

"Hey, a lead's a lead," Marla said. "I'll talk to him. Do you know where I can find him?"

"He works at a dive shop called Handsome Bob's, in Napili," she said. "Beyond that, I do not know—he is often out on the water."

"Thanks—uh, mahalo, Arachne. I owe you one."

Arachne bowed her head in acknowledgment. "I shall keep you in mind if I need future assistance. I wish you luck in your investigations. Ronin was… a good man, or at least, a man trying to be good."

"That's all any of us can do," Marla said. "Though some people don't even bother. Aloha."

Marla found Pelham looking down at one of the seven sacred pools. "What, you don't want to go for a dip?"

"It looks enticing," he admitted, "but I thought it would be ill-advised to be submerged in water, in case you had need of my assistance."

"My visit went off without a hitch, though I don't know if I accomplished much. Arachne did suggest someone I could talk to, though. You up for the drive back around the island?"

"Of course. But, may I suggest you stop for a meal along the way? I fear you don't take proper care of yourself."

Marla sighed. "I've always been better at taking care of other people, and by 'taking care of,' I guess I mean 'beating up.' Sure, let's eat. I bet you have a place in mind, right?"

Pelham drove her to Mama's Fish House, a restaurant on the North shore, about halfway back to Lahaina. At first, she objected because it was too fancy, but Pelham started going on about how she was married to a *god*, her worth exceeded those of diamonds and gold, and she agreed to eat there just to get him to shut up. The restaurant was nestled in a gorgeous cove and surrounded by palm trees, the walls of the building mostly windows, and thus largely open to the air. The place was decorated with tiki sculptures and outrigger canoes and oversized bird cages—it might have been kitschy anywhere else, but this was Hawai'i, and they were probably actual local antiques. The hostess led them to a table near a window, and a delicious sea breeze wafted through, cooling them as Marla read the menu. "Wait," she said, "this thing tells you the name of the guy who *caught the fish*."

"Let's hope it tastes good, then," Pelham said. "Or you'll know the man to whom you should complain."

"Ha." Marla was a long way from being a foodie—she tended to think of food as fuel, and got by on jerky, peanut butter, power bars, and boiled eggs most of the time. Really enjoying food seemed like an indulgence, and indulgences were for the weak... but what was the pressing reason to be strong? Sure, Nicolette and Jason were apparently coming to try and kill her, but Nicolette had never been half as good as she thought she was, and Jason... well, she still had hope she could talk to him, and talk him *out* of whatever he was doing, and anyway, *he* wasn't going to get the drop on her. Whatever chance they'd had to kill her had been blown as soon as Death told her about it, as far as she was concerned. Forewarned was forearmed and all that. Eating something opulent wasn't going to put her in mortal danger.

They ordered lobster guacamole to share—so *that's* what heaven tasted like, good to know—and she got the stuffed mahi mahi. Pelham ordered prawns, and welcome to them. Marla thought the things were too rubbery by half, though Pelly said she'd just never had a good one. They chatted, and it was pleasant. He was a lot less deferential than he used to be. Traveling the world for a few months had been good for him. He actually told her some *jokes*, though his delivery could've used a little work, and—

Marla dropped her fork, and it hit her plate with a clatter. She half rose from her chair, craning her head to look out the nearest window. Pelham looked at her with alarm until she shook her head and sat back down. "Can't be," she muttered.

"What's wrong?" Pelham twisted in his chair to look out the window. "Did you see something?"

"Some*one*. Someone who's supposed to be dead—damn it, who *is* dead, she must be. Probably just someone with a resemblance…. Listen, I'll be right back, okay?" Marla tossed her napkin onto the table and rose from her chair again, winding her way through the tables toward the walkway that led out of the restaurant. She caught a glimpse of a woman with short blonde hair, in a white silk blouse and flowy white pants, disappearing around a stand of trees.

Marla followed her, soon reaching a small but gorgeous stretch of beach, a miniature cove adjacent to the restaurant. A family was posing on an out-rigger canoe (or a prop recreation of one) on the sand while the mother took photos, and a few other tourists were wandering around, but the woman was down by the water, alone. It was hard to tell from the back, and from this distance, but the way she carried herself…

The woman turned, looked at Marla, and raised her hand to wave.

Marla hissed in a sharp breath, the same sound she might make if she'd inadvertently burned herself. Even thirty feet away, there was no mistaking the angular beauty of Susan Wellstone, Marla's onetime rival for the rulership of Felport. Susan had dropped her plans to assassinate Marla and seized the opportunity to become chief sorcerer of San Francisco instead, but that hadn't made the two of them any friendlier, so seeing her was never a pleasure.

But this time was worse, because Susan was dead, murdered many weeks ago on the West Coast. So what was this? A ghost? Ghosts tended to haunt specific people or places related to their deaths, so what would Susan's shade be doing outside Mama's Fish House? More likely it was someone wearing an illusion to fuck with Marla's head.

As Marla approached, she let her goddess-vision rise, dispelling all illu-sions… but the woman by the water's edge didn't change at all. "You're not a ghost," Marla said, stepping beside Susan. "You're not wearing a glamour of bent light and twisted perception, either. So what the fuck are you? Evil twin? Or, ha, good twin? A clone? Did Susan make herself a backup body and download her consciousness?"

The couldn't-be-Susan looked at Marla, her gaze disconcerting as always because of her heterochromia: one eye was green, the other blue. "You're go-ing to die," she said. "Your past is catching up with you—and your future is catching up with you, too, and isn't that so much scarier? I don't know why I'm not dead anymore—I *was*, they tell me I was—but I'm glad to be back, so I can see your suffering, followed by your end."

"Threatening me never worked out that well for you when you were alive," Marla said.

"Ah, but you had friends then, Marla. You had power, and influence, and artifacts." Susan—no, not Susan, don't buy the bullshit—knelt and reached into the sea, cupping her hands and lifting up a measure of glistening water. "But you let all that go, didn't you?" Susan opened her hands, and the water poured out onto the sand. Marla gasped, doubling over and vomiting up all the water she'd drunk at lunch, and pretty much everything else in her stomach, too. A simple but nasty bit of sympathetic magic, entangling the handful of sea water with the water in Marla's belly—pouring one out had caused the other to come pouring out as well. Marla straightened, wiping her mouth with the back of her hand, the surge of nausea thankfully passed. She looked around, but Susan's double was nowhere to be seen, and the family by the outrigger canoe was staring at her with horror.

"Stay away from the prawns," Marla called, and they turned away, talking amongst themselves. No one showed any gratitude anymore. Kneeling—not too close to her puke—Marla scanned the ground and tried to find a trace of Susan's footprints, but this was a popular restaurant, and a lot of customers had come down this way, so the sand was pretty well crisscrossed. With her goddess-vision still active, Marla scanned the beach, in case Susan had draped herself in a glamour, but there was no one here but ordinaries. She trudged back up the beach toward the restaurant.

Pelham was still at the table, fretfully twisting a napkin. Marla sat across from him and took a long sip of ice water to clear out her mouth. "Are you all right?" he asked.

"I think those old enemies Death mentioned have made their first move," Marla said. "They've got better tricks than I expected, I'll give them that. Way beyond what Nicolette or my brother could come up with alone. Makes me wonder who else is in on this little vendetta."

"What should we do?" Pelham asked.

Marla shrugged. "Lay traps. Get prepared. But first, we've got a murder to solve."

"Surely the case can wait, if your enemies are attacking—"

"That wasn't an attack. It was a taunt. And I wouldn't give them the satisfaction of changing my plans just because they did a little something like raising the dead."

"Are you Handsome Bob?"

The grizzled, white-bearded, sun-roughened man behind the counter grinned, showing incongruously white and shiny teeth. "Look at this face. You're telling me that ain't self-evident? Yeah, I'm Bob. What can I do you for?"

"You've got a kid working for you," Marla said. "His name's John, or Luke, or—"

"Jon-Luc," Bob said. "His parents are French, or from French Polynesia, hell, I forget which. He mess up a transaction or something?"

"Not at all," Marla said. "He recommended a great snorkeling spot on the road to Hana, and I just wanted to thank him, and see if he had any other tips."

Bob grunted. "Normally I'd be offended you aren't asking *me*, but I have to admit, even though I've lived here twenty years, that boy knows more good hidden spots than I do. He's out back hosing off some equipment."

Marla and Pelham went where he directed, down an aisle full of dangling snorkels and facemasks in assorted styles, and out the back door to a little concrete slab where a boy of perhaps nineteen with a shaggy blond mop of hair stood, washing sand off a row of brightly colored body boards.

"Jon-Luc?" Marla said, and the boy turned off the water and looked over, his face open and guileless.

"Can I help you ma'am?"

"I think we have a mutual friend," Marla said. "Glyph? My name's Marla. I'm… helping Glyph out with something. You know what I'm talking about?"

The boy swallowed, and nodded.

"Great," Marla said. "Want to take a break? I'll buy you a soda."

Jon-Luc cleared it with his boss, then walked with Marla across the parking lot to a little restaurant that specialized in mixed plates, that uniquely Hawai'ian collision of Pacific and Asian cuisine, and secretly one of Marla's favorite things about life on the island. The three of them took seats around a metal table under an umbrella in one corner of the wooden deck, just a few steps from the beach and a few yards from the ocean. Marla was hungry, having lost most of the lunch she'd eaten at Mama's Fish House, so she ordered the kalua pig and cabbage plate, which came with the traditional one scoop of macaroni salad and two scoops of rice. Jon-Luc and Pelham made do with iced tea, and once they were all settled, Marla gave Jon-Luc her best friendly smile and said, "So, which one of your friends murdered Ronin, anyway?"

The kid went all wide-eyed, mouth falling open, but Marla kept smiling. He looked at Pelham, who nodded encouragingly. "Uh," Jon-Luc said. "I don't know. I mean, I don't think it was any of my friends."

Marla leaned across the table toward him. "Here's the thing. Somebody cut Ronin's throat, which means he had an enemy. Except he *didn't*, because as far as I can tell he spent literally all his time out paddling around in the waves with his buddies. So if I'm looking for suspects, I have to look first at his friends. You get it?"

Jon-Luc pushed some hair out of his face, sighed, and shook his head. "I get it. But I don't think you do. Glyph and them… they're like *one person*. They have to remind themselves to talk out loud when I'm around. None of them would try to kill Ronin—that would be like trying to kill your, I don't know, your lungs or heart or something."

"Come on," Marla said. "There's no conflict in the group? No disagreements on philosophy—some who want to save the whales, and some who want to kill the whalers? Anything?"

Jon-Luc shook his head. "No way, they're in perfect harmony, with nature and with one another, they—"

"They tell all the newcomers that," a kindly voice said. "But it's not true, oh no, not true at all, how could they be all one mind when even one mind is all full of contradictions and conflicts and inner voices shouting, shouting over everyone and each other and everything?"

Marla twisted around in her chair, grinning at the woman in a dripping wetsuit standing on the steps down to the beach. "Well, this is really turning into a reunion show. Nice to see you."

"True true, I am very nice to see," the Bay Witch agreed.

Brotherly Love

JASON MASON HAD BEEN laying low in Mississippi, only occasionally emerging to count cards at some of the riverboat casinos to keep himself in whiskey and cigarettes, afraid to touch any of his various bank accounts in case his sister was keeping tabs on him. Who knew what people like her were capable of? She'd killed his partner Danny Two Saints, and done her level best to kill him, and she had more than connections—she had fucking *powers*.

Then his mother called to say Marla wanted to talk to him. Mom tried to lay a guilt trip on him for not mentioning he'd seen his sister recently, so he gave her a line of bullshit about how he didn't want to upset her, he knew Marla was a sore point, and all that. He wasn't fond of his mother, exactly, but he'd never quite managed to disentangle himself from her, and anyway, she was always good for an alibi, so he kept in touch.

So now he sat in the living room of his rented Airstream trailer, parked on a scraggly lot in the middle of some bare fields, nothing for miles but crows and farmhouses and leafless trees. He watched dust swirl in the yellow light coming in through the dirty half-closed mini-blinds, smoking a cigarette, and tried to work out the angles. What was the percentage in calling Marla back? What did she want? Their recent history was even uglier than their ancient history, and now she was trying to reach out. Why, why, why? A trick, a trap, a lure?

The only way to find out was to call and ask. He gazed at the disposable cell phone in his hand, the number his mother had recited repeating itself in his head—he'd always been good with numbers, almost as good as he was with people—and thought, *Screw it, why not?*

Before he could dial, someone pounded on his door hard enough to make the trailer rock on its wheels. Jason slipped out of the chair, drawing his pistol, and waited.

"Avon calling!" a woman's voice shouted, and Jason frowned. Avon? Who still sold Avon door-to-door?

"I don't want any!" he called, rising, but keeping his hand on his gun.

The door creaked open, despite the fact that he was sure he'd chained it shut, and he squinted against the rectangle of daylight. A woman climbed the steps into the trailer and looked at him, hands on her hips, just a silhouette against the brightness.

"Lady, you aren't welcome. Beat it."

The door slammed shut, apparently of its own accord, but he could make himself believe it was just the wind. When his eyes adjusted to the new dimness, he raised his pistol—because for a second, he thought it was Marla, come to finish him off. She was the right height, and the shape of her face was almost the same, but her hair was wild and long and red, and anyway, she was too young, closer to twenty than thirty. Marla didn't dress like that, either, in a scarlet silk blouse and tight skirt. The woman gave him a big goofy grin like nothing he'd ever seen on Marla's lips, and any residual resemblance dissolved then. "Cute gun!" she said, and the voice was a bit like Marla's, too, but brassier, and too loud for the small space. "Point it somewhere else, would you?"

"I don't know who you are, but—"

"I know who you are, though," she said. "A boy who can't follow directions."

The gun twisted in his hand, and he shouted, dropping it—the weapon had transformed into twenty or thirty big cockroaches, the monsters the locals called tree roaches, and he wiped his hand on his shirt as he backed away, and the bugs scurried for the corners.

"My name's Elsie Jarrow, Jason. I'm here to talk about your sister."

Shit. Marla must have sent this woman to finish him off. Figures she wouldn't bother to do it herself. Why had she tried to call him, though? Just to gloat?

Jarrow didn't try to attack. She pulled over the straight-backed wooden chair set up by the "kitchen table," a folding thing smaller than a card table, and sat down, crossing one leg over the other. "I'm told you and Marla don't get along. Why the sibling rivalry? Is it a Cain and Abel thing, or more like Michael and Fredo Corleone? Ha, I hear you tried to shoot her, so I guess it's the latter. Cain just used a rock. Oh, those were simpler times."

"What, Marla didn't tell you?" Jason had another gun, in the little built-in drawer by the bed. Could he get to it and shoot her before she turned it into a bunch of snakes or something? It was probably a longshot, but he'd beaten worse odds.

She waggled her finger at him. "Assumptions get you in trouble, Mr. Mason. Marla didn't send me. I represent a group of people whose interests may align with your own."

He lunged for the drawer, and she started laughing. When he pulled it open, dozens of pale white moths fluttered out, and flew straight for his closet. "I know what you're thinking—I turned the guns into moths. But not at all! I conjured moths who *eat* guns. Nice, huh? Of course they eat cloth, too. They're going to ruin your suits. But a bullet hole would have ruined this nice blouse, so it's only fair. Listen, sit, and tell me—why did you try to kill Marla?"

Jason knew when he was outgunned, even if his enemy didn't use guns. Better to play along and wait for an opportunity, maybe. He returned to his chair, got comfortable, picked up his tumbler of Jack and Coke, and shrugged. "It was nothing personal. Just business. Her dying would have made me some money."

Jarrow widened her eyes in mock alarm. "You would have killed your own flesh and blood? For mere filthy lucre?"

"Sure, she's my sister, but so what? She's really a stranger. I went almost twenty years without seeing her, without hearing a word, and I had to track *her* down. Hell, she was an ingrate even when we were kids, she never appreciated anything I did for her. Then she grew up and got rich, became a big boss running Felport, and she never even reached out to me. I don't owe her shit."

"Blood is thicker than water, but money is even thicker, huh?"

Jason scowled and took a sip of his drink. "Doesn't matter anyway. The plan kind of blew up in my face, and come to find out Marla's not just a criminal—she's some kind of goddamn witch. Like *you* are, I guess."

"Some kind," Jarrow murmured. "You killed a friend of hers, too, didn't you?"

Jason shrugged. "Somebody got on the wrong side of my gun. It happens. Marla came at me, tried to kill me. Didn't work. I'm not saying I don't see her side of things, but I'm not going to go down easy. Did she send you to try and see, what, if I'm remorseful? If she could get an apology? Won't happen. She was just another mark to me. My mistake was not realizing the kind of power she had, that's all. If I'd known, I would have played things differently."

"I told you I don't work for her. I don't work for anybody—I work for *me*. More fun that way. But if you keep contradicting me, you won't like what happens next. Or did you think guns were the only things I can turn into bugs?"

Jason narrowed his eyes. "What, you're going to turn me into a mosquito?"

"I was thinking more of turning your genitals into dung beetles," Jarrow said. "It's a lot more traumatic when you ruin just *parts* of someone, instead of outright killing them. Killing is boring. A good maiming will pay dividends for years to come."

Jason held up his hands. Who knew what this crazy bitch could do? "Fine, okay, you're not from Marla. So what do you want?"

"Two things: to make Marla miserable. And then to kill her. I know, I just said killing is boring, and it is, but that's what my associates want, so I'll go along with it."

Jason shrugged. "So kill her. What do you want with me? I don't know any of your voodoo shit."

"Ah, but you have other skills, and besides, Marla probably has very complicated feelings about you. Having you on our team is going to make her distracted, and it'll bother her, so it works for me."

"I wish you the best of luck. Marla, dead, that's a load off my mind. But I don't want any part of it."

Jarrow snorted. "This isn't an invitation. These are marching orders. You'll help me."

"What if I don't?"

"Well, I *could* control your mind and make you into a puppet, or even have this guy I know transform himself into your exact double, but it's more fun if you do things of your own more-or-less free will, give or take a little bit of extortion. So: this is a nice trailer you've got here. Be a shame if something... happened to it." She snapped her fingers, and the walls began to shimmer and groan, then exploded outward in a cloud of millions of small gray birds, leaving only the floor intact.

Jason tilted his head back and watched as the birds rose up into the sky, clotting together into a flock and then flying off toward the west. A cold autumn breeze blew across the fallow fields around him, making him shiver. Ha. Like it was just the wind making him do that. He was lucky he hadn't pissed himself. No way he was getting back his security deposit on this place now.

"Oops, something bad already happened," Jarrow said. "I always mess up threats that way. Those were passenger pigeons, by the way. They were extinct until four seconds ago. Look at me, I'm an environmentalist! Anyway, yes, I will do bad things to you. How'd you like to vomit tiny brass gearwheels for a week? Or have sentient shit lurking in your colon? Or have everything you touch turn to quicksilver? Much runnier than gold, and more toxic, too. All this and more can be yours for the low, low price of disobedience."

Witches. Shit. "So we're going back to Felport, then?"

"Felport? Oh, no. Marla got fired from that job. She's licking her wounds in Hawai'i. How do you feel about kicking someone while they're down?"

Jason considered for a moment, then said, "I can't think of a better time to do it."

"What are you doing here, Zufi?" Marla said.

The Bay Witch took her long blonde hair in her hands and twisted it, wringing water out onto the steps, then came forward and sat in one of the low plastic chairs around the table. "Hamil sent me a message, from you, to me, he said you wanted to talk, so here I am, for talking."

Marla blinked. "Well, sure, but—I thought you'd *call*."

"I don't have a phone," the Bay Witch said.

"So, what, you hopped the first plane?"

The Bay Witch began to draw on the metal surface of the table in a puddle of her own seawater. "Swam."

"You *swam* here? In less than a day? How did you even do that from the East Coast? Did you paddle through the Panama Canal?"

The Bay Witch shook her head. "The ocean is deep, and vast, vaster than space sometimes in some ways, it goes down as much as it goes side to side, more so. There are places in the deep deeps where space is folded over, tunnels the ancients of the drowned continents used for their wars and their business, and there are fearsome things there but they all fear me, or call me friend. You can go places fast fast if you can stand the pressures."

Marla sat back in her chair and whistled. Ancient magical (or maybe technological, or a hybrid) wormholes, deep in the ocean? First she'd ever heard of that, but then, she'd never been a big fan of the deep blue sea, ever since some bad experiences in her early twenties, dealing with a terrible tentacled thing in the ruins of an undersea megalith. "That's pretty crazy. You learn something new every day."

"When you're in the ocean, you learn something new every few *minutes*," Zufi said. She turned her blank attention on Jon-Luc, who was simultaneously trembling and staring at the Bay Witch's breasts, which probably looked pretty tantalizing to him in the slightly-unzipped damp wetsuit. "Hello. You are to be joining Glyph's crew?"

Jon-Luc managed to drag his eyes up to her face. "Yes ma'am."

She nodded. "I used to paddle with them, ride with them, ride on them sometimes, once upon. They tell you they are a perfect blend, yes yes, all together, all one with the waves, yes?"

"Sure."

Zufi shook her head. "Always there are currents, you see, always there are treacheries, because the crew reflects the sea, and the sea is all things: destroyer of sustenance and giver of food, killer and giver of life, she soothes wounds and pours salt in wounds too, she lifts you gently up and slams you cruelly down, yes? The sea is one thing that contains oh so many things, and so it is with the crew."

"Ha," Marla said. "So one of them might have killed Ronin?"

The Bay Witch cocked her head. "I will tell you about Ronin. He was once a warrior of the sky. He was the divine wind."

"A Kamikaze pilot?" Pelham said. "During World War II?"

"They taught him only to fly! But not how to land." The Bay Witch shook her head. "He loved his country. He loved the sky. He watched the planes smash into great ships and erupt in gouts of flame. His purpose, his service! But his plane failed, his engines died, he glided down, close to the water, far from the target. He tried to set off his bombs, tried to boom boom, but nothing happened. He sat and waited, ashamed of his failure. His plane hit the water. Even then it did not explode, it only broke apart."

"And he *survived*?" Pelham said.

The Bay Witch nodded. "He floated on wreckage. He floated for seven days and seven nights, very significant, he went through the door of death and looked around and came back out again." Zufi leaned forward, water dripping from her chin to *plop plop plop* on the table. "And the sea spoke to him. The ocean herself! So rare, such a rare thing."

"Hallucinations aren't that rare," Marla muttered, but Zufi went on.

"The ocean told him, I saved your life, you are mine now. You will serve me always in all things. And so kamikaze became Ronin. The man moved by the waves. He drifted. He drank rain until he learned to drink seawater. The ocean taught him oh so many things. He came here, to Hawai'i, eventually, and I met him—this was long long after the war, yes, when the Japanese were welcomed for their wallets and not hated for the actions of their ancestors anymore, and so he blended in, became the wise old man of the beach. He looked for likely ones. Prospects. He recruited me, and Glyph, and others, some others, he taught us to be one with the waves, but that means: to contain multitudes." She fell silent for a moment, staring at the puddle on the table, or somewhere farther away.

"He was a great man," Jon-Luc said. "At first he just gave me some pointers about riding my board, but later, he taught me lots of things."

"He had a sadness in him," Zufi said. "An empty place where home used to be. He knew somehow deep inside he had failed his country, even if his country had failed him by asking him to die in fire in the sky. The waves never carried him home, never never in all the drifting years. He felt himself an exile, oh, yes, "

Marla thought about Reva, the god of the wanderers, and resolved to have a little talk with him about Ronin, too.

"We spoke, not long ago," the Bay Witch said. "Ronin came to see me, we were still friends, he was still my teacher, but we had not seen each other in oh such a time. I left the crew long ago, I did not get along with Glyph, we had different ideas: I believed in protecting the life of the sea, he believed the sea should be protecting *him*, I wanted to sink whaling ships and he wanted to catch bigger waves and ride higher on the ocean's strength." She paused. "He would say it a different way, a way to make me sound crazy and bad and make him sound smart and good, but people always say things that way, don't they just. I missed Ronin, and I was happy to see him when he came, but he was sad so sad. He cried, salt tears, tears because the ocean had destroyed his home. He grew up in a little fishing village in the east of Japan, and…"

"There was an earthquake, and a tsunami," Pelham said.

Marla frowned. She'd seen some of the footage on TV, a wall of dark water sweeping across the land, burying fields, houses, and fleeing cars. She shuddered.

"Ronin knew it was coming," the Bay Witch said. "He knew the sea, knew its patterns, could read the likeliest futures in the swirling chaos, the chaos that is only part of a pattern too large to perceive, and he tried to intercede. He performed rituals, he implored, he hoped to speak to the sea again, but she would not talk to him, and his magics…. . He had great magics. But there is no force on earth like the tsunami. He had family there still, in those coastal lands, and he tried to warn them, he sent letters, he made calls, but they did not believe him: the man he claimed to be, the name he dredged up from the past, that man had died long, long ago in the war, he could not be alive anymore. The waters rushed in, and the ones he loved were lost in the dark waves." Zufi licked her lips. "He came to me, after, to talk, to tell me had… lost his faith. Strange, strange. How could I reassure him? Imagine a wise and ancient monk on a mountaintop, coming to a young one, a student at the temple, and asking for reassurance? What could I say? The ocean, it moves in mysterious ways?" She laughed, bitterly, the first hint of bitterness Marla had ever heard from the woman. "I told him the ocean does not care if we live or die. It is vast and deserving of worship, and it rewards devotions, sometimes, a bit, but there is no shortage of life. It gives and it takes. He knew, he knew, but he thought, he had a personal relationship, because once, the sea spoke to him." Zufi shook her head. "He swam away from me. He came here again, and he sat on the shore, and he didn't go back into the water anymore. He forsook the sea, as he believed he had himself been forsaken."

Jon-Luc swallowed hard and nodded. "That's true. He said he was getting too old, the ocean was getting too rough for him. He still came to the beach, he still gave us tips, but he didn't go out on the water anymore."

"They're a group, though," Marla said. "The wave-mages, they're like a hive, drawing power from each other, right?"

Zufi nodded.

"So having their eldest, most powerful member renounce his powers, that can't be good for the group as a whole, can it?"

"It would have weakened them," Zufi said. "Yes, all of them."

"Huh. So from a certain twisted point of view, killing Ronin might look like a necessary evil, or maybe even self-defense. So tell me, Zufi. This guy Glyph—is he capable of murder?"

"Anyone is capable of anything, if the current flows just right," Zufi said. She stood up. "I am sad that Ronin is dead. But he was sad to be alive. Perhaps he is happier now. But if someone killed him, yes, I want them to be sad, too. They should not gain from my loss. You will find them, Marla?"

"I'll do my best," Marla said. "And now I've got a good idea of where to look." She paused. "Assuming my enemies don't kill me first."

Zufi frowned. "Who's trying to kill you?"

Marla shrugged. "Nicolette. My brother. Who knows who else."

"I could stay and help you," Zufi said, thoughtfully. "Let me ask: if you die, will you still be able to repay the favor you owe me?"

Marla hesitated. She didn't have anything against telling lies, but when you were talking about a bargain made with another sorcerer, it was better to be straight. "No. I'd rather live, but if I die, I might actually be able to do you an even *bigger* favor."

Zufi didn't ask for details. Marla didn't understand how her mind worked, even remotely, but the Bay Witch just nodded. "Okay okay. I will swim home instead."

"Fair enough. But before you go—look at something for me." She took Death's ring from her pocket and slid it across the table.

The Bay Witch picked it up, holding it in the palm of her hand, then chewed on her lower lip. After a moment, she shook her head. "Magic. Not of this Earth."

Marla grunted. "I could tell that much."

The Bay Witch nodded, and slid the ring back across the table. "Viscarro might know more, the spider, the hoarder, the wanter-of-things, but he is dead, his soul chopped up, consumed by the monster you set loose on Felport." Zufi said that entirely without noticeable rancor, but Marla winced anyway. The Mason had killed a lot of good people in her city. Along with nasty-but-useful people like Viscarro.

"I will go now. Tell Rondeau I said: What is it I should say?"

"Hello?" Marla hazarded.

The Bay Witch considered. "Aloha," she said after a moment, and then walked down the steps, across the sand, and into the sea, where she vanished.

Everyone Is Someone's Dog

ELSIE JARROW STEPPED OUT of a rip in the flesh of reality, dragging a blindfolded man after her by the arm.

"Jesus Christ," Jason Mason said, pulling the black scarf down off his face. "What the hell was that? When you said you knew a shortcut I thought—" He looked around the assemblage in the office, then took a step back, almost bumping into Dr. Husch's desk. He pointed. "You look just like Rondeau."

"Come on," Crapsey said, striking a pose and flexing. "Why you gotta insult me? I'm way more buff than that weedy little shit."

"This is Crapsey," Dr. Husch said. "You might think of him as... Rondeau's brother."

Jason didn't look reassured. "Look, I don't know what you heard—"

Elsie patted him on the shoulder. "Don't worry, Jason, Crapsey doesn't mind that you shot Rondeau right in the guts and left him for dead, do you, Crapsey?"

"Ha. I just wish I could've seen it."

Jason twisted around and stepped away from Jarrow's touch. "*Left* him for dead? You mean Rondeau didn't die? How could he have survived that?"

"Magic, man." Crapsey shook his head. "We're all tough to kill. Which is why we're going to have to try *extra* hard to make sure Marla gets dead and stays that way. Oh, and Rondeau, too, we'll get another shot at him, he's with your sister."

"This isn't really my scene." Jason ran his fingers through his hair. "I don't really do killing, except when it's unavoidable. Don't get me wrong, I'd sleep a lot better if I knew Marla was buried six feet deep—hell, make it ten—but I don't know what I'm *doing* here."

Jason looked like Marla, sort of—same strong features, a little angular, but while Marla fell a bit short of pretty, Jason was well over the line into

101

handsome. Crapsey could see how he managed to charm desperate middle-aged women out of their life savings and family jewels, but he was nervous now, and honestly, Crapsey wasn't sure what use he'd be in their current circumstances either. But Elsie wanted him, so here he was.

"We'll all have our parts to play," Elsie said. "And it's about time we got into position. I'm just waiting for one last member of our merry band to show up."

"Who?" Husch said. "You haven't consulted me about adding anyone else to the team."

"That's just one of the many things I haven't consulted you about!" Elsie said. "Isn't it fun?"

A buzzer sounded, and Husch went around her desk to look at her computer screen. "Why is there a man with metal in his face on my doorstep?"

Elsie clapped her hands. "That's Talion! Oh, yay. Where's Nicolette? I want her to meet him."

"She's preparing some weapons for the coming war," Dr. Husch said. "She stole all my paperclips and rubber bands, a dish full of jelly beans, a box of pushpins, and one of my garter belts."

"A mighty arsenal in her hands, no doubt," Elsie said. "Well, Husch, send one of your orderlies to let our guest in, would you?"

Husch grunted and picked up her phone.

"Who is this guy?" Crapsey said.

"We used to hunt werewolves together in Europe," Elsie said.

"You have to be fucking kidding me," Jason muttered, shaking his head.

Elsie smiled, dimpling adorably. "This was back when I was just starting out, before I became almost godlike in my vast power. Oh, we'd pursue lycanthropes all night and fuck all day, good times. We had a little falling out about what to do with our kills, unfortunately. I wanted the teeth, claws, and eyes for my rituals, and he wanted intact trophies he could stuff and mount, so we went our separate ways. But he's one of the best trackers and trappers I know, so I thought, who better to join our merry band of assassins?"

The office door opened, and Talion entered. He was tall, long-faced, and broody, with spiky black hair cut in an asymmetrical style that was probably avant-garde somewhere. He had enough silver jewelry in his face to melt down and make a ten-piece place setting: half a dozen rings in his eyebrows, a large-gauge septum piercing, a labret, and what looked like fishhooks dangling from his earlobes. He looked around the room, a sour expression on his jingling face, then bared his teeth; they were all capped in silver, the better, Crapsey presumed, for biting werewolves. Talion marched up to Elsie. "You," he growled. "You dare summon me?" He had some accent Crapsey couldn't place, but that wasn't surprising—in his home universe, there wasn't a lot of communication between the continents. At least the guy was talking English.

"I am not your *dog*, and I came only to tell you I will never help you." Talion slapped Elsie across the face so hard it snapped her head to the side.

Jason cowered behind a potted plant, and Crapsey sucked in his breath and waited for Elsie to do something truly nasty, like making the guy's blood turn into maggots or something. Instead she just grinned, a handprint showing up in red on her cheek, and looked at Dr. Husch. "And the best part is, Talion hates my guts, and every other part of me! Won't this be interesting?" She stroked the werewolf hunter's cheek. "Dear boy, do you still hold all that business against me?"

"You tried to feed me to a pack of wild dogs," he said. "I stank of dog's blood for weeks afterward! And when I returned home to my estate, no one remembered who I *was*, my idiot cousin acted as if he'd been the heir forever, and everyone agreed! Security threw me out of my own home!"

"Technically not your home anymore." Elsie's nose crinkled adorably when she smiled. "Since I wiped every memory of your existence away, and rewrote all the records, and made it so you never were. I had a magic quill pen back then, good for that sort of thing. I wonder whatever happened to it? I vaguely recall stabbing a beauty pageant queen in the neck with it, but so much of that decade is a blur…"

"I have been wandering the Earth for years upon years," Talion said. "Hoping for the opportunity to meet you again, and spit in your face. I'd heard you were imprisoned. I was *glad*. But if you are free now, perhaps I should kill you."

"Better plan," Elsie said. "Help me out now, and I'll give you everything back. The estates, the family money, all of it."

Talion lifted his chin. "I have made my own fortune since then. I do not need your gifts."

"Even better plan, then," Elsie said, and stuck him in the neck with a hypodermic needle. Talion staggered backward, hand clutched against his neck. Dr. Husch opened a bag marked "Biohazard," and Elsie dropped the used needle inside. "Uh oh," Elsie said. "Tally got a boo-boo."

"What have you done to me?" he said, hand pressed to his neck.

"Injected you with a nasty infection, sweetie. Get ready to loop-the-loup-garou."

Talion spat on the floor. "Fool. I cannot be turned into a werewolf. I break my fast each morning with wolfsbane."

"That explains your breath, sweetie." Elsie sat down on the edge of Husch's desk. "And, you're right, I misspoke, you're not going to be a lycanthrope—but I hope *cyanthrope* is close enough?"

Talion paled. "No. No, there's no such thing—"

"Oh, sure there is. Not as glamorous as werewolves or even werejaguars or weretigers, obviously, but it's amazing what someone with Dr. Husch's connections in the supernatural medical community can track down. I almost went with were-hyena, but hyenas are too *cool*. So instead, you get to be a were-dog. Oh, I hope you turn out to be a sheepdog, you've already got the hair hanging down in your eyes, it would be perfect! Don't widdle on the carpet, or mommy will spank."

"This is ridiculous. I refuse to believe—" Talion suddenly screamed, clapping his hands to his face, which—alarmingly—was starting to smoke. He tore the rings out of his ears and nose and eyebrows, howling as the silver burned his fingers, bits of bloody jewelry falling on the carpet.

"Ah, were-dogs *do* have the traditional silver allergy." Elsie crouched to examine Talion as he writhed and tried to tear out his own teeth. "I wasn't sure, but I guess cyanthropes are probably an evolutionary offshoot of werewolves, just like dogs are descended from wolves. Huh, look at that, though, all your face holes are healing up nicely, that's a benefit, isn't it? Would you like me to get you a wrench to smash out those nasty teeth? You should grow new ones."

Jason sidled over to Crapsey. "This… this is so fucked up."

"What did she do to recruit *you*?" Crapsey said.

"Turned my house into bugs," Jason said. "Then threatened to turn my cock into beetles, more or less."

Crapsey nodded. "Yeah, Talion's got it a lot worse. Then again, he shoudn't have slapped her."

"Would you like another needle in the neck?" Elsie said. "I can make the pain go away."

"Yes!" Talion sobbed. "Yes, anything!"

Elsie held out her hand, and Husch wordlessly passed her another needle. "Boys, come sit on him, would you?" Crapsey and—more reluctantly—Jason stepped forward to hold down Talion's arms. Smoke and the smell of burning gums rose up from his open mouth, until Elsie jabbed her needle into the other side of his neck. After a moment, his writhing and jerking stopped, though he went on sobbing. Crapsey and Jason let go and stepped away. Elsie straddled Talion's chest and stroked his face. Without all that silver piercing his skin, he looked younger, and more vulnerable. "All better, puppy?" she said. "That's not a *cure*, now, it's just temporary relief. The cure comes later—if you always heel, and sit, and roll over when I say."

"How could you curse me?" he said, eyes so filled with tears they reflected the overhead lights like little mirrors. "I've devoted my life to fighting these monsters, and you turn me into—into something just as vile, but not even as… as…"

"As cool? I know. I was afraid that deep down you secretly wanted to be a werewolf—why else spend so much time around them? But nobody wants to be a were-schnauzer. Anyway, it fits that whole 'dog' theme you and I had going on all those years ago, with the leashes and the collars, and you remember that little cage? Super fun. So listen. This is easy. You fight a lady I want you to fight. That's all. Pretend she's a werewolf, it'll be easy. If you do a good job, Doc Prettyface here will fix you up, purge all the nasty dog-o-toxins from your system, and you won't have to sleep at the foot of my bed anymore. Deal?" She stood up, and held out her hand.

"You weren't always like this," Talion said, ignoring her hand and wrenching himself to his feet. "What *happened* to you?"

"Power corrupts?" Elsie said. "When you look too long into the abyss it also looks into you? Be careful hunting monsters, lest you become one? Ve are nihilists, ve believe in nuffink?" She shrugged. "I'm just Elsie being Elsie, baby." She snapped her fingers. "Somebody get this man a flea collar! I have to step over to Maui for a minute and see what our advance scout is up to. Marla's cage should be pretty well rattled by now."

"Lupo shouldn't be left for so long without supervision," Husch said, but without much heat. "He's unstable at the best of times."

"I gave him a few disguises to wear," Jarrow said. "Lupo's not even Lupo right now. You worry too much. Besides—what's wrong with unstable?" Crapsey expected her to tear another hole in space-time—that *couldn't* be good for reality—but instead Elsie bowed her head, whispered a few words, then took a step, and another step... and vanished. She was using her Sufi trick, then. Must be nice, to never be more than three steps from anywhere in the world.

Crapsey held out his hand to Talion, who, after a moment, shook it limply. "Since it looks like you're part of the team, let me introduce you around," Crapsey said. And what a team it was. The crazy homunculus doctor, the cowardly con man, the psychic parasite with a wooden jaw, the master of disguise who believed his own disguises, the one-armed chaos witch, and a tumor with a mind. What a bunch of freaks and misfits. *We're not the Superman Revenge Squad,* Crapsey thought. *We're the friggin' Doom Patrol.*

After the Bay Witch left, Marla finished her food, though she didn't really taste it, deep as she was in thought.

"Holy shit," Jon-Luc was saying. "The Bay Witch, wow. She is *legendary.* I can't believe you know her."

"She has been an ally of Mrs. Mason for many years," Pelham said.

Jon-Luc frowned. "I can't believe what she said about Glyph, though. He's, like, the most Zen surfer I know, all about give and take, ebb and flow. I mean, killing Ronin? It just doesn't seem like him."

Marla patted Jon-Luc on the back. "Always expect the worst of people, kid. That way, you'll only ever be pleasantly surprised. Tell me, are you integrated into the pod well enough to sense their location yet?" She tapped her temple. "Got that magical GPS in your head and all?"

Jon-Luc hesitated, obviously considered lying, then thought better of it. Smart kid. He nodded. "They're at Pe'ahi—Jaws beach—on the north shore. Maui's not the best island for surfing, but Jaws is as hardcore as it gets. We'll find them there."

"Why haven't you taken the plunge?" Marla said. "Joined up full time?"

He shrugged. "I still have my mom to think about. She's a concierge at one of the hotels. Broke her heart when I dropped out of school, but at least I'm working, you know? If I just started surfing all the time, no visible means of income…" He shook his head. "She'd get really worried. I know I want to join Glyph's crew someday, but…. Now you're saying one of them might be a *murderer*. So I don't know what I'm going to do."

The poor kid looked miserable. "It's just a theory," she said. "But I tell you what. Take me to see your friends. I'll ask Glyph a few questions, and maybe we can clear all this up. Even if he is a bad guy, that doesn't mean the rest of them are."

"I just… why would Glyph hire you to find Ronin's killer, if *he* was Ronin's killer?"

Marla shrugged. "To throw off suspicion, maybe? Because the others in the hive were demanding action and he had to do something, so he figured he'd hire the dumb haole newcomer, who doesn't know anybody or have any resources, so he can say he tried? That's just off the top of my head." She started to grin, saw Jon-Luc's stricken expression, and stopped. "I'm sorry, I know this is bumming you out, but I finally feel like I've got this thing in my teeth. The game is afoot." She paused. "You know, that expression never made any sense to me. What kind of game has feet? Clearly we're not talking about poker here."

"I understand it means 'game' as in 'prey,' Mrs. Mason," Pelham said. "It is a Shakespearean metaphor derived from the practice of fox hunting."

"Then I guess that makes me the hound," she said. "People are always calling me a bitch, so why not?" She tossed some cash on the table and rose, thinking about what she'd say to Glyph. A good interrogation was almost as fun as a fistfight, after all—

Her old mentor Artie Mann sauntered out of the restaurant's bathroom, wearing a cheap-looking aloha shirt and puffing a filthy stump of a cigar in clear contravention of all anti-smoking ordinances. And, given that he'd been dead for more than a decade, in clear contravention of natural law, too. "Do you guys see that?" she said, pointing. "That short fat bastard with the cigar?"

"A fine cigar is a gentlemanly pleasure," Pelham said, "but that does appear to be a rather cheap and unpleasant variety."

Right. Pelham had never known Artie. But at least he saw the guy, which meant this wasn't simply a hallucination. Marla stepped up her vision, and, just like with Susan Wellstone, saw no indication of illusion or ghost. The dead man caught Marla's eye, winked at her, and then kept walking, disappearing around the building and heading in the direction of the parking lot. "Give me a minute." She hurried after him, but when she reached the lot, there was no sign of the man, except a smoldering cigar end on the asphalt. Marla watched the smoke spiral up into the sky for moment before Jon-Luc and Pelham caught up with her.

"What's wrong, Mrs. Mason?" Pelham said.

"That fat guy was a dead friend of mine. That makes two dead people I've seen today."

"Ghosts?" Jon-Luc said. "You're seeing ghosts?"

"Oh, how I wish it were that simple," she said.

They stopped by Handsome Bob's, where Marla handed over a fat wad of Rondeau's money and said, "Jon-Luc's offered to give me a personal tour of a couple of good snorkeling spots, is it okay if he leaves work a little early?" She found people had a hard time saying no when they were being given money, and it worked out that way this time, too.

"Sure thing," the old guy said. "Just make sure you don't serial kill him or something, because I remember your face and your license plate and all that."

"Understood," Marla said. She paused. "Do you rent wetsuits? And, I guess, surfboards?"

Jaws

"**THIS IS VERY HAWAI'IAN!**" Marla shouted into the wind as the convertible cruised down the highway, a longboard poking up out of the back seat next to a visibly miserably Jon-Luc. "Wind in my hair, salt in the air, a song in my heart, and murderers to catch!"

"Have you ever surfed before, Mrs. Mason?" Pelham said.

"No, but I'm good at everything, so I'm sure it'll be fine."

It was hard to tell, with the wind and all, but she thought Jon-Luc groaned from the backseat.

The drive took about an hour and a half, plenty of time for Marla to prepare various strategies, even though she knew, when the time came, she'd probably just improvise. How often did a detective end up telling their client: "I think I know who did it. I think *you* did it."

Eh, maybe it was pretty often, at least in books. She'd have to ask Rondeau when they got back home. He'd read more mysteries than she had.

Jon-Luc directed them down a paved side road, and told Pelham to pull over just before it turned to dirt—or, more accurately, mud. "It rained recently," Jon Luc said. "I wouldn't try driving any farther. There's no parking or anything there anyway, it's all undeveloped land. It's only a mile or so. We can walk it."

The muddy road ahead was lined with the burned-out hulks of derelict cars. "What happened here?" Marla said. "Demolition derby?"

Jon-Luc shook his head. "People tried to block access to the beach years ago. They dragged cars across the way, and even dug trenches, so you couldn't drive this way without getting stuck. The old cars got moved out of the way, but there's still a lot of junk around. Technically, all the beaches in Hawai'i are public land, but…"

Marla nodded. "Rich assholes trying to make it a private party for themselves, huh?"

Jon-Luc shook his head. "Not this time, not exactly. See, Jaws is the best place to surf on the island, if you know what you're doing—and I mean *really* know. I wouldn't even try it myself, I'm not good enough yet. You get sixty-foot waves out here sometimes. But when the surf gets really big, tourists and posers and kuks all flock down, get in the water, and screw things up for the serious people. Back in 2004, it got really bad, and a few people got hurt, so some of the really well known big wave riders complained. After that, people took steps." He nodded toward the wrecked cars. "It's sort of an invitation-only spot now. I mean, you can *get* there, if you're willing to hike, but... you might not find the best reception."

"Ah, but you're inviting us, right?"

"I guess so." He didn't sound happy about it. That was okay. Marla wasn't that invested in his happiness.

"So, we walk from here?" Marla said, climbing out of the car.

"Unless you've got an ATV in the trunk," Jon-Luc said.

She looked at Pelham, just in case. He cleared his throat. "Alas, no, ma'am."

Jon-Luc carried the board she'd rented, balancing it on top of his head as they walked around a burned out Chevelle. "You can't actually go out on this board," he said.

"Why not?"

"I heard you say you'd never even surfed before. This isn't the place to start, okay? The water will just *destroy* you, it's carnage, it's chaos. You can't even really paddle out into the waves—people do tow-in surfing, they get a jet ski to pull them out to the right spot so they can catch the waves. The surf is biggest in the winter, and—"

"Is that what Glyph and the Glyphettes do?" Marla asked. "Tow-in?"

"No, but they're different. They're *magic*."

"Me, too," Marla said. She hadn't actually been that interested in try-ing to surf before, but if someone was going to tell her she *shouldn't*, that changed everything. They squelched along, avoiding the mudpits as best they could, occasionally walking on the shoulder, where their legs were whipped by knee-high grass. Finally they crested a hill, and Marla finally got a view of the cliffs leading down to the ocean. A few jet skis bobbed on the water, but it wasn't the frenzy she'd been expecting. "Doesn't look so scary to me."

"Water's not doing much today," Jon-Luc said. "That's how it is some-times. Getting here's a pain, and there's not much point if there's no big surf—most people will just go over to Ho'okipa and surf the Middles. On certain days, though, when you get waves taller than a building, you'll see people lined up along these cliffs, watching... it's unreal."

"So why aren't your tribe at Ho'okipa, if it's better today?"

Jon-Luc shrugged. "They don't care as much about big waves. They like them, don't get me wrong, but they're in the water every day, whether the surf is high or not. They say the ocean always whispers, but this is a place where the ocean shouts. They come here to listen."

"Preserve me from mystics, Pelham," Marla said. "If I ever start communing with giant chaotic systems, lock me up for my own safety." They followed a rocky trail down to the beach, such as it was—this clearly wasn't a place you came to set up a volleyball net or sunbathe or grill a few hot dogs. It was mostly cliffs and reefs and pounding waves, with a handful of people in wetsuits milling around. Jon-Luc handed the board to Pelham, who took it with relatively good grace, then ran down to the sand, waving, and calling out the names of his friends—"Leis! Ryan and Josh! Mad Gary! I brought the detective!" The surf-hive welcomed him warmly with embraces and shoulder-pats, then all their heads swiveled to look at Marla.

"I don't see Glyph," Marla said. "Do you—wait, you haven't met him."

Pelham nodded. "I have not had that pleasure."

Marla squinted out at the water. "There, on that wave, I think that's him surfing."

It wasn't much of a wave, and Glyph didn't look too excited about it—from this distance, at least, he looked like a guy standing around at a dull cocktail party, hoping the cute waitress with the shrimp puffs and the short skirt would come by again soon. Then, for no apparent reason, he lost his balance and fell off the board, disappearing under the waves. Marla joined the hive on the beach.

"Marla Mason," a dark-haired man—he was either Ryan or Josh—said politely. "How is your investigation progressing?"

"Not bad, I have some leads." She shaded her eyes and looked out in the water. She saw Glyph's board, rolling in on a wave, but not the man himself. "I just wanted to ask Glyph a few questions. Are you guys sure he's not drowning?"

"He won't drown," Ryan (or Josh) said, and the others chuckled. "We're drown-proof. I'm not sure why he went off the board. He must have seen something interesting underwater—" The man frowned, then shook his head. "That's... strange. He broke his connection with me."

A chorus of "Me too" rose up from the half a dozen surfers on the beach, and they all hurried toward the water, suddenly alarmed. Marla followed. Glyph's board bobbed in the water a few yards out, not floating all the way in to shore for some reason, as if anchored. Jon-Luc and the others waded out, grabbed the board, and began feeling around in the water for something.

"The board tether," Pelham said, pointing. One of the surfers pulled on the bright yellow cord trailing from the end of the surfboard... and after a few moments, they found the ankle it was attached to. The wave-mages lifted their comrade out of the water and flopped his body onto the board, then began walking it in to the shore.

Before they reached the sand, Glyph's body was already melting, his flesh crumbling like wet sand, his blood appearing briefly red before going the clear of seawater, and the other mages wailed and sobbed and scooped up bits of his deliquescing body, only to have it run through their fingers and into the water.

"Well, hell," Marla said. "So much for *that* theory." The surfers came out of the water and sat on the sand, staring blankly at one another, in shock or quiet communion, Marla couldn't tell which. She waited a respectful interval—respectful for her—then said, "You all saw that, didn't you? His throat?"

"A shark," one of them said. "There are shark attacks here, sometimes..." He subsided.

"I don't think so," Marla said carefully. "Unless it's a shark with thumbs, and a knife. His throat wasn't ripped out. It was *cut*. I saw it, before he..."

"Returned to his mother," a freckled redhead said. She blinked. "Is this... do you think..."

"It's the same person who killed Ronin?" a blond man said. "The cut, it was the same kind of cut, he was killed in the same way..."

"Is this all of you?" Marla said. "The whole family, tribe, crew, whatever?"

They nodded, all in unison, even Jon-Luc. Damn it. So much for the inside job theory, unless Glyph had cut his own throat to throw off suspicion, which was a pretty extreme tactic. Besides, the way he'd fallen off the board, it was like something had *pulled* him under. The killer might still be out there, under the water, but if it wasn't one of these people, who *was* it? "I think we have to proceed on the theory that whoever killed Ronin also killed Glyph," Marla said finally. "And that could mean all of you are in danger."

"You think someone wants to kill us?" Jon-Luc said.

"It's a possibility," Marla said.

"I understand why you think that." Reva approached from direction of the road, and Marla narrowed her eyes at him. She never liked it when gods showed up unannounced. "But there's something you don't know." He took a deep breath. "I'm the one who killed Ronin."

Marla was on him in an instant. She kicked his legs out from under him, and then knelt down on his chest, holding the dagger Death had given her against his throat. "I didn't think you were the type to go in for human sacrifice," she said. "So why'd you do it? And why kill Glyph?" She frowned. "And why tell Glyph to hire *me*?"

"I did not kill Glyph," Reva said, as unperturbed as if he didn't have an angry sorceress pinning him to the ground at all. "That's my point. It *wasn't* the same killer. If you'll let me up, I'll explain."

"Ha. Like that's going to—"

A moment of blankness passed over her, or rather, she passed through it, and in her next instant of awareness she was sitting in the sand, in a circle with all the other sorcerers. Reva was on his back in the center of the circle, and Pelham was standing over him, the unsheathed length of a sword cane pointed unwaveringly at the god's throat. "Are you with us, Mrs. Mason?"

"I, uh—the fuck?"

"Reva has the power to control the minds of any of 'his people,'" Pelham said. "Anyone who feels they are an exile, or otherwise away from home, is susceptible to his powers."

"It's not mind control," Reva said, though now he sounded a bit annoyed. "It's just a form of direct communication, stripping away all niceties, talking to the deep down true parts of a person."

"His power does not work on me," Pelham said, "for I *am* home, which is to say, by your side, Mrs. Mason. But, alas, it does work on you. He used that ability to stop you from questioning him so sharply. At least, he attempted to. I stopped him."

"I am a god, you know," Reva said. "What do you think this is going to accomplish?"

"I know that you prefer to use physical bodies," Pelham said. "I know that destroying this body will inconvenience you. And I assume you are capable of feeling pain."

"Fine," Reva said. "I'll explain. I *wanted* to explain, anyway, I just didn't want to do it with a knife at my throat."

"And look how well that turned out," Marla said. "Don't you *ever* try to mess with my head again, little god. There are things more powerful than you, and some of them owe me favors."

Reva sighed. "If I can sit up? No? Fine. I only meant to help you, Marla. I could see you were bereft, without hope or purpose. I knew you were attempting to become a detective, without much luck. So I thought… I might help you get a case."

"This is true, Mrs. Mason," Pelham said, still keeping his eyes firmly fixed on the supine god. "I regret to admit that he discussed this plan with me some weeks ago. I met him during my travels—he was in a different form then, a different body—and he said I should rush to your side, and assist you. He said he had a plan…" Pelham shook his head. "I am sorry. I should have told you."

"I see. Tell me about the plan." There was enough frost in Marla's voice to kill a thousand crops.

"Ronin wanted to die," Reva said. "We were friends—he's one of my *people*, he never got over how much he missed his home in Japan, never felt at home anywhere else, not really. He lost faith in the ocean, and he was going to kill himself. I told him there was a way his death could help another exile, and he agreed to let me stage a murder." Reva sighed. "That's why you couldn't find any traces—I *am* a god. After I cut his throat, as per his *request*, I covered my tracks. Then I talked to Glyph and the others, and told them they should hire you, and that you could find the killer."

"You set me up with an unsolvable case? Just busywork to keep me *occupied*, like a bored housewife doing crafts or something? And these people, you fucked with them, too, with their minds, with their grief? What's *wrong* with you?" The surfers nodded their heads in unison.

"Ah, not unsolvable, I thought you'd figure out it was me eventually, I hoped that you'd understand what I was trying to do—"

"Gods," Marla said, disgusted. "You're like children putting bugs in bottles, shaking them up to see what they'll do."

"I believe he did mean well, Mrs. Mason," Pelham said. "Though his methods are questionable."

"So why murder Glyph, then?"

"I *didn't*, like I said. Someone else did, the same way I killed Ronin, and I have no idea why."

Marla rolled her eyes. "Why should I believe you? How do I know this isn't another fake mystery, one set up to *seem* real?"

"What can I do to convince you?" Reva said. "There's been a *real* murder here, one that you should investigate—these people actually do need justice now, it's not playacting anymore, it's serious!"

"Huh. Jon-Luc, the rest of you—what do you think?"

"It's different, this time," the redhead said. Apparently she was the new speaker for the hive. "The killing, the method of attack was the same, but last time there were no traces at all. This time... we can sense something. Look." She scooped out a depression in the sand, while one of the others ran to scoop up a double handful of sea water. When the water was poured into the depression, it began to fizz and splash, shapes forming in the foam. The redhead said, "I see... spinning roulette wheels. Butterfly wings. A double pendulum. Three spheres, circling one another, orbit decaying. An apple—"

"Chaos magic?" Marla said.

The redhead nodded.

"What's your name?" Marla said.

"Call me Leis," she said.

"Ah, a bride of Poseidon," Pelham commented. "Very clever."

"How do you know I'm not actually *her*?" Leis said.

"She was Greek, and you appear to be mostly Irish," Pelham said politely, still holding his sword to Reva's throat.

"I know a chaos witch," Marla said, bowing her head and staring at the sand. "There was a prophecy, I guess you'd say, that she was coming to the island. I didn't think—why would she do *this*? Just to mess with me, I guess, to disrupt my investigation, to amuse herself. I'm sorry. Glyph dying—it's my fault. One of my enemies, trying to get at me, hurt one of your friends."

The surfers exchanged glances in that eerie way they had, then Leis shook her head. "You are not at fault. You didn't hold the knife. Life is unpredictable. The waves push some of us together and push some of us apart. You can't blame yourself. Might as well blame Reva, for telling us to hire you."

"That's not a bad idea," Pelham murmured.

"Or blame the sea, for sinking Reva's island, and making him a wandering god, so long ago," Leis went on. "No, we blame the actor, the one directly culpable. And we wish her brought to justice. Do you think you know the killer, Marla Mason? Then we ask only that you bring her to us."

"Nicolette," Marla said. "Her name is Nicolette."

"Can I get up now?" Reva said. "I've finally got this body broken in, and I don't want to start over with a new one."

Elsie appeared in the middle of the office, sopping wet and grinning, bringing with her the mingled smells of blood and salt. Dr. Husch started squawking about her ruining the carpet, and Crapsey said, "Did you fall off the island?"

The witch sat down on Husch's loveseat, the cushions making a squelching noise, and said, "I had a little talk with Lupo. Well, he *thought* he was Marla's old murdered mentor Artie Mann, dragged back to life and enslaved by my will, but anyway. He did some spying for me, listened in on a little lunch date Marla had, where she was playing detective." Elsie rolled her eyes. "I found out where Marla was going, and who she suspected of committing the dastardly crime she's investigating, so I thought it would be funny to get there ahead of her and cut her prime suspect's throat. Isn't that the way it always happens in detective novels? The PI thinks they've figured everything out, and they go to confront the bad guy, only to find him headless and stuffed in a closet? I love a good plot twist." She tilted her head and tugged on her earlobe, apparently trying to shake some water out. "My victim was a surfer, out in the water, so I got to play shark attack with him. Death from below! Fun, but damp."

"So was the guy you killed really a murderer?" Crapsey said.

"Don't know, don't care, don't know why you'd bother to ask," Elsie said crisply.

"Because it would be interesting if you turned out to be a tool for justice, I guess?"

"If a murderer gets hit by a garbage truck, that's not justice. It's not even karma, despite what some people want to believe. Remember, kiddies: Stuff Just Happens. Trying to figure out why will make you crazy."

"I did not release you so that you could kill innocent people," Dr. Husch said, sitting behind her big desk like a judge presiding over a particularly disappointing trial.

"Thpt." Elsie stuck out her tongue. "You can't make an omelet without stabbing a surfer in the neck. Not any kind of omelet I'd like to eat, anyway. I might have to send a few more people to the bottom of the sea before I'm done, Doctor Prettyface. Besides, maybe that guy really *was* a villainous killer, did you think about that? Either way, if you're so upset—are you calling me off?"

Husch sighed. "No. Try to keep collateral damage to a minimum from here on out, would you?"

Elsie shrugged. "We'll see, won't we? Anyway, between the dead people wandering across Marla's path and this sudden exciting development in her investigation, and the grim foretellings of oncoming doom that Rondeau told Dr. Husch about, I'd say Marla's pretty well softened up. It's time we got the whole gang over to the islands, I think, and moved on to phase two of Operation Murderkill."

"I don't guess we're chartering a plane, are we?" Jason said miserably from his seat in the corner.

"Nah," Elsie said. "I thought it would be more fun to steal one."

"I thought you were planning to teleport?" Nicolette said. "Not that I'm complaining, but—"

"Here's the thing," Elsie said. "Teleporting is like setting off a flashbang. It's noisy, magically speaking, when you rip gaping holes in the flesh of the world. When I do my little moving-the-Earth thing, that's quiet, almost undetectable. I know Marla's on edge now, so if she's got any sense, she'll be on the lookout for intra-dimensional incursions. I teleported Lupo over, and if Marla starts sniffing around, she'll find a trace of that, and a little divination will tell her that two people came through. According to what Rondeau told the good doctor, Marla thinks Jason and Nicolette are the ones coming to kill her. So—let her think you two are the ones who teleported, why not? We'll travel by more conventional means and then, boom, element of surprise, a whole crowd when she expected a duo. I doubt she's watching the airports. Everybody pack a bag, we're leaving in half-an-hour. I've got my eye on a nice redeye flight we should be able to mind-control our way onto."

"Uh, all my shit is at the apartment Nicolette and me rented," Crapsey said. "I haven't changed my shirt in two days—"

"You can steal new shirts from the corpses of your slain enemies," Elsie said. "Really, do I have to think of *everything*?"

In Flight

"**IT'S TIME TO GET READY FOR WAR.**" Marla leaned against the counter in the bookshop and surveyed her troops, such as they were: Pelham, nervous because of his little betrayal; Rondeau, who was more-or-less paying attention; and Reva, who was here only because he wouldn't go away. The wave-mages had promised to lend their support when it came to actually apprehending Nicolette, so that was something. Normally, Marla wouldn't have worried. She could beat Nicolette with one arm tied behind her back (which, given Nicolette's recent loss of limb, would be only fair), and her brother wouldn't exactly be able to con her again—she was wise to his deceit now. But Death had seen a likely future where she was dead, so it might be best to proceed with caution. Once upon a time she'd had sufficient self-confidence to believe she could defeat any challenge, but that was before Bradley Bowman got killed, and she got exiled. She was still going to fight… but maybe she wouldn't charge in with nothing but her knives and a well-honed sense of outrage anymore.

"What do you propose?" Reva said.

"Step one is to get the hell off this island. Death saw me being killed on a beach on Maui—so I might as well change that first. I'm going to stay in Hawai'i—just on a different island. I want to deal with my enemies, not run away, but I'd rather choose my own ground."

"So you want someplace nice and secluded?" Rondeau said. "Away from the ordinaries? There are some islands that are pretty much uninhabited, actually, we could dig in and—"

Marla shook her head. "Nope. Flip that 180 degrees. If I'm in some isolated bit of tropical paradise and Nicolette and Jason and some hired thugs come to kill me, nobody local is going to care—it's just a bunch of haoles killing each other. But if I'm in a nice populated area, and some nasty magic users show up and start behaving in a way that's threatening to civilians, then the local kahunas *are* going to take an interest. Just like when I was running Felport—if people came into the city itself and started making noise, I shut that shit down quick. But if people wanted to run wild in the hinterlands outside my area of interest, what did I care? I don't have the kind of support system I used to have, but if possible, I'm going to piggyback on the local system. I'll sneak inside the local beehive and let their drones protect me."

"So… we're talking about human shields, basically," Rondeau said.

Marla scowled. "That's not the way I'd put it. I don't think Nicolette is going to start lobbing fireballs through a hotel lobby—I know she likes chaos, but there's a lot of big old magic and tough badass kahunas in these islands, and she knows she wouldn't get away with that kind of assault, not without dying herself. Besides, I'll let you pick a nice resort for us to hole up in—how's that sound?"

"In that case, might I suggest the big island?" Reva said. "The most powerful sorcerers in Hawai'i live there, and the place has certain other properties that might prove useful."

Marla pointed a finger at him. "Listen, godlet. Just because you're helping me doesn't mean I'm going to join up with the Church of You once this is all over. Understood?"

"You are already one of my people, Marla. I don't demand that you become a follower explicitly. I'm a god who takes care of you even if you've never heard of me."

"I wish I hadn't," she muttered. "Rondeau, hop on the computer and make some arrangements, the way we talked about. Someplace on the Big Island, near the water in case we need help from the surfers on short notice, ideally not too close to volcanic activity just to be on the safe side—chaos magicians are fans of fire—but otherwise, please yourself. Pelham, come with me. We're going shopping." She cracked her knuckles. "It's been ages since I did any enchanting. I had people to do that sort of thing for me back in Felport. It'll be good to get my hands dirty again."

Rondeau snorted. "Yeah, that was always your problem—your hands were too *clean*."

The Marla Mason Revenge Squad breezed them through security with ease, Elsie providing fake IDs made of scrap paper and dead leaves, and cloaking them in an illusion of normalcy so thorough that none of them even got pulled aside for secondary screening. Nicolette, who was pretty good at tricking computers into doing her bidding, had gotten them all first-class tickets on a direct flight to Oahu, so they were the first ones on board, stowing their carry-ons and sinking into the luxurious seats. A couple of other people tried to get seated in the section, but Elsie made them hallucinate emergency phone calls, and they went running off the plane, leaving the whole front cabin to her own people.

Nicolette had booked herself the seat next to Elsie in the left-hand front row, but the older witch shook her head and told her to change places with Crapsey. Nicolette sullenly sat down beside Jason, who did his best to appear engrossed in a SkyMall catalog. Talion sat by himself, obsessively touching the places on his face where his piercings had been. Crapsey sat down beside Elsie—she got the window seat, naturally—and tried not to think about whether she was actively carcinogenic at the moment.

Elsie put a hand on his knee. "Cheer up, evil twin. I have a surprise for you. The Mason enchanted your prosthetic jaw, isn't that right? So you could bite through steel and eat hot lava and things like that? And there were other spells, too, laid on the jaw, things that could affect your whole body, transform you in various ways."

Crapsey massaged his chin. The Mason had ripped his jaw off when he was just a little kid, and later fitted him with a magical carved wooden prosthesis, decorated with intricate runes, though just now the jaw was glamoured to look like ordinary flesh. "Yeah, but *she* was the one who controlled the spells, not me."

Elsie tapped the side of her head. "The host body still has some memories rolling around in here, and guess what: I made a list for you." She passed him a slip of paper with a dozen seemingly random words jotted down. "All the controls were attached to this body, too, so: I hereby give you ownership of your own face. Those are the trigger words. Just be careful not to use one of them in casual conversation, or you might end up biting someone's head off. Literally."

Crapsey blinked. "That's… thank you, Elsie, this means a lot. But which keyword does what? There's no guide here."

Elsie nodded. "I know! Trial and error is so entertaining! But don't worry, I didn't include the keyword that makes your jaw self-destruct, so don't worry about stumbling across that one. Unless you accidentally just *say* it, like in the course of ordinary conversation, but it's a pretty obscure word, I wouldn't worry. Just don't go reading the entire dictionary aloud, and maybe refrain from taking up metallurgy as a hobby, or at least talking about the field too much."

Crapsey winced, nodded, and folded up the paper, slipping it into his pocket. He'd never much liked it when the Mason invoked his jaw's powers— it just reminded him of how he was damaged and weird and altered—so he was content to put the note away for now.

The flight attendants came by and checked their seat belts, and the plane took off soon after, more or less on time. Soon after they were airborne and settled in for the twelve-hour flight, the attendants took requests, and everyone asked for and received booze.

Crapsey poured his tiny bottle of Scotch over the two ice cubes in his plastic cup. He sighed. "Look, it's none of my business, but Nicolette made me promise I'd ask you—why don't you just get rid of Doctor Husch and be on your merry way?"

"I can't say I like having strings attached to me." Elsie tipped her head back and loudly gargled the contents of a miniature vodka bottle before continuing. "But it's not that easy. Husch, while she's inside the Blackwing Institute, is pretty much unassailable. She's wrapped in all the same defenses the *building* is. She's not an extension of the place, exactly, but she's definitely sheltering in its protection. A lot of that protection was designed especially to thwart little old me. Now, give me a couple of years to raise hell and get my power levels up—or hand me the right lever to pry Husch out of her fortress, where she's exposed and vulnerable—and it'll be a different story, but for now, every chain in the place leads to Husch, and I'm on one of her leashes. Besides, *you* wouldn't want me to be free—you want me to kill Marla, right? And I wouldn't have any reason to bother with some exiled sorcerer if Husch wasn't making it a condition of my parole."

"I don't really mind Marla," Crapsey admitted. "It's her friend Rondeau I hate, mostly."

"Differing agendas are so delicious. I eat them up like tasty tasty *cake*. There's nothing I love more than cross-purposes and conflicts of interests, except maybe tornadoes made of screaming glass." She patted Crapsey's knee. "You know, you only hate Rondeau because you wish you had his life."

"And here I thought I hated him because I used to be able to take over anybody at will, until he trapped me in this one body like a bug in a bottle."

"Nope, it's that thing I said. But don't worry, we'll hurt Rondeau too, I don't mind. I can do a two-for-one special."

Crapsey gestured toward Talion. "If you don't mind me asking, why'd you bring him onto the team? Just to increase complexity? More of those agendas and cross-purposes?"

"Having someone who hates me and will betray me at the first opportunity is nice, of course, but there are practical considerations, too. We've got yours truly, a master imposter, a confidence man with a personal connection to Marla, a born lackey with a magical jaw and the power to Curse—that's cute, by the way, little primal burps of chaos, I like it—and a one-armed wannabe chaos magician with an axe she doesn't know how to use. What we *don't* have, or rather didn't have, is a straight-up fighter, someone who can take the kind of punishment I hear Marla likes to dish out, and give as good as he gets. Magic's all well and good, but Marla's a face-puncher, a nose-breaker, a hamstring-cutter, and an ass-kicker by all accounts, so it might come to fisticuffs. Especially since I have another recruit waiting for us in Oahu."

"Another old friend of yours?" Crapsey said.

Elsie shook her head. "No, actually. Dr. Husch knows him. His name's Christian Decomain, and he's an anti-mancer."

"Which means... what?"

"He *negates* magic. He's a counterspell expert with an suppressive aura. Get close to him and spells fizzle, psychics lose their special insight, and levitators fall out of the sky. He'll be fun to have around. Of course, he thinks of himself as a *good* guy, so Dr. Husch had to tell him that Marla was having a psychotic break and threatening to destroy the Hawai'ian islands. He thinks we're just going to take her into custody, for her own good. It'll be fun to put him next to Marla, then let Talion try to beat the crap out of her."

"But when this Decomain guy realizes that we're not just trying to capture Marla..."

Elsie nodded. "Fun, right? He'll be super pissed. I'm not sure how that's all going to work out, since I can't mind-control him, but we'll improvise. You've got a knife, right?"

Crapsey nodded.

"Good. If Christian gets out of line, I'll need you to stab him in the neck. Negating magic means he can't use magic to protect himself, so unless he's wearing a suit of armor, he should be vulnerable to a direct attack." She reclined her seat and closed her eyes. "Don't let anyone disturb me, Crapsey dear."

"I thought you didn't sleep?"

"I don't. I'm going astral projecting. Who needs an in-flight movie when you can travel invisibly anywhere on Earth?"

"What are you planning on going to see?"

"I've been locked in a magical cube for years," she said. "What do you think? I'm going to go watch famous people have sex."

Crapsey had no idea whether she was telling the truth or not, and wasn't sure he wanted to know. He called for another drink.

"I think that's everything." Marla slipped Death's bell into her pocket, careful not to let it ring. "The other things we need we can pick up on the Big Island." She looked around the suite Rondeau had rented for her, trying to make sure she hadn't forgotten anything, though she was less concerned about leaving a hairbrush than leaving, say, a jar of cursed seawater or an enchanted nene feather.

Pelham had emptied his steamer trunk, the glamoured bedsheet now an ordinary piece of fabric again, and Marla had filled the space with those magical and practical supplies she'd managed to scrounge up that afternoon: glass vials full of rarefied airs, a box of precisely shattered pocketwatches, hatpins with blood crusted on the points, and other nice things.

Rondeau let himself in—there was no way to keep him from having a key, despite Marla's best efforts. "You guys almost ready? I booked us in at a resort on the west coast of the Big Island, and I got us on a plane tonight. It's only about a twenty-minute flight, and we're good for late check-in."

"Three rooms, right?" Marla said.

"Two connecting, one across the hall, though they all have two double beds. I like to have one bed just for jumping up and down on, so—"

"Not this time. You and Pelham can share a room."

Rondeau raised an eyebrow. "You need *two* rooms?"

"I do," Marla said.

"Then why didn't you tell me to book *four* rooms—"

Marla shook her head. "Three rooms, three people, it makes sense. When Nicolette and company come looking for us, I want them to see exactly what they expect to see. If we had four rooms, they'd wonder what the other one was *for*. Trust me on this, Rondeau. We're about to get into a fight. I'm good at those."

Rondeau raised his hands in mock surrender. "Fine, you're the boss. Oh, wait, no you're not, you're, like, my *ward*—"

Marla put her hand on his shoulder. "I know. And I'm sorry if I'm still acting like I have a right to tell you what to do without explanation. So: that extra room is going to be filled with traces of *me*, my clothes, bits of my hair, a little bit of my blood. I'm going to disguise my presence in the *other* room, and that fake room is also going to have some really nasty magical traps primed, so if anyone comes in unannounced, following a divination and looking to grab me, they'll get something more unpleasant instead. Which reminds me, we'd better keep the 'Do Not Disturb' sign on that door at all times. I'd hate to spring a nest of shadow snakes on housekeeping. Okay?"

"That kinda makes sense," Rondeau said. "But I still don't see why you get your own room and I have to share."

"Boys in one room, girls in the other. It's traditional. Plus, I'm probably going to be doing a lot of enchanting, and that means weird smells and sounds and lights. You don't want to be in there with me. You're here as my friend, Rondeau, not a guy on my payroll. I know that, and if I ask too much of you, I'm sorry. I hope you know I'd do the same for you, if you needed it."

He sighed. "I know. Just be ready. I'm going to get myself into some *hellaciously* big trouble and make you bail me out of it pretty soon, just to keep the balance right in our relationship."

"I wouldn't miss it for the world," Marla said. "Now help Pelham carry that trunk, would you?"

Reva sat next to Marla on the flight to the Big Island, unpleasantly close due to the narrow seats on the little puddle-jumper aircraft. "I love the windowseat," Reva said, once they were airborne.

Marla, who was the one actually sitting in the windowseat, grunted. She didn't offer to switch places. She was over the wing anyway, so it wasn't like the view was that great, but it was the principle of the thing.

"Looking down on the world, seeing the shape of the land, it's like being a god." He chuckled in an extremely annoying fashion. "Trust me. I should know."

"Water looks like water whether you're ten feet above it or ten thousand." Marla looked out at the wing, wishing for a gremlin to appear, "Terror at Forty-Thousand Feet"-style, because hitting something would do her good, and dealing with a supernatural incursion at high-altitude posed some interesting tactical problems. Then again, she shouldn't make wishes like that—with Pelham on board, there was a non-trivial chance the admittedly gremlin-like Nuno could appear at any moment. With all the chaos of solving a murder and preparing for war, they hadn't had time to try a ritual cleansing to get rid of his infestation yet.

After a too-brief interval of silence, Reva started up again: "I hope you won't hold Pelham's little lie against him. He was just doing what he thought was best—"

"I don't hold it against him," Marla said. "I hold it against *you*. The whole stupid plan to give me a fake murder investigation was your idea, and I know gods can be convincing. Pelham's not the most worldly guy, despite all his traveling—he still has a bad habit of taking people at face value and thinking the best of them."

"I *do* mean well, Marla—I want to help you find a new home, or adjust to the lack of a home, and at the very *least* I want to keep your enemies from killing you."

"That's why I'm not kicking up a fuss about your company—because I could use some extra firepower. Though I'm wondering what you can *do* exactly. Why are you even on this plane? Shouldn't you be able to fly to the Big Island or something?"

"And miss the pleasure of your company?" His quirked smile was almost cute, but only almost. "When I take on a human form, like this one, I take on certain human limitations. Like the inability to fly. I could give up the body, and regain greater powers, but I find it easiest to deal with people when

I'm *being* people. It makes me... think more like a human. When I'm fully a god, not using a human brain to do my thinking, not subject to the glandular passions that govern humankind, everything is a bit... cold. Abstract. Impersonal. The difference between being in the water, or thousands of feet above it. I don't like that feeling. This is better. Besides, I'm not without resources—I have a certain degree of magical ability, and as Pelham told you, I have the power to... interact at a primal level with the mind of anyone who considers herself out-of-place or away from home. Your assassins aren't likely to be local, so that could be useful."

"Mind control, huh? How... godly."

A flash of irritation crossed his face. "Again. It's not. Mind control. It just makes people receptive to bargains, and I'm always careful to give more than I get. You have a history of meddling in people's lives, too."

"Yeah, but I'm a *person*, so it's different." She yawned. "Anyway, you're going to have to get your own hotel room. I didn't book one for you."

"Oh, don't worry, I don't expect you to give me accommodations. All it takes is one clerk or concierge who isn't a native Hawai'ian, and I'll be staying in a better room than you are."

"Sounds like mind control to me," she said, and put on a pair of headphones before he could object again.

Things Are Never So Bad They Can't Be Made Worse

"**WE HAVE WALKED A MILE.** Literally a mile. Where are our rooms?" Marla paused by a piece of ornamental sculpture to tighten her shoelaces.

"Well, yeah," Rondeau said. "It's like a sixty-acre resort. We're in the tower farthest from the lobby, unfortunately. If we hadn't gotten here so late, we'd be able to take the train, or a boat, but since we had late check-in they've stopped—"

Marla stood up, scowled, and continued walking. "This is a hotel with its own *train line*. It's a hotel with *canals*. What am I doing here?"

"It's big, there are a lot of people, it's on the coast, and it's exactly what you asked for." Rondeau was cheerful. "Plus, I know you love complaining, and I figured this place would give you lots to complain about."

"It's very beautifully landscaped," Pelham offered. "And some of the artwork is quite exquisite. But, yes, it has a certain…"

"Disneyland vastness," Rondeau said. "There actually *is* a Disney resort on Oahu, but I figured that might be pushing Marla a tad too far. But basically this is a family-friendly place, you can come here, stay a week, and never even leave the hotel grounds. It's got like ten pools, and entertainment, and there's a lagoon where they truck in fresh sand every morning—"

"A fake beach," Marla said. "In *Hawai'i*."

"The coast right around here's really rocky," Rondeau said, reasonably. "I mean, you'd have to walk half a mile to get a nice sandy beach. I'm pretty sure the sea turtles and fish in the snorkeling area aren't actually animatronic, if that makes you feel any better."

"I'm not a big fan of the rustic experience," Marla said. "You know that. The whole ancient Polynesian culture thing doesn't excite me too much either, though I like their war clubs." Her Samoan club was nestled in one of the suitcases even now. "But a grass shack on the beach, even though that would be depressingly close to nature, would be preferable to this manufactured, artificial... extruded hospitality product. It's too neat, too clean, too fake, too orderly—"

"Ah ha!" Rondeau said. "What's that last word?"

"Orderly?" Marla said. She paused, then said, more thoughtfully, "Orderly. Really? You did that on purpose?"

Rondeau stopped to sketch out a little bow. "I *do* sometimes have reasons for the decisions I make, you know. Not always, but. We're going to fight a chaos magician, and this place is all about the orderliness, the schedules, the cleanliness, the high gloss. All stuff that will salt Nicolette's game."

"All right," Marla said grudgingly. "That's pretty good."

"There are also service tunnels," Rondeau said. "Running all underneath the resort, so the guests never have to see the thousand employees it takes to keep this place in operation."

"Okay," Marla said. "Tunnels, I like."

"They've also got a dolphin lagoon," Rondeau said. "I fucking love dolphins. And it's only two hundred bucks to swim with one, you believe that? A steal."

"Ah, there's our antimancer," Elsie said.

"Good," Nicolette muttered. "Maybe he can carry some fucking bags."

For reasons known only to herself—maybe for the same reasons God was such a dick to his loyal servant Job—Elsie was heaping ever more abuse on Nicolette. Besides taking an apparent shine to Crapsey, which was the surest route to annoying the younger chaos witch, she'd also ordered Nicolette to carry everyone's luggage, and as a result, she was heaped with two partially-overlapping backpacks, a messenger bag slung across her front, and the handle of a rolling suitcase in her one hand. With her buzzed hair and paint-spattered jeans and t-shirt, she looked like a furious art-school sherpa. They made an odd group overall: Jarrow in the lead, head held high, long red hair streaming behind her, heels clicking on the smooth airport floor; Crapsey in his increasingly rumpled pin-striped suit following at her heels and having unpleasant flashbacks to accompanying the Mason in similar fashion; Talion in his black leather, looking even more ridiculous given the morning heat and humidity here; Nicolette stumbling and snarling and dragging her burdens after him; and Jason bringing up the rear, no doubt thinking about making a break for it, but never quite mustering the courage to try. They all paused to allow a greeter, presumably from the Hawai'ian tourist board or something, to drape them all with sweet-smelling leis and say, "Aloha, welcome to Maui." Talion took it with exceptionally bad grace, and Nicolette groaned, presumably because even the weight of a couple dozen flowers on a string was an unwanted addition to her considerable burdens. The necklace fit in nicely with the half a dozen other chains she wore strung around her neck, all festooned with beads and charms in various sizes, shapes, and colors—since she couldn't wear enchanted items in her hair anymore, she'd resorted to wearing them around her neck, and she clattered like a dice cup when she walked. Elsie kept joking that Nicolette must have flashed her breasts a *lot* at Mardi Gras to get so many necklaces.

Christian Decomain leaned against a pillar by the curb, dark eyes watching them approach from behind his chunky Clark Kent glasses. He was a small, compact man, with short dark hair, dressed in a studiedly nondescript black-jeans-black-button-down-shirt way that actually made him stand out amid the crowds in their vacation-wear casuals. He held up a sign that said "Jarrow & Co.," and Elsie waved at him jauntily. "You must be Leda's friend!" she said, voice warm and welcoming as an old friend's embrace.

Christian folded up the sign and tucked it into his back pocket, looking them over with a frown. "And you're the famous Elsie Jarrow. Dr. Husch told me you're… no longer ill."

Jarrow beamed. "I am *entirely* cured, Christian—may I call you Christian? My antisocial tendencies have been eradicated utterly, and I've dedicated myself to making amends for all the nasty little things I did. Starting with the capture of that dangerous renegade Marla Mason."

Christian nodded. "I've heard of her, of course, even up in Portland—she was the youngest chief sorcerer ever, apart from the boy-king Jack Shaffly, but he was a conscious reincarnation, so he doesn't count."

Elsie wagged a finger. "You're forgetting the Bellingham triplets!"

"They were a tripartite soul," Christian pointed out. "Three life experiences, one mind, so really, you have to combine their ages—they were really forty-eight when they took over."

"You're such a bright one!" Elsie patted his cheek, and Christian flinched away—no surprise, Crapsey thought. This was the woman they'd called Marrowbones, after all, ostensibly cured of her bad craziness or not. "Do you have a car for us?"

Christian gestured to a dark blue van parked at the curb. "Minivans aren't really my thing, but I thought for such a large group… I got one that can seat eight, if we don't mind getting cozy, and there's a roof rack for the luggage." He paused. "I figured we might want to keep the back storage area free for, ah…"

"Bundling Marla up in a sack? Good thinking." Elsie turned. "Nicolette! Get the bags up on top. Oh, fine, you'd think I was making you eat whole lemons from the look on your face. Jason, you help her, hup hup. You can drive, too, Jason." She leaned in toward Christian, conspiratorially. "Jason here isn't a sorcerer. He's not much good for anything, really, but he's Marla's brother, so we thought he might be able to work some of that old *family* magic, talk her down from her manic arc of destruction, calm her enough for us to scoop her up and get her back to the Blackwing Institute for therapy without a struggle."

"It's a shame. From what I heard, she was so promising." Christian shook his head. "But I guess it was too much pressure for her, and she couldn't handle it. She really lost it, huh?"

"They say she was turning people into *sharks*." Elsie tapped her temple with one finger. "And just letting them drown in the air! That doesn't sound like a rational actor, does it? Paranoia, schizophrenia, posttraumatic stress disorder, who knows? Dr. Husch will handle the diagnosis. We're just in charge of bringing her in."

"This is… quite a crew for a simple apprehension," Christian said. "Who are the others?"

"Oh, just my entourage," Elsie said. "Talion does security, don't you, my good boy? And Crapsey here is an all-purpose lackey."

"And Rondeau's brother," Crapsey offered.

Elsie snapped her fingers. "Ah, that's right! You see, Marla has some misguided friends who don't want to see her committed. They're in denial, you know, poor dears, classic enablers—especially her old right-hand-man Rondeau. We're hoping his long-lost brother Crapsey can talk some sense into him. Though Marla also has a loyal-beyond-all-reason manservant named Pelham, and maybe a wayward god or two."

Christian widened his eyes but didn't say anything, and Elsie went on blithely. "So having Nicolette—that's the one-armed one, you can't miss her—around to throw some trinkets, and Talion to bite people, grr, and so on, is just us being on the safe side. Can you suppress *all* the magic in a given area?"

"Mostly, but it depends on how many sources are involved," Christian said. "And the force of the will directing the magic. I can dampen or dispel or counter pretty much anything a mortal sorcerer throws at me, at least for a few minutes, but it's like pressing against a door with a horde trying to force their way in—it takes effort and energy on my part, too. But I should be able to render Marla inert long enough to tranquilize her."

Elsie stepped close to him, so close his face was practically tucked up against the hollow of her throat, and appeared to smell his hair. "Do you think you could stop *my* powers from working?"

"I could," Christian said. "Not for long, but, yes. I've made a study of your powers, Ms. Jarrow. Dr. Husch consulted me when your cell was constructed."

The chaos witch stepped back, all smiles again. She was looking less and less like the Mason, Crapsey realized. It wasn't just the red hair and lipstick, or the fact that she smiled a lot—the structure of her face was actually changing, the cheeks rounding, the nose becoming more snub, and, yeah, her boobs were getting bigger, too. Elsie was making this body into a replacement for her own. Crapsey wondered if she was even conscious of the transformation. "All loaded?" she called.

Nicolette, huffing, tied down a last bit of rope, pulling the knot tight with her teeth. "All set."

"Then I've got shotgun," Elsie said. "Who knows the way to Lahaina?"

"There's a GPS in the car," Christian said. At her blank look, he cleared his throat. "Ah, global positioning satellite? Basically a computer that communicates with a satellite, so it knows where we are all times, and can give us turn-by-turn directions to get wherever we're going."

Elsie looked up, as if she might be able to see one of those satellites—and who knew? Maybe she could. "The world is getting so small, isn't it?" she murmured to Crapsey. "Where are the wild places anymore? I really *must* do something about all this when we're finished with Marla."

Before Crapsey could come up with an answer, Elsie was climbing into the minivan, so he got in the back. Christian and Talion sat together in the very rear, so he had to sit next to Nicolette in the next row of seats. She looked at him with eyes so filled with hate she'd probably weep cobra venom if she started to cry.

Jason, who hadn't said a word since they deplaned, drove away from the airport, following the soothing directions of the GPS as Elsie chattered at him happily about the first time she'd come to Hawai'i, which had apparently involved a horrible fire at a luau, and how she'd lived in a place down by the beach for a while. "You know, a lot of people think a sorcerer named Felix invented the spell commonly known as the Scream of Felix. Not so! That was me! Felix Garcia was my roommate. But, yes, it was his scream. You could have swept up what was left of him in a dustpan, poor dear, but he never left wet towels on the bathroom floor again…"

Nicolette leaned toward Crapsey, close enough he was afraid she'd bite his neck. "Why the fuck does she like *you*?" Nicolette hissed in his ear.

"I think it's this body," Elsie said, turning around in her seat and staring. Nicolette squirmed uncomfortably under the gaze. "I hear everything, you should know that. I hear things you haven't even said yet. Crapsey was the most trusted companion of the *last* inhabitant of this body, and you have to understand, even though I've taken over, I'm still dealing with a lot of the original *architecture*. The brain locked up in this skull has certain ingrained pathways, and I just feel comfortable with Crapsey."

"But the Mason was friends with me, too," Nicolette objected. "Or, okay, not me, exactly, but the version of me that existed in her universe."

"Yeah, but she never liked you—or your counterpart," Crapsey said. "She said you were first on the list of people she expected to betray her. Now, everybody in the world was on that list somewhere, even me, but you were right at the top. That's why she kept you close—you knew about chaos magic, which was actually kind of a danger to her, since she was so rigid and order-obsessed."

"So I'm working with those same mental grooves," Elsie said cheerfully. "I look at you and think: venomous bitch. What can I do?"

"But I *worship* you," Nicolette said miserably.

"Yes!" Elsie nodded rapidly. "It's super pathetic!" She turned around and began playing with the radio.

"Just… maybe don't try so hard." Crapsey kept his voice low, even though he knew it didn't matter. "I think she respects people who are, you know. Tough."

"But you're totally spineless," Nicolette said, glum and slumped. "And she likes *you*."

"Yeah, okay, but I'm *naturally* spineless," Crapsey said. "I'm not faking it. The whole adoration thing—it doesn't exactly fit naturally on you. You're a badass, Nicolette. You nearly killed Marla yourself once or twice—if she hadn't had the cloak, she would have died, and now, she doesn't have the cloak." It was weird trying to reassure Nicolette, but it was even weirder seeing her depressed and sulky. He wouldn't have been able to imagine her this way a few days ago—it would have been like imagining a brooding bonfire, or a depressed avalanche.

She perked up. "Yeah, that's right. I could *totally* kill Marla now. That would probably impress the shit out of Jarrow—"

Christian cleared his throat behind them. "Ah, but we're not going to kill her, I mean, we're here to get her help. Right?"

"Naturally," Crapsey said. "We're just, you know… trying to be prepared. Obviously you try to *cure* the rabid dog first, but you have to be prepared to put it down if it's a matter of self-defense—"

"There is no cure for rabies," Talion said, voice dripping with scorn. "Not after symptoms begin to appear."

"You would know, wouldn't you, dog-boy?" Nicolette said.

Crapsey smiled. Nicolette was defending him. That was something. "Huh," he said. "I didn't know that. I mean, where I'm from, there's not really a cure for *anything*. If you step on a rusty nail you pretty much just die. Measles, whooping cough, whatever. I thought you guys had cures for everything."

"Where are you *from*?" Christian asked, bewildered.

"Never mind that," Elsie called from the front seat. "Nicolette, you should call Talion dog-boy again. Or Rover, things in that vein. That's the sort of behavior that could rewire my brain's pathways in your favor."

After a few more miles of banter, snippiness, complaining, and sniping, Jason finally spoke: "This is Lahaina." Crapsey looked out the window. Cute little touristy town, right down by the water, the main street lined by buildings with wooden facades housing gift shops and restaurants and tiny art galleries. There were lots of slow-moving cars and tourists, the latter ambling aimlessly across the paths of the former with impunity. Their van crawled past a park dominated by a majestically sprawling banyan tree, and Jarrow *hmmmed*. "Pull into this next lot. Our contact is here."

Jason managed to find a spot only halfway back in the packed public lot, and they all piled out of the vehicle. "Is it okay to just leave the luggage up top—" Crapsey began, but Elsie just waved her hand, and all the luggage vanished, instantly transported inside the van.

"If you could load the van with the wave of your hand," Nicolette said through gritted teeth, "why did you make me climb up on the fucking roof?"

"Hard work builds character," Elsie said absently, then brightened. "There he is! Oh, Sam! Here we are!"

A man with sad hound-dog eyes, wearing a gray suit, emerged from the shadow at the side of a two-story building. He looked around, frowning, and twisted a fedora in his hands. "Who's Sam? I don't understand any of this." The man's eyes darted from side to side. "Who are you people? And what's with all the funny-looking cars? Is this one of those futuristic pictures, a Flash Gordon sort of thing? I think I need to talk to the director."

Crapsey looked around at his fellows, who were staring at the newcomer, all of them wearing expressions of confusion or disbelief. "What? Do we know him?"

"That's… he looks exactly like Humphrey Bogart," Christian said. "The way he looked in the '40s, in all those movies…"

"Oh," Crapsey said. "Right. Where I'm from, we didn't really have much in the way of movies. There were a lot of electromagnetic pulses, so most of the players were fried, and electricity was spotty anyway."

"Remind me to never visit wherever it is you're from," Christian said. He raised his voice. "Ms. Jarrow, what is this?"

Elsie stamped her foot. "Disappointing, is what this is." She gestured at Bogart, who looked torn between running away or throwing a punch. "This is our skinshifter, Gustavus Lupo. He can imitate anyone, perfectly. I thought maybe I could tweak him a bit, mess around with his mind and make it possible for him to imitate fictional characters. How wonderful would that be, if he could turn into, oh, I don't know, Willy Wonka, or Conan the Barbarian, or Hannibal Lector? Fictional characters have so many more obvious applications than real people do. I thought it would work—fictional creations are naturally simpler than actual real people." She looked around. "Except maybe for you, Nicolette, and you, Talion. But I thought the premise was sound! I was hoping to get Sam Spade, the private eye, but instead, I got the actor who used to *play* him…. Oh well." She took a deep breath. "Mr. Bogart, I presume?"

"Sure, that's right, and who are you?"

"You know how to whistle, right, Bogey?" Elsie said. "Just put your lips together, and..." She puckered her lips, but she didn't whistle: it was more like blowing out a candle flame, and when she did, Bogart shimmered, fedora vanishing, and the figure before them became somehow... undifferentiated, like they were looking at him from behind a pane of distorting shower glass. "This is the closest thing to a 'neutral' form he's got," Elsie said. "Kind of calls attention to itself, though, doesn't it? We can do better. I sort of miss Dr. Husch though, so..." She snapped her fingers, and the figure trembled, then became the good doctor—but with her dark blonde hair worn loose, and dressed in dark sunglasses, a clinging yellow-tank top, extremely brief denim shorts, and strappy sandals. She looked around in alarm.

Elsie jabbed Crapsey in the rib with her elbow. "You like her outfit? I did that for you."

"You're a generous soul," Crapsey said.

"What's the meaning of this?" Lupo snapped, crossing her arms and scowling. "Jarrow, how dare you teleport me against my will? For that matter, *how* did you manage to—"

"I didn't," she said. "Come on, Doctor. If I could pry you out of Blackwing, you know I would have done so first thing. You're not you. You're Lupo, imitating you."

Lupo took off her sunglasses, narrowed her eyes to glare at Elsie, then sighed. "Oh, wonderful. Not only do I have to be here with you, I also have to live with the knowledge that my entire sense of self is false, and that even this provisional consciousness could cease to exist at any moment. That's just *grand*."

"I totally missed you too," Elsie said, linking arms with Lupo, much to her apparent dismay. "Let's go break into Marla's office and put her in a straitjacket for her own protection, what do you say?"

Proverbs of the Obvious

USING SOME ARCANE SYSTEM of her own—or perhaps just acting on information from her spy Gustavus Lupo—Elsie led them to the building that housed Marla's office. "See, there's a little bit of folded space here. Plus a few safeguards against unlawful entry, but nothing I can't unpick... ." A brick wall flickered and revealed a door with a glass window decorated with flaking gold paint. "It's a used bookstore. How cozy."

"A store no shopper can find," Talion said. "It is like a Zen koan."

"Nobody said 'speak,' Talion." Elsie peered through the window—they could see shelves, and a counter, and a curtained alcove beyond that. "Hmm. It seems like someone's home—I'm getting a definite sense of habitation—but something's off. It's like cherry flavoring instead of actual cherry, if you know what I mean. Christian, why don't you work your mojo, create a nice..."

"Anti-magic shell," Nicolette said. At Elsie's raised eyebrow, Nicolette shrugged. "That's what they call it in this fantasy computer game I play sometimes."

Christian muttered, and moved his hands, and, even though nothing seemed to happen, Elsie grunted. "Yes. Nobody's home. It was a false impression of a person in there, a fake Marla, which means—probably a trap. Clever girl! Nicolette, care to lead the way?"

"So I'm a human mine detector now?" she said.

"Oh, any booby traps are sure to be magical in nature, and Christian has suppressed those. So unless there's a shotgun pointed at the door, with a string tied to the trigger at one end and the doorknob at the other, you should be fine."

"It's not beyond Marla to do something like that." Nicolette looked through the glass, sighed, and put her hand on the knob. "Uh. It's locked. And I can pop a lock with magic, but—no magic."

"Talion?" Elsie said sweetly, and they all jostled around to give him a clear look at the door. He drew a knife almost as long as his forearm from the depths of his leather jacket—good thing Elsie had been able to glamour them past airport security, or that pigsticker would belong to the TSA now, and Talion would probably still be in a holding room—and jammed it between the door and the frame, then twisted, grunted, and shoved. The door popped open with a crack, and he moved aside to let Nicolette in.

She moved fast, checking all the corners, ducking behind the counter, and looking beyond the curtain. She eyed a steep flight of stairs, sighed, and went up, returning a moment later and calling out, "Clear!"

The rest of them entered, and Nicolette walked around the room, picking things up from bookshelves, chairs, and the floor, then dumped the handful of collected objects on the counter: a nail, the skull of a bird, several black jellybeans, a fly strip, and a small glass vial. "Let's see," she said. "We've got impalement, murderous spirit birds, two kinds of immobilization traps, and, yep, straight-up poison." She shook her head. "Marla's a pretty good enchanter, you've gotta give her that. We would've been inconvenienced to death if Christian hadn't deactivated all these things."

"She knew we were coming," Husch—no, Crapsey reminded himself, *Lupo*—said. "Or that someone was coming, anyway. According to Rondeau, Death gave her a prophecy, that she would… be captured… on a Maui beach. It seems that, sensibly enough, she has chosen to remove herself from the vicinity of Maui's beaches."

"Hmm," Elsie said. "I'm sure she had the good sense to cover her tracks and frustrate divination. Is it like her, to run away from a fight?"

"Not usually," Nicolette said. She glanced at Christian. "But she's never been, ah, in the midst of a nervous breakdown before, so who knows? If I had to guess, I'd say she's just pulling back to a defensive position."

Elsie twisted a lock of red hair in her fingers. "I could just *ask* her where she went, I suppose, but making Lupo turn into Marla could backfire, couldn't it? Still, it's tempting, it's certainly *unexpected*—"

"There's a computer back here." Jason stepped out from behind the curtain. "Password protected, but they're idiots when it comes to security. I found the password list taped to the bottom of the keyboard. They cleared the browser history, but they didn't delete their cookies or their temporary internet files." Elsie frowned at him, and Crapsey didn't really follow him either, and Jason sighed. "What I mean is, I can tell what websites they were looking at recently. They booked a flight to the Big Island, and they visited a few websites for hotels on the west coast, but it doesn't look like they made reservations online, so I can't be sure which one they picked. But all the hotels are along the same stretch of highway, so we can check them out one by one, or split up and do a bunch at once." They all stared at him. "What? Not all of us have magic, you freaks. Some of us have to *think* our way out of problems and into opportunities."

"You're more useful than I thought," Elsie announced. "Though with this bunch, the bar is set pretty low. Who's up for another plane trip? Ooh, or maybe this time we can steal a boat!"

After their room service breakfast, Marla, Rondeau, and Pelham all crowded around Rondeau's laptop, trying to make sense of the milling figures that filled the thirteen-inch screen. "It would be nice if the store was wired for sound," Marla complained, watching the silent inches-high figures, filmed from a high angle, wander and gesticulate around her office.

"There's a mike set up behind some books on one of the shelves, but it's shittier than I thought, and they're not very close to it." Rondeau cranked up the volume on his laptop, and they could indeed hear some indistinct murmuring, but nothing of much use. "I didn't have time to hit a high-end spy shop, you know. I had to make do with the crappy webcam and podcasting equipment I was able to find at the strip mall. But from the tattletale keylogger software I installed, it looks like you were right—Jason went straight to the computer in the office and started rummaging through our internet history. He should be able to figure out where we are, roughly, and they'll probably expect to surprise us. So we can be ready."

"I love it when people assume I'm stupid," Marla said. "That makes it so much easier to get them to follow the trail I want."

"Like I would use that computer for anything *real*," Rondeau said. "It came with the office. It's like a decade old. Total virus bait."

"Never underestimate an enemy's ability to underestimate your intelligence. I wish they were a little stupider themselves, though. It would have solved a lot if they'd just wandered in and set off all those nasty tricks I left them." She leaned closer, crowding Rondeau and Pelham aside, her nose almost touching the screen, but all that did was make blurry things blurrier. "Who the hell *are* all those people? Isn't there some way you can enlarge or enhance this?"

Rondeau snorted. "It doesn't work the way it does in the movies. I can't infinitely zoom in—we've got a crappy webcam here. This is as good as it gets. Still, that's obviously Nicolette, and that's Jason, and that's Crapsey—I guess he just latched on to Nicolette at some point? But the other three..." He pointed. "That looks almost like Dr. Husch."

"Insofar as she's blonde and has big pixellated breasts, I guess," Marla said. "That's not how Leda looks *now*, anyway, not since the Mason tore her to pieces. That one there... could it be Talion?"

Rondeau whistled. "That guy we met in the other *universe*? Wasn't he one of the good guys?"

"With 'good guys' defined as 'somebody who hates people we hate'? In that dimension, sure, but if he's the Talion from *this* universe, then who knows? I can't imagine how he got mixed up in this, but I think he was some kind of mercenary on the other side—maybe he's just hired muscle. That little guy with the hipster glasses, I don't have a clue who he could be. And that redhead, doesn't it seem like *she's* the one calling the shots? They all keep looking at her. I'd assumed this was Nicolette's gig—but what if somebody else is in charge? If so, *why*? If I mortally offended her, you'd think I'd at least recognize her. My kingdom for a room full of obedient clairvoyants…"

"Maybe we know enough to ask the right questions now," Rondeau said. "Like, 'Who the hell are these people?' We could see about scaring up an oracle."

"Not a bad idea," Marla said. "But does that mean you want me to walk around in this ridiculous giant hotel some more?"

Following Rondeau's peculiar inner compass, they made their way through the hotel, to the artificial lagoon. There was no one else around, just water lapping at fake white sand, the waters populated by real sea creatures. Rondeau, who wore cargo shorts and sandals, strode out into the water, and Marla took off her boots and rolled up her white cotton pants to the knees and followed. Pelham, who was wearing clothing more appropriate for a day's work in a cubicle farm than a tropical paradise, chose to stay in the sand.

Rondeau went out about waist deep, and Marla sighed and followed. She hated wading in the surf in Hawai'i, especially in the dark, and even this fake lagoon was connected to the real ocean. Compared to, say, Australia, the waters of Hawai'i were fairly benign, but there were jellyfish, venomous cone snails, poisonous anemones, scorpion fish, barracudas, sharks, Portuguese-man-of-wars (men-of-war?), and—

The water frothed, and a green sea turtle with a shell roughly the diameter of a patio table rose from the water, its nose no more than two feet away. Its head was pure white, its eyes dark and strangely compassionate, and it nodded at them in a disturbingly anthropomorphic way.

"Welcome, oracle." Rondeau's voice was strained—summoning this creature had clearly cost him more effort than usual. "We seek your counsel."

The turtle spoke, the voice feminine and soothing, though its beak of a mouth didn't move. "I am Honu-po'o-kea, mother of Kailua the turtle-maiden. I will aid you if I can."

"An enemy is coming for us," Rondeau said. "She has red hair, and she comes with an army of warriors. Can you tell us her name and her nature?"

The honu bobbed in the water, her flippers moving lazily, creating little wavelets that broke against Marla and Rondeau's bodies. "She is broken shells and spoiled yolks, that one. She is water that sickens you to drink. Her name is Elsie Jarrow, and she is the fire that cracks the stones."

Marla closed her eyes. *Marrowbones*? But Jarrow was supposed to be locked up in the Blackwing Institute. She didn't even have a *body* anymore. If she was free... what was she doing here? Marla had seen her once, before becoming chief sorcerer, when Jarrow escaped her prison for one afternoon. The sight of her bloody smile had made a powerful impression on Marla, but it wasn't like they had *history*. Though Nicolette worshipped Jarrow the way Rondeau worshipped rum, and the younger chaos witch had tried to break her heroine out of Blackwing at least once before, so it sort of made sense.

"And the others?" Rondeau said. "Can you tell us who she brought with her?"

The turtle lowered her head into the water for a moment, as if thinking, then nodded again. "A one-armed witch, armed with a shard of the moon. My summoner's false brother, with a jaw of wood and stone and magic, his soul trapped in a bottle of flesh. A killer of wolves, and men who become wolves. A man who soaks up magic as the sand soaks up water. This woman's true brother, a conniver and a liar, reeking of fear and calculation. And another, a blur, not nameless, but possessed of an ever-changing name."

"That's seven," Marla muttered. "Jarrow, Nicolette, Crapsey, Jason, and we were right about it being Talion. I don't know who the guy who slurps up magic can be, and this nameless blur, *that's* not a lot to go on, but they must be the other two we saw, the little guy and the blonde woman."

"Do you have any advice for us?" Rondeau said to the honu.

"Do not trust brothers," the honu replied. "Either false brothers, or true."

"Thanks." Marla tried hard to keep the sarcasm out of her voice, because even a seemingly benevolent oracle like this one could be dangerous if treated with disrespect. But really. Telling her not to trust Jason or Crapsey was right up there with other proverbs of the obvious, like "Don't eat the rat poison" and "Don't gargle with gasoline."

"The sea calls me," the white-headed honu said, only a trifle impatiently. "Is there anything more?"

"Yes, if you can—this." Marla took the ring from her pocket and held it out to the honu. "This ring, it's supposed to be enchanted."

"It is not enchanted," the honu said. "It is magic."

Marla frowned. "What's the distinction?"

"The difference between something that is enchanted, and something that is magic, is the difference between something that is wet, and something that is *water*."

Marla nodded. "So it's an artifact. My boyfriend's a generous guy... can you tell me what it does? What happens if I wear it, I mean?"

"If you wear it?" The turtle didn't quite smile—Marla wasn't sure turtles *could* smile—but it somehow contrived to look amused. "It will be very pretty, and sparkle, and make you feel loved, if you are the sort to feel loved. But that is all."

"No power to shoot fireballs from my fingertips then? Oh well. I mean, I can do that *anyway*, it's just hell on my fingernails." She sighed. A ring that *was* magical, but wouldn't allow her to *do* any magic, struck her as an especially useless ornament.

"We thank you for your wisdom," Rondeau said. "What can we offer you in return?"

"The world is dangerous for my children," the honu said. "We lay our eggs in the sand, and the young hatch and make their way to the surf, but death is all around them: cats, rats, birds, the hated mongoose. Even a hole in the sand, or a bit of wood in the path, can delay their rush to the safety of the waves, and the false lights of humankind confuse them, and send them crawling to their deaths in the streets instead of their lives in the sea. You will go to a certain beach on a certain day next summer—I will send you a dream—and you will see to it that none of the children are lost, and that all reach the water." The honu bobbed her head again. "This you will do."

"I will," Rondeau said solemnly, and the honu vanished beneath the waves. Rondeau let out a long shuddering breath. Then he smacked Marla on the arm. "I have to go save a thousand baby sea turtles from being eaten by rats? That's a hell of a price to have to pay—it's because you ask so many questions. And what if one of the turtles gets snatched up by a seagull or whatever?"

"What, you're afraid of a turtle god now?"

"That wasn't a turtle god. That was the *mother* of a turtle god. That's even worse. You're not allowed to die in this fight, Marla. I'm making you go with me to that beach."

"It's a date."

As they waded back out, Rondeau said, "So, uh… now what? We know who, but, shit, *Marrowbones* is after us? How do we fight someone like her?"

"That's a good question. If she's here, it means she escaped from Blackwing, and somehow found a body that won't die of cancer—maybe it's a robot or something. I'm worried about what she did to Dr. Husch…"

Rondeau stopped walking. "Marla…. I just talked to Dr. Husch. Like, a *day* ago. I called her, I mean, we were friends, I stayed with her for a while, and…" He shook his head. "She sounded *fine*." His expression became thoughtful. "Better than fine, actually. She sounded like she always does, and I didn't think about it, but I thought when she got put back together…"

"Her voice was ruined," Marla said. "That's what Hamil said, right?"

Rondeau nodded. "Maybe she… got better?"

"Maybe somebody made her better. Maybe somebody made her a *deal*. And maybe getting torn to pieces tore apart something in her mind, too."

"Do you really think Dr. Husch is part of this?"

"I don't want to think so, but she went through a lot... getting ripped into little pieces probably leads to a certain amount of posttraumatic stress disorder, even if you are a homunculus."

Rondeau closed his eyes. "Shit. Marla, I *told* her things. I told her about what the eel oracle said, and about Pelham coming back, I don't remember *what* all I told her—what if she's working with Jarrow? What if I told her stuff that's going to hurt us?"Marla considered. "Well... call her again. If she doesn't answer, we'll assume she's a victim in all this, too. Then we'll get in touch with Hamil, and tell him Jarrow is loose, and that he might want to send somebody to make sure Dr. Husch is okay, and that the other patients at Blackwing are secure."

"And if she does answer?"

"Then you tell her *more*. Give her some juicy disinformation. And if Jarrow and company act on that bad information, we'll know they got it from Dr. Husch, and... we'll take appropriate action."

Rondeau nodded. "Okay. Leda. I can't believe she'd turn on us. I don't *want* to believe it." They continued on toward the shore. "What should I say to her?"

"Isn't the Place of Refuge like fifty miles south of here? I've got an idea..."

Places of Refuge

"**THE CLOSEST HOTEL IS,** let's see." Jason squinted at the guidebook in his lap and compared it to the sheet of names he'd scribbled down at Marla's office. He was in the passenger seat, next to Christian, who drove along the dark highway. "A bed-and-breakfast called the Rainbow Plantation. Doesn't sound much like Marla does it?" He yawned. "Are we really going to try to hit all these hotels tonight? Maybe you people don't need to sleep, but I do. I've been teleported, flown on a plane, and ridden on a stolen boat. I'm exhausted."

"You can sleep when you're dead," Elsie said from the first row of seats in the back, where she sat next to Crapsey, one hand resting companionably on his knee. "Are you sure you're that sleepy?"

Nicolette's phone rang, loud in the rented SUV.

"No personal calls!" Elsie snapped, turning to glare at Talion and Nicolette, or "the bad kids," as she'd started calling them for reasons of her own. Lupo was back there too, still looking like Dr. Husch, all glares and snarls.

"It's for you," Nicolette said. "It's Dr. Husch." That just made Lupo glare even more ferociously, and bare her teeth. It must really suck, Crapsey thought, to know you aren't even really *real*.

Elsie took the phone and put it to her ear. "Doctor Prettyface! Don't you inhuman homunculi *ever* take an evening off? Listen, we're on the case, don't worry—" She paused. "Oh, *really*?" She covered the mouthpiece with one hand and grinned at Crapsey. "Our friend Rondeau called Dr. Husch with another tale of woe." Back to the call: "Did he tell you anything useful, or just whine some more? Or both? Hmmm. Really? That could be fun. How long ago was this? Thanks, Doc. We're on it." She pushed a button on the phone and tossed it over her shoulder, eliciting an "Ow" from Lupo. "Christian!" she shouted. "Fire up that fancy GPS and tell it we're going to Pu'uhonua o Honaunau National Historical Park."

"Uh," Christian said, "I'm going to need you to spell that."

141

"Jason, look it up in the book, would you? Starts with a P, as in Place of Refuge, which is what it's *also* called. According to Rondeau, Marla's taking that name literally, and she's going to hole up there. Let's go pry her out of that hole, what do you say?"

"What is this place?" Crapsey said.

"You're right to ask me, since I know everything," Elsie said. "You know about taboos? They didn't have those in old Hawai'i, or rather, they did, but they called them kapu—the old Hawai'ian laws. If you commited some terrible crime—like, say, touching a chief's fingernail clippings, or wearing red and yellow feathers, or casting a shadow on the grounds of the palace, or letting a woman eat a banana—you were breaking a kapu. The punishment was usually, poof, instant death. If only we had a legal system like that now—so simple! But, just like in that great Disney cartoon *The Hunchback of Notre Dame*, there are places of sanctuary where the authorities can't get you. If you broke a kapu, you could flee to a place of refuge and throw yourself on the mercy of the priests who lived inside. They could absolve you and set you free, sometimes, or other times they'd just put you to work. People who wanted to avoid battle, or losers in a war who didn't want to get their brains bashed in, could come take refuge in a *pu'uhonua* too. The place of refuge was inviolate, nobody was allowed to take anybody out against their will, because the ground is *sacred*. Isn't religion grand? You can build stronger walls out of faith than you ever could with steel and concrete. So it makes a certain amount of sense for Marla to go to ground there—I bet there's still some magic in that place, even though the bones of the chieftains buried there were all stolen or scattered or hidden away, and the snarling tiki statues are all reproductions."

"You don't think it's a bit convenient that one of Marla's friends told Dr. Husch where she was hiding?" Christian said. "You said her psychic friend Rondeau predicted Marla would be captured—couldn't she be lucid enough to realize that Dr. Husch is the one coming after her? Or paranoid enough to suspect so?"

Elsie beamed. "You deserve a lollipop! And by 'lollipop' I mean 'head of an enemy on a stick.' Yes, it's almost certainly a trap. That makes it more *fun*. But I'm not a complete maniac. Just a partial one. We'll deploy our resources strategically and blah, blah, blah." She clapped her hands together and bounced on the seat. "Finally! Two *days* I've spent planning to catch Marla, and the time has come! I'm so glad. I was getting bored. And when I get bored, Talion could tell you, I get cranky."

"Using yourself as bait is a bad idea," Rondeau said. "Using me as bait is even worse." They sat together in a grove of palm trees, the ocean at their backs. The night was that rich quality of dark you only get some distance away from cities and their halos of light pollution, the skies clear, the air cool. They were well within the ten-foot-high L-shaped wall of ancient unmortared stone that divided the inside of the Place of Refuge from the old royal grounds and the rest of the national park. The area was guarded by fierce tiki statues, and nominally patrolled by park rangers to keep people out of the historic area after hours, but Marla had cast a little misperception loop that would keep the rangers distracted elsewhere until morning. "I feel way too exposed here." There were reproductions of traditional Hawai'ian huts on the other side of the wall, but within the sanctuary, there was no shelter of any kind—the closest thing to a structure was a massive platform of stones that had probably once been a foundation for houses.

"Nah, this is a great defensive position," Marla said. "Anybody who wants to get to us has to pass through the visitor's center, walk along the trail, either circle around the wall or come through the one opening, and then make their way across all those vicious volcanic rocks without falling in a royal fish pond or falling and getting shredded by cold lava. We've got great sightlines. I like it."

"What if they come in by canoe?"

Marla shrugged. "There's a plain of black rock between us and the water. There's no cover there at all—anyone walking in would be totally exposed. It's a good position."

"If it's so good, what do you need me for?"

"Please. Without you, this place is just a historical curiosity. With you, it's *actually* a refuge. You're telling me you can't sense the ghosts? Even I can."

Rondeau sighed. "Yeah, there are ghosts. Priests who spent most of their lives here, and some chiefs, but they're a little more faded—their bones were kept here for a while, but they got moved at some point, so the spirits are sort of doing a time-share thing between locations. There's one incredibly pissed-off old white dude in some kind of military jacket. I think he's Captain Cook, the guy who discovered Hawai'i—well, you know, 'discovered,' the way white dudes discover all kinds of places that plenty of brown people already know about. When Cook first showed up, the Hawai'ians thought he was their long-lost god Lono. He got a longer welcome than he would have otherwise, but he eventually wore it out. The locals kept some of his bones here like he was a chief, showing him respect even though they killed him themselves. I don't know how much help Cook's ghost will be, but the priests seem to accept us as legitimate sanctuary-seekers. They know they're dead, but they don't seem to mind much. They should be some help."

Marla nodded. "Good. We've got Pelham out beyond the wall, watching the road, so we should get some advance warning before the bad guys arrive."

"*If* they arrive," Rondeau said. "I'm still hoping we sit out here and nothing happens. We don't know if Dr. Husch is involved at all. Maybe Nicolette just helped Jarrow escape—" His cell phone vibrated, and Rondeau picked it up, listened, and grimaced. "Thanks, Pelly." He put the phone away. "There's an SUV coming down the road, no headlights. Pelham looked through those binoculars you gave him, the ones with the night-vision enchantment, and he says there are at least five people in the thing, and they look enough like the people in the video that he's ninety-nine percent sure they're our villains. Do you want him to proceed?"

"I think the odds that they're just tourists who didn't check the park's operating hours are pretty low," Marla said. "But tell him to stick with the strictly non-lethal measures, just in case. And call Hamil, now, I don't care if it's going to wake him up. Tell him... shit. Don't tell him what we suspect about Dr. Husch, I guess. We could still be wrong. Just tell him that Elsie Jarrow is loose, and that he might want to check on Leda, and make sure the other patients at Blackwing are secure. He's smart enough to go in on his guard."

"Fuck," Rondeau said. "Leda. I *liked* her. I always did." He made the call, keeping it short and simple, and disconnecting quickly. "He says he'll get some of his people and head to Blackwing right away."

"Good. I helped put some of those people *in* Blackwing. Somebody needs to make sure the patients stay locked up, if Leda can't be trusted to do it anymore." She ran a hand through her hair. "I wish I could be there. I *should* be there. But instead, I'm here. There's nothing I can do about what's happening in Felport. So I'd better be here all the way." Marla looked around the grove of palm trees. She'd laid out a certain number of weapons, enough to level the playing field, but the only thing that had a chance of hurting Jarrow was the dagger Death had forged for her. The problem would be getting close enough to strike. "I wish Reva hadn't wandered off," she said. "He's a presumptuous annoying little shit, but we could use some god-powers here." After their plane landed the god had promised to catch up with them later, saying he had errands to run, but he hadn't been in touch yet. "I also wish to hell this ring did something useful."

"The oracle said wearing it wouldn't do anything," Rondeau said. "But maybe you have to wear it *and* say a magic word or something? Or twist it around three times? Or stick it on your toe? Maybe there's an inscription on the inside, like people get for their wedding rings. Something useful like, 'One ring to bind them all.' Even 'insert finger here' would be helpful at this point."

Marla grunted, wishing she'd thought of the possibility of an inscription. She held the ring up to the moonlight, squinting. Was that something incised in the metal, or just a glint? She brought the ring close to one eye, closing the other and squinting—

A red-haired woman on the sand raised her arms, mouth moving in silent screams or laughter, and a flock of burning parrots appeared in the air, rushing toward Marla. She leapt to one side, diving and rolling, then bounced up to her feet—

Nothing. No Jarrow, no birds. She looked at the ring, still clutched in her hands, and lifted it to her eye again. Looking through the ring, the empty beach became crowded: there was Crapsey, holding onto Rondeau's lapels with one hand and punching him in the face with the other, and Jarrow again, now strangling a man Marla had never even seen before. The chaos witch didn't look exactly as she had the one time Marla had met Jarrow, but she *did* looked vaguely familiar—Marla couldn't quite place her. She put the ring down and frowned. "Shit," she said. "Rondeau. This ring lets you see the future."

Rondeau leaned in the doorway of the house. "Really? That's handy."

"You *look* through it," she said. "Gods, it never occurred to me… but that's one of Death's powers, to see possible futures, it's how he knows when people are going to die. Rondeau, stuff's going to get ugly here, and I'm not sure when, I don't know what kind of a delay we're talking about with this ring, how far it can see, but we'd better get ready, we—"

The phone buzzed again, and Rondeau picked it up. "Yeah, Pelly, do you—oh. Uh. Just… just a minute." He took the phone away from his ear and looked at Marla, eyes wide. "It's for you. It's not Pelham. It's…"

"Jarrow," she said, taking the phone.

"Crapsey, actually," Crapsey said. He sounded almost exactly like Rondeau, voice perhaps a bit rougher from decades inhaling the atmosphere of the Mason's version of North America, polluted as it was by the output of her vile magical engines. "How's it going, Marla?"

"I've been better. How's Pelham?"

"Little shit got away, actually. He scattered something on the road to pop all our tires, nearly rolled the SUV, but Jarrow kept us upright, and we managed to grab hold of your boy. I had him by the scruff of the neck, and we got the phone off him, but then he did some kind of crazy kung-fu shit and ran off into the dark. He's going to get himself killed on those black rocks. We could've caught him, but Jarrow said leaving him loose was an 'interesting variable,' adding some uncertainty to the situation, so we let him go. It's a chaos witch thing."

"Makes sense. So what's the big idea? Kick me while I'm down?"

"Kill you while you're weak, yeah. I mean, personally, I don't have a real grudge against you. Rondeau's the one who tricked me into drinking that potion, and trapped me in this body. He's the one I've got a beef with. Jarrow says she can settle that score for me along the way—she'll either trap Rondeau the way I'm trapped, or make him suffer some other way."

"You're an idiot, Jabberjaw. Rondeau was acting under my orders. If you want to hate someone, hate me."

"Oh, duly noted, but I was a henchman for a long time, and I believe in taking personal responsibility for your actions, even if your boss told you to do it. I want Rondeau to hurt, and Nicolette wants *you* to hurt, and since the two of you are hanging out together, hey, we joined forces."

"And got Elsie Jarrow out of the hospital to use as a weapon. Well, I must say, at least you two morons know your own limitations. If you'd attacked me on your own, I'd be picking bits of you out of my teeth right now. But Jarrow's a nuke. She's weaponized anthrax. She's not a weapon you can unleash without consequences."

"Eh, it's all under control."

"You've got Doctor Husch helping you, right?"

Crapsey laughed. "Why should I tell you that?"

"Why shouldn't you? You're pretty sure I'll be dead in a few minutes anyway. Besides, you're supposed to keep me on the phone and distracted as long as you can so the rest of the idiot patrol can surround me. So answer my question, and truthfully, or I'll hang up and start loading my rocket launchers."

"You're a pisser, Marla, I'll give you that. You remind me of my old boss, only not as pretty, of course. Sure, Husch was in on it. *You're* the reason she got torn to pieces, you know—me and the Mason wouldn't have come to this universe if you hadn't gone messing around with the fabric of reality. Husch is the one who let Jarrow out, and she's holding the leash, keeping Elsie on task. Otherwise she'd just wander off and turn the Eiffel Tower into an anthill or something. The truth is, this is Dr. Husch's operation. Me and Nicolette are just riding on her coattails." He lowered his voice to a stage whisper. "Though to be totally honest, it's Elsie's show, now. And she's a scary one. At least with the Mason, you knew what you were in for: she was going to try to kill you. With Jarrow? She could make you a palace out of emeralds or turn your liver into a swarm of fire ants, either or both for no particular reason. She's going to kill you, I guess, but I'm pretty sure she's going to play with you first, and the only reason is, she *likes* it."

"You sure have a way of picking bad company, Crapsey." Marla was walking around the site now, checking the traps she'd set up earlier, and content that all were primed, she returned to the tree where Rondeau sat cross-legged and muttered to ghosts, an enchanted lei around his neck. "Did you ever think about getting a job working for someone who *wasn't* crazy and prone to acts of senseless violence?"

"I'm not sure I'm qualified for a gig like that. Why, are you looking for another guy in your entourage? I'd make a great replacement for Rondeau."

"I have this policy against employing mass-murderers—sorry. And since you've actually lost count of all the people you've killed..."

"True. You've only killed, what, ten?"

"Seven," Marla said. "And I regret them all. Every one represents a failure on my part—a failure of diplomacy, or imagination, or preparation, or nerve."

"Only seven! You're an amateur."

"Hey, the night's young. I could have a few more failures of imagination before the sun comes up. But I never killed on a *whim*, Crapsey."

"It's not like I enjoy killing people—"

"I know. You just don't *care* if you do. And honestly? I think that's even worse. Okay, Trapjaw, are you people waiting for dawn? Where's the attack?"

"Be patient, will you? We've got a way of doing things—"

Someone screamed from off to the east, and Marla grinned. "You hear that screaming? Somebody just met one of our defenses."

"What. The. Fuck," Crapsey said. "Who are all these—"

"They're the ghosts of the priests who protected this place," Marla said. "I've formally claimed sanctuary. And since you guys are marauders, trampling through a sacred space... let's just say you're on the wrong side of some big kahunas."

"Fuck!" Crapsey shouted, and then there was a crackling sound, and nothing more.

Marla handed the phone back to Rondeau. "I think he dropped the phone, in the course of running away from some pissed-off priests."

The ghosts were becoming visible now. Rondeau's psychic field had a way of drawing latent supernatural manifestations into active status—faint ghosts became visible and capable of poltergeist activity, while presences that were more powerful to begin with could become corporeal enough to fuck or fight or drive motorcycles. The kahunas here were pretty faint, all things considered—they were from a long time ago, adhering to customs renounced by the later kings of Hawai'i, and some of them were miles and miles away from whatever remained of their mortal remains. Still, there was an impressive array: translucent kahunas in ceremonial feathers, drained of color and rendered white and gray, and furious chiefs with skeletal limbs armed with shark's-tooth war clubs. Marla had her dagger hanging from her belt, and the massive Samoan war club she'd received from Arachne was in her hand, the latter all tricked out with vicious inertial magics. A love tap from that could cave in a rib cage, and might even knock Elsie Jarrow back a step or two.

And there, stalking up the path from the direction of a reproduction of a traditional temple, dressed in the ragged remnants of a naval jacket, wig askew, was the ghost of Captain James Cook, the accidental reincarnation of the long-lost god Lono, now looking around suspiciously with pistols in each hand, obviously spoiling for a fight.

Suddenly the torches she'd placed around the area to serve as an early-warning intrusion system burst into simultaneous flame. They burned bright green: that meant four people had broken the perimeter.

Marla hefted the war club. She grinned. She still had a lot of personal, philosophical, and existential problems, true, but right now, she also had the one kind of problem she knew exactly how to solve: people who needed a beating.

A red-haired woman dressed in a pale yellow summer dress stepped into the light cast by the torches. "Marla Mason, I presume?" the woman said, then winced. "Shit, that line's from Africa, isn't it? All these hot savage places look the same to me."

"Elsie Jarrow," Marla said. "Welcome to paradise."

There's Always Someone Better Than You

THE GHOST OF CAPTAIN COOK shouted and fired his pistols at Jarrow, billowing clouds of white smoke rising from the barrels of his guns. Jarrow looked down and patted her chest. "Ghost bullets! Nice, very nice. They would have ripped my soul right out of my body, if I didn't have supernatural kevlar, but of course, I *do*."

The ghost of Cook was trying to reload his pistols, but it was apparently a very involved project. The ghosts of the kahunas rushed toward Jarrow, weapons at the ready. Jarrow took a folded bit of tissue from her pocket, dabbed at the corners of her eyes, and then blew her nose—a great, ferocious, honking blow. The ghosts stopped running and leaned back, as if being pushed by a great wind, and then burst into flower petals, blowing through the City of Refuge and scenting the air with heavy perfumes. The ghost of Captain Cook scattered as well, the last look on his face outraged and disbelieving. He'd probably worn that expression a lot in his last moments of life.

"Shit," Rondeau said, wobbling a little on his feet, and putting his hand on Marla's shoulder to steady himself. "Listen, their spirits are still here, but they're scattered, really tenuous, it'll take me a while to get them back, but when I do, they're going to be *pissed*, they're going to start calling on shark gods and the god of sorcerers and—"

"Oh, this will be over before the ghosts and ghoulies pull themselves back together," Jarrow said. "Are you two done with opening ceremonies yet? Can I start my guest of honor address? Thanks. I'd like you to meet my friend Christian Decomain." She gestured, and a small, dark-haired man with chunky hipster glasses stepped forward. His clothes were torn, there was a bruise forming on his cheek, and overall, he didn't look too happy. "Your ghost guards smacked him around a little. Not exactly what I was expecting! Those spectral shark's tooth clubs pack a pretty good wallop, if you stand around and let them hit you. I think poor Christian lost a tooth."

"Christian Decomain. That name rings a bell," Marla said. She turned to Rondeau. "Wasn't he—"

Rondeau nodded. "He was one of the freedom fighters in San Francisco—one of Sanford Cole's men. He got killed in a raid on the Jaguar, we never even met him."

"What are they talking about?" Christian said, alarmed.

"She's crazy," Jarrow said breezily. "Probably just one of her delusions."

"Wasn't he some kind of master of counter-magic?" Marla said. "An—"

"Anti-mancer," Jarrow said. She frowned. "Christian, you should have turned on your anti-magic shell when I said that, the light from the torches would have gone off, it would have been very *dramatic*."

"Ah. Right." Christian snapped his fingers, and the torches went dark. Marla drew her club. Shit. No magic, which meant her club was just a heavy stick again. The ghosts wouldn't be coming back while Christian was working his mojo, either. All Marla's fancy traps and preparations had just been made useless, their enchantments blocked. On the bright side, her enemies couldn't cast spells, either. Her dagger would probably still work—artifacts were a lot tougher to neutralize than ordinary bits of magic. It was the same difference the honu oracle had mentioned: the difference between something being wet, and something being water.

"Thanks for that, Jarrow." Marla's night vision was screwed up from the torches, but the others probably weren't much better off. "You've turned this into a fistfight, and that's kind of my forte."

"Ms. Mason, there's no need for violence." Christian's voice was absurdly soothing. "I know it's hard to believe, but we're not your enemies. You're sick, and we want to help you."

"What the fuck are you talking about?" Rondeau said, from somewhere off to the left. "You're here for an assassination, not an intervention."

"That's just paranoia talking," Christian said. "We're here for your own good."

"Is that you, Rondeau?" Jarrow said. "I've been wanting to meet you! But the grown-ups are busy now, so behave, would you?"

Rondeau squawked, and a moment later, a voice much like his, but rougher, said, "I've got the little fucker, boss." Marla closed her eyes. Crapsey had evaded the ghosts, it seemed, and found Rondeau. "The chloroform worked like a dream. He won't be stealing anyone's body for a while."

"Oh, good," Jarrow said. "I was worried. Not for myself—nobody could steal *my* body—but for my associates here. All right, Talion, get in there. Subdue Ms. Mason before she can do any harm to herself. Or others."

Marla's vision had adjusted enough to recognize the man who approached from the gloom on her right. "Talion," she said. "The werewolf-hunter, yeah? I knew you—a version of you—in another universe. He had a lot more facial piercings, though. Glad to see you've got better taste in this dimension. I see you've got all your fingers, too. A lot of those got chopped off when I met the other you, on the other side." She drew her dagger. "This is the knife that lopped those naughty digits off. And the funny thing is? We were actually on the same *side* in that universe, united against a common enemy. Imagine what I could do to you now, when you're on the wrong side?" Talion's expression was a furious snarl, but Marla had the weirdest feeling his anger wasn't directed at her. "You can walk away from this," Marla said, and Jarrow made a loud raspberry.

"No, he can't. Sic her, boy!"

Talion lowered his head, a mixture of shame and rage flickering across his face, and launched himself toward Marla, knives appearing in his hands.

He was fast, absolutely, but Marla had his number instantly. He was used to fighting werewolves, creatures a lot bigger and stronger than he was, and he expected speed to carry the day. But he had a problem: she was at least as fast as he was. He darted in with a knife, and she dove to one side, aiming a kick at his knee, intending to drop him quickly. But he turned in time, and she just ended up kicking him in the shin. He sucked in a breath but didn't stop moving, spinning toward her and weaving a net with the points of his knives. Fighting a duel by moonlight. What a bitch this was.

Christian Decomain was yelling something about how this wasn't right, what were they trying to do, *kill* her? But Marla couldn't pay any attention to that. She was too busy trying to figure out what a werewolf would do in this situation so she could do something else. Too bad she'd never actually met a werewolf—they were all but extinct in North America.

She brought up the war club to block one of Talion's knife strikes, and then bulled toward him, lashing out with her dagger, going for his belly. He managed to parry, but her dagger did its job, slicing cleanly through his blade, leaving an inch of steel sticking up pointlessly just above the hilt. Talion danced back and threw the broken weapon toward her face. Marla had to lift her club to block, and there was Talion, spinning with a kick to sweep her leg. She jumped like a girl skipping rope, but his kick caught her on the instep, sending her stumbling forward into him, both of them piling together on the ground. They rolled, and Talion ended up on top. Marla'd lost the war club, and though she still had the dagger, Talion had her wrist pinned to the ground with one hand, and a knife in the other. Marla tried to get her free thumb in his eye, or to fishhook his cheek, but he hit punched her right in the armpit with a vicious knuckled nerve strike that left her arm numb and unresponsive. She tried to knee him, but he was straddling her too tightly, and her attempts to roll failed—she couldn't get any leverage on the loose sand. "I'm sorry," he said, sweat dripping from his nose into her face. "I don't want to do this." He closed his free hand around her throat.

"Stop!" Christian screamed, and suddenly the torches flared into life as his anti-magic shell was deactivated. "You're supposed to be *capturing* her, I've got tranquilizers right *here*—"

Marla still had a little breath in her lungs, and Talion loosened his grip on her throat in surprise when the lights came on. She spat, and shouted "Conditus!" as the wad of spittle and phlegm struck Talion in the face. Latin trigger words were silly, but she'd been amusing herself by using them ever since she read the first Harry Potter book. Maybe she should have used "*Expelliarmus*" for a spell that involved hacking up a wad of spit. Next time.

Talion shrieked and fell back as the wad of slime expanded, covering his eyes and mouth, crawling around to encase his head. It wouldn't suffocate him—the mobile phlegm avoided the nostrils—but he'd be busy trying to peel it off for a while. She got to her feet, one arm still numb.

Crapsey came rushing in from the left, and Nicolette from the right—the latter was wielding a hatchet that glinted with its own inner light, and that *couldn't* be good. Before Marla needed to act, they both blundered into traps she'd scattered around the area, covered in loose sand. Crapsey stepped on a ring of shattered pocketwatches and got stuck in a moment of slowed time, his headlong forward movement changed into the merely incremental, an expression of comical surprise and outrage passing over his face in slow motion. Nicolette cracked some vials containing a few select elements—noble gases, mainly—and her body became insubstantial, turned into a misty outline of itself. The hatchet fell through her hand, still shining, and landed in the dirt. Nicolette started to curse furiously, but the words wisped away into nothingness, and she soon faded entirely from sight. She wasn't dead, or even truly transmuted, just temporarily locked into a sympathetic bond with the gases, and made immaterial. She was essentially another invisible ghost. She would precipitate out of the atmosphere again, whole and unharmed, in an hour or so. By then, whatever was going to happen here would be done.

Jarrow had knocked Christian to the ground, and had one of her feet on his throat; she was wearing golden strappy sandals. In Marla's vision, she'd been strangling the man, but any view of the future was necessarily subject to change.

"He really thought this was a mission of mercy," Elsie said as Christian writhed beneath her. She looked at Marla. "I knew I'd have to kill him eventually, but I'd heard you were a good fighter, and I wanted to see for myself, no magic involved, so I figured I'd keep him around long enough to sic my dog on you. I have to say, I'm disappointed—Talion was better than you."

"There's always someone better than you."

"Not that I've noticed," Jarrow said. "Nighty-night, Christian." She sang, just a snatch of a schoolyard verse, something about five little pumpkins sitting on a gate, and Christian Decomain screamed for an instant. His clothing collapsed, and scores of tiny golden frogs hopped away from the pile of clothes in all directions.

"You turned him. Into *frogs*." Marla stared.

"What? Turning people into frogs is very traditional for witches. You turned Nicolette into *gas*, although not permanently, I notice. You old softie. I was tempted to turn Christian into a hundred big hairy carnivorous millipedes instead, but I feel like the bug thing is so *expected*, you know? And you can't say I killed him! This is just a little transformation, though not as temporary as what you cast on my associates. Nice traps, by the way. Kind of creative."

"Can he be saved?" Marla said. "Can he be put back together, made human again?"

"Oh, sure, if you could gather all the little froglets—" She stomped down, hard, squishing a golden poison dart frog beneath her heel, then did a series of tap dance steps across the clothing, doubtless squashing dozens more. "Oops, there went his kidney. Ack, there goes his spleen. Oh, dear, I think I just stomped on his sense of right and wrong, if only he hadn't been cursed with *that* thing to begin with! You have a history with frogs, right? You fought a guy who used frogs like these to assassinate people? I researched you, in a kind of a half-assed way, I mean, I asked a few questions, just to get a sense." She put a finger to her lips. "Hmm. These things are really going to play hell with the local ecosystem, aren't they?"

Marla backed away from the frogs hopping in her direction. "What are you waiting for, anyway? Why don't you come for me?" Without Rondeau's ghosts or Pelham in a sniper position, her only remaining hope against Jarrow was luring her into the field of traps, many of which were designed specifically to combat a chaos witch, and getting in a lucky strike with her dagger. But having seen Crapsey and Nicolette felled by Marla's magics, she didn't show any inclination to go charging blindly in. Besides, this was Marrowbones; she didn't need to be close to Marla to kill her.

Jarrow pouted, but didn't make any move to approach. "You don't enjoy my company, Marla? You just want me to turn *you* into a hundred hairy millipedes? Where's the fun in that? I haven't even brought your brother into this yet. Oh, don't worry, the night is young. We'll get to the killing-you part."

"Is there even any point to asking you why you're doing this?"

Jarrow shrugged. "Actually it's very rational. I wanted a new body, and I wanted to get out of prison. Dr. Husch said I could have both if I just killed you." She covered her mouth in mock horror. "Oops! I probably shouldn't have mentioned that, huh? You've got even fewer friends than you thought!"

"I sort of figured she was behind it. But where did she find you a body? Is it a homunculus?" Marla was curious, but more importantly, she wanted to keep Jarrow talking. Marla didn't think she had much of a chance in a straight fight against Jarrow, especially with one of her arms all fucked up. Jarrow was a whole order of magnitude beyond Marla in power, someone who'd stripped away all the sensible safeguards, who'd gone way past the back of beyond in her quest for knowledge, so who knew *what* she might be capable of? Marla had to stall her long enough for Rondeau to wake up from his chloroform funk, or for Pelham to come back from wherever he'd run to, or for Reva to pop on by, or for *something* to happen. It was like that old joke, about the man sentenced to death, who convinced the king to spare his life by promising to teach his majesty's pet monkey to speak within a year. After all, a lot could happen in a year—the sultan could die. The man could die. Or the monkey could learn to speak.

Marla wasn't thrilled about staking her life on a talking-monkey long-shot, but it was the only chance she had left.

"Look at Talion wriggling around." Jarrow didn't sound amused, or contemptuous—Marla hated to even think it, but the woman sounded *aroused*. The werewolf-hunter was crawling on all fours, shaking his head back and forth, his senses of sight and hearing neutralized by Marla's enchanted spit. "He's a bad dog, isn't he?" Jarrow took a small brass whistle from her pocket and blew on it, though no audible note sounded. Talion collapsed to the ground and began to twist and howl, fur sprouting on his face through the slime, legs twisting, knees bending in reverse, ears lengthening, clothes shredding as his musculature shifted. After a few moments, the man he'd been was gone, replaced by a dirt-brown mutt of a dog, big as a Great Dane but without that breed's sense of nobility. The spit on its face blackened and glistened, oozing and changing consistency from gluey paste to something more like congealed gelatin. The dog that had been Talion ran baying across the sand and into the trees.

"Woof, woof," Jarrow said. "Don't worry, he won't suffer long. I gave him that crazy virulent face cancer that Tasmanian Devils get. Did you know those tumors are actually *contagious*? To catch them you pretty much have to bite someone who's infected straight up on the face, which isn't something most species do, except for Tasmanian Devils. Cancer can evolve in all sorts of interesting ways. The contagiousness isn't even that weird a development— it's just, most cancers are *inside* people, so it's not an adaptation that sees much use. Nobody ever goes gnawing on a guy's cancerous prostate, right?" The chaos witch sauntered over to the not-quite-freeze-framed Crapsey and thumped him on the side of the head. "Cancer's kind of hobby of mine."

"Yeah, I've heard that. Why did you do that to Talion? Because he failed you?"

Jarrow sighed. "I thought you were smarter than that. I *expected* him to fail me. He actually did better than I anticipated. I did it because I felt like it. That's the only reason I do anything, usually. Admittedly, this whole hunt-and-kill-Marla-Mason thing doesn't interest me particularly. I'm sure you have lots of epic enemies, grr, sworn to see you destroyed and ground into dust, but I'm not one of them. Still, if it's what I have to do to get Doctor Husch to fulfill her end of the bargain—"

"I don't think Husch is going to be in a position to fulfill *any* bargains." Marla saw an opportunity to stall—maybe even survive—and seized it. "We called the authorities in Felport once we found out you were involved in this, and told them our suspicions."

Jarrow picked up a handful of sand and tossed it toward Crapsey's face. The grains slowed and hung almost motionless as they entered his field of slow time. "I noticed you weren't all that surprised to see me. I know I'm famous, but I like to think I'm *unexpected*. You're in a codependent relationship with a psychic, though, which gives you an unfair advantage when it comes to intelligence gathering. So the jig is up for Dr. Husch, huh?"

"Once the Chamberlain and Hamil get their hands on her, they'll put her away forever. Whatever she promised you, she won't be able to deliver."

"Mmmm. And you don't think I'm honor-bound to fulfill my contract, even if I lose my employer?" Jarrow grinned. "Ha. Kidding, kidding. It does make things more interesting, though, doesn't it? Tell you what, I'm going to go check on the Doc, I'll be back in a little while." Jarrow touched Crapsey on the shoulder, and he was pulled back into normal time. He stumbled forward a step or two, then turned his head to blink and spit out the sand Jarrow had thrown in his face.

Fuck. Marla was chilled at how easily the woman had broken her spell. Then again, there was a lot of chaos swirling around here tonight. Things going badly for Jarrow could actually make her *stronger*. "Say good night, Crapsey," she said.

"What? What are you—"

Jarrow drew a circle in the air, and a black hole opened in space, the edges curling and appearing to smoke and burn. Marla turned her face away, because looking into the space *behind* reality was never a good idea. Jarrow stepped backward through the portal, dragging Crapsey with her, and the hole closed after them.

Marla sank to her knees, exhaling hard. That was a close one. What was Jarrow going to do? What if she attacked Hamil, tried to protect Husch? What if—

"You *bitch!*" Nicolette screamed, solidifying a couple of feet off the ground and landing with a thump in a crouch.

Claiming Asylum

NICOLETTE SHOULD *NOT* have been corporeal again that quickly—but then, she was strengthened by chaos, too. Or maybe her freedom was just a parting gift from Jarrow.

Nicolette snatched up her silver hatchet with her one hand and snarled. Shit. Leaving a weapon like that in the dirt was an amateur mistake. Marla was off her game tonight. Fighting chaos personified could do that to a person.

Marla drew her knife. That hatchet had the look of an artifact. Was it stronger than her dagger? Would they mutually annihilate one another if they collided? If only she had time to look through her ring and see what the future would bring. She'd have to get that thing fitted into the lens of a pair of glasses or something—she could see the present with one eye and the future with another—but for now, Death's gift wasn't doing her much good.

Nicolette raised her axe. "Finally. Just you and me. That's all I wanted."

"Then why did you bring fifteen other fucking people?" Marla straightened her spine. She was tired, and worried, and she had a spot of rot at the core of her sense of identity, but she wasn't going to let *Nicolette* beat her.

Or so she hoped. Then again, the outlaw Jesse James had been shot in the back by a cowardly nobody. Anybody could kill anybody, if the circumstances were right.

"You didn't like being a cloud of gas?" Marla said, as they circled one another, weapons raised. "You're worth more as a fart in the wind than you are as a sorcerer. I can't believe you're running with Jarrow. Doesn't her company just make you realize how much you suck? It's like seeing a Little League shortstop playing in a game alongside Major Leaguers. It's not even funny. It's not even *embarrassing*. It's just sad for everybody."

"I usually like a little banter," Nicolette said. "But I'm so sick of listening to you, you can't imagine."

"Then why the hell did you travel five thousand miles to the *island* where I live?"

"Because I couldn't let you—fuck! No! No talking! Murdertime!" Nicolette raised the axe, its eerie silver glow growing brighter, and darted forward.

Marla sidestepped, and Nicolette didn't even try to correct her course. She just took three more steps, swayed, and fell forward on the sand, dropping her axe. A tiny feathered dart stuck out of the side of her neck.

Pelham came limping into the circle of lights, his houndstooth jacket torn at one sleeve and smudged with dirt. He held the hollow tube of a blowgun in one hand. "I'm sorry, Mrs. Mason. I was nearly captured, and had to conceal myself, but I came as quickly as I could."

Marla grabbed Pelham and hugged him. "You wonderful Anglophile you."

"What has become of Rondeau? And of your enemies? Are they thwarted?"

"Thwart*ish*," Marla said. "Jarrow and Crapsey took off, but they might be back. Some of the others are dead. I don't even know if my brother or the mystery villain were in the van. Did you get a headcount?"

"It was difficult, in the confusion," Pelham said. "I disabled their vehicle, but before I could take up a sniper position, Jarrow somehow transported herself behind me. It was not a form of teleportation I've seen before—she did not open a portal. She merely took a few steps, vanished, and reappeared. Perhaps she has an affinity for shadows? She put me in the care of that fiend Crapsey, and I escaped. Is Rondeau..."

"I was about to check on him. I think he's just knocked out. Go into the house and find the rope, the one braided from nine strands. It wouldn't hold Jarrow any more than a pair of handcuffs would hold me, but it's good enough to keep Nicolette bound until I figure out what the hell to do with her. Maybe Arachne can tell me what they do with dangerous outlaw sorcerers around here..."

"Of course, Mrs. Mason. If I may ask... what is our next move?"

"Fall back to the hotel," Marla said. "I've got some preparations made there, too. I'm not thinking that far ahead, though, Pelly—honestly, the fact that we're still alive, and haven't been turned into beehives or library paste or something, is a major coup."

While Pelham tied up Nicolette and secured her hatchet, Marla went in search of Rondeau. He was just starting to wake up, groaning, in the dirt. Crapsey hadn't dared kill him, fortunately—Rondeau was a psychic parasite, and if his body died, he'd just find another host to occupy. "This is the worst hangover, ever," Rondeau said as she helped him to his feet. "And I didn't even get to have any fun first."

Marla surveyed the area and chewed her lower lip thoughtfully. "Okay, let's gather up the traps that didn't get set off. We might need them later—and it would probably annoy the local kahunas if we left them here for tourists to stumble across."

As they carefully disabled the traps, Pelham said, "We did well, didn't we, Mrs. Mason? The strength of our enemies has been reduced greatly, and surely your old colleagues in Felport are on their way to apprehend Dr. Husch?"

Marla shook her head. "The only enemy that matters is Elsie Jarrow. The rest of them, I can deal with, even my brother. But Jarrow… there's no stopping her if she decides she wants to kill me. I'm not saying I miss the cloak, but… it would be handy to have right now. It might make the playing field remotely level. Without that… the only reason I'm still alive is because she enjoys playing with me. Maybe she'll get distracted by something shiny and leave me alone. If not… it doesn't matter how many of her pawns, confederates, and footsoldiers we put away. We're all doomed."

"The reason you're the leader," Rondeau said, "is because you give the best pep talks."

Crapsey puked in the bushes for a while, to Elsie's amusement. "Teleporting," he groaned. "I fucking hate it. It's no way for a man to travel."

"Luckily, you aren't a man—just a psychic bug in a man-suit!" Elsie wasn't even trying to keep a low profile—she was just standing beside a row of ornamental shrubberies, watching the horde of sorcerers, mercenaries, and miscellaneous expendable personnel swarming around the front of the towering edifice of the Blackwing Institute. "Come, Crapsey, I think I see the man in charge." She pointed to a towering man pacing back and forth in the horseshoe driveway.

"Huh. Is that Hamil?"

"I believe so." Elsie strolled across the lawn toward the Blackwing Institute, Crapsey at her heels. "Mr. Sorcerer, sir!" she shouted. "Perhaps I can be of some assistance?"

When he turned and saw them, the cigar fell out of his mouth, and he didn't even notice. He made a small gesture, and a dozen people dressed in everything from white leather jackets to leopardskin coats to red-and-black opera cloaks arrayed themselves behind him in a loose semi-circle. His apprentices or lieutenants, probably. Looked like last call on Halloween. Sorcerers had the weirdest sense of fashion.

Crapsey tried to hunch behind Elsie, which was tricky since he outweighed her by about sixty pounds. If the fireballs started flying, he'd take whatever protection he could get.

"May I help you?" Hamil's voice was deep, urbane, and so patient there was no indication he was in the midst of running a siege—or that he recognized Jarrow, though from his cigar-dropping reaction, he clearly had.

"Oh, heavens no, but I bet I can help you. You're trying to crack the un-crackable egg here, aren't you?" She nodded toward the high walls of Black-wing, a building that had started life as a mansion and become a fortress. "That's the problem with making a place strong enough to hold in all the naughty sorcerers. When they start running the asylum, it can be tricky to get *in*. You're looking at a months-long siege situation here. Those walls are tough, stone and spells in a perfect marriage. Believe me. I battered against them from the inside long enough to know." She held out her hand. "The name's Elsie Jarrow. I used to live in there."

"I won't shake your hand, if that's all right," Hamil said. "You have a reputation for a certain degree of… toxicity. Why have you come here?"

"To help you apprehend the villain, of course."

Hamil frowned. "Her principle crime was setting you *free*, Ms. Jarrow."

"I know! The irony, it burns. All I ask in return is: you take all her toys away and lock her in a deep dark hole somewhere."

"Something like that may be in order," Hamil said. "Assuming she was acting of her own free will, and was not magically compelled. Certainly we would be reluctant to let her oversee patients in the future."

"Oh, this is all Husch's gig. Her mind is broken like a hand-me-down toy. If I get her out of the building, are you prepared to subdue her? Like, instantly?"

"Oh, yes. We have pacification specialists on hand."

"Great! This'll just take a minute. Everybody be quiet, would you?" Elsie waved her hand—

—and the lawn was transformed into a holocaust of flame, smoking corpses strewn everywhere, vehicles overturned, and the stench of charred humanity thick in Crapsey's nostrils. He would have vomited again if he'd had anything left in his stomach. *Fuck.* How many times had he seen scenes exactly like this in the Mason's employ? How had ended up, once again, in the company of a lunatic who preferred to do murder in bulk?

Elsie picked up a smoke-blackened bullhorn from the grass, played with the buttons for a moment, then shouted through it: "Doctor Fugitive, come on out! I've gotten rid of the first wave for you, but you know sorcerers, they'll send another bunch in no time. Come out quick, and we'll get you to safety. But this is a limited-time offer." She tossed the megaphone onto a smoldering heap of dead apprentices.

The front door creaked open, and Dr. Husch stepped out. "Jarrow… you *killed* them."

"I know! I'm very useful. Now, hurry, before the Chamberlain sends another crew."

Husch passed through the doors, then came down the steps, shaking her head. "It wasn't supposed to happen this way. You were just supposed to kill Marla. And then—"

"And then go back into my cube like a good little mental patient, and you could pretend all this never happened? No, no, no."

She snapped her fingers, and the devastation vanished. Hamil, his apprentices, and the miscellaneous others milling on the lawn reappeared, unharmed. Crapsey's sense of relief was so profound he almost fell over. It was just an illusion, a trick to get Dr. Husch out into the open. Leda looked around in alarm, and started to reach for the chain at her throat, the one that held the golden key.

A woman with blue dreadlocks stepped forward, wielding a plastic toy wand with a star on the end, trailing pale grey streamers. She waved the wand, and Husch swayed, eyes drooping, and fell face-first onto the ground. Elsie crossed to her faster than the eye could follow and snatched the necklace from around her throat. Then she streaked into the building, leaving Hamil, Crapsey, and the rest of the sorcerers staring at the front door.

"I don't suppose she's going to check herself back in," Hamil said.

Crapsey shrugged. "I'd guess no. Dr. Husch had some kind of mojo leash on her, a way to trap her again if she misbehaved, but with Husch down, and her key gone…"

"You're wanted for high crimes against Felport," Hamil said. "Perhaps I should have you pacified."

"You can try, I guess. But Elsie's kind of fond of me, in a weird way. I'm not sure she'd like it."

The chaos witch strolled out the front door, smiling. She tossed a chunk of rock up in the air and caught it in the same hand. "This is a little piece of my old cell. I thought I'd keep it as a souvenir, after I destroyed the rest of that stinking cube."

"The necklace you stole," Hamil said. "If I may ask—what was it?"

"Oh, just a key," she said airily. "An artifact. The Doc used it as the central nexus for all her security protocols. She didn't think I knew about that, but she just doesn't understand how I see the world—every linkage, every connection, every pattern, they're all *right there* for me, clear as the jaw on Crapsey's face. I could see the chains spiraling out from this key, throughout the hospital, to all the other prisoners, to me…" She smiled widely, crushed the key in her hand, and let sprinkling golden dust shower down. "Oops. I think I just unlocked all the cells in there! And I'm not just talking about the doors. A thousand bindings just went 'poof,' and this heap is nothing but a mansion now, just bricks and wood and stone. I guess you'll be too busy rounding up the all the patients to bother with little old me, huh?"

"You will be captured, or killed, Ms. Jarrow," Hamil said, as his people raced into the Institute. "You're too dangerous to be allowed to wander free."

"Oh, if you bickering old witches and warlocks can team up, you might catch me—it's happened before. But that's okay. Think of all the fun I can have in the meantime! I'm chaos, Hamil, I'm *change*, and the biggest sucker bet in the world is to bet against change." She paused. "At least until the heat death of the universe. But we've got a little while before that happens. And, besides, there are always other universes. Bye bye!" She took Crapsey by the hand, and before he could even groan, pulled him through another ragged portal from here to somewhere else.

"Hamil. Nice to hear your voice." Marla paused, listening to the air conditioner hum in her quiet hotel room. "I missed you, you fat bastard, even if you did vote me off the island. Or, I guess, *on to* the island."

"I voted against having you beheaded," Hamil said. "Gaining concessions beyond that was too much even for my considerable powers of diplomacy. But the Council of Felport owes you a debt of gratitude for letting us know about Dr. Husch's betrayal."

"You pried Leda out of Blackwing already? How is she?"

"She is… unhappy. Vocally. And, no, I didn't pry her out. We had help. From Elsie Jarrow. We inadvertently helped her escape from Dr. Husch's control, I'm afraid."

"That explains why she ran away from me so fast," Marla said. "When she heard Husch was under seige, she saw an opportunity to free herself. Shit." She filled Hamil in on the events of her evening.

"Marla, I'm so sorry. I knew you had enemies, of course, but I didn't expect *this*, or I would have made sure you were sent into exile with protection—"

"Like the Polish Lancers who went to Elba with Napoleon, huh? No thanks. I'm my own honor guard, and anyway, I've got Rondeau and Pelham watching my back, and at least two gods, though I could live without those last ones. So… what are you going to do about Jarrow? She's a fugitive from your jurisdiction."

"I'd like to apprehend her," Hamil said. "Unfortunately, the Chamberlain disagrees—she thinks that, unless Jarrow menaces Felport, we shouldn't waste resources trying to catch her."

"That's pretty small-minded," Marla said. "It's probably the same decision I would have made, though. Out of sight, out of mind."

"Do you think Jarrow will return to Hawai'i?" Hamil asked.

Marla stretched out on the bed, looking up at the white ceiling. "Who can say? If tormenting me amuses her, she might. If she decides she has to save Nicolette from our clutches, ditto. But Jarrow's a chaos witch. They're unpredictable. I really don't know what's going to happen, but I'm preparing myself for bad outcomes. Still—worst case, she kills me. And so what? It's not like I'm doing anything down here in the islands anyway. Wasting my time, and wasting my life. There's no shame in being murdered by Jarrow, either. She's killed better people than me."

"Marla—"

"Don't mind me. I got my ass kicked by a werewolf hunter tonight. I'm just off my game. Is there anything else? I know you must be busy."

"It might be nothing, but… when we secured the Institute, two of the patients were missing. Besides Jarrow, I mean."

Marla swore. "You think Husch sicced more of her patients on me? Who is it? Nilson? Vaughn?"

"Gustavus Lupo is missing, but in the confusion, it's likely Lupo just took on the form of one of the fifty apprentices and mercenaries milling around, and blended in with the confusion. He'll turn up when his sense of identity begins to fragment. No, the one I'm concerned about… I think you called her 'Beta-Marla.' The version of yourself from that other reality, the one who was dominated by the cursed cloak. She's gone. Husch isn't very forthcoming about her actions, but, well…"

Marla closed her eyes. "Shit. I thought Jarrow was using a homunculus body or something, grown in a vat in the basement under the Institute, but… she took over that body, didn't she? The Mason's body. *My* body."

"It's possible. The magical safeguards on her flesh would make for a very tempting vessel, better than any other I could think of."

"Huh. This just got personal, didn't it? That body doesn't even look like me much anymore. Jarrow's making my image over into her own. Can't say I like that. And hasn't that poor thing suffered enough?"

"Marla, please, be careful—"

"Goodbye, Hamil. You were a good friend to me, but that was in another life. Take care of yourself." She ended the call, turned off the phone, threw the phone under the bed, stared at the ceiling, and thought about what could have happened to her, in another life.

Captivities

THE LITTLE GUY GROANED from the back seat, where he was trussed up and covered with a blanket. Jason tried to ignore the noises as he drove along the highway toward the cabin Christian had booked for them to use as a base of operations. The SUV ran more smoothly now than it had before the tires got popped—Jarrow had patched them up magically, somehow. He didn't trust magic, but they hadn't given him much choice. He considered cutting the little guy loose and driving to the airport, but Jarrow had found him in his trailer in Mississippi, and he was pretty sure she'd be able to find him anywhere else he ran. Better to play this thing out, and hope he landed on his feet when it was all over.

The guy in the back said, "Hello? Who is driving, please?"

"Keep quiet," Jason said. "I'm trying to think."

"My name is Pelham," the little guy said, like Jason didn't know that. "May I ask where you're taking me?" His tone was polite, reasonable, and not even a little bit terrified. Jason had driven a few cars with guys tied up in the back seat, or in the trunk, over the years, and none of them had sounded this cool when they talked. You had to admire the guy's guts.

"Don't worry. I'm just supposed to keep you on ice for a little while."

"You work for Elsie Jarrow, the chaos witch?"

"I don't work for anybody but me," Jason said, knowing how hollow that must sound. "I'm working *with* Jarrow, all right?"

A moment of silence, and then a dry chuckle, muffled by the blanket but still audible. "You are Marla Mason's brother, aren't you? Jason."

Christ. "So what if I am?"

"May I sit up? I promise not to cause you any difficulties. I would not wish to get you in trouble with Ms. Jarrow. She seems a formidable woman." Without waiting for an answer, Pelham levered himself upright, the blanket half-falling off his body. Jason glanced at him in the rearview. His hair was mussed and sticking up in all directions, making him look like a little boy just awake from a nap. He was handcuffed, and shackled, and tied with a weird rope of Jarrow's own devising, one that twisted and squirmed like a snake. "You've certainly gone to some trouble to tie me up," Pelham said. "I'm not even a sorcerer, you know."

"Jarrow said you're an escape artist, though. She told me you don't have much in the way of actual magic, but that you know a whole lot about a whole lot of other things."

"I have some small expertise in escapeology," Pelham acknowledged. "But my lockpicks have been taken, it seems, and these bonds are ensorcelled. I am amply contained. But Mrs. Mason will be worried about me, you know. She'll come find me. She—"

"She doesn't know you're gone, Jeeves. We've got a guy, Lupo, who can make himself look like anybody. A perfect imposter. God, the scams I could run with a guy like that, too bad he's batshit crazy... anyway, *he's* being you right now. He's not even faking it, exactly—he thinks he really *is* you. I was all for putting a bullet in your head and leaving you back there at the park, but Jarrow says Lupo can do a better job imitating you if you're still alive."

"A passive psychic link," Pelham murmured. "How very unpleasant." He sighed. "At least if Lupo believes his own delusion, he doesn't pose a threat to Marla."

"Until Jarrow makes him think he's the Green River Killer or something, sure. You take comfort in that."

"If I may ask—why do you harbor such antipathy toward Marla?"

Jason wasn't in the mood to spill his guts to his sister's footman, or whatever the fuck this guy was. "We've got history. I did everything for her, and when push came to shove, she wasn't there for me. So I don't owe her anything anymore."

"She was very young," Pelham said, almost gently. "I think you would find her a loyal and indefatigable ally now."

Jason shook his head. "Too late for that. I tried to kill her. She tried to kill me. I tried to kill her friend Rondeau, though I guess he survived. Fucking magic. She *did* kill my partner, Danny Two Saints. Jarrow came to me, told me she could give me peace of mind, that I could help her get rid of Marla, so I could stop looking over my shoulder—"

"Marla wasn't coming for you, Mr. Mason. She is, I think, more sad than angry, when she thinks about you, and what's happened between you."

"Why should I believe you?"

"Don't you think she could have found you easily if she'd tried? Those who understand magic have ways of hiding from one another, but you know nothing of such secrets. She could have traced you, gone after you, with trivial ease. She did not. You should not have become involved in this."

"Too late to do anything about that now," Jason said. "I threw the dice. Now I just have to hope it doesn't come up boxcars."

"Is it true you're a confidence trickster, Mr. Mason?"

"I've made my living a lot of ways. But sure, I've spent some time on the grift."

"I don't understand why you would choose a life that revolves around hurting people," Pelham said. "I am not a religious man—I've met too many gods to be comfortable worshipping them—but I do believe there's truth in the saying that the wages of sin are death."

Jason snorted. "The wages of sin are death, sure. But so are the wages of everything else, eventually. And in the short run, the wages of grifting are *money*. Not to mention the pleasure of knowing you put one over on some sucker, or some jerk who thought they were putting one over on *you*. They say you can't cheat an honest man. That's not true, but it's a lot easier to cheat a dishonest one. The world is shit, Pelham. Most people are just *pieces* of shit. The best you can hope to be is an insect, feeding off the shit. At least then you can fly."

"You certainly have a way with colorful metaphor, Mr. Mason."

"Don't I know it. I was always the creative one in my family."

Crapsey and Elsie stepped out of the portal not far from the little beach cottage Christian had reserved for them, back before he got turned into frogs. The rented SUV was parked beside the house, hidden by the shadows of the night, and a light glowed in one of the windows, which meant Jason and his prisoner were probably inside.

Elsie took a deep breath of the warm, flower-scented air. "I love this place. Don't you?"

Since he was busy trying not to puke again, Crapsey limited himself to a grunt. He bent over and took a few breaths to get his stomach under control before straightening.

Elsie slung her arm around his shoulder. "Maybe you and I should stay here, huh? After all this business is done? Just for a while. I mean, all these volcanoes! Talk about a volatile situation. I mean, they aren't volatile *enough*, they're all pretty dormant except the one on the Big Island, but I could do something about that..."

They were alone together, and Elsie was clearly feeling cheerful, so Crapsey decided to broach a subject he'd been thinking about. "Uh, so, Elsie. I was thinking, you're probably the most powerful sorcerer I've ever met, maybe the most powerful in the world—"

"Oh, now, that's sweet of you, but really, I'm probably only in the top ten right now. But since I'm free of Husch's chains, I can really get to work, stir up some disasters, get my powers back. Check back with me in a few months, though, and I might deserve that compliment." She spun away from him, doing a little twirl with her arms outstretched and her head thrown back. "Freedom! Freedom, Crapsey! Is there a more beautiful concept?"

"Freedom's something I've been thinking about myself. You know how I got that spell cast on me, trapping me in this body. It's pretty shitty, boss. Terrifying, even, because if this body dies, there's no reason to think my consciousness will die with it. I could be stuck inside my own corpse forever…" He shuddered.

"Hardly forever! You'll rot like anybody, and since the spell is particular to that body you're wearing, you'll be free once it's entirely decomposed. Now, that means you have to avoid being buried in a coffin, because, brother, those things take *forever* to break down. You want to go all natural, ideally near as many scavenging animals and flesh-devouring insects as possible. You know, I'd say go for cremation, but there are always unburned bone fragments, and you'd have to wait for those to break down entirely too, which is way slower if you're in an urn somewhere. I mean, we're talking the rise and fall of civilizations long. No, you want to get buried in a hole, somewhere nice and hot and moist—ha, no dirty jokes now—what I'm saying is, tropical. You'll be free in a decade or two. Or three or four. I'm not sure how long it takes bones to break down and become basically undifferentiated from minerals. Now, a lot of people hate you, though admittedly most of them don't live in this universe, but still, someone could really fuck with you, take extraordinary steps to preserve your skeleton, and in that case, you're in trouble, so I'd advocate dying alone in a jungle—"

Crapsey cleared his throat. "I could go that way. I mean, that's good advice. No doubt. Or, maybe, I don't know, you could… set me free?"

Elsie cocked her head. "Are you asking me for a favor?"

"I guess I am. Is that a bad idea?"

"One of the worst! I'm a genie who just got her bottle broken to bits, Crapsey. I could do just about anything, after all. But, you know… I don't think so. I think I want you to stay trapped in your own bottle for now."

Crapsey sighed. Life was disappointment. "Why? I thought you liked me."

"Oh, I do! I do like you, and usually the kindest feeling I can generate toward anybody is plain old indifference. Consider yourself blessed."

"Okay, but… think of the chaos I could cause, if I had my old powers back."

Elsie put her hands on his shoulders and looked into his eyes. He was glad it was dark out here—her eyes could be disconcerting, so bright, so merry, so full of depths. "Your powers, let's be clear, involve leaving your body and taking over the bodies of others, destroying their souls in the process. Then you abandon their bodies, leaving them brain-dead husks. Right?"

"Pretty much. So you've got, like... a moral objection?" Crapsey was aware of right and wrong the way a color-blind person is aware of the full color spectrum: via secondhand explanations. Any conscience he'd once possessed had been utterly burned out of him during his years as the Mason's lieutenant, when atrocities became casual.

"Heavens, no! Like I said, for most people, I can barely even muster feelings of indifference. No, Crapsey, the problem is, you could be a living genocide if you really got going. You could be a one-man pandemic. And with every soul you destroyed, and every body you dropped, you'd leave the world a little less *complicated*. Me? I like complicated. I want more people, with all their tiny little drives and urges and strivings crashing up against one another. The brain-dead do nothing for me. So, no, sweetie, you just hang tight. If you get *really* desperate you can always dunk your body in a big vat of acid until it's totally dissolved."

"I hate pain," Crapsey said morosely. "Like, I hate it a *lot*."

"Those who've inflicted a lot of pain on others often do." Elsie patted his cheek. "Don't be pouty. You could live a long time in that body, and you've got that wonderful jaw! You could eat the world with that jaw! And I might change my mind. You never know. I do that. For now, let's go see how Jason's doing, shall we? I need him to call his sister for me tomorrow."

"Yeah. What are you going to do about Marla?"

"I think it would be fun to let *Marla* decide that," Elsie said. "But I think I'll let her get some sleep first, so she's not too cranky, and the same goes for you and the other remainders of the Marla Mason Revenge Squad. And our hostage. I want everyone well-rested and perky. There's plenty of time to decide Marla's fate over brunch."

"Nicolette tried to bite me," Rondeau said. "I was just offering her a Danish, you know how great the pastries are in that little cafe downstairs? She nearly took my finger off. So I, uh, psychiced her. Squeezed her brain right to sleep. I didn't even know I could *do* that, I just reached into her mind and felt around a little until I found the sleepy bit, and I gave it a little tweak, and, conk. She's snoring now." He yawned and poured Marla a cup of coffee from an oversized French press. They were out on Marla's balcony, overlooking the dolphin lagoon.

"She's still tied up in the bathtub?" Marla sipped. Kona coffee, black. That was one thing about life on the islands that she couldn't find even a speck of fault with.

"Yeah, with a bunch of pillows around her because I'm not a dick. Pelly's watching her. Your soundproofing spell is holding fine. We can't even hear her yell unless we're in there with her trying to brush our teeth or whatever, which is why we slipped in to use *your* shower this morning.

"I noticed."

"It's not like you to sleep later than... well, anybody. Roosters, early birds, worms, guys who work the night shift, you usually beat all of them."

Marla shrugged. "You're always telling me I need to learn to relax."

Rondeau frowned. "True, but maybe not when a crazy chaos magician is trying to kill you?"

"If Jarrow wants me dead, I'm dead. I don't have any more chance than the dinosaurs did against that asteroid. I can't even hurt her, let alone fight her." She took another sip of coffee. Good thing Rondeau had never learned to tell when she was lying. There *was* a way she could hurt Jarrow, she'd learned that when she talked to Hamil the night before, but it was a case of the cure being worse than the disease, and in the end, it wouldn't make any difference. Because: "Even if I took Nicolette's magic axe and put it in the hands of a god like Reva, and he managed to chop Jarrow's head off, so what? She doesn't *need* a body. It's possible that being in a body is actually making her less crazy. Hamil said she seemed sane, and it's not like she's rampaging around turning whole shopping malls into frogs."

"No, just one guy at a time. That's super comforting. So we just wait?"

"Traps are laid. Defenses are set. What else can we do?"

"Usually 'go on the offensive,' is your answer to that," Rondeau said. "Aren't you the woman who literally invaded *Hell* last summer?"

Marla grimaced. "No, Rondeau. I'm not that woman. That woman was the chief sorcerer of Felport, acting in defense of her city. In case you haven't noticed, I don't *have* a city anymore. There's not even a reason for me to get out of bed at all these days. Which is why I didn't get up this morning, until you came and poked me in the arm."

"Right, no reason at all. Except, oh, what's it called—self-preservation?"

Marla pushed her cup aside. "I didn't go to Jarrow with my head bowed and wait for death last night. I *am* fighting. I just wonder, sometimes, what I'm fighting for."

"Marla—" Rondeau's phone rang. He raised an eyebrow, and Marla nodded. Probably it was just his masseur on Maui calling to ask why he'd missed yesterday's appointment—

"Wow," Rondeau said. "I didn't expect to hear from you. I'm doing fine, thanks, totally recovered from the whole getting-shot-by-you thing. Oh, but you don't want to walk down memory lane with me. Let me get your sister." He handed over the phone. "Hello, Jason," Marla said.

"Marla. I've, ah, got a message for you. From Elsie Jarrow."

"I thought you had bad taste in friends before, but you've really outdone yourself this time. You never cease to impress."

He sounded a little shaky when he replied, but with Jason, no show of emotion was remotely trustworthy. She wasn't sure he even had emotions, apart from maybe envy and contempt. "Listen, sis, I didn't have a lot of choice. I wasn't so much recruited as kidnapped, and I still don't know what the fuck I'm doing here with witches and warlocks and guys with creepy wooden jaws. Mostly I've just been driving them around and waiting for them to get bored with me."

"Or kill you," Marla said. "That's just as likely. Maybe more so."

"You sure know how to raise a guy's spirits. But, look—I'm calling to tell you *nobody* has to die. Jarrow wants to meet with you, and talk things over. No tricks, no fussing or fighting."

"Ha. Fine. Where?"

"There's supposed to be a great buffet in that resort where you're staying," Jason said. "How about she meets you there for brunch in an hour?"

"Just me and her, alone?"

"I'm not coming, if that's what you're asking. Our tearful reunion will have to wait." There was some background noise, and then muffled noises as if Jason was covering the phone, and then he returned. "Oh, Jarrow wants to know if you've got Nicolette, or if she's still just a fart in the woods, whatever the fuck that means."

"I've got her," Marla said. "She's not hurt."

Jason relayed that. "Okay," he said. "Thanks."

"What, no demands that I release her?"

"Jarrow says if having a hostage makes you feel better, that's cool. One hour at the buffet. If you get there first, order coffee for her." He hung up, and Marla handed the phone back to Rondeau, telling him the deal.

"Normally meeting in public is a good idea," Rondeau said. "It keeps people on good behavior. But this is *Jarrow*. What if she just, like... kills everybody?"

"Then get a message to Arachne, and mobilize the kahunas against her," Marla said. "Put her in touch with Hamil, too—he was part of the team that caught Jarrow the first time, though he was nothing but an apprentice at the time. He might have some pointers."

"How *did* they catch her?" Rondeau asked.

Marla shrugged. "I was prepubescent at the time, living in Indiana. I don't know all the details. I just know it took a lot of resources. Ask Pelham— he's a walking history of Felport."

"Maybe I'll get him to tell me for my bedtime story tonight, since you're making us share a room," Rondeau said.

"Assuming you'll live until bedtime," Marla replied. "Aren't you the optimist?"

Breaking Bread

MARLA ARRIVED AT THE HOTEL'S the open-air breakfast buffet, wondering how often the birds fluttering around shat on people's omelets. She told the hostess she needed a table for two. Pelham was lurking around somewhere, keeping an eye on things to make sure Jarrow didn't bring an entourage. Rondeau was on Nicolette duty, and Marla just hoped he'd remembered to put the "Do Not Disturb" sign on the doorknob. If some poor housekeeper discovered they had a woman tied up in a bathtub, things could get awkward.

Jarrow breezed in a few minutes after Marla was seated, all smiles and cheerfully waving, dressed like a wealthy tourist from the mainland in a red sundress and lots of chunky gold jewelry and too much lipstick. Marla stood up, and Jarrow embraced her and air-kissed her cheeks. "Darling, you look tired!"

"I didn't get much sleep last night, Jarrow."

"Please, call me Elsie! I didn't sleep, but then, I never do, it cuts into my me-time, you know. I realize we have a lot to talk about, but I'm dying for something to eat. I don't actually *need* food, I subsist on other energies, but I love a good buffet—ooh, there's an omelet station!" She hurried over toward the long tables of savories and sweets.

Marla unobtrusively slipped Death's ring from her finger and peered through the circle as the witch filled up a plate with eggs and bacon and fruit. The future didn't appear to hold any surprise attacks, just Jarrow getting food and coming back to the table and talking. The ring didn't provide audio, and Marla wasn't much of a lipreader, so she didn't know what Jarrow was saying. She put the ring away. She'd find out soon enough.

When Jarrow returned, she reached across the table and took Marla's hand. Looking at her up close, Marla could see the underlying structure of

Jarrow's face, and it *was* Marla's own, though it was clearly being altered from the inside. Still, they could have been sisters, once you looked beyond the fiery red hair and make-up on Jarrow. "My dear," Jarrow said, "let there be no more conflict between us. I was hired to do a distasteful job, and now that my employer is no longer in a position to give me orders, well! Why should I bother you any longer?"

Marla frowned and pulled her hand away. "So you're just going to let it drop? No more murder or torment?"

"You understand me perfectly."

"Then why did you even come here? Why not just leave the island?"

Jarrow raised one eyebrow. "Marla Mason. I told you I did a tiny bit of research on you before I came on this mission. You're a fairly formidable person. In the past few years you've vanquished the Beast of Felport, outsmarted the time-traveling first chief sorcerer of the city—don't worry, I won't tell anyone it's really Malkin, it's cute how you made everyone think he was just some crazy guy—sent the king of elves back to his hideous little dimension, killed a resurrected Aztec god, dispelled the king of nightmares, and fought the incarnation of *Death*. Am I missing anything?"

"Lots of things, actually," Marla said. "But I guess those are some of the highlights."

"And what highlights they are! You don't look like much, forgive me for saying so, but I think you *could* make my life unpleasant, if you wanted to. You still have some powerful friends, even if you're reluctant to call on them. Why didn't you summon your friend Genevieve, by the way, the reweaver? She would have made this thing between us into a real fight."

"Against *you*? Genevieve's mind isn't all that stable, and she can alter reality with a thought—she shut herself away in a private bubble-universe because she worried about how she might mess up this world. She contains the potential for incomprehensible chaos. Throwing her at you would be like trying to douse a fire with kerosene—you'd end up using her power to make yourself stronger."

"Drat," Jarrow said. "I was afraid you'd actually thought it through. Oh well. You're a fighter, Marla, and you have a distressing tendency to *accomplish* things. You've got the one quality that's indispensable to a sorcerer: an iron will. The kind of will that says, 'I will change the world, and I will not be changed.' So I thought it best to come visit you, and formally declare an end to hostilities, and break bread together." Jarrow tore a macadamia nut muffin in half and offered a chunk to Marla, who accepted it, but didn't eat.

"If you think I could be a threat to you... why not kill me? Just to be on the safe side?"

Jarrow smiled warmly. "Why, what a cold arithmetic, Marla! I want you to live because you make the world a more interesting place. Despite your best efforts to restore things to maintain a status quo and prevent upheaval in Felport, you're an agent of turmoil. You prompted a regime change in *Hell*, Marla. You tore a big hole right in the fabric of reality and let terrible things from a dread dimension pour into this world. Thanks for that, by the way—I'm quite fond of Crapsey. You're a destabilizing force for chaos, and the adorable thing is, you think you're a force for order."

Marla shook her head. "Maybe that was true once, Elsie, but I'm not a force for anything anymore." She sighed. "But... I still try to do the right thing. And my problem is, you did bad stuff, last time you were free. It took a coalition of dozens of sorcerers from up and down the East Coast to contain you. You were a walking, talking cancer cluster. If I don't try to stop you, what am I unleashing on the world?"

Jarrow put her chin in her hand and regarded Marla seriously. "Is that... altruism? How strange. I keep meaning to try that someday—being a do-gooder for a while. Listen, Marla. Those were dark times. I wasn't entirely aware of what I was doing. My original body was ravaged by tumors. I held myself together physically through sheer force of will, but I couldn't shut out the pain without shutting off *all* sensation, so my options were utter agony or the feeling of floating in a sensory deprivation tank all the time. Neither one was good for my mental health. You have to understand, I'm not really insane—I just had a nervous breakdown, lost my handle on my powers, and... yes, people died. I know that. I've been locked in a cube for years, and for some of that time, I didn't have a body at *all*, I was so low on power I couldn't save my physical form from the tumors that consumed it. Being bodiless for long periods of time will mess you up, Marla, especially if you're a bon vivant like me. But now." She sat back and gestured at herself modestly. "I'm in a young, strong, *incredibly* well-safeguarded body. No more bad craziness in my head. Don't worry about me. Besides, practically speaking, how could you *stop* me? I mean, yes, theoretically, I won't discount the possibility—but it wouldn't be easy for you, and it wouldn't be quick."

Marla disagreed. She had a pretty good idea how she could stop Jarrow. She'd figured out the first part last night, and had woken with an inspiration for the second part. But the cost was extreme, and if she didn't *need* to do it... maybe Jarrow was lying. But maybe she was telling the truth. She was definitely weird, but she didn't seem particularly out-of-control now. Last night had been weird and ugly, but it was a duel between sorcerers—those tended to be unpleasant. Jarrow wouldn't be the only unpredictable, dangerous sorcerer in the world. And why did she have to be Marla's problem anyway? Jarrow hadn't escaped from Blackwing under *Marla's* watch. Marla didn't even have a watch anymore. If Jarrow didn't pose a clear and present danger to Marla herself, or to anyone she cared about… "I guess you have a point," Marla said.

"Truce, then?" Jarrow said.

"Until you give me a reason to decide otherwise."

"Then eat your damn muffin," Jarrow said. "Symbolism is important."

Marla took a bite, chewed, swallowed. "How's my brother Jason?"

"Surly. I see a family resemblance."

"Can you tell him I don't mean him any harm anymore? I'll leave him alone if he leaves me alone?"

"Hmm. Maybe? I'll think about it. Doesn't sound very interesting, though."

That was probably the best she could hope for. "You've decided not to try and kill me, but what about the rest of your merry band?"

"Oh, the hired guns will wander off. The ones with a personal grudge… well, there's Crapsey, I would imagine you can handle him if he gets obstreperous. And Nicolette, but you've got her, right?"

"Tied up in a bathroom. I'd like to get rid of her, by the way."

Jarrow gestured vaguely westward. "There's a whole big ocean out there you could drown her in."

"I don't go in for casual murder, or pre-emptive self-defense, either. But it would be nice if she left me alone."

"Tell you what," Jarrow said. "I'll see if Crapsey wants her back. Maybe he'll trade Nicolette's freedom for his good behavior? You can't trust him, and they'll betray you, but…" She shrugged. "It's just Nicolette and Crapsey. Knock them out and stick them on a banana boat to the mainland, and they won't bother you for a while." Jarrow leaned in and whispered conspiratorially, "Nicolette's afraid of teleporting."

"She did get her arm ripped off that way," Marla said.

Jarrow rolled her eyes. "Such a little drama queen. She lost one arm. Big deal. She's got *another* one."

"Can I ask you something? What keeps you going? I mean… what's your purpose?"

Jarrow leaned back and regarded Marla seriously. "Wow. I didn't have you pegged as the philosopher type. What's the meaning of life? Whatever meaning you give it, sweetums. I like seeing the world, meeting new people, and feeling the thrum of impossible energies filling my body. I'm basically a proponent of straight-up hedonism."

"My friend Rondeau's the same way. But for me… that's never been enough."

"Take up knitting, or join the Society for Creative Anachronism, or get into exotic animal rescue. You're retired now, right? Get a hobby."

"A hobby? Elsie, I used to have a *mission*."

"So find one of those." Jarrow shrugged. "The world's full of shit. If that bothers you, don't just bitch about it. Grab a shovel and get to work." She grinned. "People like me will help make sure there's always more poop for you to scoop."

When Marla got back to her room, Death was waiting for her, sitting in the armchair by the sliding glass door to the balcony.

"You just let yourself in, did you?"

"Death can go anywhere, Marla. That's sort of the point. I've seen the future—and your death is no longer imminent. Neither is Jason's, or Nicolette's."

Marla sat down on the edge of the bed. "You don't seem too thrilled about that."

"For obvious reasons. But you don't seem very happy, either, which surprises me."

"For a little while there, I had some adrenaline pumping, I was having fun, but… a truce over brunch? It's kind of anticlimactic. I always hated the diplomacy parts of my job the most."

"Tell me, Marla—did you discover the secret of the ring?"
"Look through it, see the future. Kind of nifty, I guess. I haven't told Rondeau about it. He'd beg me to borrow it so he could find a horse race to bet on. Like he doesn't have enough money already."

"I'm sure it's less about the money, and more about the thrill," Death said. "I'd think you could relate."

"Ha."

"Did you look at Jarrow through the ring?"

"Sure. I got to see her scoop eggs onto a plate whole *seconds* before she actually did it."

Death frowned. "The ring can do rather more than give you glimpses of the immediate, Marla. If you focus on the *person* you're watching, and let the surroundings blur, you can see farther—a view of the most likely long-term future for that individual, unfolding in a rapid flow, and by paying attention in just the right way, you can slow down and focus on particular moments. It's quite a powerful artifact." That last bit was rather peevish.

"Right. Sorry. It's a beautiful ring, and… I can see how it would be very useful."

"Perhaps, if you have the opportunity, you should look at Jarrow through it *again*."

Marla didn't like the sound of that. "Why?"

"You might see something that… makes you rethink your agreement."

"Shit. You're saying she's going to betray me?"

Death shook his head. "Not that, not exactly, but… she is a force for chaos, Marla. She is a carrion beetle that feeds on death."

"So? It's none of my business."

"Really? Well. Sometimes things get big enough that they *become* your business, whether you like it or not." He stood up. "I should be off. But one other thing. If, in the future, you have something to say to me—just say it. You don't need to send a messenger."

"I have no idea what in the earthly fuck you're talking about."

Death's expression became thoughtful. "Ah. I may have misjudged… if you don't know what I mean, never mind. I was mistaken."

"Hold on, what are you—"

"Marla!" Rondeau burst in through the connecting door. "I offered Nicolette the bathroom like ten times, but she just crapped herself and now she's laughing and rolling around in the tub—" He stopped short. "Oh. Uh. Hi, Mr., uh."

"Rondeau," Death said, voice chilly. He pulled open a door that shouldn't have been on the wall and stepped through. The door sort of sidled away and vanished after he closed it.

"What did he want?" Rondeau said. "Did I interrupt a godly booty-call?"

"Not exactly. He's pretty bummed I'm not going to die anytime soon."

A look of guilt flashed across Rondeau's face. Marla had seen that expression on him before lately. She didn't ask—he probably had lots of things to feel guilty about.

But Rondeau said, "Marla, I should tell you… I mean, it doesn't matter *now*, but… Death made me an offer, back in Lahaina."

"What kind of offer?"

"Everything I've ever dreamed of," Rondeau said. "And all I had to do in return was… stand aside and let you die. He didn't ask me to *kill* you, he just said, if it looked like you were about to get killed, if I didn't do anything, if I didn't try to *save* you, he'd reward me. I was never going to *do* it, but I didn't want to tell you, didn't want to distract you when you were in a fight for your life, but if things are cool now—"

Marla blinked. The bottom had dropped out of her stomach. "Fucking *gods*," she said.

That's when Reva knocked on the door and called, "Anyone home?"

The ropes holding Pelham hostage were unpredictable in nature: they moved, they writhed, they tightened—but they also loosened. And whenever they did loosen, Pelham shifted his body incrementally to take advantage, sliding the ropes down, edging ever closer to freedom… for what it was worth. Escaping from the ropes would take hours—but he seemed to have ample time, as they'd stuck him in a closet in a bungalow overnight and well into the morning. He was one good twist away from being loose, though what he would do *after* getting loose was an open question.

Elsie Jarrow was gone to some mysterious meeting, and moments ago Crapsey had loudly announced that he was going to take a walk because Jason kept cheating at cards, which Jason denied rather mildly. Pelham wasn't sure what Jason was doing out there. If he was napping, Pelham could escape. If he was watching the closet diligently... Pelham was fairly sure he had a gun. But two of his three captors were out of the room. When would he get a better opportunity? He—

Something moved by Pelham's foot. He squinted in the dimness of the closet—the door was slatted, allowing in some light, so it wasn't entirely black inside—and saw the carpet tear apart as a cone-shaped mound grew up through the floor. From beyond the door, Jason swore, and there was a thump, like a chair falling over.

The Nuno were coming. Pelham's curse—and, in this case, potentially his salvation. Just then the ropes went briefly slack as they slithered around his body, and Pelham slipped his hands free and tore the ropes from his ankles. Jason shouted outside, and Pelham slid the closet door open just as the first cat-sized, chittering monstrosity emerged from the hole beside his feet. He ran out into the room, where Jason was whirling around, one Nuno clinging to his arm, another trying to climb his pants leg. Pelham quickly scanned the room and caught sight of a cell phone on the bedside table. He leapt over the bed, snatched up the phone, and ran for the door. "No, stop, Goddamnit!" Jason yelled. "What the fuck! I thought you weren't a sorcerer!"

Pelham didn't bother to explain the situation. He found Jason Mason a most unpleasant man, and hoped the Nuno would find him sufficiently entertaining to avoid pursuing Pelham. He opened the door, looked out briefly to make sure Crapsey wasn't in sight, and started running. The bungalow was close to the beach, surrounded by verdant trees, quite idyllic, really, if he wasn't too busy running for his life to enjoy the view. A dirt track led off to the east, and Pelham ran into the woods parallel to the track, trying to move swiftly but not too loudly. Woodcraft was not one of his greatest strengths; he'd studied the subject, but mostly on the grounds of the Chamberlain's estate, which were not particularly wild. After he'd gone a few hundred yards from the house, and could no longer hear Jason shouting, he paused briefly in the shadow of a great tree to dial Rondeau's number.

"You again," Rondeau said. "Not that I don't love talking to you, Jason, but—"

"Rondeau! This is Pelham. I was abducted by Jarrow, and replaced with an imposter, a shapechanger named Lupo. This Lupo is wearing my face, but he *is not me*. I have escaped my captors and stolen their phone, but I am unsure of my location." It occurred to him that the phone probably had GPS, so he said, "Just a moment, I will try to ascertain my whereabouts."

"Pelly, wait, what the—"

"Drop the phone, butler boy." Crapsey appeared from the direction of the road, his face a welter of red scratches. "Those little shits you summoned were *nasty*. Elsie would approve. Definitely an eruption of the irrational. But come along home like a good little hostage."

Pelham slipped the phone into his pocket, cracked his neck, and took a stance. "I look forward to the opportunity to repay you for your impertinence," he said.

Crapsey cocked his head. "You're a fighter, footman?"

"I am skilled in many martial arts. I gather you are not."

"Nah, I usually get by on the strength of my winning personality." Crapsey grinned, and the illusion that made his grotesque wooden jaw appear normal faded away. The jaw was inlaid with strange traceries of gold. "But I do have some other resources. Now let me see, I was trying some of the trigger words earlier this morning, and I found a really great one I'd never used before—let's see: 'dysmenorrhea.'"

Pelham frowned. "A troubling condition, I'm sure, but not one that seems applicable to our current—"

Crapsey lowered his head, and his whole body trembled. His arms stretched out, growing beyond the ends of his sleeves, and his fingers and nails elongated into oversized claws. His spine curved as he hunched forward, and his wooden jaw swelled, jutting out in a profound underbite, with railroad-spike sized teeth bursting up through the wood. His eyes began to glow green, and in general he took on a profoundly bestial aspect, the stink of sulfur puffing out with his every exhalation. "Gonna—get—you," the beast growled, and reached out with those impossibly long arms.

Pelham ran. Crapsey ran faster.

An Exchange of Prisoners

"**Reva, get out of here**," Marla said, standing in the doorway. "I could have actually used your help last night, but you were nowhere to be seen." She looked him up and down. "You look like crap."

The god's hair was sticking up in all directions, and he was streaked with soot and ashes, his clothes so filthy he looked like he'd gone crawling through a volcano's cinder cone. "I should," he said. "I didn't want to give up my body—I always get so attached to my bodies—so I went to the underworld the hard way. The only local entrance to your boyfriend's realm is in a cave way too close to a volcano. It's dark and ugly down there, too, took me forever to find the landlord. Your husband is a pain in the ass, Marla. I just wanted to have a civil conversation with the guy, tell him to lay off with the enthusiasm about you dying, and he threw me out—"

Marla stepped back. "You *what*? You went to talk to Death? About me?"

Reva smiled. "No need to thank me. Like I said, you're one of my people, and I thought, as one god talking to another—admittedly much more powerful—god, I might be able to make an impression."

Marla gripped the edge of the doorframe to keep from punching him. "*Thank* you? Who the fuck do you think you are? You went and had a talk with my boyfriend, without asking me? You think I can't take care of myself? You condescending, patronizing shitheap, who the hell appointed you my guardian—" Reva shrank back under her onslaught, but before she could really work up any steam, Rondeau tapped her on the shoulder.

"Marla."

"In a minute."

"*Marla*."

"Rondeau, I'm about to ream out a god, what is it?"

"Pelham. He just called. Jarrow kidnapped him. He tried to escape, but—it sounded like they caught him again."

Marla turned and stared at him. "What are you talking about? Pelham is next door. He's been here all morning…" She trailed off. The seventh member of Jarrow's crew. The one they'd seen in the office video, but hadn't ever identified. It was Gustavus Lupo. Lupo hadn't escaped during the raid on the Blackwing Institute. Lupo was *here*, impersonating—

The connecting door opened, and Pelham stepped in. "Miss Nicolette is clean again. I now have a greater appreciation for the efforts of zookeepers. I do hope we can find a more permanent placement for her soon." He looked at Rondeau, Marla, and Reva, his amiable expression changing to bafflement. "Is something wrong? Has something happened?"

"Get Jason on the phone, Rondeau," Marla said. "*Now.*"

"I was going to let him *go*," Elsie said into Pelham's phone. "Honestly, Marla, I'd forgotten I even *had* him."

Crapsey hadn't hurt Pelham too badly when he chased him down, but the valet had sustained some bruises and scratches, and was currently unconscious, put to sleep by Elsie's magic. The chaos witch had laughed and laughed when she arrived to find Crapsey carrying Pelham over his shoulder and Jason stomping on the little ant-monsters that came crawling out of the carpet. She'd dispelled the beasts—she called them "Nunus" or something, Crapsey wasn't sure—with a wave of her hand, knocked Pelham out, and said, "Just hand me the phone when Marla calls, Jason."

So he had. "I'm *absolutely* amenable to an exchange of hostages. You bring Nicolette, and I'll bring the real Pelham. Though, really, Lupo is just as good—better! All the qualities of the actual Pelham, and capable of turning into anyone else you need, too. Admittedly, Lupo's a bit tricky to control, probably too advanced for you, but—no? The real Pelham? You're sure? Fine, fine. Where shall we meet? We'll be there in, say, three hours. I *do* hope this doesn't cause any problems with our arrangement, Marla. I had Pelham abducted and replaced last night, when things were still… tense between us. You understand. Kiss kiss. See you soon." She handed the phone back to Jason. "Your sister gets so *exercised* about things, doesn't she? I swear, you'd think she didn't have any other friends."

Jason rubbed at a cut on his cheek, from where the Nunus or whatever had attacked him. "I'm out. This is bullshit. Furry ant-creatures? I want to go home. Back to my life." He was tense, all his usual superficial charm boiled away, clearly on the edge of fight-or-flight.

Elsie *hmmed*. "Oh, fine. You can leave. Call it a gesture of good faith. You can walk out to the road and get a taxi or something. But listen—no more trying to kill Marla, either, understood? What kind of a brother *are* you?"

"I'm about to become a long-lost one. You lunatics enjoy the rest of your lives, okay?"

"Have fun scamming little old ladies until you die alone and forgotten," Crapsey said.

"At least I'm my own boss, lackey." Jason strode out of the bungalow without a backward glance.

Crapsey sat down. "And then there were two."

"Three soon, once we get Nicolette back."

"Do you think it's a trap?" Crapsey said. "Marla's going to see this thing with Pelham as a betrayal—"

"I'm sure she will. And it might be a trap. But so what? Marla can't hurt me—at least, not without destroying herself in the process. And even then, I'd just be *hurt*, not stopped. The best she can hope to do is make me mad and lead me to seek vengeance on everything she loves." She got a faraway look on her face. "You know the funniest thing, Crapsey? I really *did* forget we had her little man tied up in the closet. My mind has been on other things—what to do with my freedom. The places I'd like to visit. What would happen if I blew up the moon. How fun it would be to do a comparative analysis of the stomach contents of the world's currently operating serial killers. Whether putting a person's brain in a robot body would drive them insane. *Interesting* things." She sighed. "But I guess we'll give Pelham back. Maybe Marla will take it in the spirit in which it's offered."

"You *could* just kill her," Crapsey pointed out.

"You don't waste perfectly good nightmare fuel," Elsie said. "Marla's one of *my* people, a member in good standing of the Tribe of Discontinuity. She just doesn't want to admit it. Maybe we can still make nice."

"And if not?"

"We'll make *nasty*. Speaking of nasty, or rather, doing the nasty—we've got a few hours before we need to meet Marla for the exchange." She waggled her eyebrows at him. "Wanna fuck?"

Crapsey laughed. "You're so romantic, Elsie."

"Sometimes, when the mood strikes me, but not today. Come to bed. We won't wake Pelham, he's way down deep. Oh, and Crapsey—turn yourself into a monster again first. I'm feeling beastly."

"Of all the dangerous maniacs I've worked for, Elsie, I think you're my favorite."

"Okay, I'll tell them," Reva said. They were out in the hallway in front of her room, talking in low voices. "I think they can work up the kind of spell you're thinking about, and I'll make sure they're in place when the time comes. They don't go there often—the waves are way too gentle, usually, it's not very good surf, but they know the spot, because it has some mythic reso-nances. A chief was assassinated on that beach once."

Marla laughed, harshly. "Good thing I'm not a chief anymore, or that might worry me."

Reva looked at her curiously. "So, this errand you're trusting me with… does this mean you forgive me?"

"It means I need you," Marla said. "Look, Reva, I know you mean well—but that doesn't mean you can keep fucking with my life. You really need to *stop*. I'm starting to run out of patience."

"I used to have worshippers," he said. "They welcomed my intervention. Oh, the good old days. We'll talk about this later, assuming you survive." He left on his errand, and Marla went back inside the room, where Rondeau and… the guy who looked like Pelham… were waiting. "Pelham, Rondeau, you stay with Nicolette, see if you can get her calmed down. It would be easier if she actually walked with us to the beach when it's time."

"We have to *walk*?" Rondeau said. "Can't we drive? There's a beach ac-cess like five minutes away."

Marla shook her head. "Even with spells to keep us from seeming too interesting, it's dangerous to haul Nicolette through the resort. You want to take her out through the lobby, stand around while the valet gets our car, and give her a chance to work some mischief. I'd rather walk half a mile. Besides, if we arrive at the rendezvous point on foot, it'll give me a chance to scope things out, and make sure there's not an ambush in place."

Lupo/Pelham nodded. "We can convince Nicolette to cooperate, Mrs. Mason, but are you sure handing her over to Crapsey is a good idea?"

"I think getting them both together where we can incapacitate them and stick them on a boat headed somewhere far, far away is a good idea," Marla said. How could she tell Lupo there was going to be an exchange of hostages, and the *real* version of himself was one of the hostages? There was no etiquette for this sort of thing. Marla would just have to hope he stayed in Pelham-form, and didn't morph into Ed Gein or Ted Bundy or something, until they'd finished the exchange. "Listen, I need to prepare some things." She didn't want to say too much—it was always possible that Jarrow could listen in on Lupo's conversations. Who could say? "Just a few precautions, in case Crapsey tries something."

"You aren't worried about Ms. Jarrow?" the faux-Pelham said.

Marla shook her head. "Elsie and I have an understanding. I don't think she'll be a problem." Once Rondeau had hustled non-Pelham out of the room, Marla took her brown leather bag from beneath the bed, and began removing some of her instruments: knives, vials, candles. All the trappings of ritual magic. She tried to tell herself this was just a worst-case-scenario con-tingency plan, that she wouldn't have to actually go *through* with any of it…

but the fact that Jarrow had kept Pelham hostage was troubling, and Death's suggestion that Marla look at Jarrow through the ring again was niggling at her. What would she see? What *could* she see, that would make her take such extreme action?

She'd find out soon enough. Marla cut the meaty part of her left palm with a sharp knife, squeezed the blood into a wooden bowl, and got to work.

Nicolette was being a pain in the ass, wisecracking and walking slow and shouting "Help, help, I'm being oppressed!" before they were even out of the room, so Marla cast a look-away spell over the four of them to keep the hotel staff from getting too interested. Their tower was pretty far away from the path leading to the beach where they were supposed to exchange the hostages—Marla needed a waterfront site for her contingency plan—so they decided to take a shortcut through the service tunnels that ran underneath the vast sixty-some-acre resort. Besides… she just liked tunnels.

The tunnels were surprisingly roomy and well-maintained, and the look-away spell kept the bustling staff from noticing the interlopers in their midst, though they had to step lively to avoid being run down by the tuggers, little electric vehicles like souped-up golf carts designed for hauling luggage. They emerged from a service door near one of the hotel's myriad pools, this one a confection of waterfalls, rope bridges, multiple hot tubs, and slippery stone steps. The weather was bright, glorious, and just windy enough to take an edge off the heat.

They herded Nicolette up a set of stairs and across a swinging rope bridge that spanned a vast blue pool—*that* was a treacherous bit, as Nicolette managed to mouth half the syllables in an incantation that would have snapped all the ropes before Pelham stuffed a handkerchief in her mouth. From there they hurried past one of the resort's higher-end restaurants, one offering outdoor seating with stunning views of the Western sea. Come later afteroon, Marla figured those tables would be full of tourists ignoring their food and gazing at the colors of the setting sun. They could probably get away with sending out woefully sub-par food, given the beauty of the setting. It would be a clever way to economize.

From there it was down a set of steep steps to the shoreline. All beaches in Hawai'i were public land, by state law, and the hotel concierge had told Marla there was a path that would take them all the way to the beach at Anae-ho-omalu Bay—better known as "A-Bay," since that name was a mouthful even for the locals. They passed a place where visitors to the hotel had used small white rocks to spell out their names, declarations of love, and other ephemeral messages on the fields of black lava rock that separated the path from the sea. The path wound along, close to the water, and it was largely a trail of black and white: the black rock of the lava fields, and the white rocks composed mostly of dead coral. Such starkness; such contrast; such clarity. Marla remembered a time when everything had seemed so black-and-white to her, so yes-or-no, so all-or-nothing—when she'd stood for Felport, no matter what. Things were a lot grayer these days, like the salt-and-pepper sand composed of mingled crushed stones of both colors. The time was coming when she'd have to figure out what she stood for now.

The trip would have been pleasant, almost, if not for the moanings of the tied-up chaos witch, and the fact that a tense exchange at best and an all-out war at worst waited at the end of it. The scenery was beautiful, and the trail ran along the backside of various resorts and condos. The lavish buildings were supplanted only by the Anchialine Ponds Preservation area, where signs warned visitors away from disturbing the lava pools, where rare sea life somehow still survived amid the tourism-industrial complex. After a while they crossed a wooden bridge, then passed a small sandy cove where a pair of green sea turtles sprawled on the sand, being photographed by tourists who were far closer to the endangered animals than the twenty feet allowed by law. On another day, Marla might have given them a tongue lashing, but she had bigger problems than haole tourists annoying the local reptiles.

They finally reached the beach, a strip of off-white sand dotted with palm trees, between the ocean on one side and an old royal fish pond the size of a small lake on the other. Marla broke a carefully rotted egg against a palm tree's trunk as they arrived, casting a psychically-stinky keep-away spell to make the few tourists on the beach decide something unpleasant had died in the vicinity. Marla hoped the impression wouldn't turn out to be prophetic. There were a couple of boats in the distance, but they were way out, and, Marla hoped, wouldn't come drifting into a confrontation.

Once the place was deserted, Marla shaded her eyes and looked out to sea. A woman on a surfboard a few dozen yards out raised her hand in greeting, and as the waves moved another half-a-dozen figures sitting on boards were revealed—she spotted Reva among them, as well as the kid from Handsome Bob's who'd taken them to Jaws beach. They were all in place. Marla hoped devoutly she wouldn't need to use them.

"Okay, take out her gag," Marla said. "No reason to make Jarrow think we're mistreating her protege."

"I want my axe back," Nicolette said sullenly, once Pelham pulled the cloth out of her mouth. "You didn't have any right to take that, I stole it fair and square."

"I gave it to my boyfriend," Marla lied. "He lives in hell. He'll keep it safe. You're not old enough to be trusted with sharp things, Nicolette."

"Just because Elsie decided you get to live doesn't mean I agree," Nicolette said.

"Seriously, Nicolette, get a *hobby*," Rondeau said. "Take up underwater basket weaving, or start crafting detachable steampunk prosthetic arms. Move on with your life. You're, like, a b-grade villain. If they made a superhero movie out of Marla's life, you wouldn't get a role until the fourth movie, and even then, it would be as part of a team of four other minor bad guys."

"Marla's my nemesis."

Marla shook her head. "Not even remotely. I've had a few nemeses over the years. They're all dead now. Why would you want to be one of them?"

Three figures appeared on the far side of the fish pond, following a path from the beach's parking area. Elsie Jarrow, unmistakable with her red hair, waved, and then began walking across the surface of the pond. What a cliché. Crapsey walked the long way around with a smaller figure—Pelham!—at his side.

"Who... who is that with Crapsey?" the faux-Pelham asked, voice strained.

"Don't worry about it," Rondeau murmured. "It's okay."

No sign of Jason. Marla couldn't tell if she was disappointed or glad. He was her brother, but he was also an asshole she barely knew anymore, and what she knew, she didn't like. Still, she hoped Jarrow hadn't killed him.

"Marla!" Jarrow called from halfway across the pond. "I said I'd come, and here I am. I kept an appointment for you! You *must* know how rare that is."

The ring on Marla's finger seemed suddenly heavier. Marla slipped it off, held it between her thumb and forefinger, and lifted the ring to her right eye, closing her left.

Through the ring she saw Jarrow, walking across the pond, just a little closer now. Marla let her eye relax, allowing the background to fade out, until she was focused on Jarrow and nothing else. Time around her seemed to slow and flow like cool syrup as Jarrow's future unspooled in her view, not so much a fast-forward as a series of snapshot impressions: Jarrow in bed with Crapsey, Jarrow on a plane, Jarrow in snowy mountains, Jarrow in a forest, Jarrow on a city street, Jarrow in—Wait. She'd recognized a building in that city, the tower of the Whitcroft-Ivory building in downtown Felport. She tried to concentrate her mind and shift her focus, and the view ran backwards, then slowed down. Jarrow standing on a busy sidewalk, face all serenity, with a bundled object under her arm—something wrapped in fur. She unwrapped the object, revealing something like a ram's horn, but the same red as her hair, and as long as her forearm. Jarrow raised the horn to her mouth and blew. Marla couldn't hear what it sounded like, of course, but the buildings around Jarrow began to crumble, and the street buckled and cracked. A spidery thing the size of a car pulled itself out of a hole in the street, and dark shapes bigger than any bird swooped across the sky. Something as broad as a garbage truck, but walking on two legs, shouldered its way from an alley, shattering bricks as it came. Jarrow threw back her head, laughing, then brought the horn to her lips again.

Marla slipped the ring back onto her finger. Elsie was approaching, all smiles. She gestured, and the rope fence erected to keep visitors out of the pond fell over with a snapping of fibers and a rapid rotting of wooden posts. Jarrow stepped onto shore, still beaming. Marla forced herself to smile back. Get Pelham first. Then… think about the future.

"I really *did* forget about him," Jarrow said. "I know it sounds like a lie, but why would I lie? It's the truth. Pelham had some fun, too—did you know his little Nuno infestation had a flare-up? That's why Crapsey's face is all scratched up." She stage-whispered, "Don't say anything about it, he's sensitive."

"Elsie!" Nicolette called. "You came back for me?"

"I know! I'm surprised too! But you know what they say about chaos witches—we can't even be guaranteed to act in our own best interests."

Crapsey made it around the pond, leading Pelham with a rope tied to the valet's wrists. "Here you go," he said, studiously ignoring Rondeau. "Safe and sound."

"Shall we trade?" Jarrow said.

The faux-Pelham stared open-mouthed at his double, who looked at his own doppelganger with an expression of bemusement. "But… but this… Marla, I don't understand…" Lupo trailed off.

Jarrow clucked her tongue. "You didn't tell him, Marla? So cruel! You're not Pelham, my boy, you're *Lupo*, my dear Lupo, here." She snapped her fingers, and the fake Pelham sort of… *blurred out*, becoming a human-shaped beige smear, jittering and twitching on the sand, emitting a constant high-frequency mewling sound. "There, he's in neutral now. Crapsey, let Pelham go to his friends."

"We should get Nicolette first—"

"Marla's *honorable*," Jarrow said firmly. "She adheres to her agreements. Doesn't she?"

"Unless there's a compelling reason not to," Marla said.

Crapsey sighed and untied Pelham's wrists. The valet looked at his captor, sniffed once pointedly, and joined Marla and Rondeau. "I'm pleased to be back, ma'am," he said.

"Did they hurt you, Pelham?"

"Only incidentally, in the course of apprehending me after my attempted escape."

"Don't you want to know if they hurt *me*?" Nicolette said. "They kept me in a shit-filled bathtub and didn't feed me and—"

Rondeau shoved Nicolette toward Jarrow. "Thank you for choosing Hawai'i," Rondeau said. "We know you have a choice of vacation destinations, and we appreciate your visit."

"So, Marla," Jarrow said. "I know I told you we could drug them and put them on a boat—"

"What?" Crapsey said, alarmed.

Jarrow ignored him. "—but I'm fond of Crapsey. If I keep him on a leash and make sure he doesn't bother you or your friends, can I keep him?"

Marla looked at Rondeau, who shrugged. "I don't see why not. But what about Nicolette?"

"Ah, yes." Jarrow looked Nicolette up and down, then beckoned. Nicolette approached her, eyes downcast like a penitent. "For all the grief I give you, Nicolette, you really are a fairly promising witch. You have the right instinct for mischievous mayhem, but if you could get over your petty vendettas, you'd go a lot farther—don't you understand, seeking revenge on someone who's wronged you is so *expected*. It's much better to visit harm on those who have no connection to you. Think *random*, reject causality, do you understand?"

"So... if I stop trying to go after Marla... you'd respect me more?"

"I think you'd respect yourself more," Jarrow said. "What do you say?"

Nicolette shot Marla a venomous glare, then shrugged. "Whatever. I'm really a lot more interested in *you* than I am in Marla—"

"Good girl." Jarrow seized Nicolette's head in both hands and twisted it off. There was some magic in the act, as the head separated cleanly from the neck, with only a little blood, and Nicolette's eyes rolled in confusion and terror for a moment. Her body fell to the sand, and then Jarrow tossed the head over her shoulder, where it disappeared into the depths of the fish pond. "That's what we do with Nicolette!" Jarrow said. "Consider that my apology for the misunderstanding with Pelham. I know my girl's been a thorn in your side, and now she's gone, with no blood on your hands. Yay!"

"Shit on a biscuit," Crapsey muttered, staring at the pond, where bubbles rose among the ripples.

"She'll lose consciousness and truly die in ten or fifteen minutes, don't worry," Jarrow said. "I don't want her to suffer *unduly*."

Welcome to Death

"I CAN'T SAY I'M SORRY to see her go," Rondeau said, staring at the water with his doppelganer. "But: that is kinda *murder*. It seems more evil than chaotic."

"Silly," Jarrow said. "I'm beyond good and evil. Nietzsche wrote a book about me! You should read it."

"Okay." Marla looked at the headless not-quite-a-corpse. "Leaving aside the whole fact that you just beheaded Nicolette... do you happen to have a blood-red ram's horn?"

Jarrow cocked her head. "How did you know about that?"

"You said yourself I have unexpected resources. Tell me about it."

Jarrow *hmmmed*. "It's not a ram's horn, first of all. It's the horn of an animal called a slimestrider, actually. Stupid name, I know. I picked it up in a little imaginary fantasy universe I know. The horn was a gift from a certain Dark Lord Barrow—I think you've met him?"

"That comatose writer in the Blackwing Institute?" Marla said. *That* was unexpected, but with Jarrow, that was kind of the point. "You went into his hallucinated fantasy world and brought something *out*?"

"Oh yes. A great artifact. With another dumb name—the HellHorn, two capital 'H's—but Barrow has to name a lot of things, so it's understandable that he'd run out of ideas. But seriously, how did you know about the horn? I've got it all packed up, and I was planning on using it against you if necessary, but, well, it wasn't."

"What does it do?" Marla said.

Jarrow grinned. "It's lovely, actually. Barrow came up with a whole mythology for the horn. It's a weapon, used by countless gods, monsters, heroes, and villains in his fantasy world. Whoever blows the horn summons up the ferocious spirits of everyone *else* who's ever blown the horn, on down through the centuries. It must have been disappointing for the first guy to use it, huh? But at this point, it's got *loads* of souls attached to it, demons and giants and war-witches and all manner of nasty things. Nothing without lungs or mouths, of course, because they have to be able to blow the horn to get bound to it. That's a shame, because Barrow has some beaky tentacled things in the oceans of his world that are really marvelous—"

"I saw you," Marla said. "In a vision. Blowing that horn in *Felport.*"

Jarrow scratched under her armpit and hummed for a moment. Everyone else—well, except Lupo—stood absolutely still, sensing the tension. After a moment, Jarrow said, "So what if I did? Didn't they fire you? Kick you out? Send you to this hellish—oh, wait, paradisical—island?"

"If someone you love stops loving you," Marla said, "that doesn't mean you stop loving them back."

"A city is not a boyfriend," Jarrow said. "Are you a crazy stalker?"

"Love is just another kind of obsession. I can accept that."

Jarrow sighed. "What if I promise, double-dog-swear, not to blow the horn in Felport?"

"You'd just use it somewhere else," Marla said. "You say your reason for living is to have fun, but you consider destroying people's *lives* fun. You'll unleash hell and laugh. Won't you?"

"I'm a very naughty girl," Jarrow said. "I don't think I ever claimed otherwise. I can see your sense of righteous indignation has been activated. Fine. What are you going to do about it? Sic Pelham on me? Get your little crew of wave-mages out there on the ocean—hi there, I see you!—to summon a blue whale to crush me? I smell that little god of homesickness out there, too, how pitiful. Are you really so lost without a place to call your own? Me, I'm comfortable in any place at all—wherever I hang my severed head is home. Reva can't get to *me.* So tell me, then, what *can* you do? Ultimately, the answer is *nothing—*"

Marla pulled out Nicolette's hatchet from where it was tucked into her waistband and swung it in a flat arc at Jarrow's face. The blade struck hard enough that it should have lopped off the top of Jarrow's head, but it barely brushed her cheek, drawing a tiny speck of blood, before it rebounded hard and bounced out of Marla's hand. Oh well. Marla hadn't expected it to work, but the axe was an artifact, so it had been worth a try. If it had belonged to the great god of order Urizen or something it might have made more of a dent. At least the axe hadn't melted or burst into flames—she'd refrained from using her own dagger for fear an attack on Jarrow might destroy the weapon.

Marla's own cheek stung, of course, but she didn't let that distract her, or give her pause. She crouched and kicked, sweeping Jarrow's legs from beneath her, and dropping the witch to the sand. "Rondeau, Pelham, get out of here!" she shouted, and then began running south herself.

She glanced back. Pelham and Rondeau weren't running—they'd been drawn into the fight. Damn it. She'd wanted them to get away. But Lupo had transformed into Dr. Husch, and she was attacking Rondeau, while Pelham was crouched on top of Crapsey, squeezing his throat as the bigger man scrabbled at him ineffectually. Jarrow just stood up, head cocked, frowning, then touched her cheek and began walking slowly after Marla.

The ground underneath her moved, rising up in answer to some spell of Jarrow's, and Marla was knocked off her feet. She managed to turn her fall into a roll, not quite crashing into a palm tree. She got to her knees and glanced toward the sea. The wave-mages were there, still bobbing. They knew the time had almost come. Marla just hoped they could do their part.

Marla knelt in the shade of the palm tree and drew her magical dagger. She gently placed the blade, so sharp it could cut through hopes and dreams, a millimeter from her throat. If a powerful artifact like the axe hadn't hurt Jarrow, there was no reason to think her dagger would, either. But there were other ways to injure the witch.

"I didn't peg you for the melodramatic teenager type, Marla." Jarrow approached, moving slowly, like someone trying to avoid startling a deer. "You know I have to kill you, now. Or, I don't have to—but I'm going to. That axe might have hurt me, if someone stronger had been wielding it. Not very nice. And they say I'm a betrayer! So… what's the plan? You'll stop me from killing you, by killing *yourself*? A 'you can't fire me, I quit,' sort of thing?"

"Not exactly." Marla shrugged, the blade of her magical knife just kissing the flesh of her throat. "You *are* wearing my body, you know—or at least, a perfect duplicate of my body from a parallel universe. You put a new roof on it and did a little remodeling—though why you'd choose that nose over mine is beyond me—but the genes don't lie. I've spent the morning setting up a sympathetic magic link between us. We're identical and entangled, now, magically speaking. If I die, you die."

Jarrow shook her head. "Bluff, bluff, bluffity bluff. You're just trying to buy some time, I don't even know why. Just natural desperation, I guess. You could have done this trick to stop the *last* person who wore this body, after all, and you didn't. You let the Mason kill half the sorcerers in your city instead, you were *that* attached to living. So, no, bzzt, try again."

"I had a lot more to live for then." What would it be like, Marla thought, to cut her own throat? She'd been wounded plenty of times, but never in the throat, and never by her own hand. The blade Death had forged for her was so sharp she might not even feel the slice. She couldn't decide if that was a good thing or not. "I had a city to protect. I had a reason to live. Now, I've got nothing. But killing Elsie Jarrow—*that* would give my stupid fucked-up life meaning again."

"Oh, Marla. This is depressing. I thought I was locked in a battle of wills, facing one of the most pigheadedly tough sorcerers of the new generation, but you… you brought a spoon to a gunfight." Jarrow began piling up sand, the grains heaped and shaped by her hands and her magic into the smooth-sided walls of a sand castle that was more like a squat sand fortress. "They told me you were *smart*. We considered the suicide-murder-voodoo-hoodoo angle, of course, I mean, we looked at all the contingencies. But when I brought it up, Dr. Husch said, 'No, of course not, Marla wouldn't do that, she's too smart.' The Doc overestimated you as much as she underestimated me." Jarrow cupped more sand and let it trickle through her fingers, and it cascaded down to land on top of her squat castle and began to spontaneously form a tall, narrow spire. "Because if you kill this body, Marla, you won't kill *me*. You'll just free me from the bonds of the flesh. Now, it so happens I like the bonds of the flesh, because flesh is full of wonderful nerve endings and exciting hormone-dispensers, and it *would* be hard for me to replace this body, since most vessels are too weak to contain my awesomeness… but while I'd be sad to lose this body, I'd also be disembodied. And if that happened, oh, I have to tell you, I think I'd probably start going crazy again, and underneath the crazy, there'd be this solid core of pissed-off. This thing, with the knife and the magical link between us and all that, it's not a viable solution to your problems. Kill my body and I'll just turn into a whirlwind of black acid and maim everything and everyone you love, or once loved, or might have loved someday. I'd probably destroy a lot of other stuff in the process, too. Have you ever tried to *aim* a whirlwind of black acid? It's not a precision instrument." Jarrow shook her head. "This is the wrong approach. It's like strapping yourself into a catapult and flinging yourself against a fortress. It squashes you flat, and it doesn't much bother the fortress." She picked up a fist-sized stone from the sand and hurled it at her sandcastle, and the stone bounced harmlessly away, without dislodging so much as a single grain of sand.

"So you're saying killing myself would be an irrational act," Marla said. "Random, pointless, and bloody. Yeah?"

"As a connoisseur of the random, pointless, and bloody, that is my professional assessment, yes."

"There's one thing you don't know," Marla said.

Jarrow laughed. "There are *billions* of things I don't know! That's one of the best reasons to live forever—there's so much to learn!"

"You think you're cute. You're not cute. You're a dead thing wrapped in streamers and sparklers, an emptiness where a person used to be, a howling void in a sparkly dress."

"Projecting much, Mrs. Misery?"

Marla tightened her grip on her knife. "You aren't even curious about what I was going to say? About the particular precinct of your ignorance I'm talking about?"

The chaos witch's face took on a distant, faraway cast. "Hmm? Sorry, were you talking? I'm trying to untangle your sympathetic link here, so I can kill you before happy hour ends at the bar. Those lava flows are wonderful. This link you made between us, it's decent work, but sweetie, it's basically just quantum knotwork, and my specialty is *unraveling* knots. Or raveling. Did you know 'ravel' and 'unravel' mean the same thing?"

"You're ruining the drama of my big reveal here," Marla said. "The one thing you don't know is: when I die, I'm going to become a goddess of death. It's an awesome retirement plan. And it means I'll have the power to deal with you even in your disembodied cloud-of-cancer form."

"A goddess of death. Right. Have you always been schizophrenic, or is it a recent development? Maybe we should have checked you into the Black-wing Institute after all. Oh well. Too late now." Jarrow stuck the corner of her tongue out of her mouth and furrowed her brow in concentration. Time was running out—Marla knew the sympathetic link wouldn't survive under Jarrow's attention for long, even with all the orderly magic Marla had woven into the strands.

"Are you ready?" Marla shouted, and the surfers riding silently on the waves raised their clenched fists high in unison. Jarrow didn't pay any attention, chewing her lip hard enough to make beads of blood appear and drip down her chin. She had to be close to breaking the link.

There was a good chance this was famous last words time—or, at least, her last words as a mortal. What did you say to encapsulate—or put the capstone on—a life? "I did it my way?" True, but trite. "Suck it, fuckers?" Not very classy, and while she'd never been classy, even Marla had her limits. "France, the army, head of the army, Josephine?" The Napoleon comparisons only worked to a point. "I regret nothing?" Ha, no reason to leave this world with everyone thinking you were totally delusional.

She decided to fall back on classic apocrypha, and use the last words attributed to Pancho Villa, even though the poor bastard had died instantly, with no final words at all. But it was a good line, so somebody might as well use it:

"Hey, Elsie. Don't let it end like this. Tell them I said something."

Marla pushed in the blade. The steel was cold and hot all at once, more *sensation* than *pain*, at least at first, and then she just felt wetness, as if she'd spilled hot coffee down her front. She went lightheaded, everything going fuzzy. This was a bit like being falling-down drunk, and a bit like almost dying of exposure in the snow (the cocoon of warmth wrapped in the encroaching cold), both things she'd experienced, but not in a while. She kept her head up and her eyes open as long as she could, watching Elsie Jarrow twitch and writhe on the sand, hands clutched to her throat, which had spontaneously started jetting gouts of blood. Ha. The spells of protection wrapped around Jarrow's stolen body were impressive, but the same protections that kept magic from ripping holes in her flesh kept magic from *repairing* holes in that flesh. Even Jarrow's power to impose order and turn back entropy were useless, all her desperate death-knell spells bouncing off the hard shell of her stolen body's invulnerability. Marla could get to that body despite its safeguards because it was *hers*, really. And what she owned she could destroy.

Marla slumped, her extremities all numb and faraway, like her hands and feet had become balloons, drifting into the distance. She was fading, her sense of self dissipating, as her blood pressure dropped. No oxygen reached her brain. She felt slow, stupid, and fuzzy, and a fog drifted over her consciousness: but this was a deep blue fog, a fog made of the sky at twilight.

And then... everything was clear. *Hyper*-clear, like going from crappy low-res security video to high-definition TV. Marla blinked and stood up, looking down at her own body. She looked so *small*. She—or some part of her, a soul, or an astral body, or a stubborn conceptual persistence of shape with delusions of consciousness—walked around the tableau, which seemed frozen in time, to judge by the seagulls hovering in the air, the surfers unmoving on the waves, and the failure of the twin blood pools around Jarrow and Marla to widen and merge.

An air horn sounded, and a thousand black balloons and a rain of red confetti showered down from the sky. Marla batted aside a drifting balloon, but several others bounced off her head and shoulders. The confetti stuck to her skin, or her imaginary construct of skin, looking uncomfortably like flecks of dried blood. The balloons all settled into a mass covering the beach, jostling slightly and squeaking like well-behaved mice as they rubbed against one another. At least the balloons covered up the bodies. Marla could do without seeing *them*.

The Walking Death arrived.

"Oh," Marla said. "*That's* where you always walk in from. Why couldn't I see it before?"

"You could see it, but you couldn't comprehend it." He smiled, arms outstretched. The balloons moved aside for him, clearing a spot for his every footstep as he approached. "But you've achieved apotheosis, Marla Mason. You are a goddess now."

"I... I remember. There are things I'm supposed to do, here. Things I'm *for*." She licked her lips. "All this time, since my exile, I've been wanting a purpose, but being queen of the land of the dead—it's *all* purpose, isn't it?"

"I told you when you married me. It's not a ceremonial position. The universe needs both of us to run smoothly. There are two sides of death. One of us is annihilation and loss and abnegation and howling emptiness, destroyer of meaning, the great leveler, the despoiler of lives. One of us is the end of suffering, the giver of peace, the easer of burdens, and the necessary pause before rebirth—the fire that clears the fields, allowing them to grow back stronger than before. Both aspects of death are necessary for the workings of the world to go on. I told you about this, when we were first wed, but because such knowledge would be a burden to your mortal mind, we took it away from you when you returned to Earth." He coughed. "Traditionally, the king of the underworld is the more stark and unpleasant and stereotypically masculine side of death, and the queen is the enfolder into velvety peacefulness and reunion with the great mother and so on, but of course I'm open to non-traditional gender roles, and certainly, if you like, we can both be switch—"

Marla kicked him in the balls.

Such a Full Sea

MARLA HADN'T BEEN ENTIRELY SURE a blow to the testicles would hurt Death, since even his human form was just a convenience, but all that talk about masculine and feminine made her think it was worth a shot. His eyes crossed and he dropped to his knees, clutching his crotch. After a moment he fell over onto his side, popping several balloons in the process, and began to groan.

The new queen of the dead crouched beside him and whispered in his ear. "You shitty little fuck. You told Rondeau to just let me *die*. Did you really think he wouldn't come to me with that information? I *told* you, let me live my life in my own time, don't interfere, but you couldn't do that, could you? Between you and Reva, I've had more than enough bullshit and interference from creatures that aren't even human."

With his eyes still clenched shut, he said, "I just wanted—"

"Your queen, your other half, fine, yes, I get it, believe me, I get it *better* now. But eternity is long, and my lifespan is short. I know time goes slowly in the downbelow, but fuck, Walker, you're a *god*, you can create anything you can imagine!"

"You cut that out of me." Death's voice was small and cold, and Marla flinched. Once, the Walking Death had been her enemy, a monster, and Marla had stolen his terrible sword—a blade so sharp it could cut through anything, even time, even *abstractions*—and used it to cut the bad parts out of him: his cruelty, caprice, and sadism. She'd wanted to make him a better god, and more importantly, a better man—and she had. But she'd always worried about the deeper effects. It was hard to cut out a tumor, after all, without cutting out some good tissue, too.

"You took my desire to create baroque punishments for the souls in my realm," Death said, sitting up now, and staring down at the black balloons surrounding them. "But you also took my *capacity* to create those things,

199

and with it, the capacity to create… much of anything. In the first days after your… impromptu surgery… I was little more than a shell. Gradually, the parts of my self you cut away have been growing back, the way someone with a damaged brain can develop new pathways to route around the damage or mimic the old functions, but I'm *less* than I was. I am only meant to be half of a god anyway, Marla—we should be a duality—but I think you've cut me down to something like a third. I'd hoped you could be the other two-thirds, and that you could help *me* be more. I'll be stronger with you beside me, I'll be whole. Marla, I never sleep, I never did, but did you know, I used to *dream*, anyway, sometimes? They were not nice dreams, but they were mine, and now, I have nothing. But with you at my side… ." He met her eyes, and now that she was a creature like him, she could see the anguish in his gaze that no mortal could ever ascertain. "I might be able to dream again. To imagine. I did a bad thing. I know. I'm sorry. But I *need* you."

Marla offered him her hand, and he took it, and let her help him to his feet. "I understand all that," she said. "And, okay—it's not like you actually killed me, or killed Pelham. You could have done a lot worse."

"The thought crossed my mind," he said.

"But the point stands—we're supposed to be *equals*, but you thought you knew better than I did, you didn't *listen*. I can't have that. It's a sore point for me, and not the kind of button you want to push. How are we supposed to have a relationship if we don't even have that level of trust?"

He shook his head. "My only defense is… I'm new at this. I've never had a queen before. I'm sorry?"

She kicked a few balloons aside so she could see her own frozen-on-the-point-of-death body again. "So what happens next?"

"As per our agreement, I step in at the moment before your death—this moment, as it happens, which I've stretched out for us subjectively—and take you, living, to the underworld. There, you will ascend to your throne, though to be absolutely technical you've already ascended. There is an actual chair, though. Or an abstract representation of a chair that you and I can perceive as actual. It all gets very metaphysical down there. Starting with the fact that I call it 'down there' when it's not actually *below* anything."

"So I'm not dead," Marla said. She nodded toward Jarrow. "How about her?"

"Oh, yes, she's gone. The body is, anyway. The poor dear expired just before I froze this moment. You lived longer than your twin—but then, your will has always been greater than just about anyone's."

"Okay," Marla said after a moment. "Here's the thing. I'm not done living yet."

Death closed his eyes. "Marla. Marla, don't. Don't ask me to restore you to life. Because I'll have to refuse you, and—"

Marla shook her head. "I'm not that big of a bitch. But listen. There's actually a mythological precedent for what I've got in mind. Let's take a few minutes and haggle, what do you say? Marriage is about compromise."

After Crapsey finally managed to overpower Pelham and tossed him in the fish pond, he rushed up the beach, but it was too late: there were two dead bodies under the trees. Holy hell. Marla had gone through with it. She'd enacted what the comic books called the ultimate sacrifice: given up her own life to save the lives of others.

Though when it came to saving the lives of others, a pissed-off, disembodied Elsie was a hell of a lot more dangerous than one with a physical form to keep her contained and distracted. Basically, Marla was a shit tactician. Unless she'd just lost the will to live, and figured unleashing a bodiless Elsie as she died was a nice final "fuck you" to the universe. Crapsey could get his head around that as a motivation, at least.

The air above Jarrow's bled-out body was shimmering now, and beach sand began to swirl up and around and accrete into the shape of a female form. The whirlwind that was Elsie's consciousness picked up a quantity of the blood-soaked sand and sculpted that into hair, and a pair of red lips, but still: she was just sand. The beach-golem walked toward Crapsey, and when she spoke, her voice was all rasp and dryness. "I'm hollowed, I'm scooped, I'm uncooped, I'm free as a bird, free as a murder, I'm shadows swallowing the moon, I'm a flock of swallows, I'm starlight, I'm starlings, I'm all out of spoons, I - I - I - I—"

Crapsey backed away. Being close to Elsie right now was probably like pitching a tent next to Chernobyl. He had enough problems without bone cancer. The sand figure kept walking, leaving bloody footprints. "You, Crapsey, yes, you'll do… *your* body, yes, why not, as good as any, oh, the music I could make singing through your throat, the great workings I could work through the workings of your wonderful jaw…"

Crapsey swallowed. To have his own body stolen was a fitting enough fate, but really, as punishments went, it was a litle too on the nose. "Elsie, you're not thinking straight, it's because you don't have a brain anymore to think with. You'd burn through this body in minutes, and then we'd *both* be shit out of luck, and I wouldn't be around to help you anymore—"

"But you can *taste* things, get down and lick the salt from the sea, roll around in the warm sand, blood is pumping in you, I will take you, I will stretch time like bubblegum, I can live a lifetime before your bones turn to spun glass and black goo, shh, open wide, give us a kiss, kiss me again, kiss me like you did before." Her red mouth opened, and a tongue made from a fragment of kelp poked out.

Crapsey wanted to run, but it would be like running from the moon crashing into the Earth, wouldn't it? Maybe it would be better to stand his ground, pretend to be brave, take his last breaths as a man unpossessed by an insane chaos witch, look at the ocean—

The surfers had paddled in closer, and now they were doing something out on the waves, chanting some rhythm, and the waves seemed to be crashing in time with their chant. That couldn't be true, of course, it had to be the other way around, but it really did seem like the *surfers* were conducting the symphony of surf and tide…

Elsie reached out with one grainy hand, caressing his cheek, and she had *eyes* now, made of bits of bright seashell, and those inanimate fragments were somehow still merry. Everything was a lark: life and death and dancing back and forth across the line between the two. She stuffed her fingers in his mouth, sand on his tongue, and when he tried to pull away she seized his jaw and began squeezing. He bit down, but her hand was hard as concrete. There was a trigger word, wasn't there, something that would make his jaw activate magically, become strong enough to bite through diamonds and mithril and adamantium, but even if he could remember the word, he couldn't *say* it, because she was trying to climb into his body through his fucking *mouth*—

Then her sandy body began to come apart. Her bloody hair streamed away first, and then she lost one of her nacreous eyes. Her grip on his jaw went limp, and suddenly his mouth was just full of sand, instead of a *hand*, and he stumbled back, spitting, trying to clear his mouth. Elsie swayed in confusion, looking at the hand-less stumps of her arms, as more and more chunks of her body began to blow away—but the grains of sand were flying *against* the prevailing wind, out toward the ocean, rather than in toward the shore.

Elsie began to laugh, and then to howl, and somehow even that howling was made part of the surfers' rhythmic chant.

Crapsey didn't know what the hell was happening, but he supported it whole-heartedly. He spat toward Elsie. "You're coming apart! You're going to pieces!" "I know!" Elsie shouted. "Two-four-six-eight, look at me disintegrate!" She cackled again, and then her red lips blew away, and her face stopped even remotely resembling a face. Her human shape came apart entirely, and she became literally dust in the wind—though it was more like dust being sucked into an industrial fan.

The chanting from the surfers continued for another few minutes as Crapsey stared open-mouthed at the bobbing mages on their boards in the waves, and then their voices stopped abruptly. The waters churned and frothed wildly, great spumes of water shooting up into the air, geyser-like, as if the sea had been brought to a rolling boil and beyond. The wave-mages hung grimly onto their boards, rocking and riding out the fury, some of them leaving the water entirely and flying briefly into the air, but none of them went under. After a few moments, the sea's fury subsided, and the next few lapping waves left pinkish, blood-tinged foam on the shore. The surfers started to cheer and exchange high-fives.

"What the *shit*," Crapsey began, but then someone crashed into him from behind, knocking him facedown in the sand, and a sleep with the familiar cloying stink of magic pulled him down, as surely as an undertow drags unwary swimmers below the waves.

Marla's eyes opened, and the world was blue; and then the world was Reva, and Pelham, and Rondeau, and—*Arachne*, of all people, pressing a woven bandage down to Marla's throat and chanting, though when she did it, it was more like muttered singing. Marla tried to sit up, but Arachne disdainfully pressed a hand to Marla's chest, and managed to hold her down. After a moment, the kahuna nodded. "I think she will live. Her body needs to be replenished—she will be ravenous, and she should rest, but if she does those things, she will not die." Arachne stood up, sniffed, and said, "My obligation to you is now fully discharged, Marla Mason."

"I thought you were done for." Rondeau squeezed her hand, which no longer felt like a balloon tethered to her by a piece of string.

"Jarrow," Marla croaked. She didn't feel as bad as she should have—she also didn't, apparently, have a slit in her throat anymore—but she still felt like she'd been dragged behind a horse over lava rock for thirty or forty miles. "Elsie Jarrow, is she—"

"It worked," a new voice said. Marla turned her head, and there was the kid from the surf shop, what was his name, French-y but not—right, Jon-Luc. He squatted down beside Marla, fastidiously avoiding the drying puddle of blood. "We caught Jarrow in the tidal forces, and pulled her consciousness into the sea."

"*That* was the plan?" Rondeau said. "I thought you were going to return as a warrior Death goddess and stomp her into atoms?"

"That was plan B," Marla croaked. "Plan A was dilution." She gestured at Jon-Luc, her throat hurting too bad for her to explain.

"Marla talked it over with us," Jon-Luc said. "And asked if we could make a trap. This woman Jarrow was poisonous, right? She was basically disembodied heavy metals or carcinogens." He shrugged. "The ocean is *big*. A woman-sized dose of radiation and crazy magic, when diluted into the entire sea, is nothing. She might make a few fish sick, but her substance will become so watered-down as she spreads through the ocean, she won't be a conscious entity anymore. Not that we *like* dumping more poison of any sort into the sea, but at this point, what's another few parts per trillion?"

"What's to stop her, like, taking over the body of a shark before she gets too diluted?" Rondeau said.

Jon-Luc looked offended. "We're *good*, my crew. And we've got our own reasons to want Jarrow eliminated. She killed Glyph. We bound her up in all the orderly magic of the sea when we sprang our trap."

"The sea is lovely, dark, and deep," Reva said thoughtfully. "A symbol of order in its tidal regularity and predictable flow of currents…"

Jon-Luc nodded. "The ocean's full of chaos too, of course, the ocean's full of *everything*, but we can focus the sea's power in a particular way, and we did. Jarrow will be hopelessly diluted before she can undo those bindings."

"It's like when she turned Christian Decomain into frogs," Marla said. "He wasn't killed, just *changed*, reduced to individual component parts that don't communicate anymore, so they no longer add up to a whole. Jarrow's still down there, she's just… not Jarrow any more. She's been reduced to pieces of herself." She shook her head. "Shit. Where's Crapsey? Lupo?"

Rondeau pointed to a prone form. "Crapsey's down. Arachne dropped him when she arrived. He's alive, but out of it. Lupo… I don't know. She—he—stopped attacking me and ran away, but he was starting to blur again, he didn't look like Dr. Husch any more. I think whatever control Jarrow was exerting over Lupo slipped when her body died."

"Great," Marla croaked. "Talk about an invasive species. We'll have to track Lupo down later. We should do something with Nicolette's body. And we should get Crapsey locked up I guess. Nobody's using the bathtub anymore—"

"We'll take care of it, Marla," Rondeau said. "Pelham and me. We've got this."

Marla clutched at his arm. "Good. Can you help me back to the hotel? I need to rest. But later on, I need to talk to you. And Pelly. And Reva too. In the morning…" Marla's eyes drooped. Being on the point of death and besting a chaos witch was exhausting work. She let herself sink into Rondeau's arms, and allowed sleep to take her.

Walking the Earth

WHEN MARLA WOKE UP, HER THROAT FELT BETTER. She drank
glass after glass of water, then stepped out onto her balcony and looked down
on the dolphin lagoon. The animals were beautiful, leaping from the water to
the delight of watching vacationers. They seemed to be enjoying themselves,
but surely they'd prefer their freedom? Or maybe she was anthropomorphiz-
ing. When the sight of dolphins in a resort hotel starts to seem unbearably
poignant, maybe it's time to change your life.

She went back inside to use the bathroom—all those glasses of water
took a toll—and saw a slip of paper someone had slid under her door. Only a
couple of lines written by hand. She looked at the clock. After hurriedly using
the bathroom, she splashed some water on her face, ran her fingers through
her hair, and slipped on some comfortable clothes. In a perfect world, she
would look cool and poised and powerful for this rendezvous, but she'd just
died yesterday, and there was only so much she could do. She cast a brief
stealthy-and-silent spell (fresh cat whiskers, harvested humanely, made all
the difference) and slipped out of her room. Her friends would probably be
feeling overprotective, and this way they wouldn't hear her leaving and ask
where she was going. The spell might not work on Reva, but she hoped that
if he noticed, he'd appreciate that she was *trying* to be private, and leave her
alone.

Marla went down the elevator to the ground floor, and strolled to one
of the hotel's little cafes. Now, just past dawn, the place was nearly deserted,
except for one man seated at a small round table, his back to a pillar, two cups
of coffee before him.

She sat down across from him, and after a moment during which they
regarded one another, said, "You're looking well." She was alarmed by how
raspy her voice still sounded.

"So are you, sis."

Marla laughed, but it hurt her throat. "You are a good liar, Jason. I look like I'm half-dead—because I am. I notice you didn't come to our little final party on the beach."

Jason exhaled. "So there was something final, then? It's all over?"

She shrugged. "Crapsey is on ice somewhere, but I'm sure we'll ship him back to the mainland soon, probably tied up with some evidence of a crime in his lap. We'll see how prison suits him. And Jarrow... well. Someone like her, you can't really kill. But she's been neutralized."

"And the one with the buzzcut?"

"Nicolette... didn't make it. Not by my hand. Elsie Jarrow killed her."

"Doesn't surprise me," Jason said. "I've met a lot of dangerous people over the years, and some people so far around the bend they didn't know right from wrong, and didn't realize *what* they were doing... but that woman knew exactly what she was doing, and did it anyway, just because she liked it."

"Sounds a lot like you, brother."

"I never wanted to be part of this. I know you've got no reason to believe me, but it's true. Jarrow press-ganged me. She thought it was funny, having your brother along, making me call you on the phone, shit like that. I got away from her as soon as I could."

Marla nodded toward her coffee cup. "Is this poisoned?"

Jason picked up the cup, took a sip, swallowed, then passed it back. "If it is, we're all in this together."

Marla took a sip of her own. "Why did you want to meet me, Jason? You were the only member of the murder squad who got to walk away clean. So what are you doing here?"

"I've spent the past few months living in fear of you, Marlita. Afraid you'd hunt me down, or send a gargoyle or a werewolf or something to kill me. I'm sick of the fear. If you're going to kill me, I'd rather get it over with."

"Fair enough," Marla said. "It's not on my agenda this morning, though."

"Can I ask you a question?" Jason said. "Why did you try to reach me, a few days ago? I'd never even heard of Elsie Jarrow when I got the call from mom, telling me you'd been in touch. So what did you want?"

"It's a magic thing. I heard a prophecy, sort of, that said you would try to kill me, and die yourself in the process. I was going to call and tell you not to get involved with Nicolette, and not to come to Hawai'i. That it wouldn't end well for you. Fortunately, I messed with causality enough to keep you from dying anyway, but I wasn't sure how things would turn out."

Jason took a slow sip of coffee, both hands on the mug. "You wanted to warn me? To save my life?"

Marla nodded.

"All this time I've been hiding in shithole towns, trying to avoid detection. Once I heard you survived that… thing that happened between us… in Felport, I figured you'd come gunning for me. I mean, you're a crime boss. Or you were."

"Not really. I was a *protector*, Jason. Any crime that happened was strictly incidental."

"Funny. You being a protector. I mean…"

"Because you were the one who protected me, when we were kids? From mom's ten thousand drunken boyfriends and their roaming hands. Yeah." Marla's feelings about her brother were complicated. He was probably a psychopath—certainly he'd murdered at least a few times without any hint of regret. But he'd defended her when she was young and vulnerable, turning his cunning and his brutality toward keeping her innocence intact. "Listen, Jason. I know we tried to kill each other a few months back. But something… strange happened to me, not long ago. I know this magic stuff freaks you out, but listen. You know about parallel universes? Worlds like our own, except things are just a little different, and those little differences snowball into big changes?"

"Like places where the South won the Civil War, or Hitler didn't have a mustache," Jason said. "Like that?"

Marla nodded. "I met a version of myself from another universe. She was… seriously messed-up. She let herself get pushed around and used by evil forces. She was turned into a monster—basically, she became everything I hate. And it turns out, the thing that was different about *that* universe, was *you*. You died as a little kid over there, so you were never around to protect her—this other version of *me*—from all the things you saved me from in *this* reality. I know we're not friends now. I know you don't consider us family, anymore—that I became dead to you the moment I refused to help you bury a body and ran away from home. But I know that I literally would not be the woman I am without you. You saved me from things you didn't even know you were saving me from."

"Magic," he muttered. "I should think it's interesting. I should be trying to figure out how to make a profit off it. But really it just makes my fucking skin crawl."

Marla nodded. "Sometimes? Me too. As far as I'm concerned, this thing between us, the fact that you tried to kill me, the fact that you shot Rondeau, even this bullshit with Jarrow… we're square. I owe you that much. Go live your life." She leaned forward, and looked into his eyes, which were so much like the eyes she saw in the mirror every day. "But don't fuck with me again, Jason. Even alone, without resources, away from home, outnumbered and outgunned, I *still* won."

"Of course you did," Jason said, the ghost of a smile on his lips. "You're a Mason."

Marla snorted. "So is mom, and she never won at much of anything."

"Not true. She still brags about that wet t-shirt contest she won when she was twenty-two." Jason smiled, more openly this time. "You must have *really* wanted to protect me, if you called her. I can't believe it."

"I can't believe *you're* still in touch with her."

"She's always good for an alibi," Jason said. He dropped a few bills on the table. "I guess that's it, then. You don't try to kill me, and I don't try to kill you."

"It's a start. Maybe we can work our way up to Christmas cards."

"Anything's possible," Jason said, and walked out of her life again.

Back in her room, pretending she'd never left, Marla heard a tentative knock on the connecting door. "Come in!" she said, but couldn't quite shout. Rondeau and Pelham shuffled in, followed by Reva, who looked almost as tired as Marla felt. He was still wearing his filthy clothing. Apparently when he made a body he only conjured one set of clothes, and didn't think to buy or borrow more. Gods were such morons in some ways.

"I can order us some room service," Rondeau began, but Marla shook her head.

"Sit with me on the balcony. I've figured out some things." Once they'd joined her, Pelham and Rondeau sitting, and Reva leaning against the balcony, Marla took a deep breath. "I'm leaving Hawai'i. Not immediately—I have a couple of things to settle, we need to catch Lupo, and the surfers still owe me a secret and a trick for solving that murder—but soon."

"Where to?" Rondeau said. "I hear good things about the Caribbean. Or were you thinking skiing?"

"I'm thinking... no fixed address. With Felport closed to me, I don't have a home anymore. The home I chose rejected me, and, okay, I can even see why. And when you came back, Pelham... I realized how limited my world has been. I left Indiana and went straight to Felport, and that's where I stayed. I traveled a little as a mercenary and an apprentice, but they were always *missions*—I never got to really experience the places I went. Seeing how travel has expanded your horizons got me thinking, Pelham. It used to be, I was the worldly one, and you were the guy who'd never left home. But now, you've seen more than I have. I want to get out in the world, too. To stop looking for a fort to defend, or a rock to hide behind."

"So we're talking world tour?" Rondeau said.

Marla shook her head. "We're talking me, going from place to place, either flipping a coin or throwing darts at a map, and just... seeing what I find. Hoping I find something that resonates with me. And, for all that I think Reva is a meddling jackass, the way he lives appeals to me. Go to a place, learn to love it a little, and help the people there who need helping." She glared at the god as he began to grin. "But only people who *want* my help. Or who I'm pretty sure would want my help if they were thinking straight."

Rondeau whistled. "Wow. So you're just going to… walk the Earth? Like Jules from *Pulp Fiction*?"

"I think so. I mean… I'm happy when I get in a fight, but only when I'm fighting for something that matters. I'm kind of a crap detective, but I'm a pretty good guardian. I protected Felport, didn't I? So… maybe I can protect other places, too. Other people. Maybe wherever I *am* can be the place I protect. It seems like that would keep me occupied."

"I'm getting the sense I'm not invited," Rondeau said.

"You want to go? Walking, or hitchhiking, or hopping trains? Never knowing where you'll be tomorrow? Sleeping rough? No massages? I'd love to have you—apart from just enjoying your company, which I grudgingly admit, you're a psychic, and you'd be a great asset—but you've sacrificed enough for me."

"Hmm. How about I stay here and provide tactical support," Rondeau said. "You know. Materiel. Intel. Other things that end in 'el.' I can be your wealthy patron."

"That would be great," Marla said.

"May I accompany you, Mrs. Mason?" Pelham said.

Marla smiled. "Are you kidding? I need a seasoned traveler to show me the ropes. Otherwise I'll end up eating with the wrong fork or breaking a local taboo or accidentally marrying a guy I just wanted to sleep with. Plus I'm lousy at languages. I can't think of a traveling companion I'd rather have."

"I was really hoping that the occult detective thing would work out," Rondeau said. "Oh well. Mind if I rent out the bookshop?"

"I was only ever a squatter anyway. Suit yourself, if you can find a deed."

"Oh, Marla. It's like you've never heard of forgery."

Marla thought about how to broach the next subject, and finally decided: fuck it. Being direct had occasionally led to disaster, but there was no sense trying to change her nature. "Listen, guys, there's something you should know. When I was back on that beach, dying—I *should* have died."

"I wondered about that," Rondeau said. "Jarrow's body *did* die, and it was a sympathetic magic thing, so it seemed like you would have died, too…"

"Did the god of Death intervene on your behalf, Marla?" Pelham said.

"Ehhh… yes and no. He did restore me to life, but against his wishes, and with a fair number of strings attached. See, he *really* wants me to join him in the underworld, to reign at his side, but post-exile-angst notwithstanding, I'm not ready to leave this life yet. He was ready to schedule my coronation and polish up my throne, but I let him know that… wouldn't make me happy."

"If the goddess of the underworld ain't happy, ain't nobody happy," Reva said, grinning.

"So Death and I sat down and had a pretty hardcore negotiation, and the upshot is… I got him to invoke the Persephone clause."

Rondeau whistled. "So what? You spend six months in the underworld, and six months on the Earth? Damn, Marla. So you'll be wintering in Hell? I think that makes you the ultimate snowbird."

"Ah, but I'm a sharper bargainer than Persephone ever was, or maybe it's just because I don't have some goddess-of-the-springtime responsibilities to complicate matters. I got Death to agree that my six months in hell can be *non-consecutive*. I owe him six months a year, but I can take them whenever I want, so I don't have to say goodbye to seeing any season on the Earth for-ever. Plus, while I'm in the underworld, I don't age. So, you know. Pretty good health-care plan."

"Congratulation, Mrs. Mason," Pelham said. "And, of course, also my sympathies. I know the arrangement will be difficult for you."

"First B, now you," Rondeau said. "My friends keep turning into gods. Why don't I ever get tapped?"

"I'm sure the first time there's an opening for the god of hedonistic ex-cess, you'll make the shortlist," Marla said.

"You better not change, Marla. Or start putting on airs. I'm not going to address you as 'Your Divine Shadowhood' or anything. Does this mean you're going to go all goth, start dressing in vintage wedding dresses or black lace and spiderwebs?"

"I was thinking a black cloak, maybe with something in a matching scythe, but I'll have to see what the wardrobe department has in my size."

"This is good," Reva said. "For one thing, becoming a god yourself will help you better understand the minds of gods, and perhaps you will stop holding my interventions on your behalf against me—"

"You, shut it," Marla said. "And as a part-time goddess in training, I can say that to you without fear of repercussion. What I'm going to *do* is help Death and you and any other so-called higher powers I run into learn what being *human* is about. Which means I need to keep my humanity in the forefront for the half a year I'm allowed to be wholly a woman and nothing else. That's why you're never going to see me again while I'm up here in the world, understood? Don't take on any guise, don't come visit, don't happen to be on the same hiking trail or tour of the catacombs with me, *nothing*. You now officially have a restraining order, Reva—so restrain yourself. I've had quite enough of your meddling. I don't care if you meant well. I've learned firsthand that good intentions don't matter much, and my husband tells me we use them for paving stones back home."

"Marla, you're one of my people, whether you want to be or—"

Marla leaned forward. "Reva. You're a genius loci with no loci, right? And I'm, at least for half the year, part of the double deity that has full power over the entire sphere of death. So correct me if I'm wrong, but: don't I out-rank you?"

"That was very royal, Mrs. Mason," Pelham said approvingly.

Reva scowled. "It's not like we have *ranks*, exactly—"

Marla gave him her most withering stare. Or, at least, the most wither-ing stare she could muster as a mortal. Apparently as a goddess she'd be able to *literally* wither things. She still wasn't sure it was a good idea to let her wield that much power, but given that most stories about gods depicted them behaving like spoiled horny entitled spiteful children, she'd probably be bet-ter than most. "Don't screw around with me, Reva. I'm not condemning what you do. I plan to go into the freelance do-gooding business myself. Just stop doing it to *me*. Call it a character flaw, but I don't like people messing around with my life. Understood?"

"Yes, my queen." Reva gave an over-elaborate bow.

"Good." She leaned back in her chair. "There's one favor you can do for me, as my loyal subject. I need you to go see Death, and tell him the same thing I told *you*. He isn't to have any contact with me while I'm above ground. He gets me for half the year, and that's *it*. I won't have his long-view tainting my here-and-now. Plus, I'm still pissed at him for... well. I have my reasons, and he knows what they are."

"I could do that—"

"But listen, Reva. Take a walk with me. We need to talk. Because even though it's probably wasted, I want to try to make *you* understand why I'm doing this—for you to try and see my reasoning from a human point of view. And I want you to tell *Death* the whole story, try and get him see it from my side, from *everybody's* side, so he can understand there's a whole universe of stories that don't revolve around him, and a whole lot of things that matter other than his own convenience and contentment. He really needs to understand that people are real, all of us—every one of us—and that we mean more than just what he can *use* us for. Do you think you can do that for me?"

"You'd better do it, dude," Rondeau said. "She didn't say 'fuck' once dur-ing that whole speech. That's how you know she's serious."

"So that's why I'm here," I said, leaning back in the chair Death had grudgingly offered me. I took a sip of water cold and freshly drawn from some sunless lake. Death's meeting room was paneled in red-tinted wood, and full of heavy furniture and shelves lined with countless books, all black, their spines unmarked.

Death sat in dark leather chair, swirling amber liquid in a glass. "I told Marla she didn't need to send a messenger anymore. That she could tell me anything she had to say directly."

I shrugged. "I don't think she much cares what you want, really. Anyway, she knew I could fill in certain portions of the narrative, tell you about things she didn't see herself, and details she didn't know."

"How do *you* know all this, Reva? These stories you told, these conversations you recounted?"

"Some of it comes from direct observation—I was there for a lot of this, you know, either openly present or watching in secret. I tried hard to tell the story as objectively as I could, not to editorialize, to make myself just another one of the people in the background. Some of it I got from a little light mind-reading here and there, especially from Rondeau—I promised not to pry into Pelham's mind anymore, but I never promised that to Rondeau, so I rifled through his perceptions a bit. I also got to know Crapsey fairly well—he's the *ultimate* exile, he's not even in his home universe anymore, and after Marla and company stuck him on a boat back to the mainland I visited him, taking on the form of a crew member, and talked to his deepdown parts. Crapsey's not a bad sort, apart from being a mass-murderer. I learned a lot about Jarrow from him. Some other things Marla told me, and sometimes I read between the lines of what she told me—though you'll have to judge whether it's all true or not."

I coughed, though of course, I never really need to cough. "And, I'll admit, sometimes, I was just guessing, and making things up. Maybe I got a little carried away with the story here and there. But the point stands. Marla understands why you did what you did—and she wanted me to tell you this story so you'd understand why she doesn't want to hear from you during her six months on the Earth. She needs to know you aren't meddling, that you respect her humanity, even if you don't understand it. She needs to figure out her life, and what she's living for, and what's *worth* living for, without interference from either of us."

"Where is she now?"

"Still in Hawai'i. She's tracking down Gustavus Lupo, because she feels like that's her responsibility. Once that's done, though… Who knows? She talked about going to Malaysia with Pelham to cure him of his Nuno infestation. She's talked about walking through the American West. She's never been to Europe. She'll see the world."

"My Persephone," Death murmured, swirling the amber-colored liquid in his glass.

"No," I said. "Not your anything. She's her *own* Marla."

"You told me all this. Do *you* understand the point she was trying to make?"

"Not exactly," I said. "And I have to be honest with you… that kind of uncertainty is a new experience for me. Not a terribly pleasant one. Creatures like you, and to a lesser extent I, are used to feeling certainty in all things— aren't we?"

Death finished his drink, and we sat silently together for a while in his room at the bottom of the end of the world, thinking the thoughts that gods think, which are not entirely like the thoughts of women and men, or so I understand.

Acknowledgments

I HAVE A LOT OF PEOPLE TO THANK FOR THIS ONE. My wife Heather Shaw, of course, is first, for her tremendous support in helping me find the time (between parenting and a full-time job) to write this book. Thanks also go to Dan Dos Santos (who painted the cover art for six previous Marla Mason books!) for suggesting illustrator Lindsey Look to create a painting of Marla for this book. Thanks to Anne Rodman, the producer tirelessly working on bringing Marla Mason to the big (and little) screen, for renewing her option on the series and providing my family with enough money to take a vacation/research trip to Hawai'i. Jenn Reese and Cameron Panee gave me advice on martial arts and general violence-related matters. My copyeditor Elektra Hammond saved me from quite a few continuity errors and awkward phrases. John Teehan of Merry Blacksmith Press has agreed, once again, to produce the trade paperback print version (as he did for *Broken Mirrors*). Many of my writer friends, and longtime readers, spread the word about this novel, for which I'm eternally grateful.

And, of course, my biggest thanks go to the donors. This book would not exist without the generous individuals who gave money to me directly, or through my Kickstarter campaign: Diana Potter, Matt Yoshikawa, Alexa Spears, His Royal Splendidness Greg van Eekhout, Mur Lafferty, Samuel Montgomery-Blinn, Christian Decomain, Michael Jasper, William Shunn & Laura Chavoen, Dave Lawson, Deborah Schumacher, Ori Shifrin, Atlee Breland, Lianna Tepp, Jon Hansen, Steven Desjardins, Tiffany Baxendell Bridge, Zorknot Robinson, Natalie Luhrs, Julia Gammad, Holly Shaw, Ted Brown, Anna Enzminger, Sarah Householder, Wendy Fisher, Gary Singer, Ben Esacove, Sara, Allen Edwards, Rachael Squires, Jeffrey Reed, Ron Jarrell, Alexa Gulliford, Sharon Wood, Joshua Day, Kendall Bullen, Pedro Manuel Arjona, Dean Roddick, Scott Drummond, Max Kaehn, David Martinez, Steve Feldon, JR Vogt, Keith Garcia, Philip Adler, M.K. Carroll, Enrica Prazzoli, Samantha Roshak,

Tara Smith, Sheilah O'Connor, Kristel Downs, Lexie Cenni, Hugh Berkson, Bill Jennings, Besha Grey, Keith Schon, Heidi Berthiaume, Tina Mosca, Paul Boros, Tom Bridge, Jeanette Marsh, Kerim Friedman, Shirley Darch, Eric Altmyer, Tammy Thaggert, Adam Caldwell, Rick Cambere, Arachne Jericho, Claire Connelly, André Twupack, Claudia Sadun, Ian Mond, Dmitri, Deborah Vause, Jon Eichten, Edward Greaves, Cinnamon Davis, Catherine Waters, Susan, C.E. Murphy, Dave Thompson, Michelle Ossiander, L Wong, Russ Wilcox, Mick, Jeffrey Huse, Kristin Bodreau, Raul Francisco, Rob Hemstreet, Jason Wilson, C.C. Finlay, Marius Gedminas, Michael Jacob, Rachel Sanders, Armi Gerilla, Arlene Parker, Neil Graham, John Hathway, Alanna Maloney, David Raynes, Paul R Smith, Maureen Soar, Elektra Hammond, Renee Diane LeBeau, James M. Yager, Clara Asuncion, Ann Pino, Amanda Fisher, John Teehan, Jeanne Kalinowski, Linda Wood, Topher Hughes, Gann Bierner, Crystal Landry, Ben Fisher, Conor P. Dempsey, Mike Schwartz, Laura Cox, Jonathan Dean, Cori Lynn Arnold, Lindsay Stalcup, Danika, M D Spangler, Alan Yee, Paul Echeverri, Lilia Schwartz, Elias F. Combarro, Glyph Lefkowitz, Meredith Fletcher Hines, Tony James, Denise, Joeseph Felt, Arun Jiwa, Greg Kinney, Donald Mayne, Stephen Courson, Scott LeBeau, quiltingkitty, Lalith Vipulananthan, Margaret Klee, Tara Rowan, Bryan Sims, Kevin Hogan, Danielle Benson, Elaine Williams, Melissa Tabon, Jim Kirk, Rodelle Ladia, Paul Bulmer, Anton Nath, Jeremy, Davis, Kris, Ro Molina, Nellie Batz, Amy Gentilini, David Bennett, Sam Courtney, Mihir Wanchoo, Jess Jacob, Sarah Heitz, Rebecca Harbison, Danielle Van Gorder, Suzanne McLeod, Michael Bernardi, Kylee Livingston, Judy, Marguerite Kenner, Jonathan Spence, Juli McDermott, Kurt Miles, Jon Freestone, Jenn Reese, Dan Percival, Chris Baclayon, Sean Havins, Scott Blizzard, Sean Elliott, Josh Haas, Jamie Dawn Hickok, Kathlyn Payne, Von Welch, Keith Weinzerl, Athena Holter-Mehren, Danielle Daly, Joey Shoji, Katherin Douglas, Rion Wentworth, Nathan Bremmer, Jan WIldt, Russell Fry, Jordan Miller, Chris Kastensmidt, Gene Girard, Lynne Whitehorn, and Jennifer Sparenberg.

I hope you all like this one. It's my favorite Marla novel yet.

CPSIA information can be obtained at www.ICGtesting.com
Printed in the USA
LVOW071610210912

299797LV00012B/154/P